Ian Bruce Robertson

While Bullets Fly

*The Story of a Canadian Field Surgical Unit
in the Second World War*

Trafford
PUBLISHING

Order this book online at www.trafford.com/07-1364
or email orders@trafford.com

Most Trafford titles are also available at major online book retailers.

Note for Librarians: A cataloguing record for this book is available from Library
and Archives Canada at www.collectionscanada.ca/amicus/index-e.html

Printed in Victoria, BC, Canada.

ISBN: 978-1-4251-3512-6

*We at Trafford believe that it is the responsibility of us all, as both individuals
and corporations, to make choices that are environmentally and socially sound.
You, in turn, are supporting this responsible conduct each time you purchase a
Trafford book, or make use of our publishing services. To find out how you are
helping, please visit www.trafford.com/responsiblepublishing.html*

www.trafford.com

North America & international
toll-free: 1 888 232 4444 (USA & Canada)
phone: 250 383 6864 ♦ fax: 250 383 6804
email: info@trafford.com

The United Kingdom & Europe
phone: +44 (0)1865 722 113 ♦ local rate: 0845 230 9601
facsimile: +44 (0)1865 722 868 ♦ email: info.uk@trafford.com

10 9 8 7 6 5 4 3 2

To Tam

Contents

Foreword

This is a work of creative non-fiction. The events and activities took place when and where indicated. I have provided the creative touches – mainly the conversations – to add texture and enjoyment to the story. Many of my additions come from stories written by my father after the war, or told to me in our discussions of his wartime experiences.

I have had four main sources of information at my disposal. The first are my father's diaries written during his three years in England, 1940 to 1943. They give an interesting, personalized view of life in wartime England, and the working experience of a young Canadian doctor sent to England with the Canadian Army to assist in the war effort. The second are the 'War Diaries' that he kept faithfully, under orders, as Commander of a Canadian Field Surgical Unit. His War Diaries, and those of some of the other medical units with which he was involved (not all of them being available), give a day-by-day record of what they did, where and to whom.

The third is the Canadian Government publication *Official History of the Canadian Medical Services, 1939 -1945*. Edited by Lieutenant Colonel W.R. Feasby, MD and published in 1956, this two-volume work is a mine of information on the Canadian medical experience in the Second World War. The fourth is the wonderful book *Ortona* by Mark Zuehlke. It has been very useful as a source of facts and impressions, and inspiring as well. I am grateful to Mr. Zuehlke for the book, and for so graciously agreeing that I may draw on it as a reference. I have also used numerous other sources, internet-based and printed.

I have used the real names of the following, with permission from the families: Rocke and Rolly Robertson and Thomas Arnold, John and Trudy Leishman, Cam and Thelma Dickison, Frank Mills and General Bert Hoffmeister. I have also used the real names of the following doctors and officers: Cam Gardner, Jim Shannon, Bert Cragg, Jimmy Martin, Palmer

Howard, Keith Gordon, Phil Hill, George Raymond, George Ruddick, W.C. Hartgill, C.H. Playfair, Basil Bowman, Doug Sparling, F.C. Pace, Bill Clendinnen, Wally Scott, Peter Tisdale, Ed Tovee, Don Young, R.C. (Shorty) Long, S.J. Martin, J.A. MacFarlane, Brian Smyth, Captain Carleton, Major Diehl, Colonel Pease, Brigadier Penhale, A.J. Wiles, R.G. Donald, M.P. Bogert, G.H. Midgley, Ian Davidson, W.E. Mace, W.J. Boyd, Sandy MacIntosh, David Johnson and the Generals Bernard Montgomery, Chris Vokes and Guy Simonds. H.F. Frank appears as Harry Francis. The other officers, nurses and all other ranks (from Private to Sergeant) have assumed names except for stretcher-bearer Ted Walls, who has been a delightful source of information and anecdotes.

My thanks go to a number of people for their support and assistance. The road to this book started with my late brother Tam, who took a lively interest in family history and tried, with some success, to get me involved. My younger brother Stuart then took up the challenge of studying what our family did in the past. I am most grateful to him for his marvellous work that has drawn me in to such an extent that it now controls my life. The story of the Field Surgical Unit jumped out at me as one of historical interest rather than just family pride.

I am grateful to the Leishman and Dickison families for their support and encouragement. Thanks go to my sister Bea for her help in the field research in Sicily and Italy, her son Scott for helping with research in Ottawa, my old friend Edwy Stewart and my son Wesley who read and commented just when I needed it, and to my son Stuart for his comments and insights. I am grateful to my medical advisor Dr. Don Burrows, and to Catherine Wheeler who has served as my mentor and editor. And finally, thanks to my wife Bonnie for her constant support, and her thoughtful comments and ideas.

IBR

Introduction

Many readers will remember M*A*S*H, the wonderful TV series about an American Mobile Army Surgical Hospital in the Korean War. A series of huts set up in the hills of Korea, with operating facilities and wards and living quarters, the unit had a substantial staff of doctors and nurses who alternated between zany antics and serious medical work, including surgery, on wounded soldiers. A key scene was always the arrival of helicopters bringing in the wounded from the fighting front. The helicopters made this 'mobile' unit semi-permanent as they could deliver the wounded from near and far quickly and smoothly.

Now go back ten years to the Second World War, with the Axis powers (Germany, Italy and Japan) fighting the Allies (most of the rest of the world) in Europe, Asia and Africa. Warfare is essentially the same as in Korea, mobile and fast moving unlike the more static First World War, but there are no helicopters to transport the wounded! Consider the well established fact that the quicker you get a badly wounded soldier onto the operating table, the better his chances of survival. How, then, do you get them out of the fighting and back to a unit capable of operating on them quickly enough to save them?

The medical system used up to and at the start of the Second World War was based on the Casualty Clearing Station, a substantial unit not unlike a MASH, mobile to a limited extent but too large and complex for the flexible movement needed to keep within reasonable proximity of the troops.

The British Army worried about this issue as the war progressed. In an historic report issued in late 1941, a military committee stated clearly that this was a major issue that had to be dealt with at once. One of its specific findings was that *"casualties are not afforded the advantages which modern surgical technique can provide. Surgeons, their assistants and equipment are located too far to the rear of divisions and corps.*

The outcome was a decision to establish new mobile medical units that could move with the fighting troops, changing location even daily if necessary to be close enough to provide timely medical assistance, including advanced surgery. The units were fully mobile Field Ambulances, Field Dressing Stations, Field Transfusion Units and Field Surgical Units. All were packaged in trucks and able to set up or shut down and move within hours. The Field Ambulances brought the wounded in from the field. The Field Dressing Stations were small, mobile hospitals equipped with medical facilities and wards for patients. Field Transfusion Units were mobile blood supply units.

Field Surgical Units were mobile operating rooms that could move amongst the Field Dressing Stations providing advanced surgical services to the seriously wounded. These 'FSUs' were of particular interest because they had to deal with operating room conditions that would be condemned in any modern hospital, battling dust and dirt, heat and cold and flies as well as the challenges of the operations themselves.

This book tells the story of one such unit, the 2nd Canadian Field Surgical Unit, as it was formed, trained, and then served in Sicily and Italy up to the historic battle of Ortona. I have focused on this particular unit as my father, Rocke Robertson, was its Commander and I have lots of information about it, but the book is really about all of the FSUs and their brief, courageous and colourful careers.

Ian Bruce Robertson

List of Maps and Pictures

* Source: *Official History of the Canadian Medical Services 1939-1945, Volumes 1 and 2, 1956. Department of National Defence. Reproduced with the permission of the Minister of Public Works and Government Services Canada, 2007.*

SICILY

Cape Orlando
Sant' Agata
CEFALU
San Stefano
MOUNT SAN FRATELLO
Campofelice
43rd DIVISION
2nd DIVISION
23 JUL
30-31 JUL
3rd DIVISION
Petralia
Nicosia
28 JUL
Leonforte
21 JUL
Assoro
21 JUL
ENNA
CALTANISSETTA
PIAZZA ARMERINA
17 JUL
Mazzarino
Campobello di Licata
San Michele
CALTAGIRONE
13 JUL
Licata
Gela
SEVENTH ARMY
10 JULY
Ponte Olivo
AIRBORNE LANDING SCATTERED 10 JUL
Gulf of Gela
Comiso
Scoglitti
RAGUSA
12 JUL
MODICA
Punta Braccetto
Cape Scaramia
Pozzallo

Gulf of Palli
MESSINA
Mili Marina
Barcellona
Scaletta
REG Cala
Santa Teresa
COMMANDO LANDING 13 AUG
Taormina
Randazzo
1st DIV
Cesaro
9th DIVISION
Linguaglossa
Maletto
Fiumefreddo
Bronte
Troina
6 AUG
Mount Etna 3279
Riposto
Regalbuto
Nissoria
Agira
Adrano
Zafferana Etnea
Centuripe
Biancavilla
Trecastagni
ACIREALE
Radusa-Agira Station
Catenannuova
Paterno
CATANA
Valguarnera
Misterbianco
NO. 5 CANADIAN GENERAL HOSPITAL 18 AU - 25 JA
Gerbini
AIRBORNE LANDING 13-14 JUL
Ramacca
Gornalunga
PRIMOSOLE BRIDGE
Scordia
COMMANDO LANDING 13-14 JUL
Militello
Lentini
Grammichele
Francofonte
12 JUL
Augusta
Vizzini
Sortino
Monterosso Almo
Palazzolo
Floridia
NO. 5 CANADIAN GENERAL HOSPITAL 24 JUL-14 AUG 43
Chiaramonte
Giarratana
12 JUL
SYRACUSE
AIRBORNE LANDING 10 JUL
Cassibile
Masseria Palma
Avola
Gulf of
Rosolini
NOTO
Ispica
Noto
Marzamemi
Burgio
Pachino
Maucini
Cape Passero
RELEASE POSITION CANADIAN TROOPS
EIGHTH ARMY
30TH CORPS
13TH CORPS
10 JULY
IONIAN SEA

Scale
0   10   20   30   40   50   MILES

Canadian Forces
British Forces
United States Forces
ONLY MAIN LINES OF ADVANCE OF NON-CANADIAN FORMATIONS ARE SHOWN

Compiled and Drawn by Historical Sectio

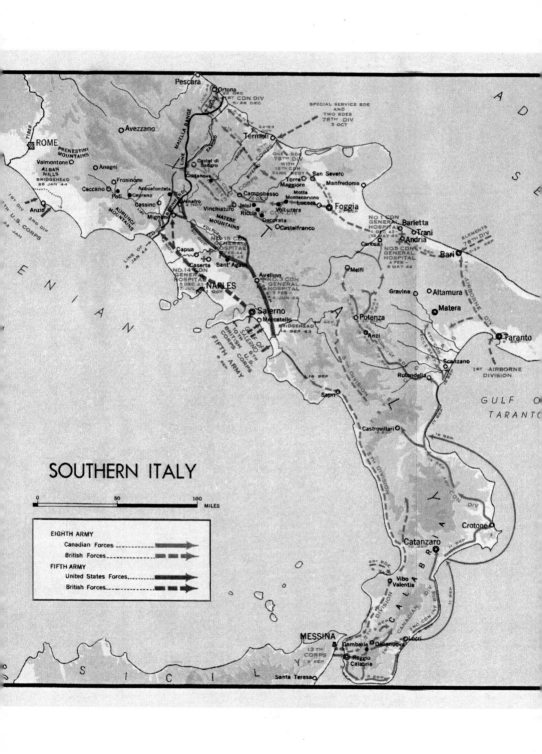

SOUTHERN ITALY

EIGHTH ARMY
Canadian Forces..........
British Forces............
FIFTH ARMY
United States Forces.........
British Forces............

0   50   100
MILES

ROME

Pescara
Ortona
1ST CDN DIV
5–28 DEC

Avezzano

SPECIAL SERVICE BDE
AND
TWO BDES
78TH DIV
3 OCT

Termoli

PRENESTINI
MOUNTAINS

Valmontone
ALBAN
HILLS
BRIDGEHEAD
28 JAN 44

Anagni
Frosinone

Castel di
Sangro

MAIELLA RANGE

ONE BDE
78TH DIV
WITH
12TH CDN
TANK REGT

San Severo

Manfredonia

Ceccano
Poli
Ceprano

Acquafondata
Cassino

Civitanova

Campobasso

Torre
Maggiore

Motta
Montecorvino

Lucera
Foggia

Anzio
1ST DIV
3RD DIV
26 JAN

Mignano
Vinchiaturo

Jelsi
Riccia

Decorata
Castelfranco

Volturara

NO 1 CDN
GENERAL
HOSPITAL
10 MAY 43

Barletta
Trani
Andria

Capua
Caserta
Sant' Agata

NO 15 CDN
GENERAL
HOSPITAL

Carbosa

Bari

NO 14 CDN
GENERAL
HOSPITAL
5 DEC 43
7 JUL 44

NAPLES

Avellino

NO 3 CDN
GENERAL
HOSPITAL
9 FEB 43
4 JUN 44

Melfi

NO 5 CDN
GENERAL
HOSPITAL
4 FEB
5 MAY 44

Salerno
Mercatello

Gravina
Altamura

Matera

BRIDGEHEAD
14 SEP 43

Potenza

Anzi

Taranto

Scanzano

1ST AIRBORNE
DIVISION

Rotondella

Sapri

GULF OF
TARANTO

Castrovillari

Crotone

SOUTHERN ITALY

Catanzaro

Vibo
Valentia

MESSINA
13TH
CORPS

CALABRIA

Gambarie
Dellanuova

Reggio
Calabria

Locri

SICILY

Santa Teresa

1. THE LANDING

The No.2 Canadian Field Surgical Unit lands in Sicily.

Saturday, July 10, 1943

"They've forgotten us, Major! The troops are all away in the landing craft and the ship is turning away from the beach. Dammit, we've gotta do something!" Lance Corporal Eric Branch is red faced with anger although he manages to keep his voice down to a moderate roar.

Major Rocke Robertson stands poised in the doorway of the ship's cabin where he and his Second-in-Command Captain Jack Leishman have been waiting for the orders to go up on deck. "Who did you talk to, Branch?" he asks. "Lieutenant Matthews, Sir. He's the deck officer, and he was very surprised to see me. He thought everyone had cleared the ship, and he'd damn well forgotten us sitting down here sweating our buns off."

"I knew it! Jack, call the other men and let's get up on deck." Jack Leishman sprints down the passageway and calls the other eight members of the Field Surgical Unit out of the cabins. They are all heavily weighed down with their landing packs and gear, their uniforms soaked with sweat. They are angry and frustrated as Rocke leads them up the stairs to the deck.

The sight that greets them as they emerge squinting into the brilliant Sicilian sunshine stops them in their tracks. The Sicilian coast stretches away in both directions. Although most of the troops have gone ashore hours ago, there are still some men and vehicles landing on the beaches and moving across them into the scrub and the country roads inland. There is some gunfire and a few explosions, but mainly the soldiers are moving unopposed. Planes are flying overhead delivering bombs inland – probably the airfield at Pachino is the main target. The sound of shells screaming overhead toward targets inland is deafening.

Offshore and all around them are British, American and Canadian ships and landing craft of the Allied flotilla: battleships, cruisers, monitors, destroyers and other warships, landing craft, motor boats, ocean liners, freighters, and tankers. It is magnificent, and exciting to be part of this huge operation – the Allied invasion of Sicily, a major turning point in the Second World War. But are they part of it?

Rocke rushes to where Lieutenant Matthews is standing with several deck hands, all staring at the team that has just emerged from below. "Lieutenant, what's happened? Why weren't we called? Where's our landing craft?"

Matthews is a tall, thin young Brit with a nervous tic, and he is clearly embarrassed to have made this mistake, especially in front of a bunch of Canadians. "I'm sorry Major, we simply forgot that you fellows were waiting below. We've sent all the troops ashore, and used up our assigned landing craft."

"So what happens now? Can you find us another craft?"

"I'm afraid not, Sir. We were told to use the craft assigned to us and no more. I'm really sorry. We're heading for Malta now. We'll have to arrange a ride for you back from there."

"Like hell you will. Jack, Eric, men – get over to the rail and find us a landing craft. Look for an empty one returning from the beach."

The men scatter to the rail, ignoring the protests of Lieutenant Matthews that this is not in the orders. Eric Branch immediately spots an empty British L/C heading away from the beach on a course that will bring it close to the ship. "There's our taxi, Major!" he yells. They wave violently at the passing craft and it pulls reluctantly alongside. Rocke grabs a megaphone and hails the Lieutenant in charge.

"Thanks for stopping, Lieutenant. Our own L/Cs have gone without us by mistake. We'd appreciate it if you would take us ashore."

"I'm afraid I can't, Sir," comes the reply. "I have no orders for your unit and I have to get back to my ship."

Rocke flashes his Major's insignia. "Lieutenant, we are Canadian army medical troops and we must be on that beach to help the wounded. You have the space and it won't take long. May we board?"

The Lieutenant thinks it over quickly: the timing and danger involved, the lack of orders, but also the implications of a junior British officer disobeying a Canadian army major in the midst of an Allied action. *And how do you deal with these medical types anyway? They aren't really soldiers, but they are damn useful. This officer looks pretty bloody angry, too. Better be careful.* The situation is complicated enough to win the day, and he calls for them to embark. He pulls the L/C right alongside, and the British sailors rush to throw the climbing nets over the side of the ship. Rocke leads his team down the nets and into the craft, which is pitching and rolling heavily in the waves.

The Lieutenant watches the team scramble down the nets and jump into the L/C. *They aren't soldiers but they do look pretty fit. Why the hell haven't they already gone ashore? Another cock-up, I guess.*

As they head for the shore Rocke asks the Lieutenant which beach they are headed for. The land ahead bears no resemblance to that shown in the aerial photographs that he has memorized so assiduously in the pre-landing briefings, but if he knows which of the three designated landing beaches they are headed for he can readily lead his team by map to the appointed rendezvous point.

The Lieutenant is still annoyed about being imposed upon, and is not helpful. "I have no idea, Sir. That's not my concern. My job is to get people ashore as quickly as possible. It's up to you blokes to find out where you are and get on with it."

The landing craft touches bottom about 100 feet from the water's edge, and the team jump into water up to their armpits and wade ashore. Rocke turns to wave thanks to the Lieutenant and receives an ironic salute in return, together with an unkind grin at the sight of the medicals struggling with their packs in the choppy sea. The water is warm and very salty, but still a relief after the long, sweaty morning they have had. They assemble on the unknown beach and scramble to the cover of a nearby bunch of scrub trees.

For the No.2 Canadian Field Surgical Unit, hot, soaked, lost and without their equipment or vehicles, Operation Husky has begun.

2. OPERATION HUSKY

The rationale and strategy for the Allied invasion of Sicily.

This was the start of Operation 'Husky', the Allied landing in southern Europe. The Second World War was four years old, and at last the Allies were returning to the continent in force to drive off the Germans and subdue their reluctant Axis colleagues, the Italians. Russian President Joseph Stalin had wanted to start the liberation of Europe with a direct invasion of France, but British Prime Minister Winston Churchill prevailed with his idea of starting by attacking from the south. As he put it, it is better to attack a crocodile through its soft under-belly than its sharp snout. The invasion of Sicily and Italy was not a 'soft' exercise, but it was successful, and it provided invaluable lessons to the Allies for their invasion of France through the Normandy beaches 11 months later.

The fleet of 3,000 Allied ships that had appeared from every direction was now churning the waters off Sicily. There were several convoys from Britain, one from the United States and one from the Eastern Mediterranean - vessels of all shapes and sizes. Each ship had a particular task, with a prescribed course and destination. The main participants were the British 8th Army and the American 7th Army. The Canadian contingent consisted of the 1st Canadian Infantry Division, the 1st Canadian Armoured Brigade, The Corps of Royal Canadian Engineers and the Royal Canadian Army Medical Corps. The Canadians were a unit of the British 8th Army, which was commanded by General Bernard Montgomery.

The storm that had rocked the ships of the convoy the previous day and almost caused a postponement of the assault had subsided around midnight. The Allied ships had started their bombardment just after midnight, lobbing shells at the targets on shore. A swarm of landing craft started moving troops and equipment onto the beaches at 0245hrs. Two thousand Allied aircraft provided air cover and bombed targets. Their main target was the airfield near Pachino on the southern tip of Sicily. The troops met very little resistance on landing, with practically no casualties at first.

The converted merchant ship M/S Batory was jammed with Canadian troops and their equipment, and they were poised and ready to go well before the initial landings began. They actually started disembarking at around 0830hrs.

The 11 men of the No.2 Canadian Field Surgical Unit were part of the Canadian force on the Batory. As they were non-combatants they had been ordered to stay below decks in their cabins, ready to go, until the combat troops were away. They were fully decked out in battle dress, with heavy landing packs, revolvers, water bottles and gas masks strapped on, and they sweated heavily in the morning Mediterranean heat. Their Commander, Major Rocke Robertson was huddled with his Second-in-Command Captain John (Jack) Leishman, discussing once again the landing instructions for the unit.

The instructions had been detailed, with maps of Sicily and aerial photographs of the landing sites and of the important landmarks in the surrounding countryside, and descriptions of every move that the unit was to make upon landing. Robertson and Leishman had memorized them, and then destroyed them the previous evening as ordered. An unwritten instruction was to find as quickly as possible their three vehicles and surgical supplies that had all come on different ships.

The unit had hoped to be kept informed of progress, but as the day wore on no word came down to them, so their only link to the action was the clatter of boots on the deck above and the roar of the barrage laid down by the monitors and other large naval craft. They longed to observe the action, but obeyed the strict orders to stay put until called for.

By 1400hrs there was very little sound from the deck above, and Major Robertson decided that, orders or no orders, they had better find out what was happening. He sent Lance Corporal Eric Branch to reconnoitre.

3. TRAINING IN MONTREAL

Rocke and his colleagues prepare for war.

Thursday, July 11, 1940

Rocke sweats into his smashing but very warm uniform in the hot Montreal summer sun, standing to attention in another endless drill. It is ironic that he is drilling here on the campus of McGill University, where he had graduated in medicine in 1936.

From his earliest days Rocke had wanted to be a doctor. His reason was simple: he hated seeing people in pain, and wanted to be able to do something about it – to help if he could. He went to McGill in 1929 to study science and then medicine, following in the footsteps of a number of family members including his Uncle Herman, who had graduated from McGill in medicine in 1897 and served overseas in the Canadian Army in the First World War.

Rocke had always been a fine student and athlete. Growing up in Victoria on Canada's west coast, he headed his class at school and was a star athlete, particularly in tennis. Tall, dark and handsome, Rocke was popular with his crowd in Montreal, and he focused first on the good life at McGill, and on tennis. Then some bad marks woke him to reality, and he eventually graduated top of his class.

Following McGill he interned at the Montreal General Hospital. He dated a number of girls, amongst them the delightful nurse Trudy Lake from Newfoundland and the petite, cute and chatty Rolly Arnold. Rolly was a Montreal girl whose father was in the steel business. Rocke met her at one of the many social functions while still at McGill, and their romance flowered during that year at the MGH. They were married in June 1937, and their first child, son Tam, was born in April 1938.

In the summer of 1938 Rocke was delighted to be offered a position as Clinical Assistant in Surgery at the Royal Infirmary in Edinburgh. Both his and Rolly's families had come originally from Scotland, and they were thrilled to be returning there. Rocke felt a strong sense of history repeating itself, as his great grandfather and great great grandfather had both been surgeons trained in Edinburgh. The former had come to Canada in 1830; the latter had practiced in India.

Edinburgh was good to the young family. Rocke excelled at this work, and in 1939 he was elected a Fellow of the Royal College of Physicians and Surgeons of Edinburgh. Rolly found their walk-up, cold-water flat much to her liking, appealing to her strong sense of history and the legendary Scottish toughness. She also had Tam to take care of, which was a joy.

Early in September, Rocke's appointment in Edinburgh completed, he took up an appointment as Demonstrator of Anatomy at the Middlesex Hospital Medical School. But the appointment was short-lived. The Second World War broke out, and he immediately applied to join the British Army. Upon being told that he would have to join up in Canada, he packed up his family and they sailed back to Canada on the 'Duchess of Richmond', landing at Montreal in late October. They settled into a house and Rocke returned to the Montreal General Hospital as a Junior Assistant Surgeon while applying to join the army.

In January 1940 he was commissioned with the Royal Canadian Army Medical Corps with the rank of Lieutenant, Staff No.1 Canadian General Hospital. His unit was mobilized in May and he left the hospital to train with the army while tending his growing family, with second son Ian appearing in June. It had been rushed and exciting and exhausting, all at once. Now he was through it and ready to sail into the war and put his medical skills to work.

The McGill University campus in downtown Montreal is an unusual place for military drilling and instruction, but these are unusual times. There's a war on, so anything goes. Now it is a training base beyond the Westmount Barracks for the No.1 Canadian General Hospital, a unit of the rapidly growing Royal Canadian Army Medical Corps. The classrooms and the gym are used for instruction, and the lower campus field for drill. The field is surrounded by stately trees that cast cool shade, but the Captain in charge of the exercise seems to enjoy roasting the 'medicals' in the direct sun. For the hundredth time Rocke wonders why they do this drilling anyway.

We're in the army but we aren't soldiers, for heaven's sake! Our job overseas will be to run hospitals and treat the wounded, not march into battles and flanking movements and the like. So why learn how to march and turn and wheel?

But then, as usual, he rationalizes. *Well, I guess that's how it works in the army. Discipline is important, even for non-combatants, so this is why we waste our time marching. At least this is the last day of it. We'll be leaving soon for England.*

Today's work ends with a photo session. "Fall out," roars the Captain, "…and report to the photographer." The 24 officers (mostly doctors) and 98 'other ranks' (orderlies, operating room assistants) move to the benches. The officers sit on the benches or the ground in front, with the commanding officer Colonel George Ruddick, cool and well pressed because he has not been drilling, placed proudly at their centre. The men stand on the ground or on the benches behind the officers. They look serious and important as the photographer records them for posterity. They are released, the men are trucked back to the barracks, and the officers head home.

Rocke gets a ride to his house with his old friend and colleague Cam Gardner. Cam has a new De Soto that he bought in March for $900. It was a lot to pay, but the car is a lovely, shiny blue and wonderful to drive, and worth every penny of it. They strip off their uniform jackets, light up cigarettes, open the car windows and get in. Rush hour on Sherbrooke Street is well under way, so they move slowly into traffic.

"Well, that's it for drilling, at least until we're overseas," says Cam, the sweat standing in beads on his forehead. "I sure won't miss it for a while. At least we're starting to look like army people." He pauses and curses as a car veers in front of him, crossing two lanes in classic Montreal fashion. "But you know, that'll be important when we have to deal with soldiers and officers who wouldn't listen for two seconds to a civilian, doctor or not. Any new word on when we'll be heading out?"

"I hear that we'll get our orders tomorrow at the barracks," replies Rocke, "but the rumour is that we'll hit the train for Halifax this weekend, probably Sunday. I haven't told Rolly yet, but she knows it'll be very soon now. That's the toughest part of all this training and waiting. You have to keep up a happy face with the family when you know you'll be leaving them soon for the war. And them knowing it too, and being so bloody brave about it. Damn the war!"

"Which speaking of," says Cam, "the Colonel reminded us again to-day about how it's our job to save lives, even if they're civilians or enemy soldiers. I find that pretty damn hard to take. It makes me feel like we're a bunch of outsiders in our own army. The boys up front work their tails off to kill Germans, and then we're supposed to save them? It's sort of like a lawyer defending a man when he knows the guy has done something awful and is guilty as hell."

Rocke blows smoke out the window and shuts his eyes against the glare of the sun, and also because he is tired. He hears Cam through his left ear, but for one moment he dozes until his burning cigarette wakens him rudely. He stubs out the butt and returns to Cam's comment about treating the enemy.

"Sorry Cam, I dozed off. Yes, I know what you mean about treating the enemy. I don't like it either. I don't mind helping enemy civilians, because they're just innocent victims – at least most of them. And I guess a lot of enemy soldiers are really the same: young guys called up to fight and hating every minute of it and wishing they were home. But maybe not. They've probably shot some of our guys, and what if it's a Gestapo officer or the like? But you know, like it or not we're in the killing game, although we have a different role in it than the soldiers. We save lives and send the wounded home alive, but we also fix up our men so that they can get back in action and kill more Germans. Just like the German doctors fix up their soldiers so that they can get back in action against us! At least when we fix up a German we know he won't be able to come back to attack us. He'll be our guest until the war is over."

Cam nods. "Right. Well, I guess we don't have a choice in the matter anyway. It's 'orders'. And you know, if the Germans invade when we're in England, we may find ourselves working for the Germans in German hospitals. Do you think they'll let us help British citizens and soldiers?"

"Not bloody likely." Rocke laughs at the thought. "That would be just great. Imagine me writing home to Rolly to say I'm at a London hospital operating on German soldiers while no Brits are allowed. She'd be on the next boat over to sort things out!"

"Is Rolly working at that canteen now?"

"Not yet. She's still pretty tired from having the baby three weeks ago, but I expect she'll start in as soon as possible after we leave. She'll want to be out of the house and busy. The canteen's a pretty neat place too. We just passed it – it's that lovely old house with the gardens around the side. She says that they're already busy with Commonwealth airmen looking for a bite to eat and a beer, but with very little money to pay for it. Those poor guys find downtown Montreal too damn expensive, so the canteen's doing good work. And there'll be more and more business for them as the Commonwealth flier training programs build up."

They turn up the hill and Rocke gets out at his house. "Thanks Cam. See you tomorrow at eight".

4. THE RCAMC

A description of Canada's military medical corps.

The Royal Canadian Army Medical Corps (RCAMC) was formed in 1920 as a reconstitution of an earlier organization. Its initial strength was 30 officers and nurses (referred to then as 'nursing sisters') and 75 other ranks. By March 1939 it had grown to 43 officers and nurses, and 123 other ranks. The head of the RCAMC was called the Director General of Medical Services (DGMS).

The Corps had been virtually ignored during the years of peace, so had a lot of work to do to get ready for the war that broke out in 1939. A report in 1938 stated that with the equipment on hand in the RCAMC, no more than a dozen regimental medical officers and no medical unit in excess of one field ambulance could be placed in the field, and that there was insufficient equipment to provide hospital facilities inside or outside of Canada. There was no comprehensive scheme for the provision of medical services adequate to the needs of any forces mobilized for duty at home or abroad.

Planning medical services for an army headed into an active war was a hugely complex task. A general guideline used by planners was that there should be hospital beds readily available for 10 percent of the fighting forces in the field. That was fine in theory, but raised many questions that had to be answered bravely and with imagination. For example: where will the 'field' be? What will be the size of our fighting force? Will we have to take care of prisoners and civilians? How about troops from allied nations…will we take care of them too?

Then there was the complex question of how to mount a medical service in a live theatre of war, especially now that warfare was becoming so mobile. You need stretcher-bearers of course, but what happens when they bring in the wounded? Do you attend to them immediately, in the field, or must they all take the Field Ambulance to a Casualty Clearing Station? How close to the fighting should a Casualty Clearing Station be? And then what? Can you operate on the really bad cases there, or do you send them over more rocky roads to the hospitals? An over-all question concerned the reporting relationships. Should medical units be attached to divisions of the army, or be under independent control at regiment level?

The declaration of war moved all of these questions to resolution at frantic speed, but many strategic issues could be dealt with only as the war progressed and experience was gained. As of September 1, 1939 the medical components of the RCAMC established for overseas actions numbered 26 units: seven Field Ambulances, two Motor Ambulance Convoys, four Field Hygiene Sections, two Casualty Clearing Stations, two medical stores depots, one mobile bacteriological laboratory, one mobile x-ray laboratory, one convalescent depot and six Canadian General Hospitals with a total of 5,400 beds. By December 1941 this had grown to 41 units, and in May 1944 the total was 93 units.

By the end of the European war, 34,786 personnel had served in the RCAMC, including 3,656 nurses, and the Corps suffered 107 fatal battle casualties.

The concept of Canadian General Hospitals (CGHs) in the RCAMC consisted of developing trained complements of doctors, nurses and other staff in Canada, and then shipping them overseas with their equipment and instruments to run fully-fledged hospitals in support of the war effort, wherever they might be situated. Their main task was to treat Canadian casualties, but they were also to treat British and other Allied troops, and civilians and even enemy casualties, space permitting. In 1939 there were six CGHs organized across Canada and awaiting orders to move overseas. Two were based in Montreal and one each in Winnipeg, Saskatoon, Hamilton and Toronto. By May of 1944 they had all moved overseas along with four others.

The Canadian medical establishment in England, at its peak, was impressive, consisting of 10 CGHs, a Neurological and Plastic Surgery Hospital at Basingstoke, three convalescent hospitals, a convalescent home for officers and one for nursing sisters, a 'Special Hospital' and four Canadian Medical Centres.

Officers and staff in these units were moved around frequently to different units, and were also recruitment grounds for smaller units such as Field Ambulances. The arrival of Canadian nurses was always an important event at these hospitals, greatly improving their efficiency and effectiveness. They also added immeasurably to the spirits of the patients and the social life of their units.

5. OVERSEAS TO ENGLAND

The 'medicals' cross the Atlantic to join in the war effort.

Sunday, July 14, 1940

The front hall of the house on Montrose Avenue is silent. The baby is upstairs, still sleeping after a very early morning feeding. Young Tam, now two years old, is playing happily in his room. Rocke and Rolly hold each other, gently and wordlessly.

They have talked everything through a dozen times over. Their loyalties are absolutely clear and unshakable. They love England and hate the war that threatens it. They love their Canada, and are immensely proud of it for getting involved so quickly to help out. Rolly is proud of her husband for signing up to do his duty. *He looks fine in his uniform. If only he didn't have to go so soon! And if only the war would end soon. Surely it will!*

Rocke knows that he is doing the right thing, and is excited about the venture. He is a surgeon, and therefore important to the war effort. But it is so hard to leave Rolly and the boys. So damn hard! They are his joy, and he can feel a loneliness, an emptiness already growing inside as the time comes to part.

It is 8:30am. Rocke pulls away, his eyes red and full of tears, and goes silently out the door. Rolly stands for a moment, staring with damp eyes at his back disappearing down the front steps. She moves to the door and waves to him as he throws his luggage into the back seat of his father-in-law's car, climbs in, and is driven away.

She already longs for his return. She worries about his safety. She has no idea that she won't see him again for over four years.

Thomas Arnold, Rolly's father, drives Rocke to the Westmount Barracks. Rocke gets out, thanks him, shakes hands and nods to Mr. Arnold's call for 'a safe return'. He hauls his bags to the luggage drop area and then falls in on the parade ground. The men of the No.1 Canadian General Hospital march to the Bonaventure Station through quiet Sunday streets peppered with onlookers calling out their support, and for the first time Rocke is glad that they have practiced their drilling. The station is a melee of relatives and friends, including two of Rolly's aunts, saying their fare-wells. The aunts present him with a dispatch case that he likes very much as he plans to keep a diary and do lots of reading and writing. He thanks them and receives a nice kiss from each.

They board the train and find their places. Rocke is in charge of No.3 Company. He settles his men in and then moves forward to the officers' car, which is very comfortable and air-conditioned. The train chugs slowly out of the station and heads for Halifax. Rocke stares out the window and thinks about Rolly.

They arrive in Halifax at 2:00pm, and the train takes them right to the docks. Colonel Ruddick is there to meet them, and orders them to form up in preparation for boarding. Their ship is the *Duchess of York*, a passenger liner converted for military use. They board the ship and head for their assigned quarters. The men of the other ranks are squeezed into stuffy bunkrooms below decks, while the officers have spacious cabins on A Deck. Rocke shares an outside cabin with his old friend and colleague Jim Shannon, and Bert Cragg who is described as an 'eye man'.

At a meeting of officers in the late afternoon Colonel Ruddick tells them that they will be sailing for England on Thursday, July 18.

-/-

They spend the following days relaxing on the ship, participating in PT (physical training), boat drills and occasional lectures, medical duty, eating splendid food and enjoying shore leaves. July 18 passes by with no word on the sailing, as do several days to follow.

Wednesday, July 24, 1940

Rocke and Jim Shannon are at the rail, smoking quietly in the lull before dinner. It has been a long and boring day, with no sign that yesterday's rumours of imminent sailing were anything but rumours. Yet there seems to be an air of excitement in the harbour. Tugs are moving about. There is smoke rising from more funnels than usual. They see the huge British battleship *H.M.S. Revenge* being towed out into mid-channel, and other ships are moving about in her wake. Things are happening.

Rocke's Diary

Shortly before 6:00pm a Polish ship was towed out into the harbour, then out came the Revenge, then ourselves. (Earlier in the day two destroyers had gone out). With the Revenge leading we steamed out in perfect order: Revenge, Polish A, Duchess of York, Monarch of Bermuda, Empress of Australia, Samaria, Antonia (our old friend) and Polish B. The two destroyers picked us up outside. The decks of all the ships were lined with troops, thousands of them (there are 1,623 men in khaki on this ship alone), and there was much cheering on all sides.

-/-

Life on board quickly settles into a quite pleasant routine. There are occasional lectures and meetings, lots of PT, good meals, medical services for the troops, and lots of time for reading and chatting with friends new and old. They all are only too aware of the threat of the German U-Boats, but the battleship and the two destroyers look awfully lethal and efficient, so they don't really think much about the danger. That being said, they welcome the first sight of land.

Thursday, August 1, 1940

After breakfast a group of soldiers on B Deck set up a loud cry that land is in sight. Everyone rushes to the rail to see Scotland in the distant mists. By 1100hrs (they are now using the military time terminology – the 24 hour clock) the ship is well into the River Clyde.

Like tourists, the Canadians line the rails to watch Scotland slide by. They pass Gurock and stop in Greenoch harbour where they join seemingly thousands of ships. All the way along there are steel yards, shipbuilding yards and plants of all kinds. They move farther up the Clyde and dock at Glasgow at 2230hrs. The officers celebrate with a cheerful party in the cabins, briefly interrupted by an air raid warning.

This is the first such warning that they have experienced, and is brings a rush of mixed emotions to the Canadians. One is fear. They are, after all, on a ship in the harbour, and if there is in fact a raid it could well be a priority target – a great fat ship full of soldiers. Another is excitement. They are in a war zone, almost, and in danger. They have been thinking about this for a long time, and now it is happening! There is some anger thrown in, for how dare the Germans threaten them and this wonderful country they have just arrived in? In the end most of them settle for a sort of quiet fatalism. If you take all the other emotions and throw in the fact that they are in the army and can't go anywhere else anyway, then what the hell? Let's drink to 'long life'!

Friday, August 2, 1940

The morning is quiet, spent mostly on deck gazing at the wonders of a huge and busy wartime port. After a quiet lunch they pack up their gear and march off the ship and onto a train that departs for southern England.

Saturday, August 3, 1940

The train from Glasgow arrives at Aldershot, 30 miles southwest of London, at 0500hrs. It has been a long night with not much sleep, and only one brief stop at Crewe to stretch their legs. The men of the No.1 Canadian General Hospital form up outside the Aldershot station and march through the town with bagpipes blazing away – to little effect, as the town is still asleep. They arrive at their billets that are called the Badajos Barracks, which they are told had been built during the Crimean War. They believe it when they inspect their quarters, which are solid but dilapidated and dirty.

-/-

Over the next few days they fix up the barracks to be quite acceptable, and find the officers' club, which is really quite nice. It has a good clubhouse, splendid grass tennis courts, and cricket and polo grounds. It feels more like being on vacation than going to war.

Monday, August 5, 1940

They start their work at the Aldershot Military Hospital, and the sense of being on holidays vanishes. They treat patients from the North Africa campaign, the recent 'miracle' action at Dunkirk, and victims of the bombing that is a constant reminder of the aerial Battle of Britain now raging in the skies over England.

Colonel Ruddick tells them that they will be at Aldershot until their own hospital facility 'somewhere up north' is completed. They find that they have great freedom to travel around, and in particular to visit other medical facilities and take courses to increase their skills.

6. LEARNING EXPERIENCES

The young doctors learn a lot as they practice in England.

Friday, August 9, 1940

Rocke's colleagues Jimmy Martin and Keith Gordon have returned from London where they have been looking into training prospects for the Canadian doctors. Over dinner they tell Rocke and his friends Palmer Howard and Phil Hill that they have been invited to go to the headquarters of the Royal College of Surgeons in London to work with Sir John Beattie.

"Wasn't Sir John a Professor of Anatomy at McGill?" asks Phil Hill.

"Yes he was," says Jimmy Martin, "but he left McGill and moved over here about 10 years ago. He's now head of the Department of Experimental Surgery at the Royal College. We didn't see his department or meet him, but from what we were told he sounds like an amazing guy to work with."

"This is terrific," says Rocke. "John Beattie was a legend at McGill. He was supposed to be a great surgeon, and evidently his classes were exciting. He didn't just talk; he asked a lot of questions and posed new ideas and theories for discussion. I guess that's why they spotted him and asked him to set up Experimental Surgery over here."

Palmer Howard is equally excited. "You know, Sir John is one of the foremost surgeons in the world. Working in his department is going to give us all sorts of insights into the most advanced thinking in surgery. I wonder why he's doing it? Does he think we're still students, or what?"

"I don't think so," says Martin." I think the Brits are bloody pleased that we all came over here so quickly to help out against the Germans, and they want to keep us busy and happy. And what better way than to volunteer us to work in places like the Royal College? And they probably also think that we still have a few things to learn, so why not teach us? That's OK with me."

"Right," says Rocke, "as long as there's no exams to write!"

-/-

This is their first intimation of the tremendous training opportunities available to them while in wartime England. These Canadians, like all Canadian military personnel who came to England at that time, have come to take part in an active war, doing their bit on Britain's side to defeat the Nazi menace. Yet they will first spend almost three years in England before being involved in an actual war zone. Germany is rampant on the continent, and this is the time of the German air raids, the curfews and the Battle of Britain. The British Expeditionary Forces have been driven off the continent at Dunkirk, and there is the disastrous Canadian raid at Dieppe. The Allies have had some successes in North Africa, but far from the Allies invading Europe to push the Nazis out of the occupied territories, there is the ever-present fear of a German invasion across the Channel.

So in England the priorities are the war in the air, preparation for the eventual invasion to liberate Europe, and home defence. Rocke's war during these years consists of medical work on civilians and some military casualties, and setting up and running military hospitals in England to support the war effort. It is a time of frustrating waiting and frequent boredom, but also of education and learning.

The young Canadian doctors have many opportunities to learn advanced medical skills directly from the top people in their fields, who make themselves available in England due to the war situation. The Canadians are almost all young and relatively inexperienced when they arrive, but in England they are greeted as well-trained officers ready to take on serious responsibilities. The work with Sir John Beattie is but one example. Rocke's diary describes many.

Rocke's Diary

Tuesday, August 20, 1940
I finished shortly before 2:00 pm and, there being no further work to be done there, I took a bus to St. Thomas' Hospital, just across

the river from the Parliament Buildings. There I listened to a well-known orthopaedic surgeon called Bristowe hold his outpatient clinic. He did it in just the way Sir John does and was, I thought, very nearly as good, providing an excellent afternoon's entertainment.

Thursday, August 22, 1940
Spent the morning at the Middlesex Hospital: first at the Tumour Clinic, then about the Radiotherapy Ward with Windiers – a very interesting morning.

Friday, August 23, 1940
Spent the whole day at the R.C.S. doing what turned out to be quite an interesting experiment. In the few days work that we have had there have been no startling results achieved, but just the same I have profited greatly by it. I have learned all sorts of things that may be of use later on.

Tuesday, September 3, 1940
Our hygiene course continued unabated today. It's really quite amusing, and keeps us busy until about 4 pm – infinitely better than sitting around all day doing nothing. We have lectures in the morning and demonstrations in the afternoon. They have gone to a great deal of trouble to prepare for us, and I think we are probably getting something out of it.

Thursday, November 14, 1940
I went into Birmingham to watch some operating. Watched a Mr. Sampson, Birmingham's top surgeon, do three very interesting jobs – the first surgery I have seen since London. It was good sport.

Saturday, January 11, 1941
In the afternoon Professor Florey arrived up from Oxford and we spent the latter part of the afternoon showing him about the hospital and talking to him. He has done a lot of work on shock since the war began, and is right in the thick of the Medical Research Coun-

cil, an interesting fellow with all sorts of good ideas. After dinner he gave a talk on his subject to the group of us – the first meeting of that sort we have had. We had quite a discussion afterwards and I found out quite a few things that I had not known before.

This session on January 11 is particularly interesting as Florey's 'subject', which Rocke cannot name in his diary due to censors' restrictions, is the new wonder drug penicillin. Florey is one of the scientists who was later knighted and received the Nobel Prize for his work on penicillin. The young doctors realize that the importance of this drug in wartime cannot be overstated. Infection is a constant, deadly threat to the war wounded; to be able to deal with it with this new drug would be a tremendous advance! But from the sounds of things it will take a miracle to have it ready for use during this war.

Tuesday, February 11, 1941
Sir Arthur Hurst, a famous medical man over here, came up from Oxford today to pay us a visit. Before dinner he went around the wards and put on a splendid show. After dinner, he gave us a lecture on some of the problems that the army medical man meets, with particular reference to gastric problems. It was really very interesting; in fact his whole visit was a great success.

Saturday, March 1, 1941
Three men came up from Oxford for lunch in the afternoon and evening. They were Professor Trueta, Professor Seddons and Dr. Scott. Trueta is a Spaniard or, properly, a Catalonian who saw a tremendous amount of war injuries in the Civil War. He was chief surgeon to the Barcelona General Hospital, and wrote a book about his experiences. He is regarded by some as a bit of a radical in many ways because he is a strong proponent of some methods introduced during the last war which have not been accepted by everyone. I have always believed him to be sound in his ideas, and everything I saw him do and heard him say today confirmed me in my opinion. … Seddons is an Englishman, an orthopaedic surgeon, quite young. He has been specializing in nerve injuries and gave us an hour's talk on the work he has been doing – very interesting too.

Thursday, August 7, 1941
Jack Garrie...and I...drove over to Park Prewett Hospital where
Jack had an appointment with Sir Harold Gillies – the big plastic
man. There we spent a most entrancing day. I saw things the like of
which I had never seen before: all types of facial deformities, several
operations during the day, and a lot of post-operative cases – some
extraordinary results – really worth seeing.

October 1941
Forgot to put in the most important thing I did last week. On
Friday, three of us went in to Birmingham to the medical school
and started a dissection in the Anatomy Department. We planned
to stick with it (once a week) as long as possible. The lab is new (a
Nuffield donation) and is quite the finest thing of its kind I have
seen. The prospects of this are very good.

November 1941
Jim Shannon and I are starting to take a great interest in knees and
have outlined a plan for clinical research. I hope we can follow it
up. Knees are certainly a very important consideration in the Army,
second only to feet.

Thursday, December 11, 1941
After lunch Cam Gardner and I drove to Dorking where we heard
Mr. Watson Jones address the Corps Medical Officers. He is one of
the outstanding orthopaedic men in the country and is a master in
his line – very well worth listening to.

In these sections of his diary written while in England, and indeed throughout it, Rocke takes a somewhat relaxed and even flip approach to what are really serious events and issues. Surgery is, for example, *'an excellent afternoon's entertainment'*, or *'good sport'*. This does not reflect a less than serious attitude to his work, but rather his wish to reassure his family back in Canada, to whom he sends his diaries in instalments, that everything is just fine and he is in good spirits. The light tone disappears when he writes his official war diaries in Sicily and Italy.

Thursday, September 19, 1940

Colonel Ruddick tells Rocke that he has been promoted to the rank of Captain. Rocke is not sure what he has done to deserve the honour, but has no complaints about it.

7. No.1 CGH, MARSTON GREEN

The No.1 Canadian General Hospital sets up near Birmingham.

Monday, October 14, 1940

Rocke joins ten other No.1 Canadian General Hospital men in the five-hour drive from Aldershot to Marston Green, a small town on the eastern outskirts of the great industrial city of Birmingham and 10 miles west of the ancient cathedral city of Coventry. They pull up in front of a new hospital building that is to be the home of the No.1 Canadian General Hospital. They are the advance party sent to get things ready for the full staff. Rocke and George Raymond embark immediately on an inspection tour.

The building is large and spacious, with a well thought-out floor plan and big, bright rooms. There are still several painters applying the finishing touches in the wards, and two plumbers are noisily sorting out a problem in one of the patients' washrooms.

George is smiling as they head for the entrance at the completion of their walk-through. "You know, it really looks quite good. Mind you, we've heard so many bad stories about what to expect, I guess anything reasonable would look just fine. But, well, what do you think?"

"I agree. It seems to be very well finished, and clean. It'll take us a while to check the layout and get it up to really efficient working order, but that's only to be expected. So, on the whole I'm delighted. And it's great to feel that we now have our own facility. If only we were still close to London. I don't think Birmingham is quite the same!"

"You've got that right, Rocke. And listen, I hear that we have some ambulances to use, and two of them came through the Canadian Red Cross Society. One was donated by the City of Calgary, and the other – wait for it – by the Capilano Brewing Company in Vancouver! Not bad eh?"

Rocke chuckles. "I guess I'll have to switch brands when I get back to Canada."

As they head out of the building they meet Cam Gardner, who is coming in to break the news to them that...."Guess what? We have this nice hospital to work in, but no place to sleep. They've forgotten to build any living accommodations for us. So gentlemen, we will be joining the local citizens in their own homes! Come on over to the office they've set up and find out who the lucky people are."

Rocke is billeted with a couple named John and Mary Fisk. They live in a comfortable house in a newly built community near the hospital. John works in a screw factory in Birmingham, and Mary runs a pleasant and efficient house and does volunteer work at a local medical clinic. They greet the Canadian doctor warmly, and work hard to make him feel at home. They agree that he will have his breakfasts with them, and most of his other meals at the village pub.

-/-

The Canadian team start their work getting the hospital ready for action. This is a new experience for Rocke and his colleagues, who have spent all of their medical lives, through training and early practical experience, in well-established hospitals. Now they have to start from scratch, and Rocke finds himself preparing inventories of supplies and equipment, re-designing operating rooms, and working on a myriad of operational details. It is a valuable learning experience for him and his colleagues, and gives them insights into the professionalism of the people who do these things on a regular basis.

Rocke's Diary

Wednesday, November 6, 1940
That night, two nurses whom we had borrowed from the Neurological Unit arrived – both well trained operating room nurses. The following day, Wednesday, I spent with them in the OR showing them what we had done. Apart from one or two stupid bits of work we had not done too badly, and they seemed quite pleased with the

place. It was very good sport to hear some of their comments on the rather makeshift and left-handed way in which we had tackled some of the problems. I have learned all sorts of things recently about operating rooms that I had never known before, and consider that the experience has been worth a lot. I had been having particular sport with the Autoclave (for sterilizing the gowns, towels, etc). I find that I knew very little about it before and I am finding out new things every day.

Friday, November 15, 1940

German bombing the previous evening has devastated Coventry, and the British authorities are nervous that Birmingham will be next. They ask if the No.1 CGH would take on some patients from Birmingham hospitals. The hospital accepts immediately, and they are even pleased in that they are all set up and ready to go, but so far have received almost no patients. This event gives them some valuable experience, some of which they hadn't planned for.

Rocke's Diary

November 15, 1940
When we got the news at about 1000hrs that patients were arriving half our men were off on leave and several officers had left, so for those of us remaining there was a good bit to do. My ward was completely empty – beds, bedside tables etc having all been taken out so that the floor could be waxed. During the day we managed to get it all put back – beds set up, tables in place and a few minutes before the patients arrived we completed the making of the last bed. At around 2200hrs ambulances and buses started to arrive loaded with children aged 0 to about 12 – 140 of them in all. The patients were all sorts: medical, surgical and nose and throat mostly. Of the 36 in my ward 16 were post-operative mastoids, a few medical patients and the rest surgical. By the next day all the cases had been switched about from hut to hut until I had a full ward of nose and throat cases. I was therefore shifted to the next hut, which contained mostly surgical cases.

Here I was very happy for a short time until word came around that 16 of the children that had been sent to us had been nursed by a nurse who had since developed diphtheria. Furthermore, one or two of the kids developed measles, and in the resulting shuffle I ended up with a ward consisting of about half medical and half surgical cases – with an odd nose and throat infant thrown in. Some of the kids are pretty ill but the majority are fairly fit. Just how long we will have them on our hands remains to be seen. I imagine the measles epidemic, which is bound to develop, and the diphtheria possibilities would complicate the picture for some time to come. In any event, it is good sport and we feel a little more worthy of ourselves than heretofore.

This is the first time the team has been faced with a sudden, heavy influx of patients, which is the hallmark of wartime medical service. It places extra burdens on the medical staff, who must deal not only with the medical situation of each individual case, but also must have efficient decision systems. In the process known as 'triage' they must quickly and accurately sort out the non-serious from the serious from the critical cases, thereby establishing priorities for treatment. There are a growing number of situations like this in England, providing excellent training for the actual theatres of war. Rocke's diary illustrates.

Rocke's Diary

Thursday, January 9, 1941
I spent the whole afternoon waiting for a convoy of patients to arrive. It finally did at 1600hrs – 69 patients in 17 ambulances, our first batch of soldiers.

Friday, January 10, 1941
During the day we learned that we were to have another batch of patients, and they arrived just before dark – 123 strong and not an exciting case in the whole lot.

Monday, January 13, 1941
A busy day – probably the busiest in a medical sense that I have had for a very long time. We had not yet worked up all the cases that arrived last week. The medical people who had a great many more patients than we had were badly bogged down. They had taken on one of the junior surgeons to help them, and today when 31 new cases arrived I was taken on to. We now have quite a houseful; eight wards full nearly, a great difference from the time last week when we had three sparsely populated wards.

Wednesday, April 9, 1941
On Tuesday night there was a raid just to the south of us, but not affecting us much until the next day when, to my great joy, the powers that be asked us to supply a surgical team. Jimmy Martin, Louis Quinn and I set off with two nurses and an orderly. We went to an emergency hospital at Warwick and spent from 1030hrs in the morning until 2000hrs at night operating on air raid casualties. All the plans that we had laid months ago bore fruit. The team worked smoothly and I think we did some quite decent work – the sort of thing we had been hoping for all along.

Thursday, April 10, 1941
That night the raid was even closer to home than it had been during the previous nights. In fact it was the first night since we've been here that I stayed up because of a raid. I don't believe that I could have slept through this one. We all stayed up until about 4 am and nearly all of us spent the rest of the night sleeping in the hospital. We expected that the team would be called out the following day, Friday, but instead we had patients admitted to us – 39 of them – mostly from Coventry, and since then we have been up to our necks in work taking care of them. We've had real trouble with two of them. One (a patient of mine) has already died, and another (not mine thank God) is well on the way. Both developed gas gangrene, which is as horrible a business as I have ever seen. It has all been very harrowing but we have learned a tremendous amount.

Tuesday, May 27, 1941
I had another couple of operations today, this time on George Raymond's patients, he having been admitted to the ward with a cough. With his practice, Cam Gardner's and my own I control something over 50 cases – a tremendous number by comparison with the usual run.

Saturday, September 20, 1941
The extra work arose out of a convoy of patients from another hospital on 28th August: about 120 patients in all of whom I drew 41 (fractures). This meant that I was given two wards, and these I still retain and sometimes I nearly have a day's work to do. Most of the cases are fractures, a few varicose veins and hand infections. At one stage I had 17 motorcycle injuries in – a most dangerous occupation, motorcycling.

December 1941
We have taken something over 500 patients in the three weeks that we have been working here, and of these I have had about a 100, nearly all fractures.

May 1942
A week or more of the usual activity during which time my own particular service swelled to 115 patients – an unprecedented number – all sorts of trash and a lot of good cases. It has also been interesting because a number of the more serious cases we had when we first came here are now coming up for final review. It's great fun when they turn out well, and awful to see the mistakes limping away, but most instructive in either case.

8. NURSES

Canadian nurses arrive at the hospital, improving its performance and enlivening the social scene.

Sunday, December 15, 1940

A group of Canadian nurses arrives at Marston Green to take up their duties at the No.1 CGH. There are smiles all around, staff and patients alike, as the nurses arrive in army vehicles and set up in the accommodations prepared for them. Without a pause they come to the hospital to receive their assignments, and move quickly to their duties. Even the weather cooperates in what is a very good day at No.1 CGH Marston Green.

Monday, December 16, 1940

Rocke is hustling along the hallway of the hospital on his morning rounds when he comes face to face with Trudy Lake, his nurse friend from the old days at the Montreal General.

"Trudy! How lovely to see you!" They exchange polite kisses.

"Rocke, it's great to see you too. Oh…oops…should I be calling you Rocke here? You're a Captain aren't you? Oh dear…will you have me court marshalled?"

They laugh together. It's good to see an old friend.

"Not unless you call me 'Rocke' on parade. Then it'll be curtains for you."

"OK. How are Rolly and Tam and the baby?"

"Just fine, thanks. Rolly and her family keep sending me tons of food and cigarettes, and of course pictures of the children. I do miss them."

"Of course you do. You've already been over here for almost half a year.

Heaven knows how long this thing will last. Let's just hope it isn't too long." She glances up and down the hallway. "You people seem to have set up a good hospital here. It's already looking like a great place to work!"

"Right, well we're not exactly experts at hospital design, but I'm sure you nurses will sort us out quickly."

"You bet we will Rocke. And I'd better get to it!"

-/-

The nurses quickly turn an adequate hospital into a very good hospital. Their unique blend of professionalism, knowledge, compassion and energy has been the missing ingredient in spite of the best efforts of the male orderlies and operating room (OR) assistants, most of whom had received only minimal training before being shipped over to England. They now pick up on their training again, this time under the instruction and watchful eyes of the nurses. The patients benefit greatly from this new situation, sensing a higher level of cooperation between the doctors and nursing staff, and also enjoying the new, warm sense of care and concern that pervades the hospital.

The presence of Canadian nurses is also a boon to the spirits of the male staff at Marston Green. There are numerous dances and teas, which Rocke enjoys. His letters home refer casually to these events, with one passing reference to 'spicy' happenings. There is also a considerable amount of dating amongst the unmarried, which Rocke observes and envies.

Saturday, May 31, 1941

A firm knock on the door heralds the arrival at Marston Green of Captain John Leishman, an urologist and surgeon from Winnipeg. 'Jack', as he is known to his colleagues, had been posted to England with the No.5 CGH from Winnipeg, based at Taplow. He has now been transferred to No.1 CGH to replace George Raymond, who is in hospital with pneumonia.

"Hello Jack, how are you?" asks Rocke as Jack enters the office without knocking. Jack Leishman is an 'A type' personality. A powerful six-footer, he marches straight ahead and is not a man to be taken lightly. Rocke knows him from several medical meetings in Montreal, and he likes Jack instinctively. He likes his power and sense of decision and movement and action.

"Fine Rocke. Great to see you. You have a nice set-up here. How's it working out?"

Rocke describes the workings of the hospital, and then fields the inevitable question, "How are the nurses?"

"They're a great bunch. They've done a lot to help us put on a really good show here. And you'll have a chance to meet them this evening. There's a dance at the nurses' quarters."

They head out of the office and onto the green for a long walk.

That evening Rocke and Jack are at the nurses' residence, sipping their scotch and watching the melee of nurses and male medical staff chatting and dancing. The noise is pleasantly loud but not deafening, mainly in deference to Matron Swanson who commands the nurses with a firm hand, and is now presiding over the party with a careful eye out for 'wrong-doing'. She has not yet had enough gin for the party to really warm up, which it always does in the end.

Jack is eying the nurses carefully, a calm and collected bachelor looking over the field. Suddenly he changes from relaxed and laid-back to alert and focused, staring at one particular nurse sitting in a chair on the other side of the room, chatting with a friend.

"Say, isn't that Trudy Lake over there? Sitting under the picture of trees?"

"That's right, Jack. She's great. She's lots of fun, and a damn fine nurse as well. Do you know her?"

· "Yes, I do," says Jack. "I met her at the Montreal General. I didn't know she was here! She's terrific." He is staring across the room, focusing on Trudy, following her every move. He is entranced.

"In fact, I'd better go and say hello right now." And without a further word he strides across the room, zeroing in on Trudy like a big game hunter. They talk, they dance, they laugh together, and by the end of the evening a romance has started. Trudy doesn't know it yet, although she does like this forceful guy from Winnipeg. Jack, on the other hand, is smitten.

Rocke watches the whole event philosophically, chatting with other doctors who are also keeping a close eye on the nurses.

-/-

Jack courts Trudy over the ensuing months, and the romance warms up. They enjoy breaks and coffee together, are together at teas and dances, and take long walks in the lush British countryside. It is difficult to find places and times to be alone together, and this becomes an increasing burden as they declare their love for each other and long to make love. Fortunately Jack is clever and inventive, and he also knows how to play the 'matron game'.

Matron Nel Swanson is in charge of the nurses, and it is her job to direct them both professionally as well as morally. A New Brunswick girl, Nel took her nurse's training in Montreal, and practiced at the Royal Victoria Hospital for five years until the war broke out. She enlisted in the army, trained in Montreal, and came overseas as head of the nursing unit in December 1940. She is a Captain in the army, a fully trained nurse and a substantial and attractive woman as well. Nel is tall and well built, with short-cropped blond hair and big blue eyes. She is very strong and athletic, and even with her normal severe expression she still looks, to most of the men at the hospital, attractive and 'not damn half-bad'.

The matron keeps a sharp eye on her charges, running them efficiently at the hospital, demanding that they take care in their dress and comportment, and watching out for them in their social lives. Her watchword, frequently uttered, is "There'll be no pregnancies on my watch."

At a dance for all ranks in February 1941 Nel meets Sergeant Harry (Hank) Money, a medical orderly from Prince Edward Island and a leader in the non-commissioned ranks at the hospital. Hank is a tall, strapping man with dark hair and wonderful brown eyes, and a lazy, casual expression that the women find magnetic. They meet by chance at the bar. After some hesitant conversation between officer and Sergeant they both realize that the difference in rank is not going to make any real difference - they are made for the same bed, and the sooner they get there the better.

The instant affair is fuelled not just by physical attraction, but also by gin. Nel loves the stuff, and drinks it with great pleasure at these social outings. She never gets drunk, but she does get tipsy and fun, and everyone knows that these are the best times to bend the rules concerning private visits to rooms for 'sport'. With Hank in the picture, Nel is drawn into bending her own rules. She is a careful and responsible person, but she is also human, and anyway she knows 'how to take care of herself' in order to live up to her watchword.

From that day on social events often feature late night disappearances of Nel and Hank, and legendary noises coming out of her room. At the same time there is, naturally, a further lightening of restrictions for everyone else. This is called the 'matron game'.

9. INSPIRATION

Churchill speaks. Everyone listens.

Wednesday, October 29, 1941

Rocke arrives home at the Fisks' house just after 1800hrs. He is feeling good: the weather is lovely, crisp and cool, and things are going well at the hospital. He carries under his arm the latest mail from Canada, which includes a wonderful letter and large parcel of goodies from Rolly. As he steps into the front door and heads for the stairs Mary calls him from the sitting room.

"Rocke, come in here, quickly. The Prime Minister is just about to speak."

Rocke goes into the room and sits down in an easy chair, joining John and Mary around their large radio set. "He's at Harrow School. They're broadcasting from there."

The radio bursts with the sound of applause, and then comes the familiar voice of Winston Churchill. He is, as usual, gruff and thrilling, and Rocke can feel the hair on the back of his head stand up in hope, fear and excitement, all jumbled together, as the great man speaks.

> *"…surely from this period of ten months this is the lesson: never give in, never give in, never, never, never, never - in nothing, great or small, large or petty - never give in except to convictions of honour and good sense. Never yield to force; never yield to the apparently overwhelming might of the enemy…"*

Rocke looks up and gazes around the tidy room and at his hosts. Mary is staring at the radio, transfixed. John is weeping silently, trying unsuccessfully to hide it behind his handkerchief.

> *"…Do not let us speak of darker days: let us speak rather of sterner days. These are not dark days; these are great days - the greatest days our country has ever lived; and we must all thank God that we have been allowed, each of us according to our stations, to play a part in making these days memorable in the history of our race."*

The speech is over. They sit silently for a full minute, absorbing the words and the lesson that comes with them. Rocke gets up and climbs the stairs to his room. He opens his letter from home and has the usual rush of pleasure as Rolly speaks to him of life back in Montreal.

Tam is full of beans now, talking a blue streak and very ready to go to a kindergarten near the house on Montrose Avenue just as soon as he is old enough. Rolly is thrilled with this sign of progress in the family, and sad that Rocke can't be with her to share the fun. It is a beautiful fall in Montreal, and Tam and Ian love playing in the piles of golden leaves in the back yard. Rocke laughs when Rolly says that she is getting quite good at raking leaves, but will definitely let Rocke take over on return. And aside from the raking, she has assembled a toolbox and is starting to learn about home repairs! She is working quite long hours at the canteen now, and is enjoying it immensely. The people are so nice there, and the young fliers are so lonely and appreciative of the meals and affordable beer. Some of them bring girls in, and Rolly is not so sure about that! Her parents are great company for her and are working hard to help her keep up her spirits.

This letter, like so many others, gives Rocke an aching vision of the joys of family life back in Canada. He usually puts the thoughts out of his mind in his busy life here in England, but the letters bring them rushing back and as always he sits in a soft bubble of loneliness, surveying his messy bachelor quarters and thinking what would happen if his family walked in *right now*. By God it would be fun!

He also has letters from his father in Victoria and his brother Bruce in Vancouver.

He opens his parcel and finds tins of cigarettes and chocolate bars, some special soap and several cans of sardines and other goodies. He has a momentary chuckle thinking about the great ships out on the dark Atlantic, braving the elements and dodging German torpedoes to bring him his chocolates!

Very funny. He stops chuckling and is totally depressed and lonely. It all seems so thoroughly stupid, and he feels so damn helpless. He is a tiny part of a huge effort, doing his part far from home by tending patients in a small hospital in the middle of nowhere – well, not exactly nowhere, but not exactly somewhere either. And hardly a part of the real war effort. He misses his family like crazy and is getting tired of it.

This is not good. *And what would Churchill think of me feeling this way? Not much!*

He always has dinner at the local pub, and it's damn well time for a beer and some laughs with friends. He takes a selection of goodies down to the Fisks, who thank him profusely, and heads out to the pub.

10. No.1 CGH, HORSHAM

The No.1 Canadian General Hospital moves to Horsham, south of London.

Saturday, November 29, 1941

Rocke and Palmer Howard leave Marston Green in Palmer's car and head to Horsham, 30 miles south of London. They eat sandwiches and cheese as they drive, stop for petrol twice, and suffer a flat tire that is fixed only after heroic efforts by Palmer. They are the first of the advance party of the No.1 CGH, which is being moved to the military hospital at Horsham and replaced at Marston Green by the No.7 CGH. They stop at the officers' mess building where they have 24 single rooms assigned to them. It is neat and comfortable, and they are delighted to find that it has central heating.

The hospital at Horsham is in an old Poor Law institution, with twelve additional huts and the finest operating rooms they have ever seen anywhere. The hospital has space for 600 patients. There is a lot of rearranging to be done for more efficient operation, but on the whole the Canadians like their new location.

-/-

Trudy Lake is very happy there, with lots of work to do and Jack Leishman ever-present to keep up the excitement. She also welcomes a new arrival at the hospital, physiotherapist Thelma Stewart. Thelma, also a Lieutenant, graduated from the University of Toronto in 1938 and joined the army in early 1941. She arrives at the No.1 CGH just as it is opening at Horsham. Trudy tells Thelma all about how the hospital works and the characters involved, and of course about her growing romance with Jack.

December 1941

The news of Pearl Harbour and the entry of the United States into the War cause great excitement and huge speculation concerning the future course of events.

January 1942

The first Americans arrive in England, and in North Africa Field Marshall Rommel's Afrika Korps begins its counter offensive against the British forces. The bombing intensifies in both England and Germany, with the first thousand-bomber air raid on Cologne and more German bombing of British cathedral cities.

In early January Rocke and colleagues attend an orthopaedic conference at Oxford, where they are housed at historic Magdalen College. Some American doctors make presentations, and there is for the first time a sort of 'hands across the sea' atmosphere that the Canadians find very pleasing.

The medical work intensifies. They handle large numbers of cases, and develop ever more efficient ways of dealing with these sudden influxes of patients. New medical personnel are posted to the hospital as the command keeps circulating staff to fill new units and departures.

March 1942

Rocke welcomes Captain Cam Dickison to the hospital as assistant surgeon in his wards. He has not met Cam before, even though they both went to McGill. Cam was just starting his medical training at McGill when Rocke was interning at the Montreal General. Cam had moved quickly to join the army following graduation in 1940.

Saturday, March 28, 1942

The pub is its usual warm self, dimly lit behind the blackout curtains, smoke-filled and humming with conversation. Most of the men are in uniform, as are at least half of the women. There are six people seated sipping their pints and gin-and-tonics around a table in the corner. Jack Leishman sits next to Trudy Lake, his hand resting on hers so that she has to drink left-handed, which is a bit awkward. Then there are Rocke and Jim Shannon, and Cam Dickison and the new physiotherapist Thelma Stewart. Jack has arranged the outing. Rocke is pretty sure why he has done so, as it is now well known around the hospital that Jack and Trudy are a serious item. He is somewhat surprised to see Cam sitting so close to Thelma, although he has heard that they have struck up a very good friendship right from the start. Rocke feels like the old married man of the group, out with his pal Jim for a few beers.

As Jack brings the drinks to the table they go through the inevitable shoptalk about patients and problems. They are all living comfortably and are only too aware of the fate of the conquered people on mainland Europe, and of the terrible cost of the German bombing in England.

"How are you settling in, Thelma?" asks Jim. "From the amount of leg and arm work I'm doing I think you're going to be pretty busy doing your physiotherapy."

"Just fine thanks," she replies, taking a modest sip of her drink and casting a quick smile in Cam's direction. "I must say we have a nice facility to work in. Don't you love it that it was a 'Poor Law' institution? I guess it's been fixed up a bit since then!"

"I should say so," says Cam. "I can't imagine the old British government treating the poor to central heating."

The talk goes on, turning more to the progress of the war and how it seems to be going on endlessly, and when are the Allies going to assault Europe, especially now that the Americans are on side? This leads to a couple of inevitable stories about Americans, after which Jack clears his throat and says that he has an announcement to make. All eyes immediately turn to Trudy.

"I'm delighted to tell you that Trudy has agreed to marry me, and we are officially engaged as of right now!" He stands up, spilling his beer in the process, pulls a small box out of his pocket, extracts a ring from it, gets down on his knees, and dramatically places the ring on Trudy's finger. She looks intensely emotional throughout, but then grins at him for the split second before he plants a kiss on her lips and then folds her in a bear hug.

The table erupts in applause and exclamations of delight, and the other men shake Jack's hand and give Trudy a kiss. Thelma gets into the act by kissing them both and then getting a towel from the bar to wipe up the spilt beer. Rocke and Jim head for the bar for another round, and the celebration is well and truly underway.

"Jolly good," says Rocke after a huge quaff of beer, thinking as he says it that he is sounding more British every day. "And it's about time too! Jim and I were thinking that we'd better tell Nel Swanson about all your goings on, not that that would do much good of course!" They all laugh, as Jack and Trudy are known to be the hospital's number one experts at the matron game. "But seriously you two, if you get married over here, Trudy, you'll have to leave the army won't you?"

"I'm afraid so, Rocke. It seems like such a quaint rule to me, but that's the way it is. However, Jack and I have looked into it, and we think the Colonel will let me continue my work at the hospital on a contract, even if I'm not in the army. I certainly hope so."

"I'm sure they will," says Jack, using a napkin as a towel to dry his sleeve that is drenched with spilled beer. "The point is they need nurses now, and will need them even more when the war heats up on the continent. If the hospital is moved out of England there might be a problem, of course, but we'll deal with that one when we have to."

"So, when's the big day?" asks Thelma.

"We're thinking of some date in late June," says Trudy. "I just hope we don't get shipped out somewhere before then."

-/-

The year goes by. They take some leave.

The attitude of Rocke and his colleagues during these long days of waiting for real action in what they call 'the war effort', meaning a fighting front, is a mixture of interest, boredom and study. They are in a country at war and being bombed mercilessly, yet they are struck by the calmness of the English people. The Brits are focused and working hard, and they are damned if they are going to let those bombs and the bad news get them down.

The Canadian doctors observe the war through the media reports and observation of the effects of the bombing: the destruction and the casualties. They discuss the war endlessly, develop and debate theories on what will happen, and at the same time write home to their families reassuring them that things are OK and everything will turn out just fine.

They have military training in such things as parade drill, the use of gas masks and firearms drill, but this does not appeal to them very much as they know that their role will always be to provide medical services to soldiers, not to be soldiers themselves. They work at their medical practices when called upon, study subjects of interest and run hospitals, but they are seldom fully occupied and have plenty of time for leisure activities such as bicycling, tennis, movies and social events including dances with the nurses. They are learning about that tried and true saying in the military, to 'hurry up and wait'. They have been rushed over to England to help out in whatever the circumstances. Now they will just have to wait for those circumstances to evolve into real, live war action.

May 1942

They carry out a training scheme to see how many casualties they can handle and what methods they should use in handling them. It all goes off quite well, although it does show up some loopholes in their systems. It also gives them a grim picture of what they will face in the event of a really big emergency.

At this time there are only 13 of the original 26 officers left in the No.1 CGH unit, due to the shifting around of personnel amongst different units and on special assignments. This is actually a remarkably stable situation; it would have been much less so had they been more actively involved in the war action.

Things continue quiet for this group of Canadians, but they are certainly anything but quiet elsewhere. June sees the Battle of Midway in the Pacific, marking the turning point in the Pacific war. The German occupation of Europe continues, but British forces under Montgomery gain the initiative in North Africa at El Alamein, and Russian forces counterattack in the battle for Stalingrad.

Sunday, June 21, 1942

Jack Leishman's long campaign to win the heart and hand of Trudy Lake finally concludes as they are married in the local church in Horsham. Under army regulations Trudy resigns from the army, and this she does with regret. Fortunately, however, Colonel Ruddick honours his promise to keep her at the No.1 CGH under contract. She and Jack share a small flat in Horsham, not far from the hospital.

Meanwhile Cam Dickison and Thelma Stewart become more and more of 'an item', and their romance flourishes within the usual confines of military life and the matron game.

11. THE NEED FOR SPEED

*The governments realize that there is need to update
the medical services NOW.*

In late 1941 a British committee under the chairmanship of Brigadier W.C. Hartgill was appointed to study the organization of the British and Canadian army medical services, with special attention to its ability to provide timely service in the field. Their report, issued at the end of December 1941, started with the blunt statement that...

"It is obvious from a study of the Spanish Civil War and from experience gained in the various campaigns of the present war, that a reorganization of the medical services in the corps and divisions is long overdue".

Their findings could be summarized by the simple statement that the medical services were not organized to keep up with the fast pace and mobility of modern warfare. The chief defects listed in the report were as follows:

1. *Field medical units are cumbersome, insufficiently mobile and not readily adaptable to changing tactical situations.*

2. *Field ambulances do not possess adequate means of communication, either with the formations they serve, or with the officers who administer them.*

3. *Casualties are not distributed directly to the appropriate units, but pass through a channel of evacuation, which causes congestion at the forward medical units. Insufficient transport leads to delay in the distribution of casualties to selected centres.*

4. *Casualties are not afforded the advantages which modern surgical tech-*
   nique can provide. Surgeons, their assistants and equipment are located
   too far to the rear of divisions and corps.

Reorganization to deal with these defects was considered to be 'imperative
and urgent', and virtually all of the recommendations were effected by mid-
1942. Changes included the introduction of three new types of units: the Field
Dressing Station, the Field Surgical Unit and the Field Transfusion Unit.

12. BIRTH OF THE FSU

Rocke is selected to set up a Field Surgical Unit.

Friday, October 30, 1942

Rocke is called to London headquarters of the RCAMC, to the office of Colonel J.A. MacFarlane, Surgical Consultant to the Canadian Army Overseas. He knocks and is called in immediately.

"Good morning Captain Robertson. Have a seat. Tea?"

"Thank you, Sir."

MacFarlane moves from the window to his desk, sits down carefully amidst a jumble of papers, and organizes a small pile of them in front of him as the batman serves them tea. The door closes and he looks up at Rocke with a slight smile pushing up his moustache.

"Well Robertson, I hear you've been impatient to get into the action somewhere. Is that correct?"

"Very much so, Sir. That's what we all came over here for."

"Right. Well, it looks like you're going to get some action. You've been selected to set up a Field Surgical Unit, which we call an 'FSU'. We don't know how it will be used, or where, but it will certainly mean action somewhere."

"That's excellent, Sir," Rocke replies. "I've heard about these Field Surgical Units, but I don't know much about them."

"You know Frank Mills over at No.15 CGH at Bramshott?" Rocke nods. "Well, we've had him set up our first FSU. It's all been very hush hush, but this comes out of a report late last year that said our medical services can't keep up with the war. It moves too damn fast now: tank units and aircraft and motorized units and the like."

The Colonel explains that there will still be Casualty Clearing Stations set up to tend to all wounded and eventually route them through to hospitals. However, the simple ambulance-to-Casualty Clearing Station system that was all right for the Great War, where they were often pinned down for months and months in one place, just won't do now. As the Stations must be set up well behind the lines, they will usually be too far from the action to help the men who are badly wounded up front – especially if the front is moving ahead quickly. By the time the ambulances can get a serious casualty back to a Casualty Clearing Station for operating he will probably be dead. He notes further that if a Station is too close to the action and things go wrong up front, it probably can't be moved out of the way fast enough and the enemy will grab it. So that won't solve the problem.

"We need intermediate, mobile units to stay closer to the action and provide medical help more quickly to those who need it. And that's where the new units come in: the Field Dressing Stations and the Field Surgical Units and, oh yes, the Field Transfusion Units.

"The Brits have tried using mobile medical units, including surgical units, down in the desert, and have had some success. The big problem for them has been getting the right people and the right equipment, because this is a new idea and it's tough to get the right things and people quickly out of traditional units. They've had to scurry around and work with what they can find, but they have at least proved the point. They've put medical men and supplies into jeeps and lorries and followed the action as closely as they can. So a wounded Tank Commander in the middle of nowhere can find himself on an operating table in hours rather than days. Great stuff!"

"It must be pretty tough operating conditions, Colonel, with all the sand and dirt and flies?" Rocke feels growing excitement, but he is a surgeon trained in sanitary conditions in hospitals.

"Of course, Robertson. This idea calls for all sorts of new thinking and organization, and a lot of imagination in the field, but it's the only answer. Now then, let's get down to it.

"Here's how it's going to work in the field from now on. As usual it starts with the regimental medical people: the Medical Officers and their orderlies. They are right up there with their units in the thick of the fighting, and they bring the wounded back to Regimental Aid Posts that they set up in sheds or barns or tents – anywhere they can find on the edge of the field of battle. It's a damn sticky business at this early stage, of course, with the stretcher-bearers under fire, as the enemy often ignore or just don't notice the red crosses on their helmets. We can expect to lose a lot of those fellows."

The Colonel stares out the window for a moment. Then he lights his pipe.

"Anyway, they bring the wounded to the Aid Post and do whatever they can to fix them up – you know, clean them up, stop the bleeding, put on splints, that sort of thing – and get them ready for the trip back. Then it's the turn of the Divisional medical services to take over.

"Our Field Ambulances set up Casualty Collecting Posts in strategic locations, and either the regimental chaps bring the wounded there, or the stretcher-bearer sections of our Field Ambulances go out and collect them. Depends on the situation – who is busier, or has the vehicles, or enough people. Sometimes the Field Ambulance bearers go right up into the field with the regimental people. One way or the other the wounded are assembled at these collection points and then brought to Advanced Dressing Stations set up by our Field Ambulances, where the Field Ambulance doctors carry out 'triage' on the assembled wounded. That is, they sort them out into three groups: Group 1 cases require further medical attention in the field, but not surgery. Group 2 cases require immediate surgery. Group 3 cases are fit enough to survive the trip all the way back to the Casualty Clearing Station before they receive more attention. These are usually the walking wounded.

"The Field Ambulances then move the wounded back: Group 1 to the nearest Field Dressing Station; Group 2 to the nearest Field Dressing Station with a Field Surgical Unit attached; and Group 3 directly back to the Casualty Clearing Station, or perhaps to a Field Dressing Station en route to the Casualty Clearing Station.

"The Field Dressing Station, or 'FDS' in our lingo, is a mobile station in tents or abandoned buildings, as close to the action as possible, with medical staff, nurses if possible, kitchens and lots of bed space. It is in effect a small, mobile hospital, with emphasis on 'mobile' as it can pack itself in trucks and be on the way in short order. It has wards for patients not ready for the move back to the Casualty Clearing Station, so this affects its mobility somewhat.

"Then we have the Field Surgical Units that move amongst the Field Dressing Stations providing surgical services to Group 2 patients. They are small and very mobile, and rely on the Field Dressing Stations for services such as cooking and laundry, and of course for all pre- and post-operative services to patients. You can picture them as simply mobile operating rooms."

The Colonel explains that the concept of the mobile Field Transfusion Unit had been developed by Canadian Dr. Norman Bethune working in the battlefields in China and then the Spanish Civil War. Loss of blood was a major cause of death on the battlefield and during the wounded's move back to medical facilities. The problem of keeping blood fresh and available for transfusion was solved by these mobile units. They would move amongst Field Dressing Stations providing blood services and assisting with the resuscitation of severely wounded patients.

"The new jargon," says the Colonel, "is that when an FSU and FTU are set up next to an FDS you have an ASC – an Advanced Surgical Centre. And when there's a Field Ambulance there as well it becomes a 'Canadian Medical Centre'."

Rocke is sitting forward on the edge of his chair, charged with excitement. "The concept is very exciting, Sir. So, how are these Field Surgical Units to be organized?"

"You'll be a small, very mobile unit compared to the others, except the Transfusion Units which will have just two vehicles. The Field Dressing Stations will have around 90 staff, headed by a Major, and 13 vehicles and a couple of motorcycles. The Field Ambulances will also be a substantial size, with 17 or 18 vehicles – lots of ambulances, of course.

The Colonel is at his diplomatic best as he slides over the fact that there are substantial differences between the British and Canadian authorities concerning the design of Field Surgical Units. Until these differences are resolved they are going with the Canadian concept which calls for three medical officers - a surgeon, an assistant surgeon and an anaesthetist, two operating room nurses, a batman, three orderlies (one of whom should be a Sergeant), and three drivers. The surgeon is the Commander of the unit, and a Major. His other officers are Captains. The FSU has three vehicles. The big one is the surgical van to carry all the operating room equipment. It has a 60cwt (sixty hundredweight or three tons) chassis and a special body for holding the unit's equipment. Then there's a 30cwt general service lorry to carry supplies and gear, and an 8cwt utility vehicle to carry people.

"That's what Captain Mills has, and it seems to be working pretty well. The surgical van is terrific stuff."

"Right Sir," says Rocke. "So you would like me to start setting up a second Field Surgical Unit. Based here in Horsham?"

"Yes. Based here, and you should try to find your staff from this hospital or nearby units. This is priority stuff so we can clear the way for you to get people from almost anywhere, but let's keep it as simple as possible. And, oh yes, you'll have to do this as Captain for the present, but we'll get your Major's stripes to you as soon as possible. Frank Mills is in the same boat."

"Thank you Sir. Shall I begin at once? How about my regular duties at the hospital?"

"I've already made arrangements with Colonel Martin to free you up. Yes, you should start at once. And in fact, Captain Mills is taking his unit out on a big training scheme called *Sawbones* starting on Monday. You should go with them to see how things work."

"Yes Sir. Thank you Sir. Will that be all?"

"Yes Robertson. Keep me right up to date on progress. Good luck."

Rocke stands up, salutes, and leaves the office. He is grinning from ear to ear. His war is finally beginning.

Tuesday, November 3, 1942

Frank Mills calls to Rocke to come and inspect the set-up. They are in a wooded grove somewhere in Hampshire, part of the large operational exercise known as Exercise *Sawbones*. The idea of the exercise is to test the validity of the new organization of medical services in the army. Just how mobile are they? Is the staffing appropriate? How well do they communicate and work together?

Frank's No.1 Canadian Field Surgical Unit has established an operating room in a tent in the grove, near a larger set of tents established by the new No.9 Field Ambulance. Their surgical van sits near the operating tent, connected to it by a wire that goes from the van's generator system to the tent's electrical systems. Rocke joins Frank and they stroll towards the tent.

Rocke has been with them since the start of the exercise yesterday morning, travelling in the utility vehicle, and has been watching them set up today. He has deliberately stayed out of the way so as not to affect the functioning of the unit. He and Frank know each other quite well, and Frank is delighted to have Rocke along on the exercise.

"OK, Rocke, so we're set up and ready to operate. It took us about an hour from the time we stopped here, which isn't too bad. It should be better, but we're all still learning. One of the biggest questions is what to have inside the tent, and what to leave out. It's tempting to have everything we might conceivably need inside, but the tents are just too small and crowded. So we're trying to get a clear picture of what the really important things are – the things that we will need quickly every time, and then the things that we can wait a few minutes for if someone has to go and fetch them."

They stop in front of the tent and look around. The three drivers are standing outside the surgical van, watching them. It is their job to keep the generator going, tidy the van and get it in order for further movement, and to be prepared to fetch any supplies or equipment from any of the trucks. They also are armed and keep a lookout for visitors, friendly or otherwise.

Frank's Second-in-Command (2 I/C), Captain Ed Tovee, greets them at the entrance, as does the anaesthetist as they move into the tent. The room is a miniature operating theatre, much smaller than one found in a hospital, but with all the essential equipment in place. It is crowded with the other members of the unit, all smiling and looking very pleased with themselves. Frank asks the senior nurse how it looks.

"It's fine, Sir, although it is a bit small. I suspect that we'll all become very good friends!" Everyone chuckles at this. She goes on. "But seriously, Sir, we will always be better to find an abandoned building or house or something than to use this tent. We really could use a bit more space, and I'm worried about the sanitary conditions in a tent. Anyway, we'll work it out."

"Quite right," says Frank. "We'll always look for the best quarters we can find. Of course it depends on where we go. If we go to France we might just be able to find a convenient wine cellar or something." There are more smiles, and the light tone prevails as they discuss the organization of equipment, sanitation, set-ups and takedowns, and other operational matters.

Rocke and Frank leave the tent and discuss the unit as they stroll back to the truck. "What are your main problems?" asks Rocke. "I need all the advice I can get."

"I'm basically happy with the set-up. But yes, there are some big issues that we'll have to deal with. One is the trucks. They're the key to our whole existence. No trucks, no mobility. They seem to be pretty strong, but they do break down fairly often, or rather they seem to need a lot of servicing.

My drivers are pretty good at it, but I'll tell you, I don't relish the thought of blowing the surgical van's engine when we're supposed to be heading into action. You should be sure that your drivers have as much mechanics training as possible, and lots of spare parts.

"Having the nurses with us will be terrific from a medical point of view, and it's certainly nice to have a couple of women with us to keep up our spirits. But I'm already worried about their safety, not to mention the lack of privacy. They seem to be very eager to be involved, so I guess it'll be ok. I hope so.

"From a medical standpoint, my biggest concern is sanitation. It'll depend a lot on where we're sent. As I said back there we could be in France and in a very nice and clean place to work. But that's not likely – the clean part, that is. There'll be mud and sweat and bugs all over the place almost for sure, so keeping the operations clean is going to be a chore. And if we go to the desert or some such hot place we'll have flies and spiders and sand and God knows what else to cause infection. But hey, it's our job to sort these things out, so we will."

"What happens now?" asks Rocke. Where to next?"

"We're through for the day. The Colonel has already been by to inspect, so we'll take everything down and pack it away in the vehicles, and go back to the same quarters for the night. Tomorrow we're going to set up in an old schoolhouse."

"I'll be heading back to Horsham tomorrow, Frank. I've seen what I have to see. You've done a great job, and I appreciate all the advice. Now then, there's a pub near the barracks isn't there?"

"Absolutely right Rocke. Good idea."

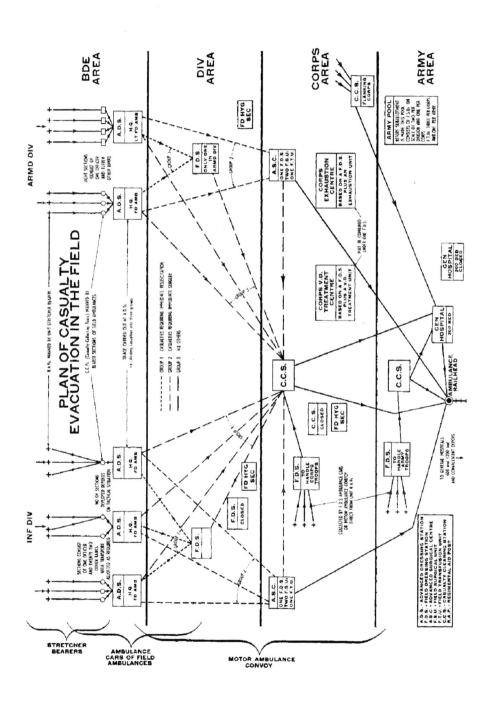

13. PUTTING IT TOGETHER

Oh, the complexities of setting up a new unit in a traditional army setting!

Wednesday, December 9, 1942

Rocke sits across the desk from Lt. Colonel S.J. Martin, Chief of the Surgical Division of the No.1 CGH in Horsham. He watches as the Colonel goes through a detailed brief Rocke has prepared on personnel for his Field Surgical Unit. Colonel Martin has been helpful in reviewing with him the officers in the unit who might be available. It has been up to Rocke to discuss the prospect with candidates to see who is interested, and to make recommendations.

Colonel Martin opens the discussion. "I like the idea of Jack Leishman as your Second-in- Command. He's a damn fine surgeon, and his work in urology will help in the field. I also think he has the personality for the job. He's tough and energetic, and the men will listen to him. And he won't be afraid to take over when necessary."

"Right, Sir. It's his personality that tipped the balance for me. Oh, and he's had some pretty good training in anaesthesia too, which is a bonus. We all have, but he seems to have taken it in a bit better than most."

"Which brings us to the anaesthetist. I think Keefer is a good choice, although I must admit I thought you would be recommending Franklin. Franklin is superb at his job, but Keefer isn't far behind. What made you lean towards Keefer?"

"Personality once again, Sir. Just as with the 2I/C, I'm looking for determination and flexibility in this position as well. After all, he'll be our third officer, and it may turn out that he has to take over on occasion. Keefer is a real driver. He punches straight ahead. He likes to control the operating room as much as possible. He treats the patient as a customer, and nothing is too good for him. He's the sort of man I want in the unit."

"OK, Rocke. I'll have a word with Leishman and Keefer and get their formal acceptances. And I'll also see to the bloody paperwork you'll need to spring them from hospital staff. You can have them as of next Monday."

"Thank you, Sir."

-/-

Jack Leishman and Frank Keefer are on the staff of the No.2 Canadian Field Surgical Unit (or the '2CFSU' as they now call it) as of Monday, December 14, 1942, and begin to learn, along with Rocke, the complexities and frustrations of the administrative side of army life. Nothing is simple. Straightforward requests for assistance are met with obfuscation and delay. Written orders are required where none seem necessary. Theirs is a particularly difficult task as the Field Surgical Unit concept is new, and to fill the staff and get vehicles and supplies they have to cut across well-known and respected lines of authority linking and running traditional units. But this does not faze them. They are moving into action, they have high-level authority to proceed, and as usual there is 'no time to lose'.

Of primary importance is finding people for the unit. They go through the staff lists of the No.1 Canadian General Hospital and neighbouring units and identify several of the medical personnel they will need. First on their list is Lance Corporal Eric Branch, an orderly from Montreal who combines good medical training and experience with an unusually strong sense of military operations and responsibilities. He answers their need for at least one team member capable of maintaining military standards within the unit. Branch is delighted with the prospect of joining the 2CFSU, noting that the position in question is rated Sergeant, which would be a great promotion for him.

He recommends two other orderlies from the hospital, Andre Boucher and James Price. These two have had some good medical experience, and he has been impressed on many occasions by their mixture of sensitivity to the demands of their work and endurance needed for the hard work involved. Boucher is from Quebec City. Perfectly bilingual, he is a reserved man with suave good looks. Price is a short, hyperactive athlete from Vancouver whose proudest boast is that he competed in the BC swimming championships in 1938 and 'did very well'.

One nurse, Lieutenant Lisa Chamberlain, is interviewed and seems like an ideal candidate. She is well trained and experienced in the OR and is tough but, at the same time, pleasant to deal with. Matron Swanson is thinking about whom she will recommend for the second OR assistant position.

These exciting times have a somewhat dampening effect on the social life at Horsham, but not entirely.

Rocke's Diary

December 20, 1942
The main feature of the past week was Cam Dickison's wedding (to Thelma Stewart) which took place yesterday. Jim Shannon and I were ushers and played our parts nobly. I think it was a big success, and certainly good fun – went off very smoothly. After it was over I had dinner in the Mess and sat about and talked for the rest of the evening. A lot of people went up to London to celebrate, but I thought I'd had enough. On Thursday Jim Shannon and I had our dinner for the bride and groom. 12 people at the local pub – an excellent dinner and all kinds of fun. These two events were the bright spots of the week.

Tuesday, January 5, 1943

Colonel MacFarlane orders Rocke to proceed to No. 1 Administrative Transport Company at Bordon, Hants, to pick up the team's surgical van and to draw equipment at the No.2 Base Depot Medical Stores at nearby Aldershot. He draws Driver Marsh from the hospital driver pool and they head first to BDMS Aldershot. The depot staff have all of the officially designated '1248 scale' issue laid out and ready for him: surgical instruments of all kinds, suture materials, drugs, Plaster of Paris, enamel ware and many other items. Rocke completes his inspection of the equipment, he and Marsh load it into their truck, and they drive to Bordon.

They check in at the office and then walk through to the yard where they are greeted by a very large, brown truck with "CL.4236160" painted on its van. Rocke is excited as he inspects his unit's most precious piece of equipment.

The surgical van consists of a Bedford 60cwt. chassis on which a special body has been built. It is 18 feet 8 inches long, 9 feet 3 inches high and 7 feet wide. The cab is a standard truck cab. Immediately behind it is a narrow compartment with a door on one side and a removable panel on the other. This compartment contains an electric generator run by a Coventry gas engine, a 65 gallon water tank, an electric suction motor, two pairs of stretcher stands, two lotion stands and shelves. Rocke is amused to see that it also has an armaments box large enough to hold six Winchester rifles. He has a momentary vision of his team of orderlies and nurses using their trusty Winchesters to hold off an attacking horde of German paratroopers. Good luck!

Opening from this compartment and extending forward over the cab is a large cupboard for the storage of such things as Plaster of Paris tins, bandages and absorbents.

The rear compartment is much larger. He enters it through the door at the back and finds himself in a narrow central corridor between lockers on both sides. There are 13 lockers containing two drawers that are easily removable, and one with no drawers. On the left side, between two sets of lockers, is a distributor box containing six electric lights. The box could be taken out of the truck and moved into the tent or other place being used as an operating room. It is connected to the generator by a 200-foot cable. On the right hand side is space for a sterilizer and shelves for holding two operating tables and two instrument tables.

Rocke completes his inspection and makes arrangements for the van to be driven immediately to Horsham. He also notes that the unit's two other vehicles are available whenever they need them. He returns to Horsham in the hospital truck with the supplies, and the surgical van arrives almost immediately to be greeted by his very curious and excited colleagues.

Over the next two weeks the team works on the van, checking the equipment and trying different configurations of storage. The work includes, for Rocke, a brief visit to Oxford to pick up missing supplies and to see the equipment of the No.1 Field Surgical Unit that is on display there for American surgical units stationed near Oxford.

Friday, January 15, 1943

Colonel Martin calls Rocke into his office, closes the door, and returns to his desk with an apologetic and frustrated look on his face. He fumbles with his cigarette, takes a sip of cold tea, and then starts in.

"Rocke, I'm afraid that the team that you've been developing has to be changed somewhat. As you know the structure was designed by Canadian authorities, and I think it is a good one. However we have now agreed to move to the British system. Don't ask me why – it's just orders, and that's it.

"Under the revised set-up FSUs are to consist of two officers, a Lance Corporal nursing orderly, two operating room assistants, two nursing orderlies, a batman and three drivers. These are to be all men; nurses are no longer in the plan. Evidently the senior people are still reluctant to send women into war zones. Comments?"

Rocke is not happy. This is a blow to the potential efficiency of the team, for two reasons. Three medical officers could, by teamwork, produce about 50 percent more operative work than two. Secondly, the exclusion of the nursing sisters will impair both the quality and the speed of the work. He states his concerns to the Colonel, but they both know these concerns are of no interest to anyone outside the unit in that orders are orders. It will be almost a year before he can prove the point about the nurses, but prove it he will.

He has the unpleasant duty of telling Frank Keefer and Lisa Chamberlain that they are no longer in the unit, and of informing Eric Branch that he will have to remain a Lance Corporal.

-/-

The team continues work on the surgical van, and on February 2 the other two vehicles arrive, with drivers from the No.1 Administrative Transport Company. The team works hard on the vehicles and their equipment, involving other people from the hospital such as operating room staff for sewing, the unit plumber and the unit carpenter. Rocke continues his search for team members.

Tuesday, February 16, 1943

They finally receive Administrative Order No.33, which formally authorizes '…the formation of a Field Surgical Unit at No.1 CGH with Captain H.R. Robertson in Command.' The order arrives while Rocke is being driven around in the rear compartment of the surgical van to see if the surgical gear and equipment are travelling well, three months and 16 days after Rocke first received orders to form the unit.

The Captain who delivers the Order tells him that as of today he, as Commander of an operational unit, is to keep a regular 'War Diary' that will be the official record of the activities of his unit. It is to have an introductory section describing actions already taken prior to receiving this Order, and then proceed on a daily basis or otherwise as appropriate. He is also advised that he is not to continue to send detailed personal diaries to his family in Canada.

He looks at the official format for the War Diary that is efficiently headed

WAR DIARY
or
INTELLIGENCE SUMMARY
(Erase heading not required)

He notes the instructions in the top right corner:
Original, duplicate and triplicate to be forwarded to O. i/c 2nd Echelon for disposal.

He knows that his typical doctor's scrawl will be unreadable to the chaps in 2nd Echelon, whatever that may be, and he decides then and there that the batman he selects for the team will have a typewriter that he is competent to use, and that the batman will decipher his scribbled notes and place them in good order on the official forms. In fact the batman can help him with all of the paperwork that is involved in army life. Problem solved. He will, however, miss writing his diaries for the family, as they have given him a sense of home and belonging that has been important to him during the long years in England.

-/-

By the end of February the unit has approvals and releases for all of the medical personnel: Captains Robertson and Leishman, L/C Eric Branch, Nursing/Orderlies Andre Boucher and James Price, and the two recent attachments, OR assistants John Pyke and David Finley. The OR assistants both come from Winnipeg and they work well as a team. They present themselves to the officers like Mutt and Jeff: Pyke is tall, thin, balding and intense; Finley is shorter, heavier, blond and jolly.

It has the services of three drivers, but not yet their formal releases. It even has the batman lined up. This is to be a hybrid job, as they want him to be both a medical orderly as well as a batman. The job is considered amusing by many enlisted men, as it seems to be sort of a glorified butler job. He is responsible for keeping the officers properly dressed and supplied, leaving them free to do their jobs without worrying about getting their pants pressed.

Bill McKenzie seems to be an ideal candidate. From Kingston Ontario, he went into the hotel business following high school, and was a management trainee when the war broke out. This gave him some training in first aid, and the army recruiters had routed him into the medical service as a result. He is an easy-going, friendly and precise man who likes the challenge that the batman assignment presents. As time goes by he proves to be invaluable, interpreting his job as caring for the whole team, not just the officers. His teammates stop considering him amusing when they realize that it's really quite nice to have someone worry about your next meal, or where you can find some clean socks or clean drinking water. The clincher in his selection is that he has a typewriter and knows how to use it. Thus he becomes the team secretary, preparing and monitoring schedules and typing up forms and reports.

They have their three vehicles in good working order, and most of their equipment and supplies checked and stored.

They go through several training exercises to test the equipment and practice in different locations. At first they clear out one of the operating theatres in the hospital and set up their own tables, anaesthetic equipment and instruments. After a few trial runs they actually operate on some patients to test the set-up. They then move out of doors to get closer to what they see as being the real thing. They choose a spot at some distance from the hospital and set up their tent and tables, spread out the instruments, get the sterilizers going and go through the motions of performing operations. After they become fairly proficient they take patients from the hospital and, to the patients' surprise, perform minor operations under field conditions.

Friday, February 26, 1943

The 2CFSU team is gathered in a meeting room in the hospital for a team discussion of progress to date. Rocke has called the meeting because they have tried many different approaches to setting up and operating, and it is time to lay down an approved procedure to be followed unless ordered to do otherwise.

"First of all," says Rocke, "I'd like to thank you all for telling me that I'm no good at setting up tents!" The team members chuckle and grin at each other. After several weeks of Rocke being directly involved in the work of bringing the tent out of the van and setting it up, they have come to the realization that he would be much more usefully employed dealing with the wounded and getting ready for surgery.

"You're not that bad at it, Sir," says Eric Branch. "It's just that some of us have had a bit more practice." More laughter – Rocke has gotten in the way more often than not when working side by side with tough team members like Branch and Jimmy Price.

"Right, well, thank you Branch. Now then, here's how I see our standard procedure from now on. This is for tents, of course. We'll have to modify it as we go along when we work in buildings. McKenzie will be writing up what we decide on.

"My job is to deal with our host Field Dressing Station: meet their Commander, agree on locations and procedures, and most importantly see the patients and plan the operating program. Captain Leishman will join me in this. He'll also be the liaison officer for any decisions that you need concerning the tent set-up – location, final approved layout of the OR, and so on. We will take the two orderlies with us to get the lay of the land in the wards and see how we can best work with the station. They can also note any requirements we might have for special equipment, and also for drugs and supplies.

"Lance Corporal Branch will be in charge of the set-up itself. He'll clear any necessary decisions with Captain Leishman, but otherwise it's up to you, Branch, to run the show.

"Branch will scout out the ground for the best location, and clear that decision with Captain Leishman who will, by that time, have established contact with the responsible officers in the Field Dressing Station. The drivers will haul the tent and all the other standing paraphernalia out of the van. They'll do any levelling or clearing required on the site, and then erect the tent and sweep and clean it, and hook up the electrical system and lights. Meanwhile the OR assistants will be bringing equipment out of the vehicles. You fellows can join the drivers in getting the tent as clean as possible, and then installing the table and sterilizer and all the other stuff. Assuming we'll be starting to work immediately, you should start the sterilizer and lay out the instruments.

"By that time we should have a pretty good idea of what sort of case load we're facing, and the OR assistants can liaise with the orderlies concerning any special needs for equipment or medicines. McKenzie, it will be up to you to have our gowns and masks and gloves ready to go, and to make sure that we have a usable wash station. You should make immediate contact with the station's kitchen so that we have a supply of food and drink. You can also look into places we can use for rest between operations, and when everything is ready to go you can help the drivers find our living accommodations. I would also like you to take responsibility for patient records – we'll advise you of the details as we proceed.

"Branch, when everything is ready you should seek approval from Captain Leishman, and then we're in business! Any comments or questions?"

"Yes, Sir," says Eric Branch. "When we're setting up in a building the drivers will have very little to do. Nice for them, but do you have any suggestions on that score?"

"Good point, Branch. Yes, they may have a lot less to do, but it will depend on the building. They should of course check the electrical situation, lighting, water supply and so on, and they should also help carry equipment and supplies into the building. The other key issue is…will always be… cleanliness. The more sweeping and scrubbing we can do before hand, the better chance we'll have of success in our operations. Any other questions?"

There is a brief, general round of comments and discussion about details, and then silence. The only noise in the room is McKenzie scratching out his notes.

"Right then," says Rocke. "That's all for now. Branch, I think you had a route march in mind?"

As they are leaving the building Rocke thinks carefully, for the first time, about the military protocol of names. He is perfectly used to the English system of calling the men by their last names, having gone to an English-style school himself back in Victoria. On the other hand it does seem a bit forced, especially in a small team of Canadians like this, working overseas and so closely together. It is, however, important to maintain at least a certain amount of protocol.

In the end he decides on a comfortable compromise. The men should always address him and Jack as 'Sir', of 'Major' or 'Captain'. He and Jack can of course use first names between themselves. They should continue to address the men using their last names, but this will likely relax to first names when they are in action. Time will tell.

March 1943

The military element in their preparation is provided through their involvement in various training exercises run by the army. The most important of these, called *Spartan*, takes place the first ten days of March. It involves the whole 1st Canadian Army on manoeuvres around southern and western England. The 2CFSU follows its Division, sets up its equipment in different places, and performs mock operations on mock casualties brought to them by the Field Ambulances. The weather is frightful and they learn a good deal about finding their way in the dark, getting out of the mud, eating cold food and finding shelter – all essential to survival in actual warfare. Three other new Canadian Field Surgical Units join them in this exercise, Nos 1, 4 and 5.

On March 5 Rocke learns that he had been promoted to the rank of Major.

The training continues, with the Field Surgical Unit working at the hospital at Horsham when not training. Lance Corporal Branch seizes every possible occasion to take them on route marches, preferably with heavy packs. He is emerging as a tough, energetic and determined military man, ideal as the non-commissioned officer for the 2CFSU that contains medical people concerned with medical issues rather than military procedure.

On March 27 the three drivers in the unit have to return permanently to their previous unit, the No. 1 Administrative Transport Company. The reason for this, as described by Rocke in the official war diary of the

2CFSU, gives an insight into the administrative complexities of war, as well as the amazing use of acronyms.

War Diary

March 27, 1943
The reason for this action is purely technical. No. 1 A.T. Coy supplies drivers to base units only, and they are not willing to allow them to be transferred to 1.C.A.S.C.R.U. from which this unit could draw them.

March 29, 1943
Three new drivers (Pte. Curran, M.P., Pte. Willmer, W.H. and Pte. Monroe, P.C.) arrived from C.A.S.C.R.U. and are posted to the Unit w.e.f. 30ᵗʰ March 1943.

Pte. Willmer does not respond well to the specialized training required for Field Surgical Unit drivers, and is later replaced with Pte. V.J. Kraft. Rocke is pleased with his team of drivers. Mat Curran is a big, easygoing farm boy from Red Deer, Alberta. He has driven a lot of different types of vehicles and rigs on the farm, and is totally at home with the vehicles of the 2CFSU. Pete Monroe is especially valuable as he has taken an intensive driver mechanics course, strengthening his life-long fascination with cars. He is a man of few words; a tough man from the sawmills of Nanaimo. Victor Kraft (always known as 'Krafty') is the most experienced of the drivers, having survived a brief but exciting stint as a taxi driver in Montreal.

April 1943

More training, setting up the apparatus in different conditions, testing new systems for the trucks such as running a suction apparatus off the windshield wipers of a truck, and practicing medical work such as setting broken bones on real, live patients. Rocke continues his ongoing fencing with the many military authorities to gain the required supplies and equipment repairs and adjustments. The war diary shows how rudimentary the equipment available to them is, and how important it is to practice and experiment.

War Diary

April 15, 1943
Whole unit went out at 1400 hours in the three vehicles to a nearby field where they set out all the equipment in the open. It took one hour to get the sterilizer to boil owing to stove difficulties, and it appears that the stoves will be a real problem until some better type of stove is evolved.

April 16, 1943
Major Robertson, Capt. Leishman and Ptes Kraft, Curran, Pyke, Finley and Keith (electrician from No. 1 C.G.H.) proceeded in the surgical van and the heavy utility to No. 2 C.C.S. near Cranleigh, where arrangements have been made with Major Campbell to investigate their electrical apparatus. It was established that the electrical equipment of the Field Surgical Unit could be easily adapted to utilize the C.C.S. light bracket, a bracket which is much more efficient than any arrangement that can be made with the lighting equipment supplied to the teams…Major Campbell demonstrated an emergency lighting device composed of two automobile headlamps set on a stand and lighted by a storage battery. He states that this will provide excellent lighting for a period of 12 hours.

April 29, 1943
The team set up the equipment in the operating room of the hospital and performed two circumcisions using Pentothal as the anaesthetic. The orderlies worked very smoothly and the whole exercise was regarded as a success.

The team has now been together long enough that they feel fully ready for action. Rumours of invasions are flying about, and they are restless to get into the action wherever it might be.

14. THE CALL

The call to war, with the usual confusion.

Thursday, May 20, 1943

Rocke is in the surgical supply room at the No.1 CGH at Horsham when he is told that he has a phone call from Colonel C.H. Playfair, the Assistant Director of Medical Services (ADMS) of the First Canadian Division. He is calling from headquarters in London to make sure that the unit is 'all set'.

"We are all set for anything, Sir," says Rocke. "Is something about to happen?"

"Do you mean to tell me, Major Robertson, that you've heard nothing?" cries the Colonel.

"Not a thing, Sir." There is a long pause.

"Well then, you'd better come up to London at once," says the Colonel, and slams down the phone.

Rocke takes a hospital car and driver, who drives like a maniac over the 40 miles to RCAMC headquarters in London, arriving just after lunch hour. He meets Frank Mills, the Commander of the No.1 Canadian Field Surgical Unit, on the front steps.

"Hello Frank. What brings you here?" asks Rocke, smiling broadly because he knows what the answer will be.

"Probably the same thing that brought you up from Horsham: a call from Playfair telling me to get here on the double. It seems we're supposed to be ready for something, but everyone forgot to tell us about it."

'Right," replies Rocke as they head into the building. "It looks like 'hush hush' and 'hurry up' don't mix very well." They are grinning as they are shown into Colonel Playfair's office.

The Colonel is not grinning and does not stand on ceremony. He waves them to their chairs. "Do you two mean to tell me that you haven't had any instructions about a move?" he asks.

"No, Sir," comes the simultaneous reply, meaning in fact yes Sir, they have not.

"Well then," says the ADMS, "I can tell you now that you are to be ready by 0800hrs tomorrow to leave for an overseas expedition. I can't tell you where you will be going, but you are to pack all of your equipment in crates each weighing no more than 80 pounds. And you will not be able to take your vehicles with you."

The Colonel explains that they are in this rush because originally the 3rd British Division and the 33rd British Army Tank Brigade were supposed to go on whatever the mission is going to be. Then the Canadians made such a fuss about so many Canadians being over here for years now with nothing to do that the British agreed to replace their units with the 1st Canadian Infantry Division and the 1st Canadian Armoured Brigade. This decision was taken quite recently, probably in early February, so the Canadian planners and everybody else have been working flat out to get things organized.

"Unfortunately it seems that we all forgot to tell you chaps to get ready. We also forgot to bid for space on the ships for you to take your equipment and vehicles! So you'll have to move smartly now, and as far as the vehicles are concerned, you'll just have to see what you can scrounge as you go along."

"Sir," says Major Mills, "we simply must have our vehicles! They are very specialized for our purposes, and we can't rely on others to move our equipment. The surgical vans are most important, of course, with their generators and operating room equipment. Without them we can't move around quickly and we can't do surgery."

"Yes, Sir," adds Rocke. "It's that equipment and all the medical supplies that make us useful. Without them we'll be a sorry lot, wandering around on foot looking for a place to go to work, and tools to work with. Surely there's some way for us to take them along?"

"I fully understand, gentlemen, but I have been told categorically that all space on the ships has been spoken for. Period. And they will not welcome further requests. The Brits are being a bit stuffy because we've taken the place of some of their boys, and they control the shipping operations. So there it is."

"Sir," says Frank, "you've always said that it's best to be very flexible and to use your imagination in working in the army. May I suggest that at least we use our vehicles to take our equipment to the port of embarkation, and then see what we can do? You never know; things have a way of changing."

The Colonel lights a cigarette while he considers this request.

"All right. Do that. I just hope you don't end up leaving all that expensive stuff sitting on a bloody wharf somewhere! Right, now, if there's nothing else you'd better get on with it."

The two Majors sprint down the headquarters steps and head back to their units at top speed. As his car careens wildly through the winding roads, Rocke thinks about the amazing ways that armies work. *They seem to be quite good at making major strategic decisions, and hopefully that will continue. But by God, at lower levels it's chaos and every man for himself. Here I have an FSU, properly established for all the right reasons, and they forget to call me to say that we're expected to go into action immediately! Christ, what a game!* He knows that he has just learned a very important lesson, namely that as a field commander he had better be prepared to make his own decisions and take the initiative. If he always waits for official orders to come through he's going to have a very bad war indeed.

Rocke arrives at the hospital at Horsham at 1630hrs and immediately commandeers the hospital's two carpenters and all the crating material that can be found. He calls his team together, briefs them on the situation, and they get to work.

The team works throughout the night, and by 0600hrs next morning they have all their equipment and supplies packed into 74 crates that are stuffed into and onto their vehicles. It all seems so horribly inefficient. The equipment and supplies that have been so carefully prepared to fit snugly into the three vehicles are now all in crates, making them awkward and much heavier.

Rocke tells the team to get some sleep, and he lies down to rest with one ear cocked to the telephone.

15. SCOTLAND

They travel to Scotland to join a convoy for destination unknown.
Administrative nightmares.

Friday, May 21, 1943

The expected orders do not come through, giving the 2CFSU team some extra time to shift things around. They also make final preparations for the disposal of equipment that will not be needed, and personal items that they will leave behind when they go to war. Rocke's war diary of these actions gives an interesting insight into the high level of secrecy that surrounds all military activity in these days leading up to the invasion of Europe.

War Diary

Saturday, May 22, 1943
The men packed their kits and stored the unwanted articles in barrack boxes in the gatehouse. These articles together with the Unit equipment stored in the gatehouse were all listed and copies of the lists were handed to Lieut. Markey of No. 1 CGH, acting Quartermaster. He was instructed that, if No.2 Field Surgical Unit did not return within four weeks time, he was to send the men's belongings to the surplus kit storage depot at Clayton Barrack, Aldershot. He was to use his own discretion concerning the disposal of the unit's 1098 equipment left behind. This was done in accordance with the verbal instructions of Col. Playfair who desired that no action that would arouse suspicion concerning No.2 Field Surgical Unit's movements be taken. It was considered that if the men's kits were

sent at once to the surplus kit storage and if the ordnance equipment were sent back to stores there would be no doubt that the Field Surgical Unit was leaving the country.

Saturday, May 22, 1943

The order to move out comes in precisely at noon. They are to drive immediately to the No.15 Canadian General Hospital at Bramshott, where they will receive further orders. They leave Horsham at 1600hrs, their vehicles stuffed with the ungainly crates containing their equipment and supplies. At 1830hrs they arrive at No.15 and are greeted by a somewhat confused commanding officer who knows nothing about their plans. This is not a surprise to Rocke in light of the confusion that has reigned so far, and in any event they are welcomed and given comfortable quarters.

Later in the evening the commanding officer finds some orders addressed to the 2CFSU saying that Rocke's unit will soon be moving to Bothwell in Scotland. This sounds like a departure order to a war zone, heightening the level of anticipation in the team.

Sunday, May 23, 1943

Rocke goes to the supplies depot at Aldershot to fix up some equipment disparities, and in the afternoon the team members are delighted when their 30cwt lorry is exchanged for a much bigger 60cwt lorry, which they bring back proudly to No.15 CGH. This exchange heightens their hopes that they will eventually be able to take their vehicles with them – otherwise why would the authorities give them a bigger and newer vehicle?

Monday, May 24, 1943

They have another round of equipment work, with visits to depots at Aldershot, Crookham and Brookwood. The orders to head for Scotland, so keenly anticipated, do not arrive, but the No.1 Field Transfusion Unit, under the jovial Captain Wally Scott, does arrive at Bramshott.

Tuesday, May 25, 1943

The daily routine is enlivened by the arrival of Frank Mills and the No.1 Field Surgical Unit. They had moved in early April to the No.1 Neurological Hospital at Basingstoke; now they are coming though their old base at Bramshott en route to Scotland. They should have arrived at the same time as Rocke's team, but their orders had somehow been mislaid.

Friday, May 28, 1943

Returning from a route march, the 2CFSU team is told that verbal orders have been received to the effect that Nos 1 and 2 Field Surgical Units and No.1 Field Transfusion Unit are to move north the following day. Written instructions follow that evening, and the teams' spirits soar as they plan their departure.

Saturday, May 29, 1943

The column of seven vehicles leaves Bramshott and heads for Scotland at 0630hrs. They skirt London through Farnham and Wokingham and stop just southwest of Oxford for lunch. They take on petrol in Kidderminster, west of Birmingham, and then travel steadily with breaks every two hours until they arrive at 2045hrs at Preston, on the Irish Sea coast. They have travelled 261 miles over roads of distinctly mixed quality, and yet are informed on arrival that they are 11/2 hours late!

The teams spend the night in Nisson Huts at the Moor Park Staging Camp in Preston.

Sunday, May 30, 1943

They depart at 0800hrs and drive north to just below Carlisle, where they stop for lunch. North of Carlisle the No.1 Field Surgical Unit team turns west and heads for Dumfries. The other two units continue north to Bothwell, just southeast of Glasgow. There they arrive at the headquarters of the No.4 British Casualty Clearing Station, which is their official destination.

They report to Lt.-Colonel Smyth, Commander of the Casualty Clearing Station. As Rocke expects, the Colonel has not heard of them, but also as expected they are welcomed and made to feel at home. They are housed in a vacant house on Bothwell Road in nearby Uddingston, and that evening Rocke telephones the ADMS office in Troon to make an appointment for next day. This is the start of what they later described as a 'great song and dance' aimed at including their vehicles in the shipping.

Monday, May 31, 1943

Rocke, Jack Leishman and Wally Scott drive south to the ADMS office in Troon, but the ADMS staff leader, Captain Carleton, is not there. They wait until 1600hrs and then return to Bothwell.

Tuesday, June 1, 1943

They are more successful in Troon and have a long discussion with Carleton concerning the importance of having the lighting system and, therefore, the surgical van.

War Diary

After some thought he (Capt. Carleton) conceived of a way of making it possible for us to take the large surgical van. He did not promise that this would be possible but he seemed hopeful.

Wednesday, June 2, 1943

While Leishman and Scott visit army depots to collect more equipment and the men work on the vehicles, Rocke spends time in Colonel Smyth's office studying papers containing instructions for a training exercise that has been planned.

War Diary

…Col. Playfair telephoned to say that arrangements were proceeding to enable us to take the surgical van.

Thursday, June 3, 1943

Colonel Playfair comes to Bothwell for consultations. He tells Rocke that it will be possible to have the surgical van taken along - that it should be waterproofed today and taken to Royal Canadian Army Service Corps

(RCASC) headquarters tomorrow. There it will be filled with anti-malarial equipment and eventually shipped off. Upon arrival at destination it will be driven to a Brigade headquarters where the anti-malarial equipment will be dumped off and the truck driven to the location of the No.4 Casualty Clearing Station. Driver Kraft is to accompany the vehicle throughout.

This sounds like very good news. At least they can count on having their van with them. The other two trucks are more generic, so will be easier to replace if lost en route to wherever they are going. Pte. Kraft is delighted to be attached to the valuable surgical van, and spends the day working on it.

Jack Leishman departs on leave to Horsham where his wife Trudy is about to produce their first child.

Friday, June 4, 1943

They complete the waterproofing of the van's electrical system and get it ready for shipment.

War Diary

> *In the afternoon the van was driven down to Kilmarnock, south of Glasgow, and handed over to Major Diehl of the Royal Canadian Army Service Corps (RCASC) at 1 C.I.B. HQ. Major Diehl seemed to be somewhat doubtful that the van could be fitted in, but he felt certain that No.1 FTU's vehicle which had gone down with our van would be able to be put aboard.*

Rocke is totally frustrated. Once again the doubts concerning the van are raised. *Just who the hell is in charge here anyway? Colonels tell me that the van will be going. Then a major tells me that it may not!*

Saturday, June 5, 1943

Rocke attends an officers' conference where they are told that all equipment will be shipped off tomorrow, and that additional markings should be painted on all cases. Nothing is simple, but Rocke also receives some good news.

War Diary

Our cases now rejoice in the following: (1) Colour bars, three buff; (2) Unit serial 1166/1; Name of exercise "Casket"; (4) Code name convoy "Herrick"; (5) SSI Number EE11/39/A. Many of the smaller cases were almost completely covered with markings.

...The ADMS assured Major Robertson that the surgical van would be taken.

Sunday, June 6, 1943

All of the cases, men's kit bags and officers' bed rolls – 97 pieces in all - are taken by unit transport to Coatbridge, east of Glasgow, where they are loaded aboard a freight car. The 2CFSU has now been in Scotland for a week. The weather has been consistently cold and rainy, but the men have been well treated by the locals and have enjoyed themselves thoroughly. With the van hopefully on the way to being loaded and all of their equipment sent on their way, they are sure that they will soon follow and finally be directly involved in the war.

Not so. They have another week to wait, a week filled with route marches (now always with full packs) and equipment checks, and constant alarums about the prospects of the surgical van making it aboard a ship.

War Diary

Monday, June 7, 1943
Major Robertson drove down to Kilmarnock to see Pvt. Kraft and the surgical van. The latter now has its stage two waterproofing complete, has its extra petrol, sandbags, etc. Major Diehl in an interview later in the morning stated that it was still not settled that the van could be taken. He did say, however, that he was not the one directly responsible – that Col. Pease would have the final answer.

Wednesday, June 9, 1943

The plot thickens when Rocke returns to Bothwell from a short visit to Edinburgh to be told by Lt.-Colonel Smyth that he has received a call from the Deputy ADMS inquiring as to the whereabouts of the van. Smyth told the DADMS (correctly) that the vehicle was at Kilmarnock. Rocke immediately calls the DADMS and is told, to his consternation, that the Royal Canadian Army Service Corps at Kilmarnock is denying that the van is in their possession! He drives down to Kilmarnock in the afternoon and finds at the vehicle park that the RCASC is just taking the vehicle away from the park to put it in a convoy for movement to port on the following day. He is greatly relieved, although not reassured about the ability of the various units in the army to communicate with each other.

Thursday, June 10, 1943

He is so relieved, in fact, that he takes the team out for a two-hour route march with full packs. Later in the day Jack Leishman calls to say that Trudy is to be delivered by Caesarean section on June 14. He asks to have his leave extended. Rocke gains that permission after some delay and several telephone calls, with the instruction to use his discretion as to when to order Leishman back.

Saturday, June 12, 1943

Rocke and four of his team go to a soccer match in Glasgow, a welcome break from the endless waiting and marching. They also learn, indirectly, that they will be moving out on June 15.

Sunday, June 13, 1943

The formal instructions for embarkation on the 15th come through. Rocke calls Jack Leishman and tells him that he can stay in Horsham until the night of the 14th, and then should take the night train back to Scotland.

Monday, June 14, 1943

Rocke distributes Tommy guns and ammunition to the three drivers, and hands over the 60cwt truck to No.4 British Casualty Clearing Station. Driver Kraft comes to Bothwell with the news that the surgical van has gone aboard ship, but that the anti-malarial equipment was never put into it. In other words, they could have left their surgical supplies properly stowed after all!

Rocke is called to the telephone at 1715hrs.

"Rocke, it's Jack. Guess what? It's a boy!"

"Jolly good Jack. Congratulations! How's Trudy?"

"She's just fine, thanks. The doctor said that everything went smoothly. And she's really happy. Wants to call him David, which sounds just fine to me. They're both sleeping now."

"Well give her my love. What time does the train leave there?"

"1745hrs."

"Well father Leishman, move your butt and catch that train!"

"Yes Sir, Major Rocke. See you all tomorrow."

Tuesday, June 15, 1943

At 0720hrs Jack Leishman strides into the officers' mess at Bothwell just as breakfast is starting. He offers cigars all around, and his colleagues offer congratulations and toast Trudy and baby David in hot coffee.

16. THE CONVOY

To sea at last, and their destination is Sicily as part of a great Allied invasion.

At 1210hrs the 2CFSU team entrains at Uddingston Station and travels via Glasgow to Gourock on the Clyde, where they embark in mid-afternoon on the converted merchant ship *M/S Batory*. The men take up their hammock quarters on D deck while the officers are luxuriously accommodated in a cabin on the boat deck.

Wednesday, June 16, 1943

The day is sunny and warm, and they spend it lounging on deck.

War Diary

There were many sights to see in the harbour – craft of all types: a battleship, cruisers, corvettes, monitors, passenger vessels, ships designed to carry tanks and vehicles, and many smaller boats such as LCTs, LCPs and 'Ducks'. From time to time Sunderland Flying Boats were to be seen landing and taking off – all in all a most impressive spectacle.

The Field Surgical Unit team is to be taken care of by Lt.-Colonel Basil Bowman of No.9 Field Ambulance. Bowman is a strapping, energetic, friendly man, and he is most cooperative in showing maps and plans of the forthcoming training scheme *Stymie*. Bowman's Second-in-Command is Captain Don Young, a friend of Rocke's from McGill days, who went on to play professional football for the Ottawa Roughriders. These medical teams share the ship with members of the 3rd Brigade of the 1st Canadian Infantry Division, which includes the Royal 22e Regiment, the Carleton and York Regiment and the West Nova Scotia Regiment.

Thursday, June 17, 1943

Details are clarified when a Brigadier Penhale, who had come on board the previous evening, calls a meeting of officers. *Stymie* is to be a practice landing. The ship's force is divided into groups of 20 (a number that even the smallest landing craft could transport), and each group has its own serial number. The 2CFSU team is broken into two, with six going in serial 2184 and the rest in serial 2185. Rocke hopes that in future operations they can be kept together. During the day the ship moves out into the Clyde in convoy, and after 'considerable circumnavigation' takes up a position off Troon.

Friday, June 18, 1943

Stymie landings start at 0230hrs. The idea is to land on Troon beach and work inland. Two Brigades land, and the 2CFSU team expect to land with the 3rd Brigade at 0930hrs. By that time, however, the sea has become slightly rough and it is decided to stop landing any further troops. In contrast to the previous day the weather is cold and very wet, and does not improve at all until later in the evening. At a meeting at 2100hrs new serial numbers are announced for landing groups, and Rocke is pleased that the whole 2CFSU team is now in one group, #2185.

June 19 and 20, 1943

The days pass uneventfully. The weather is awful and the troop ships stand offshore and wait for orders. Plans are made for *Stymie II* to start the morning of June 21, but later in the day on June 20 that too is postponed 24 hours due to the weather. Sure enough the weather continues bad, with a gale warning in effect. They stay below decks except for a brief physical training session on the deck, which they share with a group of engineers. An energetic Sergeant of the engineers runs the session, and he shows them how to forget any thoughts of seasickness for at least a brief period.

Tuesday, June 22, 1943

It is still dull, overcast and raining, and the convoy weighs anchor in the late afternoon and sails back to Gourock for restocking. *Stymie II* is cancelled and the frustration continues, thanks to the weather.

Wednesday, June 23, 1943

The ships take to sea again, and this time the 2CFSU team actually make it into landing craft and are headed ashore for a practice landing when they are called back to the ship because it is getting too rough. They board the ship and there they stay, relaxing and even sunbathing in the occasional shaft of sunlight, until June 28.

Monday, June 28, 1943

War Diary

Fine weather continues. At 2100hrs we weighed anchor and set off in convoy. It was a most impressive sight with the sea dead calm and the sun setting in an absolutely clear sky. The ships looked magnificent.

The 2CFSU is finally going to war!

-/-

They sail south, untroubled by enemy attack and dealing with a routine of food, rest, inspection, lectures, PT (physical training) and boat drills. On July 2 they are finally told their destination. The officers gather in the wardroom and learn that they are heading for Sicily as part of an Allied assault on the southern coast of Europe. The operation is called *Husky*. It is to be a major event, aimed at taking Sicily quickly, positioning the Allies to move on to Italy. They will be fighting mostly Germans, as the Italians are proving less and less willing to fight against the Allies, whom most of them consider friends rather than enemies.

They are told about the Canadian units participating in the assault. In the briefing on medical systems and units Rocke learns that, aside from the medical officers and other ranks and their ambulances attached to individual regiments, the medical establishment at Corps level, under the direct control of the Assistant Director of Medical Services (ADMS) Colonel C.H. Playfair, will include Nos 1 and 2 Canadian Field Surgical Units, Nos 1 and 2 Canadian Field Dressing Stations, Nos 4, 5 and 9 Field Ambulances, and No.1 Field Transfusion Unit, and a number of British units including a British Casualty Clearing Station.

The units are given their own specific orders. Officers are to study them carefully, commit them to memory, and destroy them before landing.

Rocke tells his team about the plans and then settles down with Jack Leishman to study the orders. They will be landing on the western side of the Pachino peninsula on the southeast tip of Sicily. They are to march five miles from landing to near a village called Maucini where they will join up with the British No.3 Field Dressing Station, which is under Canadian command. This will create an Advanced Surgical Centre close to the landing sites, able to deal with the badly wounded from the initial assault. There are maps and descriptions of the terrain.

The convoy encounters no enemy, and on the night of July 7 it sails past Gibraltar and into the Mediterranean. The mass of ships moves along the north coast of Africa and assembles south of Malta, hidden from Sicily to the north but within easy striking distance. On July 9 the convoy is blasted by a Sirocco wind coming north out of Africa. The ships are tossed and scattered, and there is great danger that the operation might have to be postponed, thereby losing all hope of surprise. Those medical people who are not seasick are kept busy treating the troops, many of whom are in terrible shape.

Late in the day the wind starts to slacken, and at 2000hrs the high command decides that there will be acceptable conditions for landing, and transmits the much hoped-for signal that *Husky* is a 'go'. Aboard the *M/S Batory* the men of the 2CFSU, along with all of the troops on the ship, make final preparations for the landing scheduled for 0245hrs. It is a sleepless night before a very big show.

17. SICILY – STRATEGIES AND PROBLEMS

The assault is carefully planned. Field conditions pose special problems for the medicals.

The Allied assault plan for Sicily called for a single concentrated effort by the British 8th Army and the American 7th Army against the island's southeast corner. The Americans were to sweep north and west, clearing the western half of Sicily including the capital of Palermo, and then moving across the north to the northeast tip. The British would drive north up the coast, and the Canadians inland through the mountainous terrain surrounding Mount Etna, joining up with the Americans at the northeast tip preparatory to crossing over to Italy.

Their opponents at the time of the invasion were two German and four Italian field divisions and between five and six Italian coastal divisions - the whole being under the command of headquarters of the Italian 6th Army which was at Enna, the hub city of Sicily. The Italian forces, particularly those of the coastal formations, were believed to be of low fighting quality, considerably inferior to the battle-seasoned troops of the two German divisions – the Hermann Goering Panzer Division and the 15th Panzer Grenadier Division. The latter Division was engaged primarily in the west of the island. The Canadians would be dealing with the Hermann Goering Division based at Caltagirone, and two Italian field divisions.

The Canadian contingent was part of the 30th Corps of the British 8th Army. It consisted of the 1st Canadian Infantry Division, which contained the Canadian Armoured Corps 4th Reconnaissance Regiment; five regiments of the Royal Canadian Artillery; the 1st Canadian Infantry Corps with the Saskatoon Light Infantry as brigade support group and three Infantry Brigades containing nine Canadian regiments; and elements of the 1st Canadian Armoured Brigade, the

Corps of Royal Canadian Engineers and the Royal Canadian Army Medical Corps.

In the initial phase most of the Canadian troops were to drive as quickly as possible into the heart of Sicily, while some of the force was to remain at the beaches forming a 'Beach Maintenance Area'.

The medical plans were very late in developing due to the late decision to include the Canadians in the plan, and then the later decisions on the assault plan. This explained, amongst other things, why so much medical equipment and so many vehicles were misplaced at the outset, as was the case with the 2CFSU. It was learned later that the decision to send the 2CFSU to Sicily, along with some other extra units, was taken no more than one week before Rocke was called to London and told to pack up and be ready to depart immediately. Another casualty of the lateness of planning was insufficient preparation by Canadian forces for the malaria menace in Sicily.

The RCAMC unit in Sicily had under its command 15 medical units: four Field Surgical Units (including two British), two Field Transfusion Units (one British), four Field Ambulances (one British), three Field Dressing Stations (one British), one Field Hygiene Section and one Casualty Clearing Station (British). Behind the Casualty Clearing Stations would be a hospital system commanded by the British and including a number of British hospitals, a convalescence depot, No.5 Canadian General Hospital and No.15 CGH. Medical supplies and equipment would be the responsibility at the outset of each unit, but once the action was established and moving forward the British would run the supply system.

The complexities of managing this medical establishment were enormous, although the concept was clear. The Field Ambulances, with their stretcher bearers and ambulance vehicles, would keep pace as closely as possible with the advancing troops, maintaining constant contact with the regimental medical teams and working directly with them to get wounded men out of the line of fire. They would set up small Advanced Dressing Stations where needed to sort out the flow of wounded coming in from the front. Field Dressing Stations, mobile but with more complete medical staffs, tents, kitchens and other facilities for handling patients, would follow at a discreet distance, as close as possible but out of the range of artillery. The Field Ambulances would bring the badly wounded to them for immediate treatment, and would take the wounded who could withstand the ride directly back to the Casualty Clearing Stations, semipermanent facilities capable of handling large numbers of wounded in transit *out of the combat zone – either to hospitals far back from the lines, or to the beach for immediate transfer offshore.*

The Field Surgical Units (FSUs) and Field Transfusion Units (FTUs) would move amongst Field Dressing Stations as required to resuscitate and operate on the badly wounded. They would normally pitch up in the same building or in tents close to the Field Dressing Stations, which would handle pre- and post-operative care, forming Advanced Surgical Centres (ASCs) when all together. The FSUs and FTUs would also use the kitchens and other facilities in the Field Dressing Stations.

So the concept was clear, but as always the devil was in the detail. First, decisions concerning the placement of the various units had to be made quickly, and often with a paucity of information. What field radio equipment there was in the army was dominated by the troops and their officers. The medical forces were for some time forced to work without radios, relying on scouts, dispatch riders and maps. Yet speed of decision was imperative, that being the whole point of the exercise.

Secondly, the constant moving of units and harsh working conditions called for the application of capabilities quite different from those expected of medical personnel in a peacetime environment. Orderlies, for example, had to repair equipment, fuel vehicles and clean large tents in addition to doing what they were really trained for, which was looking after wounded soldiers. Surgeons had to work in conditions that were so totally against all of their training that it called for a completely new psychological approach to their work. They were used to sterile operating rooms, sterilized instruments and clean, pure air. What they found in Sicily were filthy operating places, uncertainly-cleaned instruments, and extremely hot air loaded with dust and buzzing flies. To this was added the pressure of dealing with unheard-of flows of patients urgently requiring surgery that would tax the capabilities of fully equipped hospitals and operating theatres back home.

Thirdly, the flow of casualties, and the need to keep some stationary while the mobile units were compelled to move on, caused frequent problems and the temporary breaking up of integral units. In a presentation to the Vancouver Medical Association in 1945, Rocke explained.

Presentation 1945

Admitted to the ASC, (the wounded) will be treated there and re-tained until he is fit to travel on back. He may remain at this level for a period varying from 12 hours to three weeks depending upon his condition and the general situation at the time. A man with a compound femur, for example, injured in a large-scale at-tack when there are many other casualties, may be operated upon in the ASC and evacuated in a matter of hours if he is in reasonably good shape.

If, on the other hand, he is ill he will be retained. He may develop a wound infection and not be fit to be moved for days. Ab-dominal cases are routinely kept for a minimum of a week no mat-ter how well they are. Chest cases are not moved until they are free of dyspnoea at rest regardless of how long this may take – and so on.

It is, thus, quite impossible to predict how long a man may stay once the treatment is commenced. Hence the system must be elastic to handle the numerous difficulties that arise.

Picture an ASC in action with, say, 30 bed patients. The army advances. The Field Surgical Unit and Field Transfusion Unit are moved ahead to set up with another Field Dressing Station and the patients stay behind with the original Field Dressing Station. One by one as they become fit they are evacuated to the base, but it may be a long time before all 30 have moved on. Meanwhile the original Field Dressing Station may be needed forward. In such a case the main body will move ahead, leaving behind a medical officer and orderly personnel and cooking staff sufficient to care for the remain-ing patients. Such a group is called a 'nest', and it is not uncommon in a rapid advance to find several nests scattered along the lines of communication, providing a problem of supply and administration to tax the best brains.

Fourthly, the weather had a great influence on the activities of the medical units, their ability to perform and to clear cases efficiently. Wide variations in temperature had an obvious effect on their work, and of particular concern were the diseases that afflicted medical personnel and troops alike in the differ-ent seasons.

Presentation 1945

So common were malaria and dysentery in the summer months and infectious hepatitis in the autumn and winter that all the medical officers were affected to some extent by having to lend a hand in treating the cases and by falling victim to one of the diseases themselves. Then again these illnesses were complicating factors in many of the wounded. A man with a sub-clinical malaria, for example, would likely as not on being wounded develop the full-blown disease. Occasionally, particularly early in the game, his fever would be ascribed to some complication of the wound rather than to its proper cause. The effects of dysentery were probably less important…but…there were several deaths from hepatitis recorded amongst the wounded.

What this meant was that operational strengths of medical units would often be well below their official strength measured in numbers of members. It also meant that seemingly routine casualty cases could easily change through disease into much more dangerous conditions calling for more prolonged and perhaps different treatment than originally planned.

And finally there was the issue discussed with Cam Gardner back in Montreal – the need to treat civilians and even enemy troops in addition to our own. The medical units were passing through communities that had been in war conditions for some time, often without the benefit of regular medical services. Allied medical teams passing through were often besieged with requests for help, and would feel obligated to respond not only because it was their duty as human beings who had taken the Hippocratic Oath, but also because they wanted the civilians to be as friendly and helpful as possible. Enemy wounded added to the patient load. There was no doubt that Allied wounded were the priority, but these other factors had to be taken into account in the management of the medical service.

18. AND SO TO WAR

*The Canadians land and advance, with the medical units
following in support.*

July 10 -13, 1943

*By 1800 hrs the 1ˢᵗ Canadian Infantry Brigade was firmly in possession of
the Pachino airfield and the area immediately to the north and west. The 2ⁿᵈ
Canadian Infantry Brigade was equally successful on the left, and the 3ʳᵈ was
in reserve. There was some heavy resistance further to the left where a Special
Service Brigade was landing, but it was quickly repelled by mortar fire. The
day's fighting closed, under cover of darkness, with a general advance of some
four miles towards Ispica.*

*Most of the Canadian medical units landed during the day. With few ca-
sualties to deal with on the beaches, they headed inland as best they could, following the troops. The Field Ambulances, supposedly leading the charge, had
mixed success due to the missing vehicles and equipment, a problem that was to
plague most of the medical units for some time to come.*

*No.4 Field Ambulance first set up a beach dressing station to support the
invasion, but with little work to do they moved quickly inland and established
themselves in a large compound known as 'Bompalazzo', near the town of Burgio. No.5 Field Ambulance also set up a beach dressing station, and stayed one
day longer before moving ahead to establish an Advanced Dressing Station at
Ispica. No. 9 Field Ambulance, which had come to Sicily on the same ship as
the 2CFSU, lost all but two of its vehicles and virtually all of its equipment in
the confusion of the landing. It camped at the top of the beach and started to
search for its lost stuff.*

*No.1 Field Dressing Station, No.35 British Field Surgical Unit and No.35
British Field Transfusion Unit all landed around noon, and shortly thereafter*

opened an Advanced Surgical Centre in a barn about half a mile from the beach. The 2CFSU joined them the following day.

The Canadian troops advanced rapidly, moving north towards the mountains. The 2nd Brigade occupied Ispica, Modica and then Ragusa, while the 1st Brigade penetrated as far as Giarratana.

Advance units of Nos 4 and 5 Field Ambulances moved ahead to support them, while the headquarters of these Field Ambulances leapfrogged forward to open Advanced Dressing Stations, working under the direct command of the Assistant Director of Medical Services (ADMS) of the 1st Division, Colonel C.H. Playfair. No. 4 Field Ambulance headquarters ended up near Modica, and No.5 FA headquarters at Ispica.

Late on July 11 the Advanced Surgical Centre set up in the barn near the beach moved off the beach to a more suitable location in Maucini. On July 13 No.1 Field Dressing Station moved from there to Bompalazzo to form the nucleus of a substantial Canadian Medical Centre.

19. LOST AND FOUND

The 2CFSU takes awhile to get its bearings and go to work.

Saturday, July 10, 1943

Heat. Flies. Glaring sunshine in air so dry that their mouths are parched almost immediately, and the water in their bottles heating up so quickly that it removes any real sense of refreshment. Salt water chaffing their bodies under uniforms and the straps of their backpacks. Sand down their necks.

The men of the 2CFSU already have a sense of being in the war, even though they have not yet been close to any fighting or seen the enemy or a wounded Canadian. There is no action in sight from their place in the meagre shade of the scrub trees. Allied planes occasionally pass overhead, but the shelling from the big ships has stopped.

Rocke sets the plans in motion. "Strip off, men. Let's get these clothes dry. It won't take long in this heat. We'll take an hour to dry out, and then we'll head for our rendezvous with the British No.3 Field Dressing Station. It should be about an hour's walk from here, near the town of Maucini. Jack, let's get the men in shape to move out in an hour. I'm going to sniff around and see if I can find out where we are."

"Oh, and all of you…keep your eyes peeled for our vehicles and supplies. They were supposed to come ashore today, but heaven knows where they are. And everyone will be looking for their own stuff or whatever they can find to help move supplies, so we can expect them to be taken over very quickly if we don't grab them right away. Captain Leishman and I both have copies of the papers showing that we own them, so if you see any hint of them shout out right away. And McKenzie, make sure that those papers are always where we can grab them quickly."

Rocke strips down to shorts and shirt, both drying quickly, and heads along the beach. His feet squish in his soaked boots and socks. He knows that he must head inland as soon as he can, find the road to Maucini, and look for some landmarks identified in the official orders: a small chapel with a stone wall around it, and a bit north of that a large outcrop of rock that looks like an elephant's head. The rendezvous point is to be somewhere in the one-mile stretch between those two landmarks.

He turns up a gravel road leading off the beach and angling north through the coastal rubble. A group of five Allied vehicles rush past him, full of intense Canadian soldiers. The road is narrow and winding and very rough. He knows that it would be easy to get lost as the maps seem to be a bit off and most of the road signs have been destroyed. Fortunately the Service Corps people have placed temporary signs at some of the intersections.

In one clearing he passes a large body of Italian soldiers who have surrendered. They are seated in rows with their mess kits in hand, waiting to be fed by their Canadian guards. They are singing, for heaven's sake! He asks one of the Canadians guarding the prisoners what is happening, and is told that the Italians are surrendering in droves. This is a partial explanation of the ease with which the Allied landing has happened. The hard fighting ahead will be mainly with the Germans who are well established farther inland.

He comes to a rough paved road angling north and turns up it, hoping it is heading towards Maucini. It is obviously not a main road; more like a farm road running through fields of parched wheat and clumps of waving olive trees. He comes around a long curve and sees in the distance the modest spire of a chapel. The first landmark! He turns and hurries back to the beach. The team is fully dressed, dry and ready to go. They haul on their packs and Rocke leads them back along the beach.

"You're going to love the big show the Italians are putting on up ahead," says Rocke, "and I don't mean fighting. A whole bunch of them have surrendered, and they've been singing for their supper! They may do it again, just for you."

"Really sir?" asks Branch. "We must have been pretty damn good to beat them so quickly. Hell, we've just arrived here."

Rocke licks the sweat off his upper lip. "Actually, I think lots of the Italians are surrendering immediately. From the reports we were getting on board they're pretty fed up with the Germans and with the war. Half of them have relatives in England and Canada and the States, after all. They're probably getting angry letters asking them what they're doing shooting at us! Add to that the bombardment that we laid down over the past day, which must have been pretty devastating, and I think they're just saying 'to hell with it'. This lot you're going to see ahead is mighty happy to be out of the fighting!"

They come to the clearing where the Italians are now quiet, waiting patiently for their meal. The team stops and observes the curious spectacle. "I wish I had a camera," growls David Finley, who fancies himself a good photographer. "What a great sight…us feeding the guys who've been shooting at us!"

They move into the field kitchen and refill their water bottles with cool water from the kitchen's water tank, thanks to the friendly Sergeant in charge who just happens to come from Montreal. It's so hot that any water that was left in their water bottles from the landing is actually almost too warm to drink. At the Sergeant's invitation they have a wonderful meal of beef stew, bread and tea while the prisoners look on wistfully. They thank the Sergeant and move back onto the road, heading inland.

They march through a sun-bleached countryside. There are a few scrubby trees and cactus and an occasional palm tree, and even some bamboo along the roadside. There are also occasional welcome splashes of colourful red poppies and a few red tiled roofs on the peasant houses. Everything else is brown or grey, the vegetation burned to a crisp by the hot summer sun. Even the grape vines in the fields are dead and brown and, like most other vegetation, covered with the dust raised by the winds and the attacking armies.

Half an hour later they see the chapel spire in the distance, and 15 minutes later they are resting in the shade of the wall around the chapel. It is now early evening and the wall throws a long and refreshingly cool shadow over the tired men. Rocke leaves them there and walks the mile along the straight road to the elephant-shaped rock. It doesn't really look like an elephant, but it juts out enough that he is sure it is the second landmark. The trouble is, there is no sign of the British No.3 Field Dressing Station.

He walks back along the stretch, leaving the road several times to check out wooded glades and depressions in the land that might conceal it, and asking several parties of soldiers moving along the road if they have seen it. By the time he is back with his team, however, he knows that the FDS is simply not there. Night is falling and they have failed to achieve their first objective.

Rocke leads them along the road until they find a sheltered spot in a field about 100 metres off he road. They offload their packs and settle down to sleep in the open. The night is warm and clear, but they are awakened at midnight by a short, sharp air raid as enemy planes attack a nearby Allied position. They are met by a furious response from the anti-aircraft guns of the Allied ships offshore. The team feels very exposed to this battle in the air, but there is no place to hide so they listen to the bursts and watch the flashes. They wonder if they are perhaps more threatened by fragments from their own ack ack shells than by the enemy aircraft.

Sunday, July 11, 1943

The 2CFSU team is up at first light, blankets rolled and packs ready to go. They breakfast on cold rations supplemented by two delicious watermelons that McKenzie has liberated from a nearby abandoned field. Already they are carefully rationing their use of water. The dryness of the air and the ever-present dust makes them thirsty all the time, but there are no sources of water to be seen. They must rely on the army suppliers, and no doubt they are as mixed up and lost as is the 2CFSU. Pity the soldiers up ahead with their heavy packs and long marches and single water bottles! Thirst is going to be a real problem until the supply system gets sorted out.

Rocke gives his orders.

"It's clear that something has happened to our British friends, so we'll have to either find them or find the ADMS for reassignment. He's probably up ahead in the Maucini area, or beyond. Jack, you and I will head up there and try to find him for new orders. Branch, keep the men here and a sharp watch on the road. McKenzie has the papers for the vehicles, so if you spot them go after them."

Rocke and Jack head up the road, sticking to the edge to avoid the Canadian and British vehicles rushing past in both directions.

"This is the most barren place I've ever seen," says Jack. "Mind you, the shell holes and burned brush don't help, but hey, where are all the trees? It's so damn hot and dry! And from what I've seen so far, it's dirt poor here. Look at that hovel over there!"

"Right – you can hardly imagine someone living there. I've read that they've had so many invasions here over the past few thousand years that it's a wonder anything is standing," replies Rocke. "The Romans ran it for awhile, and took most of the trees out so that they could grow wheat here to feed their empire. This is the result. There're a few orchards around, like that one over there, which help. But it shows you how important forest cover is. Mind you, you come from Winnipeg…"

"That's a low blow, Rocke. We have lots of trees in Winnipeg! I guess we're also here at the hottest time of year, so everything's wilted. That and the flies! Dammit, they're worse than the black flies up north!"

In half an hour they reach the tiny village of Maucini, which is swarming with Allied troops. They ask as many as will take the time to listen if they have seen or heard of the No.3 British Field Dressing Station or the Canadian ADMS. For half an hour they are frustrated with "Can't help you, Sir," until a British Major in a jeep, spotting Rocke's insignia, stops to help.

"I haven't seen hide nor hair of the Field Dressing Station, Major, but I have seen Colonel Playfair. About half an hour ago he was heading with his staff up the road towards Pachino. That's where I'm going, so I can take you two that far." They leap into his jeep and quickly cover the two miles to Pachino, where they almost run into a jeep containing several Canadian officers. They pose the same questions and are told that the ADMS is probably headed up to Ispica as the Canadian medical units are headed that way too. Rocke and Jack thank their British friend, turn onto the road to Ispica, and thumb a ride in a Canadian supply vehicle. They cover the 12 miles in half an hour, weaving around columns of troops, and in Ispica they go through the same routine of questioning.

After further adventures they finally track down the ADMS in temporary headquarters in a house on the outskirts of Modica, six miles further on. Rocke explains his problem to the guard, who takes them in immediately to the Colonel.

"I've been wondering where you had fetched up, Major" says the ADMS over welcome cups of tea. "Your British friends never came ashore yesterday. For some crazy reason the Captain of the *Ascania* forgot about them and sailed off to Malta with them still cooling their heels below decks. Terrible balls up! Oh and, yes, they weren't the only ones. Your pal Frank Mills and his No.1 FSU team were on the same ship! And our Field Transfusion Unit. Dammit! Well, I guess there's no problem finding a doctor in Malta anyway.

"They should both be landing later today, hopefully on Sugar Beach. I'm just starting to figure out where to put them."

Rocke and Jack are chuckling at this story to the evident annoyance of the Colonel, until Rocke tells him about their narrow escape from a similar fate. Then they settle down to discuss placement. Colonel Playfair says that No.9 Field Ambulance landed with the 3rd Brigade but took heavy losses of transport equipment, and orders the 2CFSU to join them near the beach just south of Maucini to help them deal with serious casualties there. Rocke and Jack ask if they might use one of the ADMS's vehicles and a driver to return to their unit. Permission granted, and one hour later they are back with their unit and marching south to the beach, buying watermelons and tomatoes whenever offered by haggard but smiling peasants.

No.9 Field Ambulance is a sorry sight: an ambulance unit almost without ambulances. The guard at the road is a skinny, lively stretcher-bearer who identifies himself immediately as Pte. Ted Walls and leads them to the Commander of the unit, Rocke's new friend from the ship Lt.- Colonel Basil Bowman. Jack diverts the men under the guidance of Pte. Walls ("call me Ted") to the field kitchen where they exchange two watermelons for tea and sandwiches.

"It's nice to see you again, Rocke," says Bowman, "but we really don't need an FSU here right now. Our lads up ahead are having all the fun while we're stuck here without vehicles. It's a sorry situation, I'll tell you. But I'll bet they could use you over at the Advanced Surgical Centre that No.1 Field Dressing Station has set up just about a mile south of here. You know Doug Sparling don't you? That's his unit. They have a British FSU and FTU working for them, and I hear they're pretty busy. I suggest you head over there and see what you can do. In fact I'll go there with you right now to see what we can sort out."

Rocke and Bowman drive in one of Bowman's scarce vehicles over to the surgical centre, set up in a barn next to the beach. The Field Dressing Station itself is set up in a nest of tents in a grove of trees near the barn. Major Sparling welcomes them and says that he is sure the British Field Surgical Unit could use some help. He introduces Rocke to Major Tony Barnsley, Commander of the British FSU.

"I'm glad you're here, Major Robertson," says Barnsley, saluting smartly. "We've had a pretty fast start. We've been operating all night and would welcome some relief. You're welcome to use our equipment and instruments."

Bowman leaves Rocke there and drives back to his unit, where he orders his driver to ferry Rocke's team immediately to the ASC. Meanwhile Rocke works with Sparling and Barnsley at the ASC to agree on who will do what and when, and to survey the site and equipment that will be at their disposal. The team has all arrived by 1300hrs and gathers around Rocke.

"This is our first live action, men," says Rocke, looking as excited as he feels. "We won't use our tent thanks to the barn the Brits have been using, and it's all set up for us, but let's go through our paces anyway. Jack, you and I will go with Boucher and Price to look over the patients. Branch, take the others into the operating barn and surrounding areas and make sure they're clean and ready to go. The Brits have been working here all night so things must be pretty well OK, but will probably need some cleaning up. McKenzie, we'll need the wash station ready to go, and see if you can find some gowns and masks for us. And of course drinks for us all, and start checking for food we'll need later on. Questions?"

There are none, and they head off on their assignments. Rocke and his colleagues look over the patients in the Field Dressing Station and decide, with Major Sparling's agreement, that five need surgery. They have all been cleaned up and sedated by the orderlies in the Field Dressing Station, so it is time to go to work. Rocke and Jack decide that the abdominal wound will come first, then the poor guy with multiple wounds including a mashed thumb, then the buttock, the thigh, and finally the tibia.

The scene in the barn is familiar to Eric Branch; he has seen it in the many training set-ups they went through in England. But now they are in real time, and this is the real thing. Lives depend on how well they run this crude operating theatre. It is a small, very old barn abandoned years ago by its sheep inhabitants and their keepers and never cleaned up since, until now. The operating area is actually quite roomy, with a sheep stall running along one side of it and a broken down hayloft arching over it.

The British FSU team has done a terrific job setting up the area to be used for operating. They have been able to draw on the generator of the Field Dressing Station to run the lights, but there is not enough current to run the sterilizer. They have swept and scrubbed the floor and washed the walls and doorways. There is a pile of ancient sheep dung and dirt and wooden debris and cobwebs lying outside the back entrance where they swept and left it in their rush to start operating. Since they stopped operating several hours ago the wind coming in from the ocean has blown thin layers of dust on everything again, including the operating table and surrounding equipment. Branch admires the professional way that the Brits have set up the OR; now all it needs is a good re-cleaning.

He sets the team to work. Drivers Curran and Kraft take brooms and mops and start a frantic cleaning exercise. Pete Monroe, the driver/mechanic, looks to the cleanliness on the outside of the building (through which the wounded must be brought), making short work of the dung pile at the back so that the team members don't have to walk over it when entering or leaving the barn by that doorway. The OR assistants Johnny Pyke and Dave Finley give all of their attention to the layout of the OR equipment, instruments and materials, going over them with their British counterparts and requesting supplies. The Brits have been working with the limited supply of equipment and instruments carried ashore in their packs, supplemented to an extent by the Field Dressing Station. It is enough…just. Pyke takes responsibility for sterilizing instruments, which he does by boiling them over a wood fire outside the back of the barn.

Before leaving them, one of the British OR assistants hands Eric a folded picture magazine – an ancient copy of the Illustrated London News. "Here mate," he says, "you'll find this useful. It's a bit informal for an operating room, but it's a damn good tool." He chuckles at Eric's confusion. "It's a fly swatter, mate! One of you is going to have to stand over the table all the time just waving this to keep the flies off the wound. Sounds crazy I know, but – well, you'll see."

McKenzie finds the wash station used by the Brits. There are soap and towels and disinfectant and a basin, but very little water. He runs to the kitchen of the Field Dressing Station and begs for water, and they grudgingly hand over several pails of tepid water out of their precious store. He heats most of it on the kitchen stove, keeping enough to provide drinking water for the team. He finds gloves and masks in the British FSU stores, but no gowns. The Brits tell him that it's so hot they have been operating stripped to the waist, so that's what he reports to Branch.

Just before 1400hrs Jack Leishman strides into the barn and asks Eric to report. They tour the OR area and Eric tells him how the team has worked well together. He shows Jack the folded magazine and Jack laughs, knowing that it's a good idea. At the end of the quick tour Jack's surgeon's eye is satisfied. Training in the English countryside has taught him to forget the perfect and look for the practical and functional. The place is as good as it can be, although there are still lots of flies as there are open windows and doors in the barn, and no practical way to seal them up without suffocating the people inside. "Well done, Eric," he says. "Let's get to work. Major Robertson has already started to scrub, and I'm headed that way myself. You and Johnny and Dave come along and let's get ready. We've told the orderlies to bring in the first patient at 1430hrs sharp. It's an abdominal case, so we have to be in top form."

Eric is pleased with himself. He knows that he has done a good job, and it feels right. He is a proud man, with good reason. He took one year of formal orderly training in Montreal before the war came along and he joined up, and that helped him get a non-commissioned officer post in the RCAMC. The other thing that made the appointment inevitable was his excellent response to military training. Eric is a small, tough man with the energy of a coiled spring. He took to the military life immediately, excelling in all aspects of the training and showing that he had a good sense of decision-making and leadership. His assignment to the 2CFSU was the break he had needed to really show his stuff.

The Privates in the team like and respect Eric, and do what he says without arguing. He seems to know so much, and what to do in any and all circumstances. As for the officers, he has huge respect for them because he has one year of medical training and knows just how much he doesn't know, and therefore how much they do know. He is also delighted that they are not military men in any real sense of the word, and they therefore rely on him to keep the unit operating efficiently. They trust him – that's the key. Their job is to operate and save lives. His job is to set them up so that they can do just that. That's what he intends to do, and that is what he has just done. Damn fine! He heads to the wash station to prepare for the work ahead.

Starting at 1430hrs precisely the team moves into operating mode.

The orderlies wheel in the abdominal case and place him on the operating table. Working under Eric's hawk eye, they do their job gently and well. They withdraw, and Pike and Finley move in to clear back the sheet covering the soldier, and to adjust his position for the operation. The patient is not a pretty sight. He is a 20 year-old Private from the Royal Canadian Regiment who has taken a load of grenade shrapnel in his gut. It is laid open through a gaping wound, and inside is a mass of blood and damaged flesh.

Young but experienced surgeons, Rocke and Jack are used to the blood and guts of their profession, but even for them this is a terrible sight. It is far worse than any wound they have seen in civilian life, and they both feel the rush of adrenalin that comes with the frantic call for action that the case represents. They are excited that they are now doing what they came to Europe to do, but at the same time horrified by the thought that they will see a lot of wounds like this or even worse. The sight of this young man, all but dead except for what they can do for him in the next hour, gives them their first truly realistic sense of what the future holds for them.

For Johnny Pyke the thought is simpler: he almost pukes in horror at the sight of the wound. He has been trained to assist in an OR, but this is the equivalent of being thrown into the deep end of a very cold pool after one swimming lesson. He turns away briefly, gulps and swallows, mops his streaming brow, and then turns back and watches Rocke's face for the first instruction. His thoughts are crystal clear: *I'm fucked if I'm going to give in. Not now. Not ever. No way.* His crisis passes.

Dave Finley has no such problems, and doesn't know why. He has had nightmares about this moment – the first time he sees a living man turned into a bleeding mess, lying before him on the table. What will he do? Can he handle it? Now he knows: he can handle it very well. His training and thinking about it seem to have rationalized his senses so that what he sees before him is a case needing his help. It's messy, but that's the way it is, and that's the way it's going to be.

His job right now is to wield the magazine to keep the flies off, and to mop the brows of the surgeons as they work. Both are urgently required right from the outset. It is hot in the barn and Rocke and Jack are both sweating profusely, so with his left hand Dave moves the small towel back and forth continuously. The fly dispersing job is far more complex. The flies are numerous and quick, zeroing in on the wound remorselessly. He finds that if he just scoops them by passing the magazine over the wound they simply go around it and return to the attack. It takes more finesse to disturb them and move them away, particularly when the magazine can so easily get in the way of the surgeons. He starts to develop techniques that will serve him and Johnny well throughout the campaign.

As this and the following operations proceed the months of practice and training pay off handsomely. The surgeons ply their trade of surgery and anaesthetics, oblivious to the crude conditions around them except for the annoyance of buzzing flies not completely fended off by the Illustrated London News, or the sweat dripping off them and mopped frequently by the OR assistants. The injuries they are treating are rough and complex, taking all of their concentration and, particularly in the multiple wound case, a considerable degree of imagination. The OR assistant not on magazine duty moves around them sorting, handing and taking back instruments smoothly and efficiently. In some cases the shortage of instruments makes him search for substitutes to what would be ideal, leading to brief, gruff exchanges with the surgeons.

Eric directs the orderlies in their work of prepping patients and bringing them to the OR, and then returning them to the Field Dressing Station. He keeps a sharp eye on them and is pleased to see how well they work together. Their faces show a mixture of shock at the sight of the wounds and determination to help the wounded men. They are learning fast. With each new case they are more sure of themselves, learning how to transfer their raw strength into gentleness and smooth motion for the wounded.

Eric stays in the operating area while operations are in session, supporting the OR assistants and providing any link required to outside people, instruments or medicines. With the one OR assistant tied up on magazine duty he is frequently drawn into sorting and cleaning instruments and other tasks normally done by OR assistants. Like Dave Finley he has no trouble handling the sight of the wounds beyond a deep, throbbing sense of concern for the pain and the danger faced by the wounded young soldiers. The hand-over of patients after surgery to the Field Dressing Station calls for precision and clear thinking: they must transmit any instructions from the surgeons clearly and precisely to the FDS staff, who take responsibility for post-operative care. Branch keeps a pad and pencil in his pocket to jot precise notes, and he has the other orderlies do the same. They then give the notes to McKenzie as input to the patients' records.

The drivers stand guard duty, although Pete Monroe breaks off for an hour to help the FDS drivers repair a jeep that simply refuses to start.

The operating team takes a brief break between operations while the orderlies are taking the patient back to the Field Dressing Station ward and bringing the next patient over. They gulp warm tea brought to them efficiently by batman McKenzie, puff cigarettes to clear their heads, and then wash up and get ready for the next patient.

War Diary

We did 5 cases – G.S.W. abdomen, G.S.W buttock, G.S.W. thigh without fracture, a case with multiple injuries including median nerve (left) and a crunched right thumb, and a bad G.S.W. tibia. Our facilities were not of the best by any means. We were working in a filthy stable – straw and flies galore. There was no artificial light. We used what equipment 35 FSU had carried ashore in their packs (very noble of them) and there were many things that we would have wanted that we didn't have. Water was short – we didn't have enough to wash either ourselves or the patients properly. We had no sterile drapes and soon ran out of swabs. There was no proper stove for sterilizing the instruments. However we got through the cases for better or worse, and it's to be hoped that they will not suffer too much.

They finish their work at around 1830 hrs. The team is tired but elated. They have finally done what they have been training for months to do. They have operated on wounded, and perhaps even saved a life or two! They have no equipment or vehicles, and no real orders to work with, but they are working. And the team is already working well, the team members moving efficiently to compensate for the poor facilities and lack of equipment.

Rocke and Jack sit quietly with cups of tea and cigarettes, both in a state of minor shock. In quiet tones they share the idea that has come to them separately as the operations have progressed. Until today they have not seen anything like the wounds that they have worked on this afternoon, with a few exceptions back in England. Before the war they had seen very few gunshot wounds, and virtually none in the extremities. Neither had dealt with open abdominal or chest wounds. Now they have seen these as well as other open, raw injuries, and they know that this will be their professional diet for months to come. As doctors they are challenged and determined; as human beings they are horrified.

As they clean up after the operations they discuss the experience with other members of the team. The stable is a surgeon's worst nightmare, dirty and with dust in the air, and the wrong shape and size. There are flies everywhere, requiring constant efforts with the folded magazine to keep them away from open wounds. They know they must develop better ways of dealing with the flies. They themselves are tired and sweaty, and making do with inadequate instruments and equipment. But this is war and that's the way it is.

They realize that they are developing a code to live by, and they gradually put it into words. It is that the most important people in the world right now are the fighting men up front – the foot soldiers and the artillerymen and the engineers. These people are to be served with all the skill and energy that the team can bring to bear on them, no matter what the time of day, and no matter what the circumstances. The team members know that they will constantly be exhausted and dirty, and sometimes thirsty and hungry and even sick, but that is not the point. The code is, simply stated, service to the fighting men.

20. MAUCINI

They set up in a building on the south coast.

The Field Dressing Station kitchen gives them a warm meal, and just as they are finishing it a despatch rider comes roaring up on his motorcycle. He calls to the team and asks, "Where's the officer in charge here?" Rocke looks around wearily and starts to point to the Field Dressing Station tents when he remembers that he is a Major just like the other Majors, so maybe he's in charge!

"I am, Private. What's up?"

"Pte. Santer, Sir, from ADMS headquarters. This Advanced Surgical Centre is ordered to move immediately to Maucini where there's a big stone house for you to work in. Shall I give you the written orders?"

"Yes, I'll take them," says Rocke. The messenger hands him the envelope. He takes it, tells Santer to have a meal if he would like one, and sends McKenzie to find the Commanders of No.35 British FSU and No.35 British FTU and ask them to come immediately to Major Sparling's command tent in the Field Dressing Station. The four Commanders discuss the order and decide that each one should make their way over to the house in Maucini, about two miles away, as soon as they can and by whatever means possible.

Rocke returns to his team, they thank the cook (always a good friend to have), pack up their gear, and march with the British FSU and FTU to their new location. The No.1 Field Dressing Station follows in its trucks, leaving a small nest in one tent at the beach to take care of the immediate post-operative cases. They set up the Advanced Surgical Centre in the designated large stone house standing at the top of a hill overlooking the sea. The rooms are spacious but riddled with flies, beetles and lizards. The place designated for the operating room is an old wine cellar. It no longer has supplies of wine, but at least it is cooler than the other rooms. The British FSU team cleans the operating area as they are on surgical duty for the night. There are no cases, however, so they delay setting up the OR until next morning.

The house is sufficiently large that there is room for sleeping accommodations for the FSUs and the Field Transfusion Unit. Eric Branch and Andre Boucher open several bottles of wine purchased from peasants along the way. It is typical local stuff – musty and strong. The team is relaxing after their very lively day. Jack is delivering his impressions of the current situation, and they take a glass to Rocke to enjoy while he writes the war diary for the day.

There is the sound of a group of men arriving outside. McKenzie comes in to report that No.1 Canadian Field Surgical Unit and No.1 Canadian Field Transfusion Unit have arrived to join the Advanced Surgical Centre, having landed earlier that afternoon. The Commanders of the two units, Major Frank Mills and Captain Wally Scott, follow him in almost immediately, and they and Rocke have a good laugh over their adventures on the road to Sicily via Malta. The new units find sleeping places in the hallways.

Monday, July 12, 1943

There are no wounded brought in until noon, so the units have a quiet morning. They clean their gear, repack, exercise and keep a constant eye on the road for signs of their vehicles and equipment. All of the units at Maucini are short of vehicles, equipment and supplies. Pete Monroe and Victor Kraft visit the few small local stores for several more bottles of wine, and they all stock up on fresh fruit from the fields along the roads. Whenever possible they find the owner and pay for the produce.

Jack treats a local farmer whose left arm has been gashed and broken in a fall in his barn. He is shy and grateful, and offers Jack two eggs as payment. Jack is strongly touched by this gesture. The farmer is thin and clearly very poor, and probably can't really afford to give up the eggs. The two men have no common language, but Jack can see the ravages of occupation and war in the eyes of the man, and for the first time the toll of war on civilians, caught up in events they abhor and do not understand, hits him directly. This man has been downtrodden and half starved, but he knows who his friends are and he still has his pride. Jack accepts the eggs, smiles, shakes the peasant's hand and sends him away with a supply of bandages and iodine and two packages of dry rations.

Rocke and Eric Branch work with the men of the British No.35 FSU to clean and set up their equipment. The Canadian team starts the operating sequence for the day and does its first case at 1400hrs. Just as this operation is finished and they are taking a breather outside, the ADMS himself drives up and orders the 2CFSU and No.1 Field Transfusion Unit to move ahead to Bompalazzo, to the location of No.4 Field Ambulance. "No.1 FSU will stay here with the FDS and the Brits."

21. BOMPALAZZO

A strange place, not much to do, and few instruments to do it with.

The ADMS makes an 8cwt utility vehicle available to the officers of the two units, who depart immediately. The drive is a short one through undulating coastal plain that should be fine agricultural country, but is now scorched and brown. The few houses that they see are really just peasant huts, with little sign of life or habitation. They see a couple of farmers walking in their fields, but it looks like most of the inhabitants are still in hiding, uncertain how to deal with the latest invaders.

They arrive at Bompalazzo at 1700hrs. The men follow in vans also requisitioned from the ADMS. A somewhat perplexed Major Peter Tisdale, Commander of No.4 Field Ambulance, greets Rocke and Wally Scott.

"What's going on, chaps?" asks Tisdale. "I just heard that you were coming here, but I'm not sure why. We have no cases to operate on, and also, well, no equipment to operate with anyway. We're still short a number of vehicles and almost all of our supplies and equipment."

"Damned if we know," Wally Scott replies. "We've just come from operating on a pretty strong caseload with some borrowed instruments. Now we have no instruments, so if you don't either, I guess it's a good thing that there aren't any cases."

"We'll be moving out in the morning anyway," says Tisdale. "Up to Modica. No.9 Field Ambulance has just arrived from the beach, and will be taking over whatever work there is here starting tomorrow. They have a few vehicles and some equipment now, but not a hell of a lot."

"Things are moving pretty quickly," says Rocke. "We visited No.9 FA on the beach just yesterday, and now they're here with us! Colonel Bowman was very helpful to us. I'm glad some of his vehicles arrived."

Colonel Bowman and Captain Don Young join them a few minutes later, and they and Rocke greet each other like old friends. The officers share stories over tea, and then Tisdale shows them around. The Field Ambulance is set up in a large house built in a quadrangle. Once the home of a prominent local family, noisily loyal to the Fascist government, it had been requisitioned by the Italian coastal forces and the family moved to the safety of the interior. It was only slightly damaged during the invasion, and is now available as a medical centre.

It has facilities for making and storing wine, although none is currently stored there. The house has five large rooms and a kitchen. The walls are freshly white washed and the floors tiled, giving a sense of space and cleanliness. Unfortunately the nearby outbuildings have more wine paraphernalia, donkeys, chickens and cats, and the filth in them is beyond description. This in turn means that there are flies and fleas everywhere, and the officers are all scratching even before the tour is over.

"The men will be sleeping over the road in that orchard," says Tisdale. "They can join up with the men of No.9 FA who are already there. You fellows, being lucky officers, will be sleeping in the main house along with a few fleas. Ah yes, this is the reward of rank and power!"

Fleas notwithstanding, that evening the officers of the four units at Bompalazzo take advantage of the lull in work and the presence of fresh local produce and wine. They enjoy a memorable dinner in the courtyard of the main house, overseen by the Field Ambulance cook and the ever-watchful batman McKenzie. Outside on the road, between the officers dining in the big house and the men in the field also enjoying the fine local fare, sit glum representatives of each of the units watching the road for any signs of their missing vehicles and equipment. Their pals bring them plates of food from the tables and cups of wine, but it just isn't the same.

Tuesday, July 13, 1943

No.4 Field Ambulance moves out at 0930hrs, and the No.9 Field Ambulance team makes itself at home. They are still seriously short of vehicles, but have managed to find five at the beach so at least have some mobility. Jack bums a ride with a Field Ambulance vehicle to take him back toward the beaches where he is going to search for their vehicles and equipment at the main landing sites.

At 1000hrs vehicles arrive bringing No.1 Field Dressing Station and No.1 Field Surgical Unit, their colleagues of a day ago at Maucini. "Hello again, Frank," says Rocke. "Are you fellows following us around?"

Major Frank Mills just laughs. His unit, like Rocke's, is without vehicles, supplies or instruments. They are being taxied around the country like school children, hoping to find some of their things soon so that they can be independent and start doing what they came here to do. "Sure, Rocke," he replies. "Say, could I borrow some scissors and a roll of tape by any chance?"

They both chuckle, and Frank goes to look over the place and settle his team into the field. Rocke greets Major Doug Sparling, Commander of the No.1 Field Dressing Station and his host of yesterday. Sparling says that his unit has a reasonable supply of equipment and instruments, and if the Field Surgical Units need it there should be sufficient to set up an operating room. Colonel Bowman, who is the senior officer in what is now a substantial Canadian Medical Centre at Bompalazzo, joins them in their discussion. They have a Field Ambulance, a Field Dressing Station, two Field Surgical Units and a Field Transmission Unit. The Field Ambulance, still woefully short of equipment or vehicles, is to look after the admission, documentation and further evacuation of patients. The Field Dressing Station is responsible for triage and resuscitation in conjunction with the Field Transfusion Unit. With two FSUs, all they need are patients to work on.

The equipment produced by No.1 FDS proves to be inferior to that of the British No.3 Field Dressing Station at Maucini, just five miles away. They decide that until this is rectified they will do only the most urgent surgery, letting all other work flow through to Maucini.

A small group of locals forms a ragged line outside the building, waiting to gain the attention of the doctors. Some are ill. Some have cuts and bruises that need attention, and one is holding a wrist that appears to be broken. Colonel Bowman sends his orderlies to check them out, fix up the simple cases, and refer those requiring it to the doctors in the Field Dressing Station.

At 1830hrs a large unit, well supplied with vehicles, arrives at the medical centre. Lt.-Colonel Brian Smyth, Commander of British No.4 Casualty Clearing Station, steps down smartly from his van and is greeted by Colonel Bowman and the other officers. Colonel Smyth asks the other units to help his men settle in the orchard for the night, and over tea the officers discuss where the Casualty Clearing Station would best be located to anchor the work of the field units.

Colonel Smyth says that his unit landed earlier in the day along with No.2 Field Dressing Station, and they are both considering, in communication with the ADMS, where they should 'open shop'. "The FDS is camped about a mile away from here, and we'll both need a decision by tomorrow so that we can get on with it. The ADMS feels that with our rapid advances, the CCS should be as far forward as possible. He is talking about Modica, and that sounds about right to me – for us at least. I don't know about the FDS."

He then tells them about some interesting briefings his team received earlier today from a British security officer. He was talking about dealing with the locals as the Allied forces move through the country. They are dirt poor, some almost starving. They were in bad shape before the war, and with the war the German and Italian armies have taken what little they did have. The general feeling is that they will be delighted that the Allies are here to turf out the Germans. The civilians are still officially the enemy, of course, and some Italian units are still fighting, but they are pretty reluctant warriors, as can be seen by the number of surrenders being taken.

"So this means that we are to be as friendly and open as possible with civilians, and that means taking care of their wounded and sick as well, with reasonable priority. This will probably cause some problems when the fighting gets tough and we have lots of our own wounded to deal with, but that's just the way it is. The Service Corps will have translators available in the towns to help out. As to food, you may be able to buy some locally, but as often as not they'll be trying to get food from you. Just do what you can to help."

"You'll be glad to hear that we've already started working with the civilians, Brian," says Colonel Bowman. "We had quite a line-up here a few hours ago. It feels good to be helping them. They've had a terrible time."

Colonel Smyth smiles. "Good show, Basil. Now then, the security chap also talked about the Mafia. You won't likely see any signs of them, but they are all over the place. The interesting thing is that Mussolini tried to get rid of them a few years ago so that he could control things himself. They went underground, but they're still here and the word is that they're being helpful to our side because we're fighting the Germans and Mussolini's goons! This is especially so for the Americans out in the western sector. I'm told that they have a lot of soldiers of Italian or Sicilian extraction in their units, and that is helping them tremendously. It'll be tougher for us dealing with the Germans up ahead, and of course for the Yanks when they meet up with German units."

"Sir," says Rocke, "we had some experience with the Mafia in Montreal. You know that they're very active there? Well, back in mid-1937 one of our surgeons at the Montreal General operated on a young Italian boy for a ruptured appendix. The boy was in pretty bad shape when the family brought him in, and they were thrilled when we managed to save him. The boy's father took my colleague aside and said that he was very grateful, and that he owed the doctor a favour, and if there was ever anything he could do for the doctor, just let him know. The doctor thought nothing of it, of course. However about six months later a similar case came in – another young Italian boy in trouble with his appendix, and this time my colleague couldn't save him. The family was grief-stricken, and the father took the doctor aside and told him 'Doc, you messed up the operation and you didn't saved my son, and I'm going to get you'!"

The Colonel is looking interested but sceptical. "Is this really true?" he asks.

"Absolutely true, Sir. So once again the doctor thought nothing of it, but then he started to notice that things were happening that weren't nice. A car just missed hitting him, and a tool kit just happened to fall off a building and barely miss him. That sort of thing. He started to worry, and he remembered the warning he had received…and also the earlier promise of help he had received. So he phoned the first father and told him what was going on. The father said 'OK Doc, now you just go home and don't come out, and read the papers, and come out when it's OK to come out'.

"And that's what he did. He stayed at home and read the papers every day, and by Jove if he didn't see an article in the Gazette one morning about a week later saying that a well-known local criminal had been found dead, bound and gagged, floating in the St. Lawrence River just downstream of Montreal. That was, of course, the second father! So my colleague came back to work, and everything was fine!"

The group is momentarily stunned into silence. Then Colonel Smyth speaks up. "That's some story, Major. And now we're at the heart of the

Mafia system, and thank heavens they're on our side! So one way or another, keep it in mind. The civilian you're saving might just be a godfather or capo or something! You'd better be nice to him, because he might turn up in Montreal to visit you some day."

Wednesday, July 14, 1943

The 2CFSU team has a midnight to 0800hrs shift, but there is no work to do so they sleep right through the night. No.1 Field Surgical Unit has several cases during the day, and 2CFSU has one in the 1600hrs – midnight shift, but that is it. It is a quiet day that is seen by all as a blessing. Few casualties means that the war is going well, and anyway they have very inferior equipment to deal with cases when they do show up. There is another line-up of locals, easily handled by the Field Dressing Station.

Jack arrives back at 1730hrs, filthy dirty after having spent 30 fruitless hours at the beach. "The organization there is a shambles, Rocke. There are people going every which way looking for their stuff. Some guys are just grabbing anything they need and taking off with it. There seems to be no real system. I think the organizers have moved inland with the troops. God knows when our vehicles will be unloaded. Nobody seems to have seen them – at least nobody will admit to it.

"I've been thinking that seeing as all of our units are missing stuff, maybe we should send a team down there to set up camp and keep watch over all offloading operations. Whenever they see any of our stuff they can grab it and send it up to us here. If we don't do this it'll just continue to be catch as catch can – whatever we can spot as it rolls by."

This seems like a good idea, but the other units don't agree so nothing happens.

22. FAST PROGRESS

The war goes well for the Canadian troops

July 14–18, 1943

The Canadian advance was resumed on the night of July 14, directed on Vizzini, Grammichele, Caltagirone, Piazza Armerina, Valguarnera and Enna. This was pursuing General Montgomery's strategy of seizing control of the central group of road junctions around Enna. With the Americans sweeping through the western part of the island, the capital Palermo and the left centre of the core, and the British moving up the east coast and mountainous areas around Mount Etna, the Canadians had the task of driving straight up the centre of the island on a path between Enna and Etna. The overall objective was to subdue the forces on the island and, by moving north quickly, to cut off any escape routes to Italy via the Strait of Messina on the northeast tip.

As they moved north the terrain grew increasingly mountainous and difficult. Off-road movement was next to impossible in many places, and many of the towns in the area had been built on hilltops with defences that took advantage of the rugged geography. The Germans utilized this rough terrain to telling effect, fighting rearguard actions from strong positions of their own choosing and igniting ingenious demolitions along the narrow and tortuous mountain roads.

The Canadians moved up with little opposition through Vizzini, and then on the morning of the 15th met their first serious German resistance near Grammichele, on the road to Caltagirone. The column of tanks and vehicles full of soldiers were caught in the fire of a German artillery and tank detachment from the Herman Goering Division. They engaged the enemy and the 48th Highlanders, supported by the tanks of the Regiment de Trois-Rivieres, were able to drive the enemy back. Both regiments pursued the enemy as far as Caltagirone, which they entered the next morning.

There was then some bitter fighting in the hills south of Piazza Armerina, but the Canadians forced the Germans back and on July 18, after more heavy fighting, occupied Valguarnera, southeast of Enna. In a single day, near Valguarnera, the Canadians had 145 casualties including 40 killed.

The Command then decided that the Canadian advance would be directed northwards towards Leonforte and Assoro, leaving Enna to be taken by the Americans.

This very rapid advance placed a strain on the medical services. It was only 40 miles as the crow flies, but much longer on the tortuous Sicilian roads. Several of the medical units were still short of vehicles, and equipment and supplies were scattered. The shortage of vehicles taxed the available transport to the limit. Of key importance was establishing the Casualty Clearing Station as a secure base for the advanced medical operations, as well as the medical supply depot for the whole operation. The ADMS decided on Modica late on July 14, and a major effort was launched to establish it there as quickly as possible.

One of the problems that they had to deal with was the 40 tons of unaccompanied medical stores dumped on the beach on July 13 when the Casualty Clearing Station landed. The stores were to be controlled by the CCS, which was originally scheduled to set up on the beach. With the rapid advance of the troops, the CCS was now to set up at Modica, so this large volume of valuable medical supplies had to be moved there as well.

In spite of the heavy usage of vehicles moving these major units and supplies into position, the field units were now urgently needed to support the rapidly advancing Canadian troops. This led to a brief period of highly flexible transport management, with vans and ambulances and jeeps being begged, borrowed, traded and operated almost around the clock. As this frantic activity proceeded more vehicles did appear, coming from later landings, so that the units slowly managed to gain their prescribed vehicle strength. Supplies and equipment continued to be scattered.

When the forward troops moved out towards Vizzini, No.5 Field Ambulance had already been ordered forward from Ispica to Monterosso Almo. On July 15 they established an Advanced Dressing Station there in a large municipal building. No.1 Field Dressing Station and No.1 Field Surgical Unit arrived there late in the afternoon of the 15th. and set up an Advanced Surgical Centre in a building opposite. With Monterosso Almo just 10 miles south of Vizzini, this seemed to have placed medical services sufficiently close to the frontlines. The troops, however, were moving ahead so quickly that late that evening the

ADMS ordered No.4 Field Ambulance to have an Advanced Dressing Station open even farther ahead, in Grammichele, by first light.

No.4 Field Ambulance received this order when it was still back at Modica. Many of its vehicles were involved in moving units and supplies forward, and also it had been instructed to retain all casualties save urgent surgical cases with a view to transferring them to the Casualty Clearing Station as soon as it opened. Thus it received the order to move when it was loaded with patients and struggling with limited vehicle capacity. Fortunately this was the sort of challenge that its Commanding Officer, Major Peter Tisdale, enjoyed the most. With an heroic effort he delegated a reserve company to stay behind to tend the patients on hand, divided supplies, had most of the available vehicles loaded, drove through the night along the twisting, dangerous roads through Ragusa and north past Vizzini, and proudly opened his Advanced Dressing Station as the sun peeped over the hills to the east of Grammichele.

23. MOBILE AGAIN!

They finally recover their vehicles, lost in the landing.

Thursday, July 15, 1943

At 0600hrs Colonel Bowman tells Rocke that he has received word that the Germans have landed paratroopers at Augusta, out on the east coast. "This is going to really get things going, Rocke. It looks like the Germans have decided that we're here in force, and are strengthening their forces to stop us. Our troops are moving up already to get in better positions, and the Brits moving up the east coast really have their work cut out for them.

"The ADMS has ordered No.1 Field Dressing Station and Frank Mills' team to move up to a place called Monterosso Almo. They're going to set up an Advanced Surgical Centre there. Frank will have to ride with the Field Dressing Station, as he still has no vehicles. You'll be staying here with us. We have some surgical equipment and supplies, and you're welcome to use them to set up your OR."

"Thank you, Sir," replies Rocke. We'll get right at it." Colonel Bowman moves to the door and calls out "Pte. Walls, take Major Robertson and his people to the equipment vans and help them get any things they need to set up an OR."

"Yessir" says Ted Walls. "Good morning, Major. The vans are over there." The 2CFSU team, minus the watchers at the road, take the equipment and instruments from the Field Ambulance vehicles and move them into the room just vacated by the departing No.1 Field Dressing Station. They scrub the room as best they can and set up the table and equipment, ready for action.

At 0930hrs an ambulance with four stretcher cases comes to a gentle stop in front of the building. Colonel Bowman and Rocke receive a quick briefing from the accompanying orderly and look the patients over. "What do you think, Rocke? I would say that you could do a good job on the leg wound and the shoulder case. They're nasty but they look like they're pretty straightforward. But the other two are abdominals, and I wonder if you would be comfortable doing them under these conditions? We could get them back to Maucini pretty quickly."

"I agree. I would hate to have to work on an abdomen here, unless of course there's no alternative."

"Right," says Bowman. He gives the orders, the two lighter cases are taken off the ambulance and prepared for surgery, and the ambulance moves off towards Maucini. The 2CFSU team completes the two operations at 1230hrs.

At 1430hrs Jack is in the operating room going over the instruments when he hears a shout from Dave Finley, who is on duty at the road. "Sir, the vans! I think I see them starting up the hill towards us. There's a whole lot of them." Jack rushes to the road, yelling over his shoulder to McKenzie to bring the papers for the vehicles. McKenzie has already heard the news and is there almost before Jack, along with four others of the team. As the vehicles grind up the hill towards the house they recognize the lead vehicle with the red cross on the side as their surgical van. The number CL.4236160 is there, clear as a bell for all to see. Several vehicles past the van are their other two vehicles, and all are loaded with supplies.

As the van comes abreast of the house Jack steps out on the road and signals it to a stop. It does so immediately, and those behind it follow suit. Jack walks to the driver's open window. "Private, you are driving a surgical van that belongs to the No.2 Canadian Field Surgical Unit. It is essential to our operation, and we need it immediately. I must ask you to step down so that we can take it over. These are the papers."

The startled driver turns to the other man in the van, a Lieutenant from the Supply Corps in charge of this convoy of vehicles that is taking rations to a forward supply depot. The Lieutenant steps out of the van, comes around the front and salutes smartly. "Lieutenant Morse, Captain. What's this about your vehicle?"

Jack repeats his order and hands the papers to the Lieutenant. "And Lieutenant Morse, I also see that our two other vehicles are in your convoy: the 60cwt lorry four back from you and the 8cwt utility vehicle just behind it. These vehicles are essential to us, so we will take them as well."

"Sir, these vehicles are loaded with rations for the supply depot up at Modica. Can we take the stuff there and then bring the vehicles back to you here?"

"I'm afraid not Lieutenant. We're desperate for them as we could be ordered to move on at any minute. Hang on." He turns to Captain Ted Conway from No.9 Field Ambulance, who has been listening to the exchange. "Ted, if we offload the rations here, could you fellows take them up to Modica for the Lieutenant? I know he'd appreciate it." He winks at the Lieutenant, whose worried expression is slowly turning to one of hope.

"Sure Jack. No problem. We can send the supplies on later this afternoon. Oh, and Lieutenant, Captain Leishman here has eyes only for his own vehicles, but I see a few other red crossed vans farther back. One is clearly another surgical van. That belongs to No.1 Field Surgical Unit that has just moved on to Monterosso Almo. It's getting pretty hot up at the front, so these special vehicles are really important to our medical units. Please be sure that you get them over to Monterosso Almo as quickly as possible after you dump your loads at Modica. I'll call your Commander at Modica to make sure that he has the message. I'll also call Major Mills up at Monterosso. You'll probably find him waiting for you when you get to Modica!"

"Thank you, Sir," replies the Lieutenant. "May I leave these vehicles with you to unload?"

They pull the three vehicles over to the side of the road and the drivers get out and climb into other trucks. Lieutenant Morse salutes unhappily, climbs into the new lead vehicle, and the shortened convoy rolls on its way.

The 2CFSU team watch quietly and happily until the convoy has passed. Then they break out in happy cheers and whistles, climbing over their vehicles like long-lost friends. Victor Kraft is close to tears. He has mechanically nursed the surgical van tirelessly for so long that it seems like his firstborn, and he has felt devastated thinking that it might be lost. Now he has it back, and within seconds he has the hood up and is inspecting the engine.

Rocke returns from his walking visit to a peasant's hut where he has treated a farmer with a nasty puncture in his leg, and shouts with joy upon seeing the vehicles lined up beside the road. "Well done Jack," he says after Jack briefs him on the hand-over. "Now we have transport...wouldn't it be nice if we had something to put in them?"

After the team have inspected and cleaned the trucks, Rocke has driver Pete Monroe take him in the lorry back to the beach to see if he can find any equipment or supplies. They return at 2200hrs empty-handed, having stopped for dinner with the No.3 British Field Dressing Station that has finally landed after first going off to Malta, and is now set up at Maucini.

Friday, July 16, 1943

Rocke and Wally Scott drive back to the beach to look for equipment. The scene is incredible. The men who should have been unloading equipment and supplies have given in to the hot conditions and are idling about or swimming. Rocke and Captain Scott roam the beach and manage to locate some of their crates, which they load into the lorry with the congenial assistance of the swimmers. They have a swim themselves and then drive back to Bompalazzo.

There are no cases, so the teams go to work unpacking the crates and loading their contents into the vehicles. It feels good to finally have a few instruments and supplies of their own. At 1700hrs Colonel Bowman finds Rocke with his head in a supplies cabinet in the surgical van. "Rocke, we'll be moving out some time later this evening, so you'd better get all your gear loaded."

They are fully loaded and ready to go by 2000hrs. After dinner (without wine) they move their three vehicles into a convoy of 23 vehicles consisting of 2CFSU, No.9 Field Ambulance, No. 2 Field Dressing Station and No.1 Field Transfusion Unit.

They are ordered to drive with headlights on at low beam. At first this strikes them as odd, using lights at night in a war zone. But they realize that they will be driving through countryside and towns already liberated by Canadian troops, so it should be safe. And of course, the glow of the lights will illuminate the red crosses on the vehicles. Equally important is the state of the roads. They are rough, narrow and twisting even here close to the coast, and will inevitably get worse as they move inland into the increasingly mountainous heart of Sicily. There are occasional washouts and other obstacles, and in many places ancient stone walls, picturesque to look at but deadly to hit, line the road. Driving without lights would be suicide.

They have very little means to defend themselves against attack, counting on the facts that this is conquered territory, and also that there will be Canadian troops stationed in the towns that they will pass through. Each unit is ordered to have one weapon per vehicle ready to deal with nuisance situations. This is a problem for the 2CFSU, as their Tommy guns have not yet arrived. The two officers give their side arms to drivers Curran and Monroe, and tell Krafty that he'll just have to keep his head down.

The convoy starts to roll north at 2330hrs.

24. THE ROAD NORTH

The medicals travel north by night, following the troops into the heart of Sicily. Operating in tents.

Saturday, July 17, 1943

The night is clear and cool, with a beautiful full moon. They pass through tiny Ispica with no difficulty, but the following towns are a different story. Towns in Sicily were often built on hilltops for defensive purposes. This means that the road through the town usually rises through tight switchbacks to the edge of town, takes an agonizingly complicated route through the town itself, and then falls away on the other side through more switchbacks. Driving through them in daylight, with a good map and all road signs intact, is difficult enough. Doing it at night, with faulty maps and most of the road signs destroyed or skewed, is a nightmare.

Modica gives them their first taste of it. After squeezing up the twisting road to the town's border they are faced immediately with unsigned options in the form of dark streets heading off steeply at difficult angles. Colonel Bowman in the lead vehicle is close to despair as he pores over his map until his driver announces the approach of two Canadian soldiers, a Corporal and a Private.

The Corporal salutes smartly. "Good evening Colonel. We've been expecting you. We're here to guide you through Modica."

"Well thank God for that," grunts the Colonel, returning the salute and folding the useless map. "Climb on board, Corporal, and let's go." The Corporal climbs onto the running board of the van, leaving the Private on watch for stragglers, and guides them through the sleeping town. At the other end, with the road running ahead of them in the moonlight clear down the hill through rocky fields, he tells the Colonel that there will be similar services in the other towns along the way and that he will call ahead to be sure they are awake. He salutes quickly and then jumps down from the slowly moving vehicle. Colonel Bowman shouts his thanks, and then breathes a sigh of relief and lights up cigarettes for himself and his driver.

Ragusa is a similar challenge, and once again a friendly Corporal helps them. Giarratana and Monterosso Almo are too small to warrant an escort, but they do benefit from the directions received from sleepy Canadian soldiers at checkpoints on the road. Vizzini presents a challenge similar to Modica and Ragusa, and has the same splendid service to guide the convoy through.

They finally come to rest at 0800hrs in an olive orchard that offers some welcome shade, at a point halfway between Vizzini and Caltagirone, just to the east of Grammichele where Canadian troops have recently fought their first major engagement. They wash up, have breakfast, snooze and laze around in the morning, discussing the war situation. They know that the troops ahead have done some heavy fighting, with more on the way, but they still have a lull before their heavy duties begin. They have a tremendous sense of anticipation…they want to be there.

They move on at 1330hrs, drive past Grammichele for another 10 miles, and set up their sleeping tents in a field beside the road. They know that they are close to the fighting now. This seems to be an assembly area for the army, and they watch with interest the movement of troops up the road. They all look so young – too young to be marching into such a battle. But the soldiers also look tough, very tough. The medicals also see the vehicles of No.4 British Casualty Clearing Station, their home station, passing by towards Caltagirone. They hear that Caltagirone will be the location of the CCS, which means that they will be moving ahead of it very soon – probably tomorrow morning.

Sunday, July 18, 1943

At 0630hrs Rocke meets with Major Bill Clendinnen, Commander of No.2 Field Dressing Station and Captain Wally Scott, Commander of No.1 Field Transfusion Unit, to discuss their orders to move closer to Valguarnera to set up an Advanced Surgical Centre. "There's fighting going on right now in Valguarnera. No.9 Field Ambulance is going ahead right behind our troops, and No.5 Field Ambulance is setting up a dressing station in an orchard ahead of the artillery batteries, just this side of Valguarnera. Our orders are to move ahead to that orchard," says Clendinnen. "Looks like they're taking this 'advanced' thing seriously!" They all chuckle nervously, and move the discussion quickly on to order of convoy, rest stops, emergency signals and other operational details.

The convoy moves out at 0715hrs, heading northeast. They stop in Caltagirone, where the officers meet briefly with Colonel Smythe at the Casualty Clearing Station to confirm their orders and receive any fresh briefings. "The only thing I can tell you is that the fighting is getting very hot up there, so you should be ready to go to work the moment you arrive. Oh, and we're still trying to locate more of your supplies and equipment. But you should also keep your eyes open for hospitals that have been closed. They often have good equipment in them. I'm not saying that you should loot the places, but it's OK for you to take what you really need. If you see the ADMS you can clear this with him."

The convoy drives on. They pass through San Michele where No.1 Field Surgical Unit and No.1 Field Dressing Station have a hard-working Advanced Surgical Centre in an abandoned warehouse, and Piazza Armerina, the scene of bitter fighting just hours ago. As they climb along the twisting road towards Valguarnera they can hear the sound of artillery ahead. They pass the Canadian artillery unit two miles out of the town, and half a mile on they are signalled into an olive orchard by an RCAMC staff Sergeant, and join up with No.5 Field Ambulance.

They set up their Advanced Surgical Centre as quickly as possible, sweating heavily in the hot morning air. Jack takes Eric and two of the drivers over to the Field Dressing Station to beg for surgical instruments and equipment. A key piece of equipment is the operating tent, and they return with the smallest, most unlikely tent imaginable.

Based on the team's first experience with flies back on the beach, the drivers know that they must minimize the number of flies in the OR right from the start. They have developed a service that they provide on arrival at this and all future operating sites. They call it 'Fly Patrol'. It consists of securing the operating area and any surrounding medical installations from invasions of flies. They seal all entrances and windows as best they can, preferably with sheets of screening, and spray copious amounts of 'Flit' at the droning flies, and on all exposed walls and other surfaces. They follow up with a rapid and violent fly swatter attack, and then finish with a sweeping operation to clear the area of fly corpses. They are proud of their work; it is immensely valuable in an operation that is horribly exposed to infection.

As they are setting up the tent the Canadian artillery opens up behind them, and they can hear the shells whistling over their heads. The din is terrific, knocking them back momentarily from their tasks to watch and listen.

Then it's back to work, and as they begin operating the true nature of the tent reveals itself.

War Diary

The tent allotted to us was one of the smallest variety called, by some optimist, an operating tent, measuring about 12x15 feet with a very low sloping roof. The floor is dust and the tent is insufferably hot in the daytime and difficult to black out at night. We started to operate at about 1500hrs and worked almost continuously until midnight doing six cases (compound tibia and fibula, compound humerus, two abdomens and two sucking chest wounds). The congestion in the tent made a rapid handling of cases almost impossible. During the day the artillery opened up from time to time to add to our discomfort...Considering the natural difficulties the work done was quite good...One of our patients with a sucking chest wound was a German of the Herman Goering Division. He was very friendly though he had no English.

During the operations the drivers work on their vehicles, continue to secure and improve the camp, fetch supplies and equipment when ordered, and act as security patrol. McKenzie, the batman, sees to the substantial housekeeping needs of the team, fetching and serving food, water and tea, and supplying fresh clothing and clearing and cleaning bloodied clothing. He finds a copy of Macleans magazine to replace the over-used and filthy Illustrated London News in warding off the flies during operations. He has his typewriter set up in a convenient place so that he can do the patients' records quickly and efficiently.

At midnight the unit feels, for the second time, the heavy fatigue that comes from long hours of concentrated medical teamwork in very trying conditions.

25. BATTLES AND STRATEGIES

The troops are involved in fierce engagements.
The medical units move to support them.

July 19 - 22, 1943

The march through the inland mountain region became more and more difficult for the Canadian troops. The enemy was stationed around Leonforte-Assoro, where rocky outcrops jut out from the bed of the River Dittaino, buttressing Mount Etna. Mount Assoro reached 920 metres and the German positions seemed impregnable. From this natural stronghold the German 15th Panzer Division controlled the road to Messina.

This was not enough to stall the Canadian troops. On July 20 at Assoro, strongly defended by German positions in commanding high ground, soldiers of the Hastings and Prince Edward Regiment, 1st Infantry Brigade scaled cliffs at night and attacked the surprised Germans from higher positions at dawn. Fierce fighting went on until noon on July 22, and Assoro remained under Canadian control.

This battle exemplified the bravery and ingenuity of the Canadian troops in Sicily. Assoro had been successfully defended for thousands of years, often by minimal forces. Defenders had always assumed that the cliffs at the back, with almost impassable country at their base, were insurmountable, and had successfully focused their attention on the approach road at the front. The small Canadian force that launched the surprise attack had hiked all night over impossibly rough terrain, silent and in pitch darkness. Starting at around 0430hrs and already very tired, they then scaled the high cliffs, bringing with them their weapons and ammunition and, importantly, a huge and ungainly radio and battery. When German artillery started to take part in the counterattack the Canadians, using this radio and an artillery spotter's telescope captured from the Germans, were able to call down accurate Canadian artillery fire to silence the German guns.

Soldiers of the 2nd Infantry Brigade engaged in fighting equally tough but also successful at Leonforte. The enemy's destruction of the bridge carrying the main road across a deep ravine south of the town seemed to have given them immunity from attack by Canadian armour. Soldiers of the Loyal Edmonton Regiment and the Princess Patricia's Canadian Light Infantry made a frontal attack, and their tactics caught the Germans by surprise. The assault was so fast and so efficient that the German guard posts at the entrance of the city surrendered. The infantry companies, under cover of a heavy bombardment, fought their way into Leonforte on foot while engineers began bridging the 50-foot gap. A fierce struggle developed in the streets and the Canadians were cut off from outside support, but thanks to the strenuous efforts of the engineers the bridge was completed during the night, and at daybreak a flying column of infantry with tanks and anti-tank guns burst into the town. There was more bitter street fighting, but by mid-afternoon of July 22 Leonforte was clear.

The 3rd Infantry Brigade, meanwhile, was routed eastward by a more southerly route to attack the town of Catenanuova, opening a southerly approach to the key centre of Adrano.

With Canadian fighting units on the move north to Assoro and Leonforte and east towards Catenanuova, the ADMS had to place his Field Ambulances strategically to support this broad span of operations. On July 19 he moved No.4 FA into Valguarnera to serve the troops moving north.

He decided to leave No.5 FA where they were in the orchard near Valguarnera for the time being to act as a staging post for casualties en route south to the Casualty Clearing Station at Caltagirone. Then on July 22 it was moved to a point four miles north of Valguarnera, only partially opened but well positioned for future requirements farther forward.

On July 21 he moved No.9 FA, finally well equipped with vehicles and equipment, eastward into the Dittaino Valley in support of the Canadian 3rd Brigade's assault on Catenanuova. It opened an Advanced Dressing Station near Raddusa-Agira Station, eight miles east of Valguarnera.

With Valguarnera clearly the centre of action, and decision taken to place No.4 Field Ambulance in that town, the ADMS decided to establish the main Canadian Medical Centre there. This decision was supported by the presence in Valguarnera of an abandoned schoolhouse that would make an ideal medical *facility. The Italians had used the large, rambling school building as a temporary hospital.*

On July 19, No.1 Field Dressing Station and No.1 Field Surgical Unit moved up from San Michele to join No.4 Field Ambulance in Valguarnera, based in the school building. The 2CFSU and No.1 Field Transfusion Unit joined this substantial medical centre on July 20. There was plenty of room for all of the units, including large rooms for wards and masses of parking for the medical vehicles. The facility was filthy and dishevelled when they arrived, but it was easy to clean and had excellent electrical and water supplies. It contained large stocks of medical supplies including surgical instruments and dressings, and these were invaluable to the medical teams still awaiting the arrival of much of their own supplies. Living quarters were in tents in a nearby orchard.

The one sour note was the 60 enemy patients, civilian and military, who had been left behind by the fleeing hospital staff and whose condition, along with that of the building, was indescribable.

No.2 Field Dressing Station moved to a reserve position near the Canadian Medical Centre in Valguarnera. They did not open for business, but were poised to move quickly when ordered.

26. MEDICAL ISSUES

The changing face of war surgery.

Monday, July 19, 1943

"Major Robertson, we have an abdominal case that needs work immediately."

Rocke struggles out of his exhausted sleep at 0200hrs on the quiet urging of driver Kraft, who had unluckily drawn first sentry duty when the unit finished operating two hours ago, at midnight.

"What's the status, Krafty?"

"The Field Dressing Station says it's a lad from the PPCLI. Name is Pte. John Henderson. He's taken a hunk of shrapnel right in the gut. There's lots of bleeding, and the FDS guys say that we'd better see to him right away or he's a goner."

"OK," says Rocke, climbing off his cot and reaching for his shirt. "Call Captain Leishman, Finley and Price. Get the generator going and the lights on, and start the sterilizer. You can help move the patient over here. You'd better get Monroe to take over sentry duty. And tell McKenzie that we're going to need some coffee."

Fifteen minutes later the team is ready – still somewhat bleary-eyed, but there is no complaining, no comments on the time of day. They have moved quickly from deep sleep to operating status, their mood heightened by the sight of the wounded soldier who is carried into the operating tent. The Field Dressing Station team has cut away his uniform around the wound and cleaned the area as best they can. He is mercifully sedated and almost asleep, but manages a weak smile when he sees the masked surgeons staring down at him. His wound is awful. The shrapnel must have come at him from the right front, tearing into his lower abdomen and passing through to his back, almost but not quite exiting next to his spine. The steel shard is still in him.

"Good morning Pte. Henderson," says Rocke. "We're going to fix you up and have you back on your bicycle in no time." There is no reply.

For once the tent is almost cool, and there are fewer flies to contend with. They go to work quickly and efficiently. As Jack applies the anaesthetic Rocke examines the wound while, at the same time, enjoying a sense of accomplishment in the smooth running of his team. They've had a long time to practice as a team, and it is great to see it all working – even in the middle of the night.

They complete the job at 0345 hrs. They have found and removed the shrapnel, cleaned the wound completely, and done some suturing inside the wound. They have not, however, sewn the wound up completely, holding it in place by a large abdominal bandage. This represents an evolutionary approach to the treatment of wounds in the military.

Issues in the Treatment of Wounds

Up to the First World War methods of treatment of wounds were primitive. Most wounds were caused by relatively small calibre bullets. Treatment consisted of basic cleaning of a wound, pouring in a disinfectant such as iodine or carbolic acid, and sewing it shut. In 1914, however, surgeons found that the nature of warfare had changed drastically: the introduction of larger and more irregular missiles, problems of transport, and an unprecedented volume of cases meant that they were now dealing with a grotesque variety of complex wounds.

Simple cleaning and suturing no longer did the trick. Internal damage would inevitably cause infection to occur inside the wound. There was now a need for more complex surgery, clearing out damaged tissue (called 'debridement'), removing all debris, and giving due attention to reviving the vital processes in a complex wounded system. An initial response was 'open wound treatment', in which they would clean the wound and then let it heal naturally, without suture. This dealt somewhat with the problem of infection, but had its own associated problems, in particular the need for lengthy immobilization of the patient and very extended healing periods.

This led to evolving approaches to suturing. 'Primary suture' – sewing up the wound immediately - was pursued in the simplest cases. The concept of 'delayed primary suture' involved wound closure 4-7 days after initial treatment, often following minimal debridement and cleansing. This gave a few days to ensure that the wound was really clean, so that suturing could be done without fear of infection.

'Secondary suture' was much more delayed, generally following debridement associated with extensive tissue damage. The wound would be closed only after one to three weeks, being kept dressed and immobile until obviously clean and free from infection, and until healing was already underway. This sometimes involved skin grafts.

Two key related issues were immobilization systems and infection control. Unsutured wounds must be kept immobile if healing is to have a chance, and also to save the patient from unnecessary pain. The use of Plaster of Paris casts became widely accepted around 1940 as the best way to immobilize wounds to arms and legs. In many cases it removed the need for suture altogether.

Infection control was always a key factor in the treatment of wounds. Before penicillin was introduced in the middle of the Second World War, doctors applied cleansing agents such as sulphonamides to wounds in an effort to keep them clean, thereby preventing the onset of infection. Penicillin, the first antibiotic, changed the rules of the game in that it was now possible to halt the spread of infection once started.

Excerpts from "Wounds and Infection" H. Rocke Robertson, published 1953.

Source: Official History of the Canadian Medical Services 1939-1945, Volume 2, 1956. Department of National Defence. Reproduced with the permission of the Minister of Public Works and Government Services Canada, 2007.

Private Kraft and colleagues from the Field Dressing Station move the unconscious patient back to the FDS ward. The surgical team members go back to their cots.

There are no new operative cases in the morning. Rocke and Jack visit their patients in the Field Dressing Station post-op ward. It is a hard experience.

War Diary

One of the sucking chest wounds we did yesterday died this morning. The post-operative care of these desperately ill patients is a tremendous problem. The FDS personnel which is almost entirely untrained and whose equipment inadequate is forced to look after cases who would tax the ingenuity of well trained nurses in the best-equipped hospitals. The heat in the tents during the day is almost unbearable; there is no space for moving about; the flies are a constant menace and the stretchers miserably uncomfortable. At the moment there are no better conditions in the rear – if there were one would be tempted to send these people back in spite of the experiences in North Africa and Spain. As it is we have to do the best we can and pray that there will not be many casualties.

The surgeons return to their unit and supervise a complete cleaning and overhaul of the operating tent. The drivers do Fly Patrol and then spray light oil on the floor of the tent to keep the dust down. The generator motor has broken down. Pete Monroe takes it apart and finds that the connecting rod and piston are both broken, and they have no spare parts. Fortunately the Field Dressing Station has a functioning system that they can draw on, but they need to fix their own motor as quickly as possible.

At 1400hrs Rocke, Jack and the officers of the Field Dressing Station drive into Valguarnera to the new Canadian Medical Centre for a group meeting and briefing with the ADMS. Rocke tells him about the generator problem and Colonel Playfair says that he will try to get a new one for them from the supply depot. He also authorizes Rocke to pick up any supplies he can from deserted hospitals along the way.

His medical briefing includes the issue of foot problems. Like the medicals, a lot of the front-line troops are also waiting for their first shipment of replacement clothing and materials, and that includes socks and boots. They've been doing some terrific hiking through really tough terrain, and many of them have worn right through their boots. Some have developed wounds from sharp rocks or just plain wear and tear. The soldiers are a tough bunch and don't complain about it much, but he suggests that the medical units check everyone coming into the station for foot problems.

Several of the doctors have already met with this problem, and there is a brief discussion concerning the types of injuries and treatments.

The ADMS continues. "Another common problem to keep in mind is dehydration. They're having a devil of a time supplying the troops with water, and some of the lads have actually passed out from dehydration. All of them say that they are thirsty all the time. So if you have good supplies of water, be sure to get it out to the troops, even just when they are passing by. And you should just assume that every patient who comes in has some degree of dehydration.

"Malaria and dysentery are already a problem, and you can assume that they're going to get worse. Obviously the water problem is at the core of the dysentery problem, as the men will sometimes drink anything they can find and a lot of the natural sources of water around here are contaminated, mainly with farm waste. Do keep this in mind with the water you are using. A bit of old fashioned boiling never hurt anyone! As to malaria – you have a few cases now, and you're going to have a whole lot more as we move through the incubation periods. It's just very difficult to convince a soldier under fire that it's the mosquito on his arm that's going to kill him before the bullets do! We'll have the consultant on malaria through here in a while, and he'll brief you on the latest techniques for prevention and treatment."

· The Colonel then takes some time to discuss the scary subject of shell shock. This was a subject of great concern and misunderstanding in the Great War. Most men who suffered from it were looked at as cowards, and many of them were shot for it – cowardice and desertion of duty. A lot more is known about it now, but it's still a tricky question. There are always examples of men simply being scared and faking it to get out of the war, but most of the cases are genuine. They range from troops who just get too tired and battered and need a rest to regain their spirits, to men who go completely out of their minds. They lose their senses and their ability to perform, and sometimes they go really mad and babble and swear and shout at everything and everyone.

He stresses the fact that a shell shock case can be a real danger to a man's comrades, citing the example of a man sent to scout out the enemy who is afraid to lift his head above the grass to look around! Or a soldier gabbling away rather than providing covering fire. The worst cases concern officers who gradually lose their courage and ability to make decisions. Sometimes it's difficult to detect until it's too late and they make some terrible blunder.

"I don't expect you chaps to be experts in this, but please keep in mind that shell shock is a real thing, and men who have it are wounded and need treatment. Don't just set them aside; make your judgement as to how bad their case is and deal with it accordingly. We do have psychiatric consultants to help you, and as you know we have a Corps Exhaustion Centre to deal with the tough cases. Here are some written materials on the subject.

"Oh, and I should also remind you that we have a Corps Venereal Disease Treatment Centre as well. But of course, you know all about that." There are nervous smiles all around.

When he has finished the medical briefing, Colonel Playfair clears his throat and theatrically announces, "Gentlemen, I am pleased to bring you a great new piece of technology. You know all about it, but you haven't had it yet. Sergeant, bring in the wireless set!"

A Sergeant and two Privates enter the tent carrying a large, complex piece of equipment. It is a new wireless with its heavy, ungainly battery attached. They place it on a bench and the two Privates withdraw. The Sergeant is a trained wireless operator and stays to demonstrate if ordered to do so.

"This is the first time our signals chaps have been prepared to let us have some wireless equipment," says Colonel Playfair. "They've kept it all pretty busy up at the front, but we've finally managed to convince them that our Field Ambulances, at least, simply must be able to communicate more efficiently if they are going to be able to really do their jobs. They've finally given in and loaned us four sets, one for me and one each for the Field Ambulances. So Major Tisdale, here is the set for your No.4 FA. Sergeant Frost will stay with you for a couple of days to train your chaps to use it."

"Thank you, Sir," says Tisdale, beaming and running his hands over his new toy.

Major Rocke Robertson, War Surgeon   *personal picture*

Captain John 'Jack' Leishman, War Surgeon   *personal picture*

Major Frank Mills, War Surgeon, personal picture

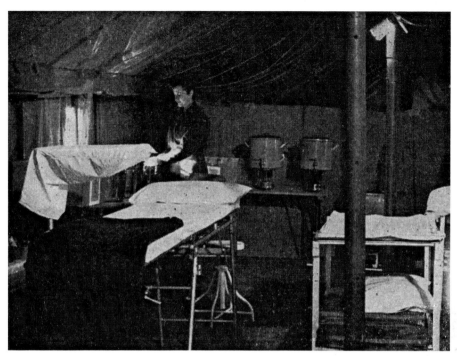

A Field Surgical Unit   *Vol 1, page 91*

A jeep ambulance   *Vol 2, page 352*

Advanced Dressing Station in San Vito Chietino   *Vol 1, page 169*

A ward in a Field Dressing Station   *Vol 1, page 370*

Leishman and Robertson –
two very tired surgeons in Sicily

personal pictures

27. VALGUARNERA

A full Canadian Medical Centre goes to work in the town.
The 2CFSU raids an abandoned Italian hospital for supplies.

Tuesday, July 20, 1943

There are no new casualties today. Rocke and Jack drive in the lorry to the Casualty Clearing Station at Caltagirone to see if any of their equipment or supplies has shown up. Only three crates have arrived and are being held for them, one containing the Tommy guns for the drivers. But a visit to the supplies depot proves to be more profitable. They find that Colonel Playfair's orders have preceded them and a new generator is waiting for them. They manage to secure a large supply of Plaster of Paris and splints, some medicines and a small selection of instruments.

They also find a bag of mail for the medical units at Valguarnera – the first mail that they have received since leaving England. Rocke finds three letters from Rolly, and hands the rest over to McKenzie to distribute. For half an hour he loses himself in news of home. The letters cover a period in which Rolly has taken the boys by train to the west coast to visit Rocke's family in Victoria. He grins and chuckles as he reads of the boys' shenanigans on the train, vexing the elderly conductor to the limit. He is delighted to hear of the wonderful time they have in Victoria. His parents are so sweet and welcoming, and the boys have tremendous fun playing on the beaches and meeting several relatives for the first time. The third letter was posted just before they boarded the train to return to Montreal.

In one of the letters there is a great picture of the three of them. Tam is now a handsome five year-old, and the baby is three and smiling at him. Rolly is as lovely as ever. Rocke feels a moment of loneliness so intense that he must hug the great, hollow space in his chest. He has the awful feeling of life passing him by while he lives and works in this barren, dangerous, foreign land. It's just so bloody stupid!

He folds the letters, puts them into his kit bag and goes back to work.

The 2CFSU and No.1 Field Transfusion Unit teams load their vehicles in the late afternoon, and after an early supper they move into Valguarnera to join the Canadian Medical Centre already operating there. They stop at the school building to unload their equipment and to meet and greet Frank Mills and the other unit Commanders.

"How's it going, Frank?" asks Rocke. "The building is certainly big enough, with lots of room."

Frank leads the way down the main hall to the area set aside for operating. "Yes, it's a good place for us. This was used as a hospital, and we've managed to find some instruments and equipment in excellent shape to help us get up to strength. I suggest you do the same. I'll get my batman to show you around. But we have had a problem with the inmates already here. When we got here yesterday we found about 60 Italian patients, abandoned a week or two ago when our troops were advancing towards here. They're a mixture of soldiers and civilians. They were in terrible bloody shape, I can tell you. Only a few of them could get up and walk, and they had tried to help the others, but there's shit and blood everywhere, and they're all dehydrated and almost starving. Fortunately for us only two of them have required surgery. The rest are in the charge of the FDS boys, and they're moving the civilians out to a civilian hospital near here as quickly as possible.

Rocke is disgusted. "How on earth could the Italian doctors abandon so many patients? Don't they take the Hippocratic Oath like we do? Did they honestly think that our troops would kill them when they're taking care of their people? What sort of outfit are they anyway?"

"Rocke," says Frank, "I think that this sort of thing just happens in war. Perhaps the doctors figured that these cases were pretty far-gone anyway and they wanted to stay out of our hands so that they could treat more of their own people. Hell, perhaps the Germans just told them to get out so that they wouldn't be around to help us, and there was no way to carry all these patients with them. Who knows? One way or the other, it's our problem now.

"As for us, we've been working flat out, and I'm damn happy to see you here. There's a lull right now, but it's not going to last long. When we see what comes up we can get our shifts sorted out."

152 ∴ WHILE BULLETS FLY

Rocke and Jack find a few useful instruments and two stretchers in a storeroom down the hall from the OR. Aside from that there is nothing that they need, and they gather the team and drive over to the campsite used by the Canadian medical teams – a rather dingy orchard on the edge of the town. They set up camp, service the vehicles, and have an early supper at the field kitchen of No.1 Field Dressing Station, their hosts.

At another table, away from the officers, Pete Monroe and Dave Finley are chatting with despatch rider Billy Santer, who has become a friendly acquaintance after several stops at their unit. "So how's it going, Billy?" asks Pete.

"It's going just fine, thanks. In fact, I'm having a ball. The roads aren't too bad on a motorcycle. I can go around most of the traffic, and so far I've managed to miss any mines in the roads. Mind you there have been a few tough times. The Colonel has me working my balls off most of the time, mainly because we haven't had any radios for a while. It's a bit better now, but there's still a lot of detailed orders that have to be delivered, plus messages and other junk. So, how are you guys doing?"

"OK I guess," replies Pete, "but it's pretty damn boring in these towns. How do you work, Billy?"

"Well, I'm sort of a one-man unit. You know, self-contained. I have a change of clothes and other stuff in my saddlebags and enough supplies and money to live on the road, and I just go where the boss sends me. The boss is usually the ADMS, but when I'm away from headquarters I take orders from any of the officers. The ADMS likes me and the other two riders to be at headquarters, ready to go, as much as possible, but he knows what the field units are up against and understands when they send us off somewhere. And you know, it's not just the medical officers I'm dealing with. I also have a lot of contact with the army units, helping our medical guys keep in close touch with them."

"Sounds like fun," says Dave. "You roam around the country on that big fuckin' Norton, stopping whenever you want and doing what you want. What a great job!"

"Yeah, it's not too bad. Mind you, most of the places I go to are pretty badly shot up, just like here, so there isn't much to do there. But there are a few places where there's some action, and of course the women are always delighted to take care of one of their 'liberators'."

"What?" cries Pete. "Women? Don't bloody well tell me you've found women around here. Hell, I thought they were all hidden by their families to protect them from people like you. And me too!"

They laugh. "Yeah, actually you're right," says Billy. "I haven't had any luck yet. I've seen some beauties in a couple of towns, but they're always too shy to talk, and there's usually some evil looking brother hanging around them. Anyway, I'm going to keep trying. You guys do the same, and we'll see who scores first!"

After supper Rocke and Jack drive with Wally Scott to a tiny nearby mining town where there is a small, modern and deserted hospital. This experience is a memorable one for Rocke, as recorded years later in his memoirs.

Personal Memoir

It gave us an eerie feeling to walk into an absolutely empty hospital. There was a large, unexploded bomb on the floor of the main entrance hallway. The beds in the ward were all dishevelled. In some there were the bodies of patients who could not make their escape when the bombardment started. The doors of the cupboards were open and there were clothes scattered about on the floor. Everything pointed to a frantic exodus.

All was shipshape in the Operating Theatre suite. It was spotlessly clean, obviously ready for the next day's slate. I had the difficult task of choosing the instruments that I needed – and only the instruments that I needed. I was sorely tempted to open my haversack wide and fill it with everything that it would hold. For the most part I held my hand. I did find, when I returned to my unit, that I had come away with one or two articles that I could not possibly use in an FSU. But, after weeks of deprivation, one's ability to pass up such an opportunity is enormously reduced – especially, one rationalizes, when the unexploded bomb at the front door may explode at any moment!

They drive back happily to the campsite. The 2CFSU now has come a long way in its restocking of supplies and equipment, although there are still some annoying gaps. When they were training back in England they had not had much practice at foraging and scrounging, but they are now thoroughly accomplished at these very useful skills.

Wednesday, July 21, 1943

At breakfast a tired and somewhat embarrassed Jack Leishman tells the team about a little adventure he had last night.

"Yes, I am tired Eric, and I'll tell you why. It's really stupid, but, well, you know all the stories we've been hearing about snakes all over the place, eh? So last night I was just going off to sleep when I heard something under my cot. I leaned over and looked under it, and there was a snake lying there! I was bloody petrified! It was too dark to see what colour it was, but I wasn't about to take any chances. I lay there all night, hardly sleeping, and I couldn't even get up to take a pee! I didn't want to yell for any of you guys – we all need our sleep. So anyway, at first light I checked under the cot again and there was my belt lying there! The noise I had heard must have been the belt slipping off the chair next to my cot."

The story is greeted with hoots of laughter, and the batman promises that in future he will "do a snake sweep" every evening to make sure the Captain is safe.

No cases come in during the day. A small shipment of supplies comes in from the stores depot early in the afternoon: marginal things for the most part such as rubber boots and lanterns, but there are a few good drugs and the foot suction. The Field Dressing Station handles a steady stream of locals, shy and smiling and thrilled that the war is over for them and they can get some medical help.

Rocke and Frank Mills have tea in the afternoon and discuss shifts. They decide on 12-hour shifts for the two FSUs and toss a coin to see who gets to choose. Rocke wins and picks the night shift, thinking that it will be good to work in the cool of the night.

They get to sleep early, and are awakened at 2200hrs by an orderly from the Field Dressing Station telling them that cases are coming in and they should be ready to operate at midnight.

Thursday, July 22, 1943

They operate continuously until 1000hrs. There are six cases, most of them large and long ones – an abdomen, a compound femur and several multiple wounds including a penetrating wound of knee joint and a sucking chest. The OR is hotter than they had expected it to be at night, and growing hotter as the morning progresses.

At 1000hrs they leave the hospital, passing the No.1 Field Surgical Unit team on the way in to take up their day shift. They return to the orchard and settle in to sleep, and it is only then that Rocke realizes the mistake he made in taking the night shift. It is unpleasant working in hot conditions, but it is even worse trying to sleep in the stifling tents. The team sleep fitfully though midday averaging about four hours, eat a couple of light meals, and return to work at midnight feeling thoroughly the worse for wear.

28. THE ADVANCE CONTINUES

The horrific battles at Assoro and Leonforte. Complex medical manoeuvres.

July 23 - 28, 1943

As soon as Leonforte and Assoro were under control, Major General Guy Simonds ordered his Brigades to attack Agira, roughly 10 miles due east of Leonforte on the main road to Adrano. Along the road to Agira they also had to subdue enemy troops in the town of Nissoria. The General deployed an artillery barrage comprising five field artillery regiments and two medium artillery regiments. The Canadian guns pounded the German positions, with regular pauses to allow the infantry to move forward, while RAF Kittyhawks bombed the German positions.

The enemy resisted fiercely and it took five days to capture Nissoria and Agira. The Canadian losses were heavy, but the enemy, which retired towards Regalbuto, had been severely hit. Meanwhile the US Army was moving east along the Canadians' left flank, Palermo being already captured.

In the evening of July 25 the Rome radio station broadcast the astounding news of the resignation of Benito Mussolini's Fascist government.

On July 28, towards the end of the afternoon, a thunderstorm broke over the hills. This was the first rain to fall since Allied soldiers had started their exhausting progression through the Sicilian furnace.

When this assault north and east started the Canadian medical units were focused on the town of Valguarnera, roughly 20 miles south of Assoro and Leonforte, with the flow of wounded back down the road and through the Casualty Clearing Station at Caltagirone. Now the troops were sweeping on and it was time for the medicals to move on with them.

As usual the Field Ambulances led the charge. No.9 Field Ambulance had already set up its Advanced Dressing Station in the Dittaino Valley to support the Canadian Third Brigade in its approach to Adrano from the south, through Catenanuova. Late on July 24, when the fighting was in progress on the eastern side of Nissoria on the more northerly road to Adrano, No.5 Field Ambulance opened an Advanced Dressing Station in an orchard about one mile south of Leonforte, alongside the main road from Valguarnera. No.4 Field Ambulances, after remaining in Valguarnera functioning as a staging post, closed completely on July 30. Its staff was dispersed temporarily to strengthen the other two Field Ambulances.

On July 25 No.2 Field Dressing Station, No.1 Field Surgical Unit and No.1 Field Transfusion Unit also moved out of Valguarnera and joined No.5 Field Ambulance near Leonforte, setting up an Advanced Surgical Centre on the opposite side of the road. They had wanted to set up in a school building right in Leonforte, but were thwarted by enemy artillery.

No.1 Field Dressing Station and 2CFSU stayed on in Valguarnera to handle overflow cases from Leonforte and post-operative work. This was a time of very high casualty rates. Canadian casualties from July 25 to 30 inclusive, which period saw the 1st and 2nd Brigades take Agira and the 3rd Brigade capture Catenanuova, totalled 119 killed and 446 wounded. The sick rate at this time also climbed another notch. Gastro-intestinal disturbances continued to head the list of causes, but cases of fever were becoming increasingly common. For the six days slightly more than 650 battle and non-battle casualties were admitted to No.5 Field Ambulance at Leonforte.

Meanwhile No.9 Field Ambulance at Raddusa-Agira Station, to the southeast, was also receiving a substantial flow of casualties, and on July 28 the 2CFSU was ordered to move from Valguarnera to join them to help out.

The occupation of Leonforte had a tremendous positive side effect for the Canadian medical establishment in Sicily. The Canadian troops found a large cache of enemy medical supplies in a warehouse. When the ADMS heard that the No.5 Canadian General Hospital in Siracusa, on the east coast, had lost almost its entire equipment in enemy action, he immediately undertook to re-equip it at least partially from this source. Within 48 hours, with the assistance of the Royal Canadian Army Service Corps, some 40 three-ton lorry loads of hospital equipment and supplies were transferred to Syracuse. Another 12 tons were sent from Canadian stocks in Modica.

29. EVENTS AND AN IMPORTANT LESSON

The 2CFSU has a sad, costly lesson. Rocke falls ill.

Friday, July 23, 1943

Once again the night shift is a busy one, with eight cases passing through the unit between midnight and 1030hrs. The heat is surprisingly oppressive and the flies are a miserable nuisance in spite of a noisy and violent Fly Patrol by the drivers just before the start of the shift. But the team is now used to these conditions, and can at least enjoy the luxury of operating in a reasonably well set - up operating room inside a building rather than in a close, stifling tent.

Rocke is particularly interested in a case involving a neck wound, a case that in the end serves as a painful lesson. The young Private from the Loyal Edmonton Regiment has taken a bullet through the neck, entering in the left side and passing through his throat near his tonsils before exiting right front. He is conscious on arrival at the OR, but deeply shocked and gasping for breath. As they set him up for surgery and seek to improve his breathing he lapses into unconsciousness, and shortly afterwards his breathing becomes so laboured that they perform a tracheotomy by cutting into his windpipe to provide airflow. Almost immediately they notice paralysis on the left side of his body. They conclude that the bullet has severed his internal carotid artery, and with his rapid deterioration there is nothing they can do for him except provide supportive services. He is bound to die; they move on to the next urgent case.

They finish work and return to their camp. The heat is intense, but they are getting better at dealing with it and manage an average of six hours of sleep, a vast improvement.

At 1800hrs Rocke and Jack walk into town and visit the makeshift officers' mess that has been set up in an abandoned restaurant. It's good to have some more of that challenging local wine, and a meal that isn't from a field kitchen.

"How's Trudy doing with the new baby?" asks Rocke.

"She sounds just fine thanks. The baby's keeping her up at night so she's pretty tired, but she sounded really happy in her letter. She does fret a bit about the bombing, but there's nothing to be done about that. Knowing her she'll be looking for a nanny soon so that she can get back to work. She's not exactly the type to sit around, you know. How about Rolly?"

"Oh, she's full of news about the boys. They're just on the way back from a visit to Victoria to stay with Mum and Dad. They had a great time. Tam will be going to kindergarten this fall, in a small school just a couple of blocks from the house. Ian's still at home, so Rolly has arranged for a friend to look after him while she's working at the canteen. She says that the canteen is really busy now. The pilot training programs are pumping out pilots, and she says that they all seem to be short of cash but still need a beer or two. They deserve it too, the way they're being shot down over England! I really do miss the family – it's been over three years now."

"Agreed, Rocke. Mind you I had a bit better time than you did in England!"

Saturday, July 24, 1943

They complete 10 cases between midnight and noon. Everyone is very tired, and nerves are raw. Their lives are now filled with a constant stream of blood and agony, of young men – boys really – torn apart and hoping that the team will put them back together again. They hold lives in their hands, and those hands are tired. Many of the wounds they are dealing with are, in a sense, routine – dislocated knees and broken arms and crushed hands. But some are truly spectacular and call on all of their imagination and skill – the abdominals, of course, but also grotesque head wounds and mangled genitals. None of them are immune to this terrible display, not even the surgeons who have by far the most experience and training to draw on. Some of the men are having nightmares: rows and rows of bloody meat marching past their tired eyes, with no hope of it ever stopping. They talk a lot amongst themselves, trying to maintain at least a minimal sense of life and the living. This is their trial by fire; they must get through it.

Andre Boucher, one of the team's three nursing orderlies, is particularly worried. He sits on the steps of the hospital, smoking a cigarette and gazing absently at the passing military traffic. He knows he should get straight back to camp for some food and then sleep, but he just needs to think things through a bit. Andre was just starting to think seriously about what he would do for the rest of his life when the war broke out and, for a while at least, made up his mind for him. He wasn't sure how he ended up in the medical corps, but he sort of liked the idea and applied himself hard to the training. It included advanced first aid and a lot of instruction in patient care, and by the time they all sailed for Sicily he felt confident that he was ready for the job of orderly – helping wounded men in an all-male and very violent world.

Now he isn't so sure. In fact he's not really sure about anything. Now that they are actually at war, and the patients are coming in thick and fast and terribly wounded, he is finding that the gap between theoretical knowledge gained through training and the realities in the field is huge and, well, unexpected and damn worrying. It's just that nothing ever seems to work like they said in the textbooks or the classrooms, or even in the training exercises back in the English countryside. The basics are there of course – types of bandages and how to turn a patient and so on. But it's the unexpected that always seems to happen that shows him how shallow his training really is.

Take a case from last night for example – the one he can't get out of his mind. They had a soldier with severe chest wounds. He'd been ripped up by an exploding grenade and had huge gashes across his chest and very likely all sorts of metal pieces and dirt in the wounds. Andre had worked with an orderly from the Field Dressing Station to get the man ready for surgery. They had cut away what remained of his uniform and cleaned the areas around the wounds as best they could. They had laid a sheet over him and moved him to the holding area at the edge of the tent ward, ready for the OR which should be ready for him in about 15 minutes. Andre was sitting with the sedated patient, and after a couple of minutes the poor guy had lifted his head and vomited blood – spewed it all over the sheet. Then he lay back, breathing uncertainly. Andre felt panic seizing him like a great, cold hand. There were no doctors in sight, and the other orderlies were too busy to help him – this was his case to deal with!

So what should I do? Is this a good thing, perhaps clearing an obstruction in his throat? Or is it the sign of a serious internal rupture of some sort? What if the man is choking on his vomit? How the hell do I work on a choking man whose chest is a mass of wounds? What if he stops breathing? Should I clean out the man's mouth? What if he does it again? Should I yell for a doctor? I can't – they're all so damn busy and this is my job. In the end he cleaned the man as best he could and just prayed out loud for him not to die. When the endless15 minutes were up and he got the word to move the man into the OR he was so grateful he wept.

There have been lots of cases like that already, cases where he has to use his judgement and deal with a situation that is really way beyond his trained level of competence. Now he understands why those cute nurses he used to date back in Quebec City had to work so long and train so hard before they graduated. But the nurses aren't here, and the place is full of guys like him, with enough training to do a lot of things, but not enough to judge complex options and make the tough decisions.

But fortunately, Andre is a practical man, with a tough core that he is now starting to know about and appreciate. He closes his eyes and the cigarette tastes good. He knows that he is as good as any of the other orderlies, and all he can do is his best. He flicks the cigarette butt onto the street and heads back to camp.

Before returning to camp Rocke, Jack and orderly Jimmy Price visit the post-operative ward to check on the progress of their patients. They are terribly uncomfortable with the hard cots and heat and flies, but there is not a murmur of complaint, and most of those who are awake give the team a thumbs up or a weak "hi doc". The doctors have brief conversations with those who can speak. The star of the ward is a Corporal from Edmonton who has suffered a broken hip and leg diving into a ditch to escape rifle fire, and having a large boulder disturbed by a nearby mortar blast roll in on top of him. He is heavily bandaged and lightly sedated most of the time, which sets him drifting and dreaming, and when he drifts he sings. He makes people smile every morning when he sings his favourite children's song:

Good morning merry sunshine.
How did you wake so soon?
You scared away the little stars
And shined away the moon.

His other songs, sung periodically throughout the day, include such classics as "The North Atlantic Squadron," and are equally well received.

An orderly tells the surgeons that the young soldier with the neck wound is in another room, still alive and sleeping. Rocke feels a tingling sensation of concern. Perhaps he wasn't as badly wounded as we thought? Perhaps we should have operated? No, he is sure they were right; the paralysis was a sure sign that there was no hope. He is too tired to think any more about it.

As they are leaving the building they meet two military police shepherding a miserable looking Italian youth. One of the MPs, noticing Rocke's Major's insignia, says "Excuse me Sir, are you Major Robertson?"

"Yes," replies a sleepy Rocke.

"Sir, this man was arrested three days ago carrying a map showing the position of some of our artillery batteries. We've been noticing that the Germans seem to know an awful lot about the movements and placements of our guns, meaning that someone's tipping them off. So this man was suspected, and yesterday a military court here in Valguarnera tried him and condemned him to death as a spy. Trouble is, when they gave him a quick once-over before putting him in jail they found some sort of painful swelling in his crotch that they said might be something called a 'strangulated hernia'. The Colonel ordered that he be examined immediately. I take it that if he has a bad medical condition they have to deal with it first. Seems crazy to me if they're going to shoot him anyway, but there you are. The ADMS gave us your name to examine him."

"Now?"

"I'm afraid so Major. I know you're just getting off a long night of it, but we need to get this thing done right away. Could you do it in here?"

They take the man to a small examination room and Rocke looks him over while the MPs hover outside the door. The prisoner is terrified and submits meekly to the examination. There is a swelling there, but it is clearly not a strangulated hernia. Rocke opens the door and nudges the prisoner back into the waiting hands of the MPs.

"I'm not sure what it is, Corporal, but it's not a strangulated hernia."

"Right, Sir. Thank you. Now, could you just make a brief written report on your finding, please? The Colonel will want to see it at once. Here is the form and a pen."

Rocke returns to the room, sits at the desk, and writes the craziest report he has ever written or would write:

"With respect to Prisoner Maroni, I have examined the swelling in his lower abdomen. This is not a strangulated hernia. In my opinion, this man is fit to be shot."

Sunday, July 25, 1943

There is only one case during the night, and the team gets a good sleep. Starting at 0830hrs five more cases arrive, and they are busy operating until noon. By 1100hrs Rocke is feeling rotten and asks Jack to take over the last case and any more surgery that comes up, and to do the ward rounds at the Field Dressing Station after the surgery is finished. Rocke has diarrhoea and feels testy and hot. He is used to feeling hot here in Sicily, but this feels much worse.

As he leaves the hospital for the comfort of his tent he passes Frank Mills, who tells him that No.2 Field Dressing Station, No.1 Field Transfusion Unit and his No.1 FSU are moving north immediately to set up an Advanced Surgical Centre next to No.5 Field Ambulance's Advanced Dressing Station at Leonforte. Rocke wishes them well, and then hurries on to the latrine in the orchard, and then to his cot.

At 1430hrs Jack looks in on him and reports that most of their post-op patients are doing fine. "I also was told that our young Edmonton lad died around 1000hrs this morning. You know, Rocke, that really has me worried. He stayed alive for a very long time for a guy with a severed internal carotid artery. I'm wondering now if that was the case. I told the orderlies that we would be doing an autopsy tonight, and they said that they would have it set up for us. I hope you agree. I would really like to know what happened there."

"Yes, I agree. It's damn troubling, that case. I was so sure that we made the right diagnosis, but now it looks like we may not have. My God, what a mistake...if it was one! I hope I can be there with you for the autopsy. If not please just go ahead, and let me know."

Jack is now in charge of the unit. With Frank Mills' team having moved out, the 2CFSU is responsible for all operating in Valguarnera. There are not likely to be many new cases as No.1 Field Surgical Unit is now closer to the action and will bear the brunt of the influx of wounded, but there is still a lot of post-op work to do. Jack orders the team to get to bed in good time so as to be as ready as possible.

Monday, July 26, 1943

It is 0900hrs. There are no new cases, so Jack and Ptes Pyke and Boucher bring the corpse of the young Edmonton soldier into the OR to perform the autopsy. Jack makes the first incision into the neck and examines the carotid arteries. There are no lesions to be seen. Further examination does, however, indicate some brain damage, probably meaning that the internal carotid artery had at some stage gone into spasm for a sufficient length of time to damage the brain irreparably. That had caused the paralysis.

With no cases requiring operation the team goes to the wards to help with the patients there in any way that they can. Jack goes back to the camp and checks on Rocke. He finds him in bad trouble, his face flushed, sweating profusely and wracked with cramps. "Rocke, it looks like we'd better do something about you," says Jack. He fetches a thermometer and finds to his alarm that Rocke's temperature has soared to 104 degrees.

"I'm going to send you back to the Casualty Clearing Station. They have some cooler space back there and will get you better in no time."

"OK Jack. But listen…how did the autopsy go? What did you find?"

Jack hesitates. This is a bad time to deliver bad news, but then…there never is a good time. He sits down beside the cot and describes their findings. "I'm afraid we messed up. The carotid artery had not been severed. It had spasmed, and that caused some brain damage that in turn caused the paralysis. If we'd just opened the neck up right when we did the tracheotomy we'd have seen that the artery was not ruptured, but was in spasm. We could have applied some heat or injected some Novocain, or even done a periarterial sympathectomy. That might have prevented or at least limited the brain damage and perhaps we could have saved him! It all happened pretty quickly, but we might have done it. I wish we'd tried."

Rocke groans. "Dammit, dammit, dammit! Why the hell didn't we think of that? Now that you think of it, with a neck wound like that we should have been into there right away. Well, I do know what we did. We were in such a fuss to get him breathing properly first that we waited too long to check the wound itself. Then we saw the paralysis and figured we knew what had happened, and just let him go. I guess by then the brain damage had been done, but…"

"It's scary isn't it?" says Jack. "With these rushes of serious cases we have to make very quick decisions about who we treat first and what we do, and also who we have to leave out because they have less chance of making it. We're playing God, is what we're doing. And everyone accepts our decisions because we're the best trained to make them. But I wonder if they know how much judgement goes into those decisions? There's lots of science involved, but in the end we just have to use our heads and make a choice. In this case we were right to deal with him first because of his breathing problem, but then we didn't really think through what to do. But then we didn't have much time…we needed an instant decision and we made it and we were wrong. Don't beat yourself up about it, Rocke. Let's just learn from it and move on. This sort of thing is going to come up again. We'll be better prepared next time."

Rocke is sitting on the edge of his cot, his hands covering his face to hide his anguish. "Thanks Jack. I know you're right. But man, I still hate to lose that soldier. I'd rather have him alive than have our lesson. And… well…what is the lesson? Aside from using our damn heads?"

Jack thinks for a minute. "I guess what we've learned is never to be diverted from wounds by secondary symptoms, no matter how visible or dramatic they are. In this case we got carried away with the breathing problem and forgot to deal with the wound itself before it was too late."

Rocke climbs wearily from his cot and heads to the latrine. Jack orders McKenzie to find an ambulance to take Rocke back to the Casualty Clearing Station. The ambulance arrives. Rocke climbs in and lies down heavily on the stretcher. McKenzie hands him his shaving kit and change of clothes in a bag. As they are about to pull away Jack, leaning into the ambulance, says, "Rocke, we can't be right every time. Forget about it and get some rest. We need you back here."

"Thanks, you're right. But by God, it hurts to make a mistake like that."

As the ambulance pulls out of the orchard and heads down the road towards Caltagirone, Rocke settles onto his stretcher and feels fiery hot, light headed and thoroughly silly. *Here I am, the big-shot surgeon, deserting my unit because I have the shits! And I've just made a stupid blunder that cost a man his life! And there's so much work to do. And I need to give the orderlies some more training. And perhaps we should go back to that hospital and get some more supplies. And how is Tam doing in kindergarten? And is Rolly really OK? And does she really miss me? And why is Sicilian wine so weird? And…*he leans out of the stretcher, vomits into a can offered by the attendant, and falls back into a delirious sleep. Two hours later he is in a cool bed in the

Casualty Clearing Station ward at Caltagirone, a drip in his arm, a compress on his forehead, and a long and delicious sleep ahead of him.

Tuesday, July 27, 1943

There are still no new cases coming in, even though there is news of tremendous action up along the road to Adrano as well as farther south in the attack on Catenanuova. No.1 Field Dressing Station is busy in the Valguarnera schoolhouse with a large inventory of sick and post-operative patients, but the 2CFSU team is restless. The flow of seriously wounded from the Adrano road is obviously being handled by the Advanced Surgical Centre up at Leonforte, and the flow from the action around Catenanuova hasn't started yet. They want to help.

They spend the day cleaning up their equipment and restocking supplies. At 1540hrs Major F.C. Pace, Acting Commander of No.1 Field Dressing Station while Doug Sparling is on sick leave, finds Jack at the camp and tells him that orders have come for 2CFSU to move over to the Dittaino Valley and set up with No.9 Field Ambulance. The action in the move on Catenanuova is really heating up and the Field Ambulance there is not equipped to handle the seriously wounded. They do however have enough bed space to support an FSU for a short time. The 2CFSU team is to move out at 1000hrs tomorrow. This seems to be a late hour to move, but the story is that the ADMS wants to have enough time in the morning to ensure that the army's drive towards Catenanuova is still progressing before the 2CFSU moves forward.

"I thought we'd be coming with you, Jack," says Major Pace, "but we have a heck of a load of patients here."

Jack orders his team to clean things up, load the vehicles and be ready to move in the morning, and they go happily about their work. Part of this work is a brief visit to the deserted hospital in the mining town where they pick up some more instruments, still in beautiful protective cases. They also take a magnificent hospital tent, double walled and roomy, and other much needed equipment. By nightfall the vans are packed and ready to roll. With no new cases to deal with, they get to bed early.

30. RADDUSA-AGIRA STATION

A brief stop for the 2CFSU. Rocke returns to action.

Wednesday, July 28, 1943

The cook in the No.1 Field Dressing Station kitchen in Valguarnera goes all out with pancakes for the 2CFSU team at their 0800hrs breakfast. They thank him and his crew. Jack does a final ward round at the Field Dressing Station with Major Pace, they shake hands and Jack returns to the camp.

The unit hits the road at 1000hrs sharp. The surgical van is, finally, almost full with the equipment and supplies so carefully planned in their training days back in England. The big lorry is also well loaded with supplies and medicines, as well as rations and extra clothing and materials, and that beautiful Italian tent that is too bulky to fit in the surgical van. The small utility vehicle contains six rested and eager team members ready to get back into the forefront of the action. Jack rides up front in the surgical van with driver Kraft, and batman McKenzie rides in the big lorry with driver Matt Curran. They have no military protection except the drivers' Tommy guns and the red crosses painted on the sides of the vehicles.

They head north for five miles on the road to Leonforte and Assoro, and then swing east on the road to Catenanuova. They cross the Mulinello River on a bridge built by Canadian engineers after the retreating enemy destroyed the original bridge, and then drive on tiny, winding country roads over the ridge that marks the southern edge of the Dittaino valley. After eight more miles they come to the Raddusa-Agira Station, a settlement of several demolished buildings on the banks of the Dittaino River, next to the bridge that crosses the river carrying the road from Raddusa in the south to Agira in the north. The station is less than 10 miles from Catenanuova.

The Advanced Dressing Station of No.9 Field Ambulance is set up in an open field on the south side of the road. There are large trees along the edge of the field where some of the sleeping tents rest, but this cover is very limited and the space too cramped for the ADS. They are working in tents in the field in the blazing morning sun. Some of the tents are open-sided, and there are also several of the Italian tents similar to the one that the 2CFSU took from the deserted hospital near Valguarnera. They are wonderful looking things, very large, and with huge red crosses on their sides.

The 2CFSU vehicles park next to the station and Jack finds and salutes Colonel Bowman. "Nice to see you again Jack," says Bowman, sweating profusely into his uniform collar. He has bloodstains on his shirt, showing that he is a hands-on Commander of the station – a reason that he is so popular with his men. "And hey, where's Rocke?" Jack tells him that Rocke is back at the Casualty Clearing Station, hopefully on the way to recovery.

"It's bloody hot here," says Bowman, "but there just isn't any other place to set up at the moment. We've had a fair stream of wounded, but not a lot of serious cases, fortunately. Our ambulances are having a grand old time bombing up and down this road, too. It's a helluva lot better than pitching cross-country! But I'll tell you, the stretcher-bearers are working their butts off, because a lot of their work is actually off-road. The regimental aid posts are scattered in the hills, so some of our guys are racking up some very long carries."

A familiar face appears by the Colonel's side. It's stretcher-bearer Ted Walls, their old friend from back on the beach near Maucini and then at Bompalazzo. "Hi Captain," he says. "How's it going?"

"You remember Pte. Walls, I'm sure," says Col. Bowman with a grin. "He seems to be everywhere these days. These stretcher-bearers are the damndest lot, I'll tell you. Walls here has just come back from up the road with a couple of fracture patients, and that was his third trip of the day, and right now he's decided that he's on water duty and is topping up all the tanks! Terrific stuff. Walls, show Captain Leishman's people where they can set up their operating tents will you? And also help them to find a space for sleeping."

"Jack," Bowman continues as Ted Walls moves away to follow the orders, chatting with the 2CFSU team as if they are family, "we have four cases for you to do, starting probably at around 1700hrs. They've come in this morning and they all need a bit of work before we put them on the table. So you've got lots of time to set up your OR. And while your lads are setting things up I wonder if you could look at a couple of other cases that have me a bit worried?"

"Of course, Sir," says Jack, and they head into one of the stifling tent wards.

The team work like a well-oiled machine, following precisely the system laid down on that rainy day back in England. Eric directs them with the élan of an orchestra conductor, sensing problems before they occur and heading them off, leading where he must and observing when he needn't lead. And most importantly, keeping the men cheerful and congratulating them when the job is well done.

They have more than enough time, and by 1700hrs the operating tent is set up and equipped, generator firing away and sterilizer steaming, and they are ready to take their first patient. Jack has borrowed a doctor from the FA to do the anaesthetics. The Italian tent is luxurious: very large, with a high ceiling and screened windows and entrance that have made the Fly Patrol doubly effective. The double sides ward off the sun and keep it reasonably cool. The surgical team is delighted. They operate on the four cases, breaking for dinner after the first two, and finish at 0200hrs in the morning.

Thursday, July 29, 1943

In spite of the large crowd of wounded in the tents of No.9 Field Ambulance there is little surgical work to do. One case comes in at 1000hrs, an artillery gunner with a torn shoulder, and Jack operates on him at 1130hrs. Aside from that Jack and the orderlies are kept busy helping the Field Ambulance team tend to the wounded in the tent wards. The drivers, meanwhile, work over the vehicles, and also help with some badly needed repairs to two of the Field Ambulance lorries.

At 1300hrs Colonel Bowman receives radioed orders from the ADMS to open an Advanced Dressing Station in Agira as the start of a medical centre closer to the troops than Leonforte or their current location. Bowman is in his element as this order, while seemingly simple, causes enormous complications for him. He explains the situation to Jack.

"I still have two vehicles away helping that delivery of equipment from Leonforte to the hospital in Syracuse. That leaves just three here, plus the ambulances, and one is a permanent store of supplies. I also have, as you well know, over 50 patients in those tents. If we're starting to move up to Agira they'll almost certainly want us to complete the move within a day or so, so we've gotta bind these poor guys up as best we can and get them out of here, back to the Casualty Clearing Station or wherever. In fact we really have to start doing that now, and hope we aren't pushing them too hard.

"So what I've decided is to use two of the vans to ship the advance crew up to Agira, along with two ambulances. One of the vans can stay there, along with the ambulances, and the other should be back this evening. I'll send Lieutenant Askew in charge – he's a good doctor and loves to run something when he can - and I'm going to send three orderlies along. That'll have to do for the moment. One of the trucks will carry equipment and supplies, the other people and more supplies, and of course the stretcher-bearers will go with the ambulances. See any problems?"

"How about the four abdominal cases?" asks Jack. "Isn't it too early to move them?"

"I don't think so, Jack. They've all had several days of recovery time, and none of them were really bad. If we hold them until the last minute I think that they should be able to handle the trip back. But Jack, please take a careful look at them and give me your opinion."

The station becomes a beehive of activity, with Field Ambulance staff and 2CFSU members sorting out supplies and equipment and loading vehicles. A gentler crew is working with the wounded, binding them up as best they can for the accelerated movement back to the Casualty Clearing Station. The convoy to Agira heads out of the field at 1515hrs, passing a jeep coming into the field. The jeep skids to a stop in front of the operating tent and Rocke climbs out.

"Welcome back, Major," calls Eric, who is just passing by with his arms full of boxes of bandages. "How are you feeling?"

"A lot better thanks, Eric," replies Rocke as he hauls his bag out of the jeep. He tells the driver to check with Colonel Bowman over at the Field Ambulance tent before he goes back to the Casualty Clearing Station in case there is something that needs transporting back. "Where's Captain Leishman?"

"He's right inside here, Sir". As Branch speaks, Jack emerges from the tent, sees Rocke, walks over to him and claps him on the back. "Good to see you back, Rocke. How are you?"

"Well Jack, I've just had three really tough days in bed in a cool room with lots to eat and lots of sleep, but I'm still OK. It's a tough war!"

They laugh, and Jack leads Rocke away to check in with Colonel Bowman and to visit the wounded. Within 10 minutes of arriving back Rocke is working with Andre Boucher resetting a broken arm and applying a cast.

Over dinner that evening they discuss the progress of the war. The news of the victories at Assoro and Leonforte, and of the great successes of the Americans up north and the Brits to the east, is discussed and rehashed, drawing on snippets of news and gossip interspersed with an occasional authoritative comment by Colonel Bowman, who has his radio and access to more senior levels of intelligence. He reports that his convoy covered the ten miles to Agira without incident and are set up there in a schoolhouse on the southern edge of the town. They are busy already with a stream of wounded coming in from the action towards Regalbuto, and also with a bunch of locals who evidently are gathered in a cathedral.

They are all heading to bed when there is an eruption of artillery fire to the east. The horrifying rumble of the guns is accompanied by flashes of explosion that seem to light up the whole eastern sky. That is where Catenanuova is, and they know that they are watching the opening of the offensive by the Canadian 3rd Brigade to capture that town.

31. END GAME IN SICILY

The final phase of the Sicilian campaign.

The British and Canadian forces were now starting to merge in combined efforts as the advance swung north towards Messina, which would be the escape hatch to the mainland of Italy for the German forces. As the advance continued they would also be in increasing contact with the American forces sweeping east across the northern part of the island.

In the Dittaino Valley, the 3rd Canadian Brigade launched its attack on Catenanuova on the night of July 29, and captured it the following day. It then pushed past Catenanuova, moving on the left flank of the 78th British Division and under British command to clear the hills between Regalbuto and Centuripe. Regalbuto, nine miles east of Agira, and the lofty hill town of Centuripe southwest of Regalbuto, were the main outposts in front of the key crossroads town of Adrano. The task of clearing enemy-held heights towering more than 1000 feet above the river flats involved fighting on foot over rough, trackless terrain, with mules carrying wireless sets and supporting weapons and ammunition.

By August 3 the Canadians had cleared the hills of enemy, and on the same day the Centuripe stronghold fell to a full-scale assault by a brigade of the 78th British Division.

Further north the 48th Highlanders, the Royal Canadian Regiment and the Hastings and Prince Edward Regiment took part with the 231st British Brigade in the battle for Regalbuto and the surrounding hills. The battle raged from July 30 to August 3. Pounded by major artillery and air bombings, Regalbuto lay in ruins and rubble blocked the streets. This time there were no cheering crowds to greet the Allies as they entered the town.

With Regalbuto and Centuripe cleared, the 78th British Division took over the main road to Adrano, and the combined forces of the Canadian 1st Division swung north across the Salso River. On the morning of August 5 General Simonds sent forward a tank-infantry force with mobile artillery which, paralleling a successful attack on the right by the 78th Division, in a brilliantly-executed operation cleared the north bank of the Salso to its junction with the Simento River.

On August 6, as the Canadian forces were moving towards Adrano, orders were received that Adrano was to be left to the British. The British and the Americans, between them, then completed the liberation of Sicily with some further tough fighting northwards and westward to Messina. The Canadian 1st Division was drawn into reserve, its work over for the time being.

In order to relieve some of the pressure on the medical installations at Leonforte, the ADMS ordered No.9 Field Ambulance to open the Advanced Dressing Station at Agira on July 29. As they set up in Agira they were asked to attend to a dozen civilian casualties being held in a cathedral near the school. They called for assistance, and this accelerated the plan of the ADMS to establish his new Canadian Medical Centre at Agira. On July 30 the 2CFSU moved up to Agira, and on July 31 the No.9 Field Ambulance closed its Advanced Dressing Station at Raddusa – Agira Station and moved its remaining staff to Agira. All other Canadian medical units moved to the Centre in Agira over the next few days except No.5 Field Ambulance and No. 2 Field Dressing Station, which remained at Leonforte to handle the large inventory of patients.

From July 31 to August 6 the Canadians lost 106 killed and 345 wounded. The sick rate during the same period showed a decided tendency to drop, but this improvement was more apparent than real. By August 6 gastro-intestinal disturbances had been supplanted by fevers as the chief cause of sickness, marking the onset of what was shortly to become a serious epidemic of malaria.

During this final phase of the Canadian campaign in Sicily, most Canadian casualties and many from the 231st British Infantry Brigade were cleared from the regimental aid posts in the first instance by No.9 Field Ambulance at Agira. Seriously wounded were sent across immediately to the Advanced Surgical Centre, with its two FSUs and FTU. Others were further evacuated to No.5 British Casualty Clearing Station at Ramacca until August 5, then to a British Field Ambulance at Catenanuova. So far as possible Canadian sick were retained at Agira, the overflow being sent back to No.5 Field Ambulance at Leonforte. At both Field Ambulances accommodation for the sick was provided in tents.

No. 9 Field Ambulance at Agira took the brunt of the incredibly difficult task of bringing wounded out from the mountain country surrounding the roads to Adrano. In this almost trackless and extremely rugged terrain wheeled transport, even the ubiquitous jeep, was useless. Reliance had to be placed on the old-fashioned method of hand carrying by stretcher, since neither cacolets (a chair suspended from a pack saddle to carry wounded) nor litters were available. Particularly in the case of the Loyal Edmonton Regiment, which lost 26 killed and 60 wounded between August 2 and 6, this was no light assignment: on August 3 the hand carry involved was over 3 miles.

The withdrawal of the 1st Canadian Infantry Division from the line on August 6 brought little respite for medical units, nor did its subsequent move to a concentration area south of the Catania plain, near the east coast. The fighting was over for the moment, but it had left a cruel legacy of wounded. Hardly had these been evacuated when the problem of malaria became acute. The period following the cessation of actual fighting proved to be the most difficult of the whole Sicilian campaign for the RCAMC.

32. AGIRA

A major Canadian Medical Centre.
The 2CFSU helps an important group of local citizens.

Friday, July 30, 1943

The 2CFSU team work in the Field Ambulance ward tents in the morning, filling in for the FA staff now up in Agira, preparing as many patients as possible for the ride back to the Casualty Clearing Station. Three new serious cases arrive late in the morning and they start operating at 1130hrs. At 1500hrs they have completed the three operations, and as Rocke leaves the operating tent a stretcher-bearer calls him over to see Colonel Bowman.

"Rocke, you have orders to leave right away and get up to Agira. They have a ton of work coming in and they can't just keep sending the serious cases on to Leonforte. And they have that bunch of civilians who need looking after. Doug Sparling is back from sick leave now, and his Field Dressing Station will be moving over there from Valguarnera tomorrow, and we'll probably all be up there by the end of tomorrow once we clear off the rest of our patients here. Do you think your three cases today will be able to travel?"

"I think so, Sir. They're all extremity wounds, and we're getting them well covered with casts. As long as you fellows are nice and gentle."

"Oh, of course! Good. OK, carry on. See you tomorrow."

Rocke issues his orders, and in just over an hour the 2CFSU is on its way over the bumpy 10-mile road to Agira. The countryside is beautiful, with lovely rolling hills and deep valleys. Mount Etna rises in the distance, a slight wisp of steam rising from its summit. The fields are mostly parched brown, but there are sprays of colourful cactus and palm trees to relieve the dullness.

As they approach Agira they see a typical hilltop town, this time resting on an almost perfect cone-shaped hill. The winding road turns upwards, and after some impossibly sharp curves they drive through the outskirts of the town. A military police officer directs them to the Canadian Medical Centre, and at 1730hrs they wheel into the playground of a school that was until recently a propaganda machine for the Fascist Mussolini government. A Field Ambulance van and one of the ambulances are parked outside, watched by their armed drivers. Rocke goes in the main door and is greeted by Lieutenant Askew.

"Hello Major, welcome to Agira," says the cheery doctor. "We have a few things for you to do here, Sir, but first I think you had better take your team up to the cathedral near the top of the hill. You can't miss it; it's the only building that's still intact in the centre of the town. It's called St. Antonio di Padova. Here's a rough map. There's 12 civilian casualties in need of treatment there.

"It seems that after the battle here the locals brought wounded civvies to the cathedral. They had no other place to take them as the hospital had been demolished. We've been told that they are high priority, so I took an orderly with me and a translator from the Service Corps over there after we arrived yesterday and we looked them over. It was quite a scene: 12 wounded people lying on blankets on the floor, each surrounded by family members moaning and groaning louder than the casualties! Some of them were covered with blood. Others had been washed, but nobody seemed to want to get too close to those wounds.

"We went through them one by one, and I found that most of them could be treated quite easily, even though a few were in considerable pain. Two will definitely need surgery: an older man with a bad wound in the buttock and a woman with quite extraordinary injuries to her feet. We've cleaned them up and given them all a shot of morphine. My orderly Eddie Zimmer and the translator are there now continuing the work, which includes directing all those family members to keep out of the damn way! Anyway there's no problem with feeding them; the families have brought some food and drink, and they offer it to us too whenever we look at them! I think they're glad we're here."

"OK Lieutenant," says Rocke, "we'll head straight over. I assume we come back here to sleep?"

"Yes Sir. We have masses of room here. I've set aside a bunch of rooms over there for your sleeping quarters, and down the hall there's an ideal operating room – lots of light and air. It's hot and has a few flies, but it should do fine for you, and it's very convenient to the wards."

They drive out of the schoolyard and follow the directions on the map, guided also by the cathedral spire rising above all of the other buildings. A precipitous climb through narrow streets brings them to the cathedral that is situated on a triangular square, with a road cutting across it as the long side of the triangle. They park beside the ancient and very beautiful building and a small group of locals, expecting their arrival, directs them with hand gestures to a side entrance that is used to access the assembly rooms.

Rocke, Jack and Eric enter the first assembly room, right inside the door, and there is the scene exactly as described by Lieutenant Askew. It is a sea of humanity, most of them seated or standing or kneeling around wounded people lying on blankets. The delicious aroma of garlic almost overrides the stench of too many people in the room, and the acrid hint of blood. Some people are eating from meagre stores of food, and there are open bottles of wine.

Eddie Zimmer sees them from across the room and comes over immediately. He is accompanied by the translator, a huge Italian Canadian from Toronto who answers, wonderfully, to the name Luigi. They both have blood on their tunics; Luigi feels right at home here and, in spite of having no medical training, likes to help out.

"I'm glad you're here, Major," says Zimmer." We have most of these people pretty well under control, but our two serious cases over there under the window need your help badly. Lieutenant Askew says that they're the only ones needing surgery. I think there may be a couple of others, but you can see for yourself."

"OK Eddie. We'll start right away. Where should we set up our OR?"

"Over in that room, Sir. The one with the door closed. It's not too bad, and I've kept everyone out of it."

"Well done Eddie. Eric, would you please get the OR set up and send Boucher and Price in here to join us? We're going to have a quick look at these people with Eddie, and then we can get started. Luigi, when you have a moment I want you to go around to each of these groups and ask them, politely of course, if they would limit themselves to two relatives per patient. Tell them that there are simply too many people in here and that it will hurt the patients with all this noise and people breathing on them. Oh, and also, tell them that the two who stay should do everything they can to keep the flies away from the wounds."

They go to inspect the serious cases first. One is an elderly man who had stayed in his house too long rather than fleeing like most other civilians did when the fighting broke out in the town. When he finally decided to get out he was running up an alleyway when a stray bullet ricocheted off the pavement and hit him in the right buttock. The ricochet had made the bullet spin, so that it tore into the buttock creating a terrible, wide gash. In trying to clean the wound the orderlies had found chips of bone but no exit wound, so it seems that the bullet hit the hip bone and did some damage, and is now resting somewhere inside the wound. The man is heavily sedated but still groaning softly.

The other is a youngish and attractive woman, lying on her back with her legs slightly elevated on a pillow and covered with a towel. Her feet under the towel are at an impossible angle, almost horizontal. Zimmer explains that she had been sitting in her kitchen when a stray shell hit the roof of her house. She had looked up when she heard the kitchen ceiling cracking, but then moved too slowly to avoid the falling tiles. A heavy chunk smashed into her lower legs, breaking her ankles and crushing her feet.

"You're right about these two, Eddie. We'll take the man first because I'm worried about his bleeding. Then the woman immediately after. Andre, you can start prepping them now. Luigi, tell their family people that we are going to operate on them, and it would be best for all of them to leave now. If they wish to leave someone outside we will keep them informed of progress, and when they can visit. But it won't be before tomorrow morning at the earliest. Eddie, let's take a look at the others."

Rocke is amazed at the array of things that can happen to civilians in time of war. He had seen lots back in England, treating victims of the bombing, but this scene in the cathedral adds imaginatively to the variety of problems that war inflicts on its innocent victims. There is only one other bullet wound: a woman who was rushing out of her back door at the sound of gunfire when a stray bullet took half her ear off and ploughed an ugly wound in her cheek. There are several broken bones from falls while escaping to shelter, and one poor man who broke his nose and cheek when he ran into a dark lane and bounced off a Canadian jeep ambulance coming the other way. Falling debris has caused some ugly but not very serious cuts and abrasions, and then there is Luigi's favourite.

"This guy has a farm, Major, just outside the town. He keeps cows, and he put them into his barn when he heard the fighting coming through. Then he saw some Germans running past, so he hid in the barn himself. Then a shell went off nearby and the cows panicked and tried to stampede, and that ain't a good idea inside a barn! They ran right over him! He's lucky, though; they missed all of his important parts, but he's pretty badly scratched and bruised!"

Luigi bends down and says a few words in Italian to the farmer, who looks sheepishly at Rocke and mutters something back to Luigi. "He says that he's not a good farmer, Sir, and is ashamed. But he also says thank you for coming to help him and the others." Rocke smiles and shakes the man's hand that is offered in a formal gesture of thanks.

The OR is well set up. It is a clean room, though still quite hot, and with the inevitable flies buzzing around. The lights work and there is a basin with running water in the corner. They start operating at 2100hrs after a snack organized by Luigi with food happily contributed by the families. They finish the two operations just after midnight and head back to the school to sleep.

Saturday, July 31, 1943

Eric and the OR assistants and two of the drivers set up the operating room in the schoolhouse while Rocke, Jack and the orderlies visit the cathedral ward to check on the civilian casualties. The two patients from last night are resting quite well, although the man continues to groan. He is forced to lie uncomfortably on his side on the hard blanket, and that probably hurts as much as the wound. All of the other patients are improving nicely. The woman with the head lacerations is clearly unhappy about what the wounds will do to her looks, and therefore her prospects. Rocke tells Luigi to reassure her that the RCAMC has a unit that does reconstructive surgery, and he will ensure that she sees them. She smiles for the first time in days.

Luigi has clearly been persuasive with the families as each patient has just two relatives in attendance, although there is a small crowd of them camped outside the doors of the cathedral.

They finish their rounds and return at noon to the schoolhouse to find that Wally Scott and his Field Transfusion Unit have arrived from Leonforte, as has Doug Sparling with his No.1 Field Dressing Station team. They are setting up quickly, so the Canadian Medical Centre at Agira is now substantial and will be even more so when Colonel Bowman arrives this afternoon with the remainder of this Field Ambulance team, and Frank Mills arrives tomorrow with his FSU.

There is a heavy flow of casualties coming in, and Rocke and his team are preparing to start surgery at 1230hrs when two very interesting visitors walk into the centre. They are Brigadier A.J. Wiles, Orthopaedic Consultant and Colonel R.G. Donald, Surgical Consultant to the British 8th Army. These two immensely experienced doctors suit up with Rocke and his team and share the burden of operating, which goes on until 2330 hrs.

33. WONDER DRUG

An important visitor tells them about penicillin.

Rocke and Jack learn a lot from the two experts, and also provide them with a few useful thoughts based on their recent experiences. In the course of their conversations Brigadier Wiles tells them that he is running some tests with the new wonder drug penicillin, and will be reporting his results to army headquarters very soon. He feels that the drug could be of terrific benefit to the medical services as, for the first time, they will have a weapon to deal with infection once it has started. The trick is for the authorities and companies back home to produce enough of it as soon as possible so that it can really make a difference.

During a tea break between operations he gives the Canadians an overview of penicillin and how it is being developed.

The Battle Against Infection

Infection is the scourge of the wounded. It can quickly turn a manageable wound into a killer wound, so the battle against infection has always been a vital component of military medicine. Until the mid-1930s infection was fought through cleaning and protecting wounds in the hope that infection-causing bacteria could be kept at bay until the wound healed. This of course is not a simple matter in war conditions, complicated by the fact that infectious organisms can come from so many sources: weapons and flying objects (although bullets are often sterile), the patient's skin itself, clothing especially if it is driven into wounds, and from secondary sources such as the nose, throat and hands of attendants, or from soiled dressings, instruments, bed clothing, flies and other insects, or contaminated dust.

A complicating factor is that the variety of bacteria found in wounds tends to increase over time. Too frequent examination of wounds in surgical wards can itself increase the incidence of serious infectious organisms.

In the mid-1930s it was found that sulphonamides could retard the growth of bacteria. Sulpha drugs could be given by mouth or used as a powder applied directly to wounded tissue. Dramatic results were obtained before the war by the use of sulphonamides in the treatment of certain types of septicaemias (invasion of the bloodstream by virulent micro-organisms from a local seat of infection), lobar pneumonia, meningitis and some surgical infections, and this raised the hopes that the use of these drugs in wounds would greatly lessen the ravages of infection.

The practice that was developed was the introduction of sulphonamide powder into the wound as early as possible to prevent the propagation of the bacteria introduced at the time of wounding, with any bacteria surviving dealt with, after surgery, by post-operative administration of the drug orally or intravenously. A survey of the results of this practice as applied in civilian cases in the United States showed, unfortunately, that this local application of sulpha drugs directly to wounds did not cause any diminution in the incidence or the degree of wound infection. Its impact in the theatre of war in Europe was never thoroughly assessed by control studies, but the results were observed to be similarly disappointing. It was also observed, however, that oral and intravenous administration of sulphonamides did prevent or minimize septicaemia, the spread of infection, in many cases.

There was still a huge gap in the weaponry available to doctors in the battle against infection. Sulpha drugs had some impact, but it was a limited victory in a very large and complex war. What was needed was a drug that would deal with a much broader spectrum of bacteria, and could cure infection rather that just preventing it.

This was penicillin.

Sir Alexander Fleming discovered penicillin in 1929 at St. Mary's

Hospital, London, through the astute observation of a chance happening. Working with culture plates in the lab, Fleming noted that some of them showed areas of inhibition of culture growth. These areas were ones where airborne moulds had fallen on the plates. He surmised that the mould was producing a material that inhibited the growth of the bacteria. After further studies he suggested that penicillin, which he named after the generic name of the mould that produces it, might be an efficient antiseptic for application to, or injection into, areas infected with penicillin-sensitive microbes.

In the early 1930s Drs Raistrick, Clutterbuck and Lovell at the London School of Hygiene and Tropical Medicine contributed important information on yields of penicillin from selected media and also on chemical extraction with ether. Unfortunately their work seemed to indicate that penicillin was a most unstable chemical that was produced in very minute quantities by the mould, so that there appeared to be little hope of clinical application. There the subject rested for seven valuable years.

In a paper published in August 1940 there appeared the results of a group of Oxford workers under Prof. H.W. Florey and Dr. E. Chain. Their studies announced the preparation of penicillin as an impure, water-soluble brown powder, and showed that the material was effective in treating patients. The paper gave ideas concerning methodologies to be pursued for the production of penicillin in large quantities. Their work was of such obvious importance to the medical world that financial aid was provided by the Rockefeller Foundation, the Medical Research Council and the Nuffield Trust.

They proceeded with their work with the utmost vigour, driven by the knowledge of how important penicillin could be in the war. They did not solve the production problems —how to produce sufficient quantities of a substance that emerged in tiny quantities from complex extraction processes - but their studies did show that penicillin possessed an anti-bacterial activity and was effective in dealing with infections. Since it was clear that this work could not proceed quickly in England under war conditions, it was decided that help should be sought from the United States and Canada.

In July 1941 the Rockerfeller Foundation arranged for Prof. Florey and colleague Dr. Heatley to come to North America. Their visit aroused interest in penicillin in important places. Through the National Academy of Science in Washington they contacted Dr. Robert D. Coghill and the staff of the Northern Regional Research Laboratories of the US Dept. of Agriculture. These labs had extensive experience in moulds of various types that fitted into the problem of producing penicillin. By December their work in production techniques had progressed to such an extent that four commercial houses, Merck, Squibb, Pfizer and Lederle could be put to work to produce enough penicillin for clinical testing.

Research on penicillin was also proceeding in Canada at the Banting and Best Department of Medical Research of the University of Toronto. The project was led by Dr. Philip Greey, assisted by Dr. Alice Gray. The National Research Council made arrangements for Dr. Greey and Dr. Ronald Hare to visit the Northern Regional Research Laboratories in the USA to ensure that there would be full cooperation and no wasted time. Early in 1943 the first batches of therapeutic penicillin were made in Canada, and were used successfully in the treatment of staphylococcal septicaemia that had failed to respond to sulphonamide drugs. The supplies of penicillin above those required for investigational work were offered to the armed services, which distributed them to overseas units on a strictly prioritized basis.

The findings in Europe were that, as with sulpha drugs, early application of penicillin to wounds as a preventative measure had little impact, and in some cases even had the negative effect of building immunity to penicillin treatment later on. It was, however, a powerful weapon against infection once started, permitting healing in what would otherwise have been impossible cases. Thus the new wonder drug was to be used only in cases where serious infection had set in, for example the horrible gas gangrene.

The clinical testing program in the United States was run under the direction of the National Research Council of the United States. It soon revealed the remarkable curative powers of penicillin, and by May 1943 it was apparent that very large quantities would be needed to satisfy military and civilian requirements.

Responsibility for production was given to the War Production Board. In all, 21 plants were erected in the United States and Can-

ada, with full cooperation between the two countries, at a cost of about $20 million. In Canada, plants were constructed by Connaught Laboratories, University of Toronto, and Ayerst, McKenna and Harrison Co. Ltd., Montreal. Some time later Merck & Co. in Montreal constructed a penicillin plant as a private venture. All of these plants in both countries were built at lightening speed. The specialized equipment required in the plants flowed to plants in an almost miraculous manner, permitting production of penicillin to begin even before the builders were out of the plant. Within nine months production of penicillin had increased a hundredfold, quality was steadily increasing and cost per unit was falling.

By the end of the war thousands of servicemen and women owed their lives to this historic exercise in international cooperation and efficiency. Drs Fleming and Florey were knighted in 1944 for their work, and in 1945 they received the Nobel Prize in Medicine, along with Dr. Chain of Oxford.

Excerpted from "The Development of Penicillin," Philip Greey, published 1953, and "Wounds and Infection," H. Rocke Robertson, published 1953.

Source: Official History of the Canadian Medical Services 1939-1945, Volume 2, 1956. Department of National Defence. Reproduced with the permission of the Minister of Public Works and Government Services Canada, 2007.

"It sounds like a miracle, Sir," says Rocke as they are scrubbing up before the next operation. "How long will it be before we can get hold of some?"

"It's still in very limited supply. We know from our test program that it's going to be a tremendous help to us, but as I understand it the problem is production. It takes a lot of work to produce the stuff. I have heard, however, that the Americans and your chaps in Canada have already decided to go after it on a priority basis, and are rushing a number of plants into production. All I can say is 'keep your fingers crossed' that they get those plants going quickly. In the meantime you may get some experimental-size batches."

34. THE WOUNDED

One man's painful experience in the field.

Tuesday, August 3, 1943

Lieutenant Tony Miller is having a pretty good war. A strong, good-looking man from Belleville, Ontario, he graduated from Queens University in 1938 with a degree in philosophy and a letter in football. He was heading into post-graduate studies when the war broke out, and he immediately signed up with the Hastings and Prince Edward Regiment, commissioned as Lieutenant. After a training program that almost killed him but that he enjoyed immensely, he shipped out to England with his regiment in the fall of 1942. Their landing in Sicily with the 1st Canadian Brigade on July 10 went well, and they fought their way up through the country with distinction.

Tony has a personal philosophy that is, simply stated, to be happy and positive and things will do just fine. He brings this philosophy to his work, and it has rubbed off on the men he commands. In spite of the heat and the flies and the exhaustion and yes, the casualties, they are a positive bunch of tough guys, and that makes them very effective in the field. Tony never actually thinks about this being a 'good war' for him, but he is very aware of the success the Canadian army is having, and he is hugely proud of his unit. He knew they would be winners, and they are.

Tony's good war comes to an abrupt halt at 0937hrs today. Leading his men through a series of side roads on the outskirts of Regalbuto to clean up some German positions, he takes a bullet square in the right knee. The knee is shattered, he spins and falls and hits his head on the rocky ground. His helmet saves his life, but he has bitten his tongue and blood is trickling out of his mouth. The force of the concussion knocks him mercifully un-

186

conscious for several minutes.

When he comes to his mouth tastes of blood, his head is ringing from the concussion and his leg is in such agony that it is all he can do not to scream and scream. He dares not move; any move sends out a rocket of pain that makes him want to buck and kick, and that will make it hurt more. He rasps his dry tongue over his bloody lips as he turns his head slowly to see where he is.

There is a soldier kneeling next to him - Jimmy Cain, a wiry fighter from Gananoque known for his horrific joy in hand-to-hand combat. Cain is yelling to the unit's Sergeant who has taken cover nearby. Tony wants to tell the soldier to keep things rolling and he'll be just fine, but he can only croak through the blood. Sergeant Andrews comes into his view, looking down at him with anguished concern in his eyes. Tony knows he doesn't have to tell Andrews what to do, so he just closes his eyes and keeps very still. He hears the Sergeant ordering Pte. Cain to guard him until the stretchers arrive, and then moving off to take charge of the advance. *That's good.*

Tony looks up through his daze and sees that Cain actually looks scared. This makes him chuckle in spite of the pain. *Hey, here's a guy who will take on anyone anywhere in a fistfight, but who is terrified at the thought of even touching a wounded man! Perhaps he's just squeamish. Perhaps he's afraid of hurting me more. Who knows?* Pte. Cain is crouching behind the low wall right next to Tony – the wall he was just about to climb over when he was hit. *Good idea.* Tony prays for the stretchers to arrive.

At 0946hrs Tony hears more movement. He jerks out of his reverie and sees four regimental orderlies just coming up to him, carrying a stretcher. One is actually the regiment's chaplain, who presides over the souls of the troops and their dead but prefers to help out with the living. They are talking to Cain.

"Hi soldier," says the first bearer to arrive. What have we here?"

"This is Lieutenant Miller. He's taken a bullet in the knee, and he's also hit his head pretty hard on the ground."

"Have you moved him at all?"

"Nope."

"OK soldier, we'll take him from here."

"Thanks guys." Pte. Cain mutters, "Good luck Lieutenant," and moves gratefully away to rejoin his unit.

"Hello Lieutenant, we're going to get you out of here. How are you feeling?"

Tony wants to tell them how much his leg hurts and not to move it, but he still can't speak. He is in shock, his tongue is badly swollen and his mouth caked dry. He is desperate for water, and for some release from the pain. The bearers are working quickly and efficiently. He feels a needle jab and knows it's morphine. *Good idea.* They lift his head gently and give him a swig of water so delicious he almost swoons. Then, morphine notwithstanding, he does swoon as they put a bandage and splint on his leg and move him gently onto the stretcher. Even semi-conscious he is wondering if they will be able to lift him. He is thinking that he is pretty big, and these guys aren't.

No problem. They lift him smoothly and set out at a quick walk down the road. Tony is flowing gently along on the stretcher. The ride is incredibly smooth. *Perhaps it's the morphine?* After 200 metres they cross into a field heading west, and after 15 minutes of trudging through rugged terrain they come to a broken down shed surrounded by a grove of scrub trees. They place him on the floor inside the shed along with three other men on stretchers. Two of them are unconscious. The third is awake and groaning loudly, his left arm a mass of oozing blood covered by a crude bandage. Tony is fully awake now but feeling very little pain. He wonders if he should perhaps get up, but decides against it.

The stretcher-bearers leave immediately, jogging back towards the action. An orderly squats down beside Tony, checks his pulse and bandage, gives him some more water and tells him "hang in there Lieutenant. This is your friendly Regimental Aid Post, and you're in good hands. We expect a Field Ambulance will get here soon to take you back to Agira for treatment." Tony nods and dozes.

At 1115hrs three more wounded come in the door. They are walking, all of them with relatively light but painful wounds to the upper body. The orderly who escorts them in leaves immediately, back to the action.

At 1143hrs a team of five stretcher-bearers arrives at the RAP. Their leader is a small, tough and cheery man named Ted Walls. "Hi Billy," he says, addressing the RAP orderly. "What have you got for us today?" He then turns to the wounded. "Hi fellas. We're from the No.9 Field Ambulance and we're here to take you back to more comfortable surroundings. OK, Billy, let's sort 'em out."

They start moving the wounded out quickly. The four bearers carry one of the unconscious wounded in the stretcher, with the three walking wounded leading the way, guided by the fifth member of the FA team. After a 20-minute hike they come to a road where there is a crude FA Casualty Collecting Post. There is one ambulance there with two wounded already aboard, tended by an orderly, and a driver ready to roll. The walking wounded climb onto benches in the ambulance, and the team loads the stretcher case onto a cot at their feet. There is still room for one more, so the team turns and sprints back to the RAP. At 1255hrs they return to the ambulance carrying Tony Miller on their stretcher. They load him in and the ambulance roars off for Agira. The bearer team heads back to pick up the next patient for the next ambulance that will arrive at the collection point within half an hour.

The road is bumpy and Tony is glad he has the morphine in him. They wind through the streets of Agira, passing locals who silently watch the ambulance go by. They come to a stop in front of a schoolhouse that has lots of Canadian army vehicles parked outside. The stretcher-bearers take him gently off the ambulance and into the entrance of the building, which has a screen door that shuts with a loud bang right behind them. In spite of the morphine he will be very glad indeed when they can stop moving.

Tony finds himself on a table in a small room with stuff on shelves around the walls. Two men with masks on are moving around him and doing things. It hurts when they cut away his trousers. He croaks for water and they give him some. They are examining him all over, and talking to each other, not to him. They leave and he is alone. He dozes.

At 1530hrs Tony comes out of his reverie lying on a table under bright lights. A man with a white mask is gazing down at him, saying nice things about how good his knee is going to be. Another man is waving a magazine over his knee. *He must be crazy!* Somebody puts an ether mask over Tony's face and he drifts off to sleep.

At 1845hrs Tony comes slowly and painfully to the surface. His mouth is horribly dry, he has a crushing headache and his leg is throbbing mercilessly. He opens his eyes and there, looking very relieved, is Sergeant Andrews.

35. CLUBBING

Interesting conversations at the Agira officers' club and a local bar.

Tuesday, August 10, 1943

Almost the day after the Canadians occupied Agira, the stores and bars and restaurants started to reopen. Some were in bad shape, but with ingenuity and energy the owners put them back to work as quickly as possible, for three reasons: to make money, to serve the locals, and to serve the substantial number of Allied troops in the town. This is a great comfort to the soldiers and medicals and other allied personnel. The army field kitchens do heroic work, but most of the troops are tired and thirsty and ready for a brief stint of serious relaxation. And of course, the company of an attractive 'working girl' is always nice.

A Service Corps Sergeant has convinced one restaurant owner to use his place as an officers' club while the troops are there. The smiling owner appreciates the extra supplies this brings him, and although he has to keep his prices down and he always has a Canadian soldier watching over him, he still has a good business going, with no rowdy stuff to worry about. The place is rough but clean and pleasant, and the code is 'first names only' for all officers while in the mess, no matter what their rank. This was ordered by Colonel Bowman, and has been problematic only once, when a boyish Lieutenant hailed a visiting British Colonel as 'Freddy'.

It is 2115hrs in a reasonably cool evening, and Rocke strolls to the mess with Jack for some wine. It has been another 12-hour day and they are both very tired. Acquaintances in England would not recognize them now. They have both lost a lot of weight thanks to the heat, the work and the dysentery. They are tanned, but still manage to look gaunt in their uniform shorts and blouses. They definitely need a drink after the last case they did

190

before Frank Mills took over for his night shift. It was an artilleryman with a spray of shrapnel wounds across his back, taken when an enemy artillery shell exploded just behind his own gun. It had taken a long time to find and remove all of the fragments and clean up the dirt in the wounds, and there were early signs of some infection. They wish they had some penicillin to give him. They hope he lives.

They are sitting quietly, looking around and sipping their wine, when Tony Miller wobbles in on crutches. He sees Rocke and Jack and lunges into a chair at their table, his leg cast stretching out across the aisle between tables.

"Tony," says Jack, "I guess you've heard enough jokes about being kneecapped in Mafia country?"

"Yes Jack, I have. You know, I used to think that 'kneecapping' sounded sort of quaint, but now I know better. It's bloody awful! I've never felt anything like the pain. I'll tell you, I was happy when those stretcher-bearers came along!"

"They really are amazing people, aren't they?" says Jack. "That guy who brought you in ... Ted Walls? He came to check on you several times while you were still in bad shape. He seems to take all his customers personally. And you should hear what he says about the regimental orderlies! He says they must be crazy to do what they do. But then, Ted and his buddies are often up in the fighting themselves, so I guess they're all crazy."

"That's right. You know, I really didn't think they could lift me. They're all smaller than I am, and they had to carry me over some really rough country. But it was no problem. Those guys are tough as nails. And they don't seem to care at all about flying bullets. They just go wherever they have to and do their work, and trust in that little red cross to protect them. I wonder if many of them get hit?"

"Oh, I think they do," says Jack. "They're right in the thick of things. But changing the subject, did you see who pulled into the parking lot today? The Dental Unit! Here we've all come all this way to get out of having dental appointments, and they follow us here!"

"Yes, I saw them," says Tony. "I'm very glad that they're here too. I heard that they went around the wards and were surprised at how many of the patients had some sort of complaint about their teeth. This is aside from the wounded mouths and jaws too. It seems that a tooth ache in the battle-field is no more pleasant than one at home."

"That's for sure," says Rocke. "So now that we have them here, let's be sure they stay until we get everyone fixed up."

The conversation drifts on, and Rocke leaves at 2230 hrs. He has to get a good sleep, and he also has to bring his War Diary up to date. There just hasn't been time to write it for the past week or so, and every day that goes by adds to his guilty conscience. He sits down at the desk in his room, yawns, and gazes for a minute at his latest picture of Rolly and the boys. Then he starts to write.

War Diary

August 1, 1943 to August 10, 1943
Ten days inclusive were spent working in the Fascist school at Agira. During this period we brought our total number of cases up to 105, of whom 19 have died. The most outstanding group of cases were admitted on the night of 6-7 August 43. A number of men of the 2nd Cdn Fd Rgmt RCA were sprayed with burning petrol from a crashed plane. 27 in all were burned, about 10 seriously. We undertook the treatment of the most serious cases and four of them died shortly after admission. On the 1st of Aug 43, Capt. Leishman left with two lorries in search of equipment. He returned on 3 Aug 43 having been in Siracusa, Pachino and right back to the beach. (Back South). He had found a number of kit bags, and about 30 of our crates. He had not been able to find any of No.1 FSU's equipment. We now have all but about 15 boxes of our equipment, and fortunately we are not lacking any essential supplies.

That same evening Eric Branch and Johnny Pyke are enjoying a beer at a recently opened local bar. Eric is feeling very good about things. The Major has told him that he has put in a recommendation for him to be promoted to Corporal (forget the 'Lance'). It hasn't come through yet, but it's nice to know that it might happen, and soon. The place is hopping. There must be 30 Canadians there, all eyeing the seven prostitutes who are working the room. Two Sergeants from the Hastings and Prince Edward Regiment (known as the 'Hasty Pees') ask them if they can share their table.

"Sure thing gentlemen," says Eric. They sit down and call for their drinks. Eric introduces Johnny and himself and the newcomers respond. "I'm Jock Harding and this is Al Percival," says the larger of the two Sergeants, a huge man with a vast, craggy face. "We're with the Hasty Pees. You fellas are medicals?" "That's right," says Eric. "We're with the No.2 Field Surgical Unit, stationed here in Agira … for the moment at least. How about you; what brings you here?"

"We're moving through from Leonforte," says Al Percival, who is smaller than his friend but just as tough looking. In fact, Eric has never seen two tougher looking people in his life. It's not a question of size – Jock is big but Al isn't. No, it's the way they walk and talk and look. They are rawbone tough, with not an ounce of fat between them. They are both tanned dark and have a look of controlled violence in their eyes. They are friendly but they don't smile a lot. Eric is glad that he is on their side in the war.

"We've heard a lot about Leonforte and Assoro. What was it like?"

"It was bloody tough going," says Jock. "We came so close to losing it! But by God we did it, and I'm fucking proud of it. I'll tell you, it's not a great idea to climb cliffs in the dark with a bunch of Germans at the top. It was just lucky that they didn't think anyone could do it, so they weren't expecting us. Too bad for them. So here's to the Hasty Pees, lads."

They drink, Eric calls for another round, and the Sergeants ask him about the work of the 2CFSU. Eric and Johnny describe what they do, and the Sergeants are way more impressed than they expect them to be. "You guys are damn important to us, you know," says Al. "Christ, I'd hate to do what we have to do without you guys behind us to pick up the pieces. Me, hell, I can't even stand the sight of blood! And that's the way it is with a lot of us. We'll knock the shit out of anyone, but once one of our guys is hit we get scared as hell, and just hope you medicals are around to help out. Actually, we've had several of our own medical staff killed or wounded over the past few weeks. The enemy don't seem to notice red crosses when it isn't convenient. Bastards."

Soon it's the Sergeants' turn to buy a round, and so the evening goes until the Hasty Pees decide to take two working girls for a walk. Eric and Johnny return to their quarters feeling drunk and elated.

The hard work continues over the following days. They have had a few new cases over the past week, mainly from the British army, but the main concern is second-round surgery: resetting broken bones, delayed and secondary suturing and battling infection. Added to these surgery-related duties are medical assistance to the many cases of sickness, mainly malaria, and a busy clinic for the local residents. The Field Ambulance is going crazy with action.

Thursday, August 12, 1943

Rocke walks into the officers' mess for a brief lunch break and runs into Don Young, Second-in-Command of No.9 Field Ambulance. They have seen each other a couple of times in the hospital, but this is the first time they have had a chance to talk.

"How are you, Don?" asks Rocke, worried to see that his athletic friend looks thin and very tired. They all look that way these days, but it comes as a surprise in a man as strong as Young.

"OK, I guess," comes the reply. They order their meals and then Don explains. "We've had so damn many casualties pouring in – by ambulance and by foot. We've lots of civilians, of course, with all that artillery action, and we also have about 20 Germans to take care of.

"We were working right around the clock for awhile. You know what it's like, Rocke. You see someone, whether a soldier or a civilian or even a Kraut, and they're beat up and bleeding and in real pain, and you just have to do something about it! Like, right away! We had some little kids brought in; there were four of them had been caught in a cellar when the roof collapsed. Christ, they were a mass of broken bones and really big wounds. The nuns who brought them in were almost hysterical, and most of us were in tears working on them. You'll remember you took two of them in for surgery, and one of those died.

"But I'll tell you, the worst cases are what we call the 'home runs'. These are our soldiers who've been hit with everything. I'll give you an example. A week ago our stretcher-bearers brought in a Private from the Hasty Pees who had taken a big load of shrapnel in his shoulder. He was soaked in blood and sweat and in God-awful pain in spite of the morphine, but that was only the start of it! His feet were a bloody mess because his boots were worn down to nothing. He was almost totally dehydrated from all the marching and the heat and lack of water, and also because he had dysentery. So the final straw was that he'd shat himself and was a total stinking mess from the waist down. So here's a tough, hard working guy from Ontario who's in the worst shape you can possibly be in, and you know what?

He's embarrassed to be putting us to so much trouble fixing him up, and thanks us for the help! Christ!"

Don is leaning almost half way across the table to make his point, and has to sit back as their soup arrives. Rocke seizes the moment.

"Yes, we've had a few of those here too. I know you ambulance people really get the brunt of the urgent work, and you're all doing a great job. How about your stretcher-bearers? Are they surviving?"

"All but one. The poor guy took a bullet square in the face while he was carrying. He was dead by the time he hit the ground, and the guy on the stretcher took a beating when the stretcher fell over. The other three bearers had to carry the wounded man out themselves. Fortunately it wasn't too far to the ambulance. Then they went back and brought out their pal's body. But anyway, aside from that, all of our guys are OK."

"Don, I hear you had a visit back to Leonforte? What's it like over there? Did you get to Assoro?"

"The towns are both badly beaten up, but there's a bit of life there now. Yes, I have been to Assoro, and I went up to the top and looked down the cliff that the Hasty Pees climbed. I'll tell you I couldn't have done it. It's a real cliff, and a bloody high one at that. It was an amazing feat. They climbed it at night, you know, after marching for hours and with all their gear on! Oh and Rocke, I should tell you that we've had a bunch of American wounded to take care of over the past week. As you know they're moving east along the roads north of us, and we turned out to be the closest medical facility for some of their badly wounded people."

"That's interesting. I haven't seen any of them. What are they like to deal with?"

"Oh, just fine. Just like our guys, really. The only real difference is the equipment they have. It's great – the latest and best in everything. Hell, even their boots have our guys drooling."

The conversation moves to cases and incidents.

36. TIME FOR A REST

The Canadians move to a concentration area to rest and prepare for Italy.

August 13 – September 2, 1943

Until August 12 there was no change in medical dispositions. The medical centre at Agira and No.5 Field Ambulance at Leonforte were fully occupied with battle casualties requiring post-operative care or with sick. There were around 250 on the sick lists, with malaria increasingly predominant. A divisional anti-malaria officer was therefore appointed and charged with improving the state of unit precautions, which were in sad shape due to losses of equipment and supplies at sea and in transit inland.

Between August 12 and 15, after the patients on hand had been either discharged to their units or evacuated to a Casualty Clearing Station or hospital, all medical units moved with the Division to a concentration area near Siracusa on the east coast, bounded by Scordia, Lentini, Sortino, Francofonte and Militello. This was a time of rest for the troops, but the medicals still had lots to do.

No.4 Field Ambulance established an Advanced Dressing Station near Francofonte to serve the Brigades stationed nearby, with car posts at each Brigade headquarters. These took care of casualties from the continuing mopping-up operations and fighting to the north. Those with wounds beyond the scope of the field medical facilities were evacuated to No.7 British Casualty Clearing Station at Lentini. The rest were sent to No.5 Field Ambulance in the medical area east of Sortino. This unit held and treated all but malaria cases, which were transferred to No.2 Field Dressing Station nearby. No.1 Field Dressing Station opened at Sortino on August 20 to increase the capacity of the medical centre there.

37. OH THOSE FLIES!

A patient is driven mad by the flies.

Friday, August 13, 1943

The officers' club in Agira is crowded for its last evening of operation. The owner is officially saddened by the well-known plans for departure of all remaining Canadian units tomorrow. Privately he is quite pleased with the timing. He is pleased with his earnings from the officers' club, and with their generous supply clerks, but local business is starting to come back to the town in force and he doesn't want to lose out. He is quietly friendly and solicitous, offering free glasses of local brandy to anyone brave enough to drink it.

Rocke and Jack join their many colleagues for farewell drinks. The hospital is almost empty of patients, packing and loading of vehicles is proceeding, and they feel good about what they have accomplished here in Agira.

They enjoy a round of small talk, and then drift over to a table and in more serious mood discuss the case of Pte. Jon Robson. Robson is a British gunner who was brought in four days previously with a shrapnel wound in his abdomen. The operation went well, but he is still in serious condition. The concern is that they will be moving out tomorrow, but to move him would be against strict RCAMC guidelines that abdominal cases should not be moved for at least a week after their operation. This rule had been written based on the experience in the fast-paced Africa desert war when many abdominal wound patients had died or developed serious complications when they were moved too soon.

"Whatever you say, Rocke. I'll be happy to stick around for a few more days if you like."

"Jack, I've thought a lot about it and I think I'd better do it. Why don't you take the surgical van and the utility vehicle? I'll keep the lorry, and we'll clear some space in it to fit the stretcher, and a place for an orderly to sit with him. I think I'll keep Bill McKenzie and Jimmy Price with me to help out, and Matt Curran to do the driving. We should be able to get away by the 16th, or the 17th at the latest. You can take the unit down to Sortino and get us settled in."

Jack is relieved. He is ready to move on. "OK, will do. But hey, what are you going to do here with all these bars and restaurants, and grateful people?"

"I think I'm just going to have a nice, long sleep!"

Saturday, August 14, 1943

Rocke watches the long line of Canadian military units move slowly along the street, heading down the hill to the main road that will take them east and then south to various rest stations, some at the concentration area near Siracusa. This will be, for most of them, a time of at least some rest before the expected attack on Italy itself. It is an impressive show – a long line of tanks, artillery, infantry, medical units and Service Corps, the medical vehicles with big red crosses in various positions. A sizeable crowd of citizens of Agira lines the street to wave them off, some of the women looking unusually sad.

The medical units have left the schoolhouse/hospital almost empty, although there is a fair amount of stuff left behind – some food, used equipment and cots, and extra medical items no longer needed and with no place on the crowded trucks. Rocke still has his own sleeping room near the back of the building. He has had McKenzie and Curran take over a nearby room, and put Price with the patient in an adjoining room with whatever equipment and supplies are needed. They have some food, but plan to rely for the most part on the nearby restaurants.

It is 0830hrs by the time the trucks have disappeared and the dust has settled. Matt Curran is working over the lorry in the front yard, sorting the load in the back to be sure that it will be a reasonable ride for Pte. Robson and Jimmy Price when they eventually take off for the coast. Price is inside the hospital sitting beside the patient, reading while the patient sleeps fitfully. Rocke walks into the building to cook up a cup of tea and catch up on his diary. The schoolhouse is eerily quiet and growing warmer in the sun. The really good thing about it, still, is the virtual absence of flies. When it was a busy hospital the orderlies and drivers had gone to great pains to spray the rooms and halls regularly and to brandish fly swatters whenever necessary, and that had kept the fly population to reasonable limits. They have a few cans of Flit with them still and plan to keep at least their own rooms clear until they depart three days hence.

Rocke is just settling at his desk when he hears footsteps running along the hall towards his room. Matt Curran bursts in through the open door. "Sir, there's a great bloody crowd of locals coming into the building. I don't know what they want. They seem friendly enough, but they look damn determined."

Rocke closes and locks his door and heads down the hallway. Before he gets close to the front entrance he finds almost swimming against a stream of local citizens moving quickly down the hallway and into the many rooms. A few are heading the other way, back out the door with boxes and bits of furniture in their hands. The people smile at him but don't wait to talk. They are looking for stuff. They are looting the building!

Rocke orders Curran to get outside with his firearm nearby and protect the truck. He turns and runs back to the rooms that he shares with his three staff and the patient. He orders Price to sit in the door of his and the patient's room, and McKenzie to salvage the food supplies and guard all three rooms. That done, he moves back down the hall and positions himself near the front entrance to keep an eye on the action.

Initially he is outraged by this invasion of the hospital. The mayor had promised the Canadians that the locals would stay away! Then, as he watches the action more closely he starts to reconsider. These people have been living in the middle of the war, with German occupiers, for a long time. They have seen their own sons going out to fight against people they thought were friends, and many sons have not come back. They have been deprived of many of the necessities of life. They look thin and dishevelled. They need things, there are things to be had in this building, and the Canadians have left those things behind to be taken. It's as simple as that.

He smiles at a few successful raiders and receives some sad but grateful smiles in return. Then he notices something else that is truly unwelcome. The great influx of people off the street has broken down the defence against flies. Attracted by the people and by the smells of food and blood, they are swarming into the building. In ten minutes there seem to be clouds of flies everywhere, just as there had been in the tents the medicals had used in previous weeks. The flies aren't biters, but they seem to get in everywhere: his ears, his nose, even his mouth. They are distracting and annoying.

One hour later the building is quiet. The visitors have left; the building has been stripped to the walls. There is not one piece of equipment or furniture anywhere except in the three rooms that Rocke's team shares. The raiders have heeded the warnings of the smiling Canadians with polite and understanding smiles of their own, and left them completely alone. Outside, Matt Curran had the same experience: people simply waved at him and passed by.

Rocke tells McKenzie to get some tea, and Curran to stay by the truck for a while to make sure there are no rear-guard actions. Fortunately the tea things and other food supplies, and the tiny cooking stove, are now in McKenzie's room, so have been spared. He goes back to their rooms, has a brief word with Price, and they check on the patient. They move to his bedside (actually a stretcher with short legs) and stare at a most unpleasant sight.

Robson has a mosquito net strung over his stretcher. Few flies have found their way inside the net, but the outside of the net is black with a blanket of flies stretching almost two feet up from the floor. They are crawling around busily, desperate for his blood and searching for gaps, and the ugly mass is emitting a small, persistent drone. Inside this living tent Pte. Robson is awake, his eyes are wide and staring, and he is sweating profusely.

He doesn't wait to be addressed by the Major. "Sir," he whispers urgently, "please sir, I can't stand this. These flies! I can't stand it. Please sir!"

Price is on his knees trying to sweep the blanket of flies away from the netting, but to no avail. It is like using your hand to sweep water off a hard surface: you get some off in a spray, but then it just rolls back again. Rocke is horrified. He has worked with the most terrible wounds imaginable over the past month. He has seen blood and agony and disfigurement and hopeless disease. He is a surgeon and it is his job and his calling to deal with all that. But this?

He knows that if they try to move Robson to another room the flies will simply follow, and they don't have the means to get rid of them. He also knows that he simply must not move Robson away. It is too soon. The rule is clear and it makes sense. Robson's insides are at a very delicate stage in their healing. Jostling him along in a truck might well kill him.

He tries the military approach. "Now then Robson, I know those flies aren't too pleasant, but they aren't going to hurt you, and in three days we'll have you out of here. See if you can get some rest. Price, give him a shot will you? Through the netting."

Robson listens, but his eyes are on the swarming netting. "Sir, please, I don't want to sleep! These damn flies will get to me. I know it! Please Sir, let's just get out of here! I feel fine. I'll be OK!"

Rocke turns to leave, repeating his order to Price. He goes to his room, sits on his cot, and covers his face in his hands listening to Robson's moans from the next room. He wants to puke. He hears Price give Robson the sedative and then leave and sit outside in the hallway.

The sedative does not work and Robson does not sleep. As the hours go by his moans turn into cries for help, and by mid-afternoon Rocke knows that, orders notwithstanding, it will be more harmful to keep him here than to move him. If they don't get him away from those flies he will inevitably try to flee on his own, and that will kill him for sure.

He goes with Price and faces those staring eyes. Robson is panting with desperation. "Alright Robson, we're going to get you out of here today. Now close your eyes and just hang on. We're starting to load up right now, and we'll be heading out as soon as it's cool enough to drive." Robson nods his head, mumbles "Thank-you, Sir," and closes his eyes.

At 1800 hrs the truck is loaded and ready to go. They have cleared a space in the back for the stretcher, with a naso-gastric suction unit and intravenous ready to be hooked up. McKenzie and Curran lift the stretcher gently while Price shakes the flies off the mosquito net. They move out of the building and place the stretcher in position in the lorry. Price climbs aboard and hooks up the equipment to Robson, who has succumbed to more sedatives and is in a deep sleep. Price and McKenzie spray Flit around the interior of the van, and then sit down beside the patient. Rocke and the driver close the doors, climb into the cab and drive slowly away from Agira.

They drive at a snail's pace through the cool of the night. At 0515 hrs they deliver Pte. Robson, exhausted but finally smiling, to the hospital at Catania. "Thanks Major," he says as he is about to be wheeled away.

"You're welcome Robson," replies Rocke. "I just hope you get better. Please do let me know."

"I will Sir."

Three hours later they arrive at the 2CFSU camp at the medical rest station in an olive grove not far from Sortino.

38. THE LESSON

An anatomy lesson for the orderlies.

August 15 – 31, 1943

The unit enjoys two weeks of relative relaxation, good food and sleeps at the rest station. There is still a substantial amount of medical work to do, mainly taking care of malaria victims, but the rest from dealing with the onslaughts of new war wounded is a great relief. They spend long hours with colleagues from all the units discussing cases and devising new and better ways to deal with the terrible results of modern warfare. They are all amazed at how little they knew when they landed in Sicily just over a month ago, and at how much they have learned since then. They have crammed years of medical experience into a month.

They follow closely whatever news is available about the course of the war. They are thrilled that the Germans have been tossed out of Sicily, and they know that their next move will be into Italy. The success in Sicily has given them confidence, but the thought of landing on the mainland gives them pause. It's not going to get any easier!

Tuesday, August 17, 1943

In response to the urgings of several of the stretcher-bearers from the field ambulances and regimental medical units, and orderlies from nearby units, Rocke and Jack give a training workshop in anatomy. It takes place in the 2CFSU operating tent, the large Italian job, and there are 19 visitors perched on borrowed stools for the show.

They start by taking questions to see what the main areas of interest are, and it becomes clear that these men, who have seen so much carnage and savaged flesh and done so much invaluable first aid work, still have only a rudimentary sense of how the various parts of the body's systems work together. So they start with some general lecturing, using charts from medical journals to illustrate. This goes over well, but nothing like what comes next.

Jack has managed to rescue an arm amputated the previous day from a soldier with a huge wound in the upper arm. He gained the soldier's permission to use it for scientific and training purposes, and he now brings it out proudly and lays it on a slab on the operating table. With 19 pairs of wide-open eyes watching their every move, Rocke and Jack dissect the arm, explaining as they go. The audience is totally absorbed, firing detailed, intelligent questions and discussing amongst themselves.

The session takes almost four hours. At the end of it they thank the two surgeons for teaching them so much. The demonstration has answered "…a million questions that we have had but haven't had time to ask."

39. MONTY

General Montgomery praises the Canadians.

Friday, August 20, 1943

This is a red-letter day for the Canadian forces, although you wouldn't know it from the way the men grumble as they get up in the morning. This is the day that General Bernard Montgomery, Commander in Chief of the British 8th Army, is to visit. It sounds like an honour, but the troops are thoroughly annoyed about it. They are exhausted and need their rest, and now they have to polish their boots and put on their best uniforms and actually parade and be inspected. It just isn't worth the effort!

Like most of the officers, Rocke is somewhat more pleased with the prospect as he looks forward to having a look at, and perhaps meeting, the hero of the war in North Africa. He is, after all, their Supreme Commander, and highly successful, and Rocke is proud of the accomplishments of the Canadians and figures that Monty is probably proud of them too. Rocke does, however, share with the men the irritation of having to dress up and parade. This is the first parade they have had since England, and his good clothes are in sad shape in spite of the energetic ministrations of his batman.

At 1030hrs Rocke is at the head of his small unit, formed up with all Canadian personnel in three sides of a square in a field near the rest station. The troops are still disgruntled, knowing that they will inevitably have to wait for Monty to arrive. Inspecting officers are always late. After an hour of standing in the blazing sun they are becoming very restless, some of them grumbling loudly about the heat and probably being late for lunch.

Just before noon a cloud of dust appears in the distance. It is raised by Monty's little open car that is, in fact, a captured German jeep. It drives into the field, and as it approaches the parade Monty stands up and waves to the men. The car comes to a halt in the middle of the square and Monty calls out "break your ranks and gather round me. I don't want to inspect you. I just want to have a few words with you. I'm sorry I'm late. I know you must be awfully hot, but I've had so many people to see today!"

The Canadians break ranks and move *en masse* around the car. Rocke is tall enough to see over the heads of the crowd in front of him. Monty turns to his adjutant and asks in a loud voice "tell me, are these Canadians from the east or the west of Canada?"

"Both, Sir," says the adjutant.

Monty turns back to the troops and shouts a question. "Which is better, the east or the west?" The men, now beginning to think that the General is not all bad, respond with deafening shouts. Monty then explains that it doesn't matter where in Canada they come from, all Canadians have been magnificent fighters and he wouldn't dream of undertaking the attack on Italy if he didn't have the Canadians with him. His final words are historic.

> *"The people in Canada, in your home country, will know how proud they should be of what you have done here, fighting in Sicily. I regard you now as one of the veteran Divisions of the British Army – just as good as any other, if not better."*

The effect on the men is miraculous. They roar their approval of Monty's words and cheer him as he is driven away, still waving. Monty has won them over completely; the men are proud of the recognition he has accorded them.

Some of the officers are cynical of the performance, however. One of them tells Rocke that he has heard that Monty is saying the same thing to all of the units in the army, just to make them all feel good and ready for more hard work in Italy. Rocke doesn't care. He feels good about Monty's words, and ready for Italy.

-/-

The sentiments expressed by General Montgomery that day were, in fact, genuine. In his memoirs written after the war, Field Marshall Montgomery wrote:

> *The Canadians were magnificent in the Sicilian campaign. They had done no fighting before, but they were very well trained and they soon learned the tricks of the battlefield, which count for so much and save so many lives. When I drew them into reserve to prepare for the invasion of the Italian mainland, they had become one of the Eighth Army's veteran divisions.*

-/-

Wednesday, September 1, 1943

At 0600hrs the 2CFSU loads up the vehicles and joins No.2 Field Dressing Station driving north and east. They drive steadily until 1400hrs, passing Catania en route. They bivouac that evening on the banks of a dry riverbed about half a mile from the seashore, just north of Taormina.

Thursday, September 2, 1943

They pass a quiet day in the bivouac, briefly interrupted by a rapid inspection by the Brigadier in charge of the 1st Brigade. It is their last day on Sicilian soil.

40. ITALY – THE STRATEGY

The Allies plan for the invasion of Italy.

President Roosevelt and Prime Minister Churchill did not at first agree that it was a good idea to continue the action in the Mediterranean by attacking Italy. Taking Sicily had proven the point that the Allies could win against well-defended German positions on European soil, and Roosevelt was not keen to divert any more attention or resources from the massive attack on northern France that was being planned. Churchill, on the other hand, was convinced that it was vital to keep on attacking the soft underbelly of Nazi Europe. They eventually agreed on limited involvement in Italy, one key objective being to force the Germans to continue to commit forces to the southern front, thereby weakening their ability to deal with the planned Normandy invasion and the battle with Russia.

The initial goals of the Italian campaign were to capture Naples and the airfields at Rome and Foggia. Hitler would realize that the airfields could be used as bases to bomb Germany, thus ensuring that he would defend Italy vigorously. In anticipation of this he did in fact reinforce his army divisions already stationed in southern Italy, with orders to defend Rome at all costs. With the Italian surrender on September 8, 1943, the Allies no longer had to face Italian troops, but were in for a terrific battle with the experienced German forces of Generalfeldmarschall Albert Kesselring's 10th Army.

The Allied plan of invasion involved a three-phased attack. On September 3 the 13th Corps of the British 8th Army, including the 1st Canadian Division and the 5th British Division, would cross the Strait of Messina and land on the toe of Italy (Operation Baytown). The 5th British Division would start up the west coast of the peninsula to support the Americans as needed in their drive to Rome, and then cross over to help clear the centre and the eastern side of the peninsula. The Canadians would land in the vicinity of Reggio di Calabria and advance to the northeast through the Aspromonte range of the Apennines on the general axis Reggio-Delianuova. They would move through the foot of the Italian boot and then drive up the eastern side of the peninsula in support of the 78ᵗʰ British Division, which would effect landings on the eastern side of the peninsula.

On September 9 the 6ᵗʰ U.S. Corps and the 10ᵗʰ British Corps, under the command of the US 5ᵗʰ Army, would launch an assault in the Gulf of Salerno, to the south of Naples (Operation Avalanche). On the same day the 1ˢᵗ British Airborne Division would be landed by sea at Taranto, giving the British Army more strength to move up the east coast (Operation Slapstick). These combined efforts would, it was hoped, eliminate all enemy forces in the foot of the Italian boot and open the way to Rome both directly from the south, and from the east on roads across the Italian boot.

The German strategy was to withdraw slowly from the most southern areas, but make the Allied advance as difficult as possible by mining and destruction of bridges and roads. They would toughen up their resistance as the fighting moved north, and under direct orders from Hitler would defend to the death the last line of defence before Rome, the combined 'Bernhard Line' and 'Gustav Line' stretching from Ortona on the east coast to Gaeta on the west coast. It was a sound defensive strategy, and it cost the Allies dearly.

The medical plan for Operation Baytown was similar in principle to that for Operation Husky: mobile medical units advancing closely behind the troops, managed on a day-to-day basis for maximum flexibility, and backed up by slowly advancing Casualty Clearing Stations and stationary hospitals. The circumstances were, however, much different. The medical units were now fully equipped and experienced, and had but a brief amphibious crossing rather than a lengthy sea voyage to contend with.

Once the landing over the Strait of Messina was effected, all casualties were to be held by the rear-most medical units, mostly in Reggio, until arrangements could be made for their evacuation by empty tank landing craft to Sicily or beyond. This system would remain in place until hospital ships could enter the harbour at Reggio. As a supplement, evacuation by air was to be instituted as soon as landing strips became available. Special attention was paid to the malaria menace, and the medical authorities even recommended that all units shift from short to long trousers, the better to ward off mosquitoes.

The purely Canadian medical plan was quite simple. No. 9 Field Ambulance was to be the first unit ashore and quickly open a temporary beach dressing station for the 3rd Infantry Brigade. On the beach they would work alongside the British No. 34 Beach Brick Medical Section, which was charged with the chief responsibility for the reception and treatment of casualties on the beaches. No. 9 Field Ambulance would then establish an Advanced Dressing Station in Reggio. No. 2 Field Dressing Station and 2CFSU would cross and as soon as possible join No. 9 FA to form a Canadian Medical Centre in Reggio.

A detachment from No. 4 Field Ambulance was to remain in Italy and supply personnel for the care of wounded ferried to Sicily on tank landing craft. The balance of No. 4, with No. 1 Field Surgical Unit and No. 1 Field Transfusion Unit attached, were to land under command of the 1st Infantry Brigade, move into Reggio and be prepared for further orders to move ahead behind the troops.

No. 5 Field Ambulance was to cross and remain in reserve, awaiting orders.

The plan was to be flexible from then on, under the direct control of the ADMS.

41. A GOOD BEGINNING

The invasion starts out well.

September 3-13, 1943

The Anglo-Canadian assault on September 3 met negligible opposition. By the end of the day the attackers had secured their initial objectives and begun to push inland, the British along the western coast road, the Canadians through the rugged mountains of the Aspromonte.

On September 8 the Italian surrender was announced, to the joy of the attacking troops. They knew that they were now fighting just the Germans. So the fight was still on against a very tough foe, but at least the Allies could count more on the cooperation and even support of the local citizens.

With the going through the mountains very tough, the Canadian command decided on that day to switch the main Canadian axis of advance to the eastern coast road, and by nightfall the leading elements of the 3rd Brigade had made their way down from the hills to Locri. Within a few days most of the Division was concentrated in the vicinity of Catanzaro, with patrols occupying Crotone on the coast to the northeast. Here they had to pause to permit the administrative units to catch up with the fighting troops.

The joint U.S./British assault at Salerno, being much closer to Rome, met strong resistance from the outset. The Germans were determined to drive them back before they could be supported by the British troops advancing up the west coast from the south. Violent fighting took place around Salerno until September 14.

The chief medical problems in the south, during this first phase of the Italian campaign when casualties were light, were to maintain an efficient system of evacuation over the rapidly lengthening lines of communication, and to deal with the very heavy flow of sick, mainly from malaria. These alone accounted for approximately 1,500 admissions to medical units in September.

There was little for No.9 Field Ambulance to do on the beach, and late on September 3 they joined up with No.2 Field Dressing Station and 2CFSU as planned in a large school building in Reggio. This substantial Canadian Medical Centre was to remain the pivot of Canadian medical arrangements until a base could be established further forward, probably in the Catanzaro area.

As the Canadian troops advanced through the Aspromonte Mountains up the toe of Italy, the ADMS moved his mobile units forward in support. On September 6 No.5 Field Ambulance opened an Advanced Dressing Station in Gambarie, northwest of Reggio. The next day No.4 Field Ambulance set up its Advanced Dressing Station at Delianuova, farther to the west.

With the prospect of heavy inflows of wounded to these two stations from fighting in the mountains, the ADMS also sent No.1 Field Surgical Unit and No.1 Field Transfusion Unit to the Gambarie station on the 7th. They had hardly set up, however, when he ordered them next morning over to the Delianuova station to assist with an inflow of casualties from the West Nova Scotia Regiment. These troops had the misfortune of entering into a brief but bitter battle with Italian paratroopers on the very day that Italy surrendered.

Also on the 7th, No.1 Field Dressing Station opened a medical staging post at Locri on the coast to treat wounded coming back down the coastal road, and to facilitate their movement back to Reggio.

While the dressing stations at Gambarie and Delianuova were on the route originally planned for the Canadian advance, their locations were problematic. Evacuation back to Reggio from them was slow and difficult by reason of congested traffic on poor roads made worse by enemy demolitions. Thus when the infantry regiments were ordered to move down from the mountains to the east coast, the ADMS was only too pleased on September 11 to order these stations closed, and the medical units to move over to the better conditions in the coastal area and join the army convoys heading northeast.

No.4 Field Ambulance left Delianuova and was on the move in convoy for almost two weeks.

No.5 Field Ambulance moved in the convoy all the way to Catanzaro where, on September 12, it formed the ambulance component of the substantial Canadian Medical Centre being established there as part of the original medical strategy, taking over from the centre in Reggio. This new centre benefited greatly from its location in a modern hospital building that had been used as a sanatorium. No. 1 Field Dressing Station joined them there on the same day, having been replaced at the staging post at Locri by No.9 Field Ambulance that was moving up from Reggio. No.1 Field Surgical Unit and No.1 Field Transfusion Unit joined the centre in Catanzaro the following day.

By September 13 the line of evacuation back to Reggio, ending either at the Canadian installation there or at a British Casualty Clearing Station that had opened there on September 5, was over one hundred miles in length. Treatment of Canadian casualties was being done mostly at Catanzaro, and British casualties from the 13th Corps were being routed to another British Casualty Clearing Station located well forward at Vibo Valentia near the west coast. A British Field Ambulance moved into the Canadian building in Reggio to handle transmission of patients out of Sicily.

The Canadian Medical Centre in Reggio, now consisting of No.2 Field Dressing Station and the 2CFSU, thereupon closed down and moved up to the main body of the Division.

42. THE MIRROR

The crossing to Italy is held up by a bizarre incident.

Friday, September 3, 1943

The 2CFSU team are dressed, trucks loaded and ready to go at 0230hrs, the appointed time for the start of the Allied assault on the mainland of Italy. They have been listening to the opening artillery barrage across the Strait for several hours and now, as ordered, they are 'standing ready and awaiting orders to move'. They can see much of the fireworks – a spectacular display of explosive power. They are tense and ready to roll.

At 0430hrs Rocke orders McKenzie to bring the team some breakfast. The batman cooks up some tea and hands out the sandwiches he made the previous evening. Still no orders.

The sun rises straight into their eyes, a great golden ball heralding another stinking hot day. The flies wake up and start their swarming and annoying. The artillery is occasional now, and there are Allied planes patrolling the skies. They can see landing craft of all shapes and sizes moving back and forth across the Strait. Still no orders.

At 1215hrs Rocke orders McKenzie to find some more food for the team. Several of the men join the batman in preparing a lunch of mixed scraps and cold rations, washed down with lukewarm water.

At 1600hrs Rocke orders Eric to go down to the embarkation area at Dog Beach and find out what is going on. Eric returns at 1645hrs and, with the team gathered around, says "Sir, it's like the Sicily landing all over again. It's bloody chaos over there. I couldn't find anyone in charge, and there's all sorts of units just looking for a boat to take them across. So it looks like we've been forgotten again and we're on our own!"

"Right," says Rocke, "then we'd better do the same thing too. Men, lets

214 ∴ WHILE BULLETS FLY

get into the vehicles and down to that beach. I'll go in the surgical van up front. Jack, will you please bring up the rear in the lorry, and let's all stay right close together."

They drive the short distance to the beach and start moving back and forth along the road at the top of the embarkation zone. The area is several miles long, covered with vehicles and units of soldiers, engineers and medicals milling around, loading onto vessels or just searching for orders. At 1740hrs they are turning around at the southern end of the embarkation area to head back for another run when Rocke spots a vehicle transport vessel, an 'LST', beached nearby with its gates open, ready to receive passengers. Without a second's hesitation he orders the driver to turn down to the beach and head for the vessel.

At 1745hrs the three vehicles of the 2CFSU drive straight on board the LST and are hoisted to the top deck. Still no orders, but now it doesn't matter! The team climb down from the vehicles, check and lock them, and then head to the rail to watch the fun. At 1900hrs the vessel sails for the mainland in a beautiful, calm evening with no enemy action in evidence.

Eric asks Rocke if the men can have permission to take showers in the washrooms on board. "We have lots of time, Sir, and the showers have obviously been well used by previous passengers." Rocke hesitates. *Surely there must be some military reason why this is a bad idea?* Branch persists. "Sir, we haven't had a proper hot shower for two months, and it would do the men a lot of good." Rocke relents. "OK Eric, you can have your showers. Make sure that just two are in the showers at any one time; the others should be fully clothed in case there's an emergency."

Forty-five minutes later a clean and cheery Eric Branch reports that all showers have been completed and the men are 'damn happy about it'. Rocke sends Jack to take a shower, and then enjoys the wild luxury of a hot shower himself. At 2100hrs the LST touches down on the beach near Reggio di Calabria, on the tip of the toe of the Italian boot. There is no enemy gunfire opposing them.

The team are in their vehicles, waiting to be hoisted down to the lower deck. Rocke hears the loading portal open and two or three vehicles drive off onto the beach, but then there is silence. He senses that something is wrong and sends Eric down to find out what is going on. Eric reports back. "You won't believe this Sir, but the naval Lieutenant at the portal says that

215 Ian Bruce Robertson   ∴   215

someone has stolen a mirror from the washroom and the Commander has ordered that no-one can leave the ship until the mirror is returned."

Rocke goes down to the portal and finds the Lieutenant. "Lieutenant, what's going on? Are you seriously keeping us all on board because of a lost mirror?"

"Yes Sir," replies the harried Lieutenant. "Commander's orders. He says that sailors are very superstitious about mirrors, so we have to find this one before anyone can disembark. He let the Colonel and his staff go, but nobody else."

"Good Lord, man. What steps have been taken to find the mirror?"

"None yet, Sir. I think it's up to the army to do the search."

"Right," say Rocke. "Who's the senior army officer on board now?"

"I don't know, Sir."

Rocke asks the Lieutenant to summon all army officers to the portal deck immediately, using the ship's PA system. When they gather Rocke sees, to his dismay, that with the Colonel having gone ashore he is now the senior army officer of the group, so it's up to him to solve this impasse, and quickly. *Actually it's becoming rather fun working without orders from above!* He orders the officers to break into pairs and go to each vehicle on the ship and tell the occupants to surrender the mirror if they have it, and that no questions will be asked and no disciplinary action taken if they give it up.

They reconvene twenty minutes later with no mirror. Rocke goes up to the cabin and is greeted by an agitated navy Commander. "Of course I know why you're here, Major," he says, "and I have just given orders to let the troops disembark with their vehicles. But I hope you can appreciate my reason for taking such an extraordinary action – to, so to speak, interrupt the invasion of Europe because a mirror is missing. You know, the sailors are a very superstitious lot and they regard the loss of a mirror as a sign of bad things to come, just as does the breaking of one. I had to do everything in my power to find that mirror so that my ship won't be regarded as an unlucky one."

Rocke is relieved that the crisis is over, and he sympathises with the Commander's dilemma. He salutes, thanks the Commander, and as he dashes back to the surgical van he sees that the promised orders are already being carried out and vehicles are streaming out onto the beach. The 2CFSU drives off the LST at 2135hrs.

43. REGGIO DI CALABRIA

A Canadian Medical Centre opens on the tip of the toe of Italy.

They drive slowly through the streets of Reggio. Their first impression is that this is a real town with modern buildings, unlike the more primitive development in Sicily. There is an unfortunate amount of damage from the Allied barrage and bombing, but that is a fact of life in war, and anyway there is a fair amount of the town still in reasonable shape. They pass some groups of Allied soldiers who have looted deserted shops in the town. One group, riding on a tank, is sporting top hats and ladies' garden party hats. They are laughing and waving at any onlookers they spy.

Using their maps the 2CFSU team soon pull up in front of a large, modern school building in the heart of the town. They park next to the trucks of No.9 Field Ambulance and No.2 Field Dressing Station and join these units in setting up a very complete Canadian Medical Centre in the building. They break for sleep at midnight, with sleeping quarters in offices at the rear of the building.

Saturday, September 4, 1943

The Field Dressing Station kitchen staff, working in the school's well-equipped kitchen, produces an excellent breakfast for all units at 0700hrs. Rocke joins Colonel Basil Bowman of No.9 Field Ambulance and Major Bill Clendinnen of No.2 Field Dressing Station to discuss the layout of the centre. They are thoroughly pleased with the structure, having found that there is lots of room to meet all of their requirements. It is dusty but easy to clean, and has electricity and water. The building divides nicely into the

216

separate units, with the reception and examination areas in the front of the building, holding wards in the middle, and operating rooms and testing areas at the back. The longer-term wards are in a wing out to the left, over-looking some unkempt gardens and a deserted town square.

The operating room is a spacious and well-lighted classroom with an adjoining bathroom that can be used for sterilizing and washing up. The room holds all of the equipment easily, with shelves along the wall ideal for holding instruments and supplies. There are some flies in attendance, but a Fly Patrol makes short work of them, and the drivers then move on to patrol the reception and examination areas and holding wards. The medical staff feel very much at home here. They have the sterilizer going full tilt, the OR swept and clean, all surfaces scrubbed and the equipment and instruments laid out and ready to go when the first case arrives at the front door.

He does not arrive by ambulance. He is a small Italian boy, no more than 6 years old, and he is carried into the hospital by his nearly hysterical mother, supported by Victor Kraft who has been sorting out and cleaning the surgical van just outside the front entrance. By a stroke of luck the translator Luigi, still connected with No.9 Field Ambulance, is in the re-ception area cleaning with an orderly from the Field Ambulance. He strides over to the woman and in rapid Italian finds out what has happened.

"Christ almighty, the kid was playing with a grenade he found in the street! She says that she saw him playing and yelled at him and he threw it·in the gutter, but it went off too soon. He's got some bad wounds in his chest and arms."

The orderly tells Luigi to bring the mother and child along the corri-dor and into one of the examination rooms. He asks Kraft to get a doctor, and Victor heads for the OR and returns quickly with Jack Leishman. Basil Bowman joins them almost immediately, and they enter the room where the orderly has laid the boy on the examination table and is starting to disengage the bloodied towels. Without waiting for the obvious orders, Luigi takes the mother gently by the arm and draws her out of the room. He sits her down in a chair just down the hall and calls to another orderly to bring her a cup of hot tea with lots of milk. He speaks to her quietly, calming her and reassur-ing her that her son is in good hands (albeit the enemy), and will be fine.

In the examination room the doctors are surveying the awful damage that a grenade can do to a small person. It had exploded when on the ground, dislodging and hurling a cloud of rock fragments in every direction. The boy's face and chest are a mass of contusions, some still bleeding freely, with the remains of his shirt stuck deeply into some of the wounds. His left arm is not too bad. His right arm, which he had brought up to protect himself, is a mess. It has obviously stopped several shards of rock that were heading for his face, and one piece of rock has done bad damage to his hand, almost severing the ring finger.

"Jack," says Bowman, "You and Rocke had better get this lad on the table as quickly as possible. That hand is going to need a lot of work and some of those contusions look very deep – especially that one on his left cheek and the ones across the lower abdomen. And there's probably some debris from the road in there."

"Agreed, Sir. You fellows can get him cleaned up and prepped. We'll scrub up and be ready to go in about 20 minutes. Just roll him in when you're ready."

Jack rushes to find Rocke and the OR assistants, and after twenty minutes of frantic scrubbing and organizing they are in place as the boy is wheeled into the OR. The mother is still in the care of Luigi, who has found it helpful to supplement her tea with a sedative. She sits outside of the OR, silently holding her rosary with her eyes closed, for the two hours that it takes for the 2CFSU to save her son's life. She has already lost her husband to the war. She will not lose her son.

They do two more operations in the afternoon, both Canadian engineers injured by enemy bombing.

Pete Monroe takes the 60cwt lorry to the Canadian military workshop set up in Reggio to see about repairs to the gearbox. It has been slipping and neutralizing since they left Sortino, finally succumbing to the hard work it has done through the mountains of Sicily. The mechanics say that it is probably the transfer case, and say it will be ready in the morning.

September 5-7, 1943

The workload continues to be light, averaging three cases per day. There are far more sick patients than wounded patients in the hospital, and the 2CFSU team pitches in to help deal with them. They also have some good exercise in walks throughout the town. Rocke and Jack are pleased to see that an officers' club has opened in the next block.

One of the sick patients continues to be the 60cwt lorry. It is 'ready to go' on the morning of the 6th as promised, but has the same problems when tested on the roads just outside Reggio. Pete takes it back to the shop and they try another new transfer case. Same result.

Pete takes it back on the 7th and finally gains the interest of the head mechanic. He checks over the lorry for 10 minutes and announces that "…It ain't the transfer case at all. The damn chassis's bent!" They promise to call the hospital when they have fixed it.

Wednesday, September 8, 1943

Colonel Bowman tells Rocke the welcome news that the airfield at Reggio has been opened, so they can now evacuate patients by air to Sicily or the hospitals in North Africa. They have no patients ready for evacuation, but still appreciate this sign of progress.

He has also received a message for Rocke that Eric Branch's promotion to Corporal has been approved. Rocke is delighted. He knows that the official model of the FSU has the non-commissioned officer as a Lance Corporal, the lowest NCO position in the army. He also knows, however, that rules are made to be changed, and with two months of experience under their belts it is clear that this position deserves at least a Corporal designation – *hell, the guy is, in effect, running the unit!* The senior officers have seen fit to agree, so there it is. He asks McKenzie to find Eric and bring him to the surgeons' office.

Eric appears, somewhat concerned that he has been summoned so abruptly. Rocke smiles, shakes his hand, and says "Congratulations Corporal Branch. Your promotion is effective as of today." Eric smiles from ear to ear. "Thank you, Sir. I appreciate your confidence in me." They grin at each other but there's nothing more to say. "Jolly good," says Rocke finally. Eric salutes (for the first time in two months), turns and walks out humming to himself.

Late in the day a battered ambulance brings in five wounded from the engagement near Delianuova between the West Nova Scotia Regiment and Italian paratroopers. The Canadians are a private soldier with a neck wound and Captain Hardy, the medical officer of the West Novas who was shot through the foot while dressing a patient. He receives some good natured kidding for 'shooting himself in the bloody foot', arguing vehemently that he didn't do it himself and that it was a crazy stray bullet that did the job. The three Italians are all badly wounded and sedated.

A Canadian soldier with severe leg wounds is brought in during the evening. He has been treated two days ago farther up the line, and is here to stabilize before being evacuated.

In the evening the officers from the centre toast the surrender of the Italians at the officers' club. Their mood is quiet; the Italians were as good as out of the fighting anyway, and the real problem is the German army. However it's good to have the Italians neutral or even on our side.

Thursday, September 9, 1943

There is only one new case today, another Italian paratrooper injured in the scrap with the West Novas. There are more sick to treat, which keeps them busy.

At noon No.9 Field Ambulance packs up, clears out of the building and heads to the east coast road. With so few wounded coming in here they are needed closer to the action.

In the afternoon the soldier with the leg wounds dies, and Rocke does an immediate post mortem examination.

At 2030hrs Rocke leaves the hospital and goes directly to the officers' club. He needs a drink – a very large one. He sits at a table with Bill Clendinnen.

"Rocke, you look a bit shook up," says Bill. "What's up?"

Rocke takes a large slug of his scotch, lights a cigarette and leans back with his eyes closed. "We've had another gas gangrene case in and we lost him late this afternoon. Christ it's a terrible thing! I'd rather treat anything than gas gangrene. Honestly Bill. Have you seen much of it?"

"Just a couple of cases. One we lost because it was way too late to save him. The other we saved because the moment we saw a bruise on the forearm changing colour we took a chance on what it was and had Frank's team take the guy's arm off at the elbow. We could see the infection growing even while we were setting up to operate! And the smell was there when we had the arm off. It was like a freight train coming down the track at us."

"Well," says Rocke, "we weren't so lucky with this guy. He was wounded in a mine explosion. He had a compound fracture dislocation of his right ankle region, with some exterior wounding, and simple fractures of his left tibia and left femur. The station up front felt that the wound of the right ankle joint wasn't too severe, and they treated it by simple excision and a plaster cast. The left lower leg was grossly swollen and the circulation was seriously impaired, so they put it in traction in a Tobruk splint. Two days later they sent him back to us, still seemingly in good condition. He arrived here last night.

"This morning he was in considerable discomfort, but there were no visible signs of the cause. So we left him to rest and watched him carefully. Still for no apparent reason he just got worse and worse and finally died this afternoon. We felt bloody helpless watching him go and not knowing what to do to help him.

"We did an immediate post mortem, of course. The original wound in the right ankle was perfectly healthy and showed no signs of infection, nor was there any evidence of infection in his right calf or thigh. What he had died of was a gross and fulminating gas gangrene of the muscles of his left calf and left thigh."

"There were no outward signs of the gangrene?"

"No, none. What we figured was that the portal of entry of the infection was the small wound of the right ankle. The organisms entered his bloodstream and lodged in the damaged muscles of his left leg and thigh, and there they set off the gas gangrenous process. No doubt the damaged blood vessels in that region helped the infection along."

"My God, Rocke. So it started in one leg and moved across to the other before digging in?"

"Yes, that seems to be what happened. The left leg was a stinking mess when we opened it up. I don't think I'll ever forget that smell."

"Maybe another scotch will help," says Bill, heading for the bar.

September 10 – 12, 1943

The 2CFSU has one case each day, and otherwise they help with the sick and keep an eye on post-operative cases. The young 'grenade boy' is doing well, responding to the constant care of the orderlies and his mother. On September 12 she records her first smile – a fleeting smile at Luigi as she asks him to thank the team for her. She has been thrilled that Italians are no longer enemies of these nice people. She gives the team a loaf of bread.

The weather is starting to show early signs of fall. The heat has broken and there is occasional rain. Pete Monroe receives his call from the mechanics and is greatly relieved when he picks up the 60cwt lorry and it works just fine.

The fighting is now over one hundred miles ahead, and the unit is keen to get moving.

Monday, September 13, 1943

A dispatch rider brings orders from the ADMS that 2CFSU and No.2 Field Dressing Station are to move up along the east coast tomorrow. Rocke orders the team to pack the supplies and equipment and load the trucks. At 1530hrs No.7 British Field Ambulance arrives to take over the building. Their Commander, Major Pat Dumfries, is frustrated at this posting so far away from the action, but resigned to their role of staging for casualties being evacuated. He joins Rocke, Jack and Bill Clendinnen in the evening for a farewell drink at the officers' mess.

"Well, I wish you chaps well," says Dumfries, who has bought the first round for the smiling Canadian doctors. "I hear things have been pretty light up the coast, but it's bound to get busier soon."

"It has to, Pat," replies Bill. "The Germans aren't going to let our troops move so fast forever. The closer we get to the Rome line, the tougher it's going to be, so we'd better be there. Look what's happening up at Salerno!"

"Yes, that's been very tough," says Pat. "Our troops landed on the 9th and they're still having a very hard time of it. From what I hear they should be able to break out soon, but they're taking a lot of casualties. I guess we'll be handling many of them in the coming weeks. Our chaps in the 5th Division are moving up the coast pretty well, so that should help. I think the plan is that as soon as we've secured the Salerno area we'll move our Casualty Clearing Station up from Vibo Valentia to Sapri."

"That makes sense," says Rocke. "What are you hearing about Taranto?"

"I think the landing went fine, and we have a medical centre set up there. It should help support your troops when they get to that area and turn up the coast."

44. CONVOY TO POTENZA

It's time to move up the boot of Italy. Complex moves and slow going.

September 14 - 30, 1943

The 5th British Division driving up the west coast of Italy re-opened the general advance on September 14, and on the 16th it finally made contact with the right flank of the U.S. 5th Army's bridgehead just south of Salerno. The Canadian Division meanwhile had seized the principal towns in the highly malarious plain lying inland to the east and southeast of Castrovillari. To strengthen the link with the 5th British Division as they started to swing east now became the immediate objective in order to secure the eastern side of the peninsula. The Canadians were therefore ordered to seize the important communications centre of Potenza and, as a subsidiary task, to join hands with the British force landed in the Gulf of Taranto.

The 3rd Brigade, headed by a highly mobile striking force, reached Potenza without encountering serious opposition, but had a stiff fight with German defenders before occupying the town. The West Nova Scotia Regiment under Lieutenant-Colonel M.P. Bogert and the engineers provided a special force to deal with the obstacle course of mines and blown bridges leading up to the town. On September 20th the 'Boforce', as it was nicknamed after its commanding officer, entered Potenza and enemy resistance collapsed immediately. The 2nd Brigade, following closely, promptly began to patrol vigorously in the direction of Melfi to the north. The 1st Brigade, in carrying out the Division's secondary task, had meanwhile dispersed itself over the wide expanse of country separating the British forces in the Taranto area from the main body of Canadians in Potenza. The end of September found these positions basically unchanged, with the U.S. 5th Army and the British 8th Army forming an uninterrupted front line that reached all across the Italian peninsula from Salerno in the west to Bari in the east.

When the northward advance was resumed the ADMS was faced with highly complex issues in managing the medical forces. First there was the need to provide mobile medical support to the troops moving rapidly ahead on the coast and then increasingly in the mountainous interior regions. This was similar to the challenges faced in Sicily, but the complicating factor here was the long distances involved, with advanced medical units having to move along rough roads jammed with military traffic. Then there was the need to maintain an evacuation system back from the front-line areas hundreds of miles to the safety and complete medical and rehabilitation facilities at Reggio and beyond in Sicily and North Africa. This latter issue was exacerbated by the roughness of the roads, which made ambulance riding extremely bumpy and therefore dangerous for wounded men. The ADMS solved these problems in a remarkable display of leadership and management.

The Field Ambulances, with their responsibilities for first contact with the wounded cleared from action by the regimental medical teams, moved ahead with the troops. Fortunately these forward Field Ambulances had to open infrequently while the line Potenza – Taranto was being seized, mainly to evacuate sick troops.

No.4 Field Ambulance accompanied the 1st Infantry Brigade, establishing an Advanced Dressing Station at Scanzano on September 19. They remained there until the 27th, and then moved to a new site inland just north of Gravina to continue serving the 1st Brigade which was now turning north, passing the heel of Italy.

No.5 Field Ambulance was directed to open an Advanced Dressing Station just north of Crotone, right on the coastal road, as a precaution against a sudden rush of battle casualties. It was the clearing station for all Canadian casualties being moved out of the battle zones ahead. As the action moved forward, this station became over 100 miles from the forward troops, even as the crow flies, making evacuation by road uncomfortably long and bumpy. On September 19 arrangements were made for evacuation to it by sea in infantry landing craft plying between Crotone and beaches close to the forward divisional maintenance area near Rotondella. From Crotone the seriously ill and the relatively few battle casualties were evacuated by air to Sicily, while most of the minor sick were retained pending recovery.

No.9 Field Ambulance moved up from its staging post at Locri to accompany the 3rd Infantry Brigade in its attack on Potenza. They arrived in that town on the afternoon of September 20, just hours after the town had been secured.

The Field Dressing Stations moved behind the Field Ambulances, building the base of support for wounded and sick brought in by ambulance.

No.1 Field Dressing Station remained at Catanzaro to evacuate or complete the treatment of approximately 130 patients being held there. Having completed this task it opened partially on the 23rd at Anzi, about 10 miles south of Potenza.

No.2 Field Dressing Station stayed at Reggio until September 14, and then moved forward with the last of the divisional convoys. When the ADMS saw that Potenza was going to be an important medical centre for a while, he sent this unit there on September 22 as the base unit of a full Canadian Medical Centre.

The two Field Surgical Units and the Field Transfusion Unit also arrived in Potenza to complete the Canadian Medical Centre. Their work was surprisingly quiet through to the end of September, the main medical issues being sickness and civilian problems. The weather was cool and rainy. Due mainly to concerns about mines and booby traps left behind by the rapidly departing Germans, until September 29 Potenza was out of bounds to all troops, and the men of the medical units were confined to barracks. It was a boring time in the midst of a war zone.

-/-

Tuesday, September 14, 1943

The hospital in Reggio is alive and bursting with activity starting at 0300hrs. Rocke and Bill Clendinnen compare notes and maps over breakfast in preparation for the departure up the coast. Jack reports the unit's vehicles all loaded and ready to roll at 0515hrs, and the convoy of 16 vehicles rolls out of Reggio at 0530hrs, driving through light rain and early morning mist. They stop for lunch in a grove of trees near the beach 10 miles north of Locri. At 1830hrs they settle in an olive farm just south of Catanzaro.

Both teams are alert and smiling as the farmer and his attractive daughter come out to offer to sell them tomatoes, blackberries, watermelons and figs. The girl is in her late teens. Her simple dress covers but does not disguise her shapely figure, and she has lovely flashing eyes and long dark hair. The men haven't been this close to such beauty for a long time, and

226 : WHILE BULLETS FLY

they flirt and stare unabashedly. She smiles back at them, safe beside her nervously smiling but tough looking father. They take their time negotiating for the goods, with Luigi leading the Canadian side at his charming best. They are delighted with the produce, which adds immeasurably to their evening meal. The daughter does not, alas, accept their invitation to dinner.

Wednesday, September 15, 1943

Rocke, Jack and Bill Clendinnen have Victor Kraft drive them through Catanzaro to visit the Canadian Medical Centre set up by No.1 Field Dressing Station, No.1 Field Surgical Unit and No.1 Field Transfusion Unit in the sanatorium. They find Frank Mills supervising his team in cleaning and checking their equipment and supplies in the vehicles. Frank leaves the work in charge of his Second-in-Command and goes for a cup of tea with the three doctors in the hospital canteen, now being run by a highly efficient crew from the Field Dressing Station. Major Doug Sparling, Commander of the Field Dressing Station is there and joins them.

"It's good to see you fellows again," says Rocke. "We've been awfully quiet back at Reggio for some time now. How's it going here?"

"We had four cases yesterday," says Frank, blowing on his tea. "Two of them had the same problem with their left foot. It seems that they were blown up by the same mine while marching a bit too close together. But generally it looks quiet for us too, and I think we'll be moving up the line soon."

"We've got a lot more to do," says Doug. "There's just a helluva lot of sickness around – malaria and hepatitis and the usual dysentery. I thought with the weather getting cooler and damper the troops would be in better shape, but it seems not. A lot of them are very tired from the long, rough marching, and I guess that contributes to it. Right now we have well over 100 patients in the wards. That includes three civilians with injuries from mines and four German prisoners. They're tough customers, I'll tell you. These ones were part of demolition teams messing up the roads ahead of our troops, and they got a bit too close to their work. Our drivers are having great fun guarding them."

"The big problem I see coming up is evacuating the patients back to Reggio and out of Italy," says Rocke. "The troops are moving ahead so quickly it's going to be a damn long ride back for the ambulances, and those roads are going to kill off some of the bad cases. No.5 Field Ambulance has set up over at Crotone as a clearing station so that will help, but there's still a lot of distance on both sides of his unit. Have you heard of any plans for evacuation by sea or air?"

"Not directly," replies Doug, "but when I was briefing the ADMS staff they did mention that plans were being worked on for something like that. I agree with you that this is top priority. And it's not just the state of the roads. I think that all of us are having problems with the vehicles, and the breakdowns are bound to get worse."

The talk moves on to interesting cases. Frank tells of a recent patient who had taken a shell fragment in the chest. When they opened him up they could not find the fragment in spite of a diligent search including x-ray, and eventually had to close the wound and consider the case unsolved. The patient got better and was about to be discharged when he complained of soreness in his lower abdomen. They diagnosed the pain as appendicitis. When they opened him up, however, they found that the appendix was fine, but that there was a large shell fragment in the lumen of the terminal ileum, or in other words in his lower intestine. Reconstructing the case, they figured that the missile entered the left chest, passed through the diaphragm directly into the stomach, and thence found its way down the gastro-intestinal tract until it lodged in the terminal ileum. The x-ray had not spotted it because it had not covered such a low part of the abdomen. It was incredible that the soldier had no symptoms of this passage through his body until it lodged lower down and its sharp edges started to cause pain.

This story leads to several comments about the strange routes that bullets and other projectiles often take through the human body. The doctors agree that the general conception that bullets go in one side (the entrance wound), pass straight through and come out the other side (the exit wound) is by no means the general rule. The body has all sorts of ways of deflecting objects, and Rocke produces his own story on the subject.

"Back in Agira we had a soldier brought in complaining of pain in the left chest and trouble breathing. We took an x-ray and it showed a bullet in his left chest and a massive effusion that later turned out to be blood. The trouble was, we found no entry wound! We searched carefully, but could find nothing. So we removed the bullet from the lung and drained the blood and fixed him up, and he was recovering well when one day he complained of a sore right ear. We checked his ear, and I'm damned if there wasn't a wound far inside the ear canal. This was the wound of entry! We took another x-ray and traced the subsequent course of the bullet. It went in his ear, deflected off and fractured the spinous process of one of his cervical vertebrae, was deflected down towards the root of his neck on the opposite side, and then passed into his left lung!"

"Jesus, Rocke, he sounds like a human pinball machine!" exclaims Doug. "We've had a few strange cases, but none as weird as that. Changing the subject, we have some mail here if you're interested."

They are, and carry the mailbags happily home to the camp at the farm, buying some more fresh produce along the way. Most of the men have letters from home, so there is a brief silent period of reading and reflection in the camp, and not a few silent tears of loneliness.

Eric then reminds Rocke that they are only 500 yards from the ocean where there is a good beach for swimming. Rocke gives the order, which includes the suggestion that they get Luigi to invite the farmer and his daughter to join them. The invitation is politely refused, with some regret on the part of the daughter, and 10 minutes later the team is romping in the cool waters of the Mediterranean, engaging in fierce splash fights with the men from No.2 Field Dressing Station.

Thursday, September 16, 1943

A farmer from a nearby farm brings his young son to see the doctors about his son's sore eye. Rocke examines the boy. The eye is swollen and red, and weeping copiously. The farmer says, through Luigi, that he thinks the boy has been stung by some sort of bee or wasp. Rocke takes the boy to the hospital in Catanzaro where they have an eye specialist, and returns around midday with the boy's eye dressed, medicinal ointment in hand and the gift of a small pocketknife to cherish. The farmer offers a chicken in thanks for the service. They accept it graciously, and purchase three more from him for good measure.

In the afternoon the two units move three miles north and camp again. They are told that this is to put them in better position 'for the start of the big move tomorrow'. This appears to mean that they will be joining up with rear elements of the 2nd Infantry Brigade, who are moving up to Potenza.

Friday, September 17, 1943

The two units hit the road in the morning, headed for Villapiana which is roughly one third of the way up the Gulf of Taranto, but they don't nearly make it. Near Cariati, not far north of Crotoni, they catch up with the rear of the 2nd Infantry Brigade, slow to a crawl and camp near them overnight. The medical officers mingle with the infantry officers and it is a pleasant evening, with infinite mutual respect on display.

Saturday, September 18, 1943

They are off to an early start, following the troops grinding their way along the coast road. By 1800hrs they reach a point near Villapiana and are signalled to the side of the road by a military police officer who tells them that orders have not yet arrived for them for the next segment of their journey to…where they don't know anyway. They are to send a dispatch rider ahead to Division Headquarters near Scanzano to get their orders. Rocke instructs their favourite messenger, the motorcyclist Billy Santer, to do the job.

They wait and wait, have a cold meal beside the road, and bed down in the open next to the vehicles. At 0100hrs Rocke receives the news from Santer that they are to remain where they are until first light, and then move forward.

Sunday, September 19, 1943

The two medical units are up at 0400hrs and on the road at 0500hrs, travelling free of the 2nd Brigade trucks which were on the road even earlier. They make relatively good time and reach Division headquarters at 0915hrs, where they again line up with the divisional convoy.

Jack mingles with some of the infantry officers and learns that the 3rd Infantry Brigade is fighting up near Potenza and is expected to take the town shortly. That is probably their destination. He and Rocke check their maps and see that if that is so they will soon be turning inland onto the mountainous road to Potenza.

At 1000hrs No.1 Field Surgical Unit and No.1 Field Transfusion Unit catch up to the convoy, parking behind the No.2 Field Dressing Station vehicles. Frank Mills loudly tells Rocke that he has been having 'enough goddamn trouble with my trucks to last a goddamn lifetime'.

At 1050hrs they join the rear of the divisional convoy and head towards the mountains. They grind along on quite good roads with few diversions, but the going is slow behind the long convoy of military vehicles. At 2330hrs the convoy finally stops for the night, and the medical units camp in the inevitable olive orchard. They are too tired to socialize.

Monday, September 20, 1943

They remain in camp all day, and only after vigorous questioning of all officers in sight do they find out that they are near Laurenzana, southeast of Potenza. Their campsite is the most beautiful they have had so far, thickly wooded with oak and with heavy underbrush. It is very like England in many ways, and totally unlike the arid country that they have come through.

At 1600hrs they learn that the 3rd Division has taken Potenza and moved on, and that No.9 Field Ambulance has already moved into the town in support.

45. POTENZA

An uncomfortable place to work. Billy Santer and his women.

Tuesday, September 21, 1943

The infantry units move off towards Potenza in mid-morning. The medicals follow soon after and stop near the tiny village of Rifreddo, about 10 miles south of Potenza. They stay packed and ready to move, awaiting orders. At 1600hrs 2CFSU and No.1 Field Transfusion Unit receive orders to join No.9 Field Ambulance in Potenza. They drive slowly along the 10-mile stretch of road into the town, manoeuvring carefully around the debris of the recent battle.

The town has suffered extensive artillery damage but most of the streets are passable. They navigate their way to the municipal building that has been taken over by No.9 Field Ambulance. It is spacious and well laid out, and the Field Ambulance crew has done a good job organizing it.

The 2CFSU team sets up the OR and other facilities in the building under Eric's watchful eye while Rocke and Jack renew acquaintances with Basil Bowman and visit the cases already brought in. None requires immediate surgery. The West Nova soldier guarding the entrance to the improvised hospital tells them that the men are to stay in quarters until further notice, and the officers are advised to do the same. "The Krauts got out so quickly that we figure they've probably left behind a whole bunch of mines and other stuff to keep us busy, and we wouldn't want you guys getting into any trouble. Hell, even our own guys aren't allowed in except on duty assignments."

Wednesday, September 22, 1943

Around 30 cases come into the hospital, but none require surgery. At 1100hrs Colonel Bowman tells Rocke that No.2 Field Dressing Station, No.1 Field Surgical Unit and the Field Transfusion Unit have also come into Potenza and are setting up at a nearby special eye hospital.

At 1430hrs Rocke and Jack leave the building and visit a nearby bombed-out hospital. As usual they feel a twinge of regret at seeing a well-structured hospital in such shocking condition. The halls are littered with rubble and two of the four walls are seriously holed. They find the operating theatre area and salvage a few useful instruments.

At 1930 Pete Monroe and Dave Finley are drinking coffee in the hospital canteen when they spot the dispatch rider Billy Santer at another table. They call him over to their table.

"How's it going, Billy?" asks Pete. "You must be having a helluva time driving around on these crazy Italian roads. But you look like you're still in one piece. Had any luck with the women?"

"Yeah, in fact I have," says Billy.

"You're kidding," says Pete. "You've gotta be bull-shitting. As far as we've seen, the good looking ones are all Catholics and kept locked up by their parents. Are you saying you've found some?"

"Oh yes," says Billy. "But there's a few tricks you have to learn first. You see, you can't just look for the young ones. Everyone does, and they're all protected by their families. It's actually a bit like at home. I think I told you that I worked for an insurance company before the war? In the mailroom?

"Well, there were cute secretaries and clerks all over the place there, and I had lots of chances to chat them up, but I could never score. They were always married or engaged, or just going out with someone, or too shy, or whatever. I managed to get one quick blowjob in the storeroom, but that was all. She got scared and embarrassed and never came back. So, like, I was frustrated as hell, and then one day the secretary of one of the Vice Presidents came to the mail-room when I was there working late. I'd seen her many times and we were friendly, but she was way into her 30s, so I figured she was definitely too old for me. But that day she looked terrific and sexy.

"We got to talking, and she was smiling at me, and then she got this strange look in her eyes. She kind of leaned into me, and all of a sudden there we were fucking like crazy on the floor. The damn mail sacks got in the way, but I didn't even notice! It was great, and made me look at older women differently. And I figured that older women probably like younger men too. We screwed around a lot after that until the war came along and I joined up and came over here. I missed her for awhile, but hell, she was married with two kids so it was better to get away."

"OK Billy," says Dave, "that's very interesting history. But how about here in Italy?"

"Yeah, I'm just coming to that. In England I was too busy to do much hunting for women, and I was totally unsuccessful when I did manage to sniff around. It was the same at the start down here, as I told you before. I just couldn't even get close to the girls. Then my luck changed one day in Valguarnera. One evening I dropped into a small local laundry to get some things washed. It was run by a woman who was older than the young ones I'd seen so far, but not yet nearly old. We started to talk (I speak Italian you know – our family name used to be Santini), and she told me that her husband had been killed a year before. She had no children and was alone with this tiny place.

"Well guys, it was just like back in that mailroom in Canada. She gave me some coffee and we were talking and laughing, and she got that same strange look in her eyes. And pretty soon there we were rolling around on the laundry floor. And hey, she may have been a bit older, but I'll tell you she knew how to screw. Talk about passionate!

"I went back to the laundry the following morning to get my laundry, and I'm damned if she didn't close up the shop and we went at it again! Only this time we used her bed! It was a riot…people were knocking on the door and going away all mad, but she didn't care. Hell no. She even gave me a cup of the best cappuccino I've ever had before she let me out the back way!

"So that got me started with the widows of Italy, and I've done pretty well. Laundries and small stores are the best places to look."

"Billy, you are some lucky bastard!" says Pete. "Shit, man, everyone in this damn army is horny as hell and just dying to get laid, and you've got one in every bloody town!"

"Well, not quite, but yeah, it has been good. But hey Pete, let's just keep it to ourselves. OK?"

Billy gets up, says "See yah guys," and leaves two thoroughly depressed medicals mumbling into their coffee.

September 23 – September 30, 1943

War Diary

This very quiet period was spent in Potenza. We continued to be with 9 Cdn Fd Amb and did a small amount of work averaging a little over one case a day. Until 29 Sep the town of Potenza was out of bounds to all troops and men of the unit were confined to barracks, which added to the boredom. The weather is now quite cool and on the night of the 28th there was a violent thunderstorm accompanied by much rain.

Tuesday, September 28, 1943

Frank Mills tells Rocke over tea that he has had an interesting visit with the 1st British Field Surgical Unit that is also staying in Potenza. They had similar experiences to the Canadian FSUs in Sicily, but were chagrined to have to report that none of their abdominal cases in Sicily had recovered. They gave as reasons the extremely unsanitary conditions for surgery and the occasional need to move abdominal patients too soon.

Rocke gulps his tea and prays silently that he will soon receive some sort of communication from Private Jon Robson, his last surgical patient in Sicily, saying that he is OK.

46. BATTLING UP THE BOOT

The fighting gets tougher as the Allies move north.

October – November, 1943

At the start of October the Allies held a line extending from sea to sea roughly north of Naples to the west and Foggia to the east, but bulging considerably southward in the central region. On the eastern flank forces of the British 5th Corps occupied most of the vital Foggia plain, and patrols from the 2nd Canadian Infantry Brigade had entered Melfi on September 27. British 5th Division troops were probing the area further to the west and maintaining contact with the U.S. 5th Army around Naples. The British were developing the Taranto area as the 8th Army supply base in place of Reggio.

Several factors now made the Allied attack even more difficult than it had been to date. The first was the terrain. There were the rough, mountainous regions up to and then beyond the Foggia plain, and they were faced with a series of rivers running northeast across the country to the Adriatic Sea. These all had to be crossed and some of them posed serious obstacles, particularly the more northern rivers such as the Sangro and the Moro.

A second problem was the weather. As the fall turned into winter there were cold and torrential rains. This contributed to miserable living conditions for the soldiers, bogged down transport and even movement by foot in fields of mud, and turned rivers that should be easily bridged into near-impassable torrents.

And then there was the enemy. The Germans were now offering increasingly stubborn resistance, making skilled use of the numerous defensive advantages conferred by the terrain and weather, and retiring only under strong pressure. Hitler had ordered them to defend Rome at all costs, and that meant holding the line across Italy, from Rome to Pescara. Their reinforcements were battle-hardened paratroopers.

With Rome remaining their principal objective, the Allied command decided that the 8th Army should now seize the line from Campobasso to Termoli, roughly along the Biferno River. This would be a major step on the way to Pescara. The 13th Corps was to launch an attack from the Foggia plain with the 1st Canadian Division and the 78th British Division, each supported by armour. The Canadians were to advance through the difficult mountainous region to the west and capture the two important towns of Vinchiaturo and Campobasso, while the British moved on Termoli by land and sea along the coast.

The main body of Canadians moved from the Potenza - Melfi area on September 30 to concentrate with the 1st Infantry Brigade along the southeastern edge of the Foggia plain southward of Canosa. On October 1 the 1st Brigade, preceded by a strong advance guard that included the 14th Tank Regiment, surged forward across the plain to take the main road to Campobasso through Lucera and Volturara. Behind it was the 2nd Brigade, which was to strike off over secondary routes and open country to secure Vinchiaturo and thus approach Campobasso from the south. The 3rd Brigade was held in reserve for the moment.

The Canadian Division had hard fighting before finally capturing Campobasso on October 14. They then continued on through the latter half of October to drive the enemy beyond the Biferno River so that they would be out of artillery range of Campobasso, which had been designated as a major administrative centre for the Allies. Most of November was relatively quiet, though they maintained constant pressure on the enemy. In the latter half of the month the 3rd Canadian Infantry Brigade joined elements of the British 5th Infantry Division and the 8th Indian Division in a diversionary mission along the upper Sangro River, one purpose of which was to mask the preparations being made for a full-scale British attack across the lower Sangro River through Ortona to Pescara. General Montgomery hoped that this action would draw substantial German forces away from the more important coastal area.

On November 28 Montgomery launched the assault north along the coast, involving the British 78th Division and, farther inland, the 8th Indian Division and the 2nd New Zealand Division, supported by the British 4th Armoured Brigade. They battled their way across the Sangro River, and then met ever-increasing resistance as the Germans rushed troops back from the diversionary action to the west. The Germans withdrew reluctantly, making their next determined stand in entrenched positions on the northern ridge of the Moro River valley, seven miles north of the Sangro.

The stiffening enemy resistance encountered by the Canadians during the drive to Campobasso was reflected in the casualty figures. From October 1 to 15 there were 147 Canadians killed and 401 wounded. Clearing the banks of the Biferno cost a further 251 casualties, 58 of them fatal. In November the toll dropped to 39 killed and 102 wounded. Sickness continued to present huge medical problems. In October there were just under 2,600 non-battle casualties in the Division, and in November almost 1,900, mostly cases of undiagnosed fever, malaria and infectious hepatitis (jaundice). As the main reinforcement pool was still far to the rear this meant that every effort had to be made to cure the sick within a reasonable period of time.

In response to this crisis the ADMS sent No.5 Field Ambulance forward on October 1 to Lucera, near Foggia, to establish a post in a large school building to handle fever and jaundice cases. They stayed at that location throughout October and November. He managed the other medical units in a complex, fast-moving wave of activity across the Foggia plain and up to Campobasso and the surrounding area.

No.4 Field Ambulance acted as an Advanced Dressing Station to deal with casualties from all three infantry brigades. It set up first at Lucera on October 1, and over the next two weeks moved to Motta Montecorvino, Volturara and then Riccia, before finally settling in Campobasso on October 20. 2CFSU moved up from Potenza to join it at each stop after Lucera: on October 3 at Motta Montecorvino, on October 10 at Volturara, on October 12 at Riccia, and finally at Campobasso on October 20.

The Canadians were now fighting close to the British forces, and in many cases replacing them in the lines and medical responsibilities. In response to a direct request from the British Deputy Director Medical Services (DDMS) for the 13th Corps, No.2 Field Dressing Station, No.1 Field Surgical Unit and No.1 Field Transfusion Unit were ordered to Foggia on the night of October 5 to assist the British medical units there in handling the casualties suffered in the fighting around Termoli. In two days Frank Mills' team carried out an incredible 31 operations.

No.1 Field Dressing Station joined the Advanced Surgical Centre in Motta Montecorvino on October 5, working with 2CFSU and replacing No.4 Field Ambulance, which moved on to Volturara. No.1 Field Surgical Unit and No.1 Field Transfusion Unit then moved to Motta Montecorvino on October 8 directly from Foggia to support 2CFSU and No.1 Field Dressing Station there. These 4 units then moved to Volturara and set up their Canadian Medical

Centre in an old monastery. No.4 Field Ambulance was still there, but moved two days later to Riccia.

This left No.2 Field Dressing Station at Foggia to handle a very large number of post-operative and other cases already there, and also flowing in from the fighting. Its war diary on October 8 said that it had just completed 'the hardest task that the unit had undertaken', having admitted 269 patients in under two days.

A reserve company of No.9 Field Ambulance moved on October 8 to Castelfranco, directly south of Campobasso, to provide a casualty clearing service from the 2nd Infantry Brigade to the southern evacuation route.

On October 15 the ADMS started to concentrate his units in Campobasso, the major town in the Matese mountains that was designated as the administrative centre for the Allies in southeastern Italy. No.9 Field Ambulance and No.1 Field Surgical Unit arrived there on October 15, No.1 Field Transfusion Unit on the 16th, No.4 Field Ambulance and 2CFSU on the 20th and No.2 Field Dressing Station on the 22nd. All Canadian casualties were now collected there, and Campobasso soon had a constant population of patients of around 300. Evacuation back from Campobasso was effected by the volunteer American Field Service Ambulance Company, and then by a British motor ambulance convoy.

The No.2 Light Field Ambulance, responsible for supporting the tank units, had a difficult time fulfilling its intended role due to the wide dispersion of the tank regiments. They established dressing stations as best they could to serve the units, near Foggia, and then near Iesi and later at Riccia.

During November the only medical development of interest was the dispatch of No.4 Field Ambulance and 2CFSU to the upper Sangro River with the 3rd Infantry Brigade taking part in General Montgomery's diversionary attack. Their Advanced Dressing Station was at Civitanova, whence casualties were sent back 40 miles to Campobasso.

47. MOTTA MONTECORVINO

Working in a tiny village. Frank Mills describes his 48-hour operating marathon.

Saturday, October 2, 1943

The quiet time in Potenza continues. Word is that the troops are moving ahead smartly, so the urgent work is going to have to be done farther up the line.

Rocke visits driver Victor Kraft who has been confined to his bed for several days with a rising temperature and developing symptoms of infectious hepatitis. A close examination confirms the diagnosis. Rocke arranges for Kraft's evacuation to Sicily and submits a request to ADMS Headquarters for a replacement driver. Krafty is sorry to leave, but is consoled by the thought that at least he has worked closely with the other drivers and they are all good at mechanical work on the vehicles. He knows he has done a good job.

At 1630hrs orders come in from the ADMS for all units at Potenza to move up as soon as possible. Rocke rolls out a map and briefs his team. "The ADMS wants us all to get up much closer to the fighting, which has already moved past the Foggia plain. So we're all going up to Foggia or past it. We'll get our specific orders when we reach ADMS headquarters near Foggia. No.4 Field Ambulance is up at Lucera already, and No.5 Field Ambulance is on the way to Lucera where they're going to handle all of the fever and jaundice cases, and there are a lot of them right now. You've seen what happened to Krafty.

"So gentlemen, I know that you're going to miss the wonders of Potenza, but let's get cracking. We'll make an early night of it and get on the road early tomorrow morning."

Sunday, October 3, 1943

The 2CFSU team is up at 0400hrs and manages to hit the road at 0515hrs, just ahead of the other medical units. The three vehicles are in great working order thanks to the rest in Potenza and the ceaseless ministrations of the drivers, and they make good time on the road north. There is one short diversion through a riverbed around a blown bridge, but otherwise the trip is uneventful.

Andre Boucher drives the utility vehicle, replacing Pete Monroe who has taken on the surgical van. Andre is not a professional driver, but claims that if he can drive in Montreal he can certainly drive in Italy. Rocke is in the surgical van with Pete. It is cold in the early morning and the heater provides a welcome blast of warm air. Rocke lights cigarettes for them both and hands one to Pete.

"You fellows have the vehicles in great running order, Pete," says Rocke. "I know you've had a lot of problems with them, but you've done a great job."

"Yes Sir, thank you. These babies are pretty tricky to fix up. They're basic stuff, sort of rugged but easy to mess up too. I guess Krafty and I must have rebuilt the engine in this van about 3 times, more or less! But I love it. This is one important piece of equipment, and I'm damn proud of it."

"That's good, Pete. I think we're all proud of the job we're doing. How do you like it…being in the medical service, that is?"

"It's OK, Sir. You know, sometimes I wish I was up front with the troops taking shots at the Germans, but then when I see them coming in wounded I'm pretty happy to be doing this. It damn near makes me sick to see the mess some of them are in. I've sort of gotten used to it, but it actually gives me nightmares sometimes. And hell, I'm not even working with them like the orderlies or you folks in the OR! How about you, Sir? How do you feel about it?"

"About the same as you do, Pete. I just can't stand to see men wounded and in pain. It seems so crazy that people would do such things to each other, and it makes me mad! But they do, and so I look at ours as a job that has to be done, and I've had the training that lets me do it. Mind you, as a surgeon it's a great experience. I've done more work over here on wounds and fractures and other serious stuff than I would have in years at home. And of course we're doing it in some pretty tough conditions, so we have to use our heads and our imaginations, and that's good too."

"Do you ever have nightmares about the wounded?"

"Maybe not nightmares, but rough dreams – yes. You know, people think that doctors don't worry about seeing awful wounds and disease – that it's just part of our job. Well, it is our job, but most of us hate to see bad wounds. We know what the patient is going through, and that's what let's us do what we do. We know that with our training we can help out, so we do. But we're not immune to it. And I'll tell you, the toughest cases of all are the children like that lad back at Reggio. They're totally innocent. All they want to do is play, and they get injured or even killed for it."

Pete is quiet for a minute as he steers around a pile of rubble on the road and checks his mirrors to be sure the others are keeping up. He is being especially careful about the small utility vehicle where Andre Boucher is at the wheel. Then: "That's interesting, Sir. So you doctors are actually human!" They laugh.

They wind down from the mountains, skirt around Melfi, and at 1530hrs reach the ADMS headquarters on the outskirts of Foggia. Rocke finds Colonel Playfair in a talkative mood, clearly excited and on edge about the moves now going on.

"I've sent Peter Tisdale and his No.4 FA over to Motta Montecorvino, and I'd like you to join him straight away. That'll give us surgical capability right up close to the fighting, and I'm afraid we're going to need it as our troops continue the drive to Campobasso. As soon as Doug Sparling's No.1 FDS can get up to Motta he'll replace the Field Ambulance who can then move on somewhere else. I haven't decided on that next move yet."

"Right sir," replied Rocke. "Can you tell me where Frank Mills will be going?

"Frank and the FTU are going to work with the No.2 Field Dressing Station right here in Foggia. There's a real load of casualties coming in, mainly Brits from the fighting at Termoli out on the coast. Their DDMS himself has asked for our help, which makes me feel good. But as soon as they can get the situation under control I'll be moving our three units up closer to you as well."

"It's a bit of a chess game, isn't it sir!"

"That it is, Rocke. A very big one, and it's going to get a lot bigger soon. The sickness business really has me worried. I hate having the Field Ambulance at Lucera tied up treating fever and other ailments, but there's no way around it." He pauses to light a cigarette. Then: "Anyway, enough of that. The Sergeant will give you a new map on the way out. Off you go and good luck."

Rocke heads back to his vehicles, passing Frank Mills who has just arrived for his orders. The 2CFSU convoy drives through Lucera and across the Foggia plain towards the mountains. As they approach the foothills they see two very small towns sitting on the tops of hills. The one on the right is Motta Montecorvino. The slightly larger one on the left is Volturino. They turn off to the right at the sign pointing to Motta. The road starts to climb, and after a numbing series of switchbacks they arrive at Motta at 1745hrs. There are numerous signs of war along the way, but they are unimpeded and arrive without delay or incident.

Motta is tiny and dull, a small grouping of houses along the roadside. The vehicles of No.4 Field Ambulance are parked in front of a house that is quite modern and remarkably intact from the shelling except for one room that is riddled with shells. The FA staff are still unloading the vehicles and preparing the house for use as the medical centre, and there are already around 20 casualties waiting for attention.

Rocke and Jack leave Eric to supervise the unloading and set-up of the OR and post-op ward, and of their sleeping quarters in a similar abandoned house next door, and join Peter Tisdale in the examination of the casualties. There are a variety of minor wounds, six cases of fever, and one serious case – a soldier from the Royal Canadian Regiment with a badly torn abdomen. They start operating on him at 2130hrs and finish on the stroke of midnight.

October 4 - 8, 1943

The weather is turning bad. There is almost continuous rain, and cold winds whistle through the holes in the wall of the room in the medical centre that had been riddled with machine gun fire. Soon there is mud everywhere. The situation is totally different from Sicily where the problems were heat and dryness and dust and flies. Here there are flies, but now the main problems are cold and mud and a pervasive dampness. Every person entering the centre tracks in mud and often sprays of rainwater. The wounded who are brought in are often covered in mud, soaked and shivering with cold. The cleaning details for the orderlies and drivers are endless, and the doctors turn their attention to the important issue of keeping their patients warm. They had better get good at it, because this is just the fore-taste of the Italian winter.

On October 5, No.1 Field Dressing Station joins them in Motta, re-placing No. 4 Field Ambulance that immediately moves up to Volturara. Doug Sparling tells Rocke that he has heard that Frank Mills is looking at a landslide of work back at Foggia, with a heavy stream of wounded coming in from the fighting at Termoli. He is right.

Frank Mills' War Diary

October 5, 1943
Order received at 2300hrs to proceed to 132 Fd Amb (Br) located in an old hospital in Foggia. Started to work at 0130hrs and did six cases between then and 0700hrs. No.2 British FSU was there and continued to carry on after we left. No.1 FSU moved to 2 FDS about half a mile from where the English Ambulance was located and set up there.

October 6, 1943
Major Mills did a bowel resection at the RAF hospital in Foggia. Started to work at the FDS at 1930hrs and worked through the night. Cases were from the 78ᵗʰ British Div, which had run into troublesome German opposition near Termoli on the east coast.

October 7, 1943
Worked all day and night. A good assortment of cases presented themselves at the FDS. Rained copious amounts.

October 8, 1943
Finished working at 0130hrs having finished 48 hr stretch straight through. Visited by the DDMS 13ᵗʰ Corps. Did 31 cases while in Foggia. At 1500hrs moved to 1 Cdn FDS at Motta Montecorvino where we joined No.2 FSU. We are to alternate with them, work-ing 24-hour stretches.

On October 8 No.1 Field Surgical Unit and No.1 Field Transfusion Unit pull up outside the medical centre in Motta. Both teams are totally exhausted from their marathon operating schedule at Foggia. "I think I have the world record," Frank tells Rocke. "Thirty-one operations in two days, for heaven's sake! We worked for 48 hours straight. The cases were all Brits from the 78th Division, who seem to be having a tough time over on the coast near Termoli. The Germans are really starting to tighten up now. I think we'll be seeing a lot more work from now on.

"And you should see what Bill Clendinnen and his people are going through. They've had a great long queue of wounded and sick lined up for admission at their station in Foggia for the past several days. I think they've taken in almost 300 patients in two days! They're all absolutely fagged out back there."

"I'll bet they are," says Rocke. "And you look pretty tired yourself. I suggest you fellows get some rest. We'll handle things until you feel a bit better, and then we can see how we split up the work. I've been thinking that it might be best for us to work 24-hour shifts, starting at 1800hrs. Jack and I have talked it over and think that it would be worth a try. I think it would be better than working just all night or all day, and with an occasional catnap we should be able to do it. What do you think?"

"Sure, let's give it a try, Rocke...as long as you start today!"

There is work for the surgeons, averaging about 5 operations a day. That plus consultations, post-operative work and help with the sick keeps them busy, which is good because there is nothing else to do in tiny Motta Montecorvino. The only diversion is the current resident population of 45 people who have welcomed the Canadians as saviours. They are desperately short of food and very hungry, so Doug Sparling orders his cooks to supply them with whatever food they can spare. There is also one civilian casualty who visits the centre. He is one of the several young men who went into hiding a month ago to escape the German work details. He almost starved during the month, and then broke his ankle climbing out of his cavern when he knew the Germans had left. He seems more embarrassed than hurt when his friends bring him in, but the break requires setting and a cast, and he is grateful for the help. He devours a bowl of soup while his cast is drying.

Saturday, October 9, 1943

At 1000hrs the ADMS, Colonel Playfair arrives at the medical centre in Motta and meets with the commanding officers of the units there: Rocke and Frank Mills of the FSUs, Doug Sparling of No.1 Field Dressing Station and Wally Scott of the Field Transfusion Unit.

"You fellows are doing great work. I'm proud of you all. Frank and Wally, the Brits were extremely grateful for your work back at Foggia. You seem to have developed a bit of a reputation there. Well done! And Bill Clendinnen would like to send his greetings, but he's too damn busy to do so! He has close to 400 patients there now, most of them sick with malaria or jaundice, but also quite a few wounded from the action up ahead. This sickness business is no joke. I have No.5 Field Ambulance settled down at Lucera and that's about all they are doing – handling fever and jaundice cases. They are absolutely swamped, and I don't know when I'm going to be able to move them up closer to the action. One of the most important problems, of course, is that it's such a long way back to the Casualty Clearing Stations and the hospitals. The ambulances are going flat out but the evacuation is a mighty slow process.

"Anyway, we're here and now, and it's time for you fellows to move up again. The troops are moving slowly on Campobasso." He points out this strategic town on his map. "It's a good location for a medical centre. The idea is that we'll clear it out, and also push the Germans back over the Biferno River so that we'll be safe from any artillery action. This is going to take a while as the Germans are really digging in, but we will certainly get there."

"Sir," says Frank, "how far do you think this offensive will go with the weather closing in the way it is? It's a terrible mess out there now, and it's going to get a lot worse. Pretty soon the tanks are going to start bogging down, and so will the men. Is there any thought of shutting down for the winter?"

"I don't think so, Frank. Monty seems to really have the bit in his teeth. The story is that he's frustrated with the slow progress we've been able to make moving up to the Pescara-Rome line. He wants to be at least at Pescara so that we can launch a spring offensive on Rome from there as well as from the south. But he didn't bank on this early winter weather. We have not only the mud, but also a bunch of rivers that are swollen and bloody difficult to cross in this weather. And of course, they're easy to defend too.

246 ∴ WHILE BULLETS FLY

The Brits have had a terrible time crossing the Biferno south of Termoli, and then there's the Triono and the Sangro and the Moro before we even get to Ortona. Those plus lots of smaller rivers. So I think the answer is no, there won't be any winter vacations for us.

'I'd like you fellows to move forward tomorrow to Volturara. It's only a few miles up the road, but it'll put you right on the road to Campobasso with easier access to the troops. I'm told that there's a nice cozy monastery for you to set up in. Peter Tisdale is already there enjoying himself. So finish up your cases here today. I've instructed Basil Bowman's ambulance team, back at Castelfranco, to come up later today and start clearing out your patients from here. Doug, you may have to leave a small nest here for a couple of days until this evacuation is completed, but I'd like you all up at Volturara as soon as possible.

"Now, something to watch out for is an increase in the number of civilian patients. The closer we get to the areas that the Germans are determined to defend, the worse off the locals are going to be. Evidently the men are being pressed into slave labour building defensive positions, and the Germans have taken damn near all the food. Lots of people are in hiding, and some of them are getting themselves killed on mines when they come out looking for food. So you're going to see some wounded and starving people coming in to see you. I don't need to tell you that they deserve a warm welcome. They've been through hell."

The ADMS departs and the medicals go back to work. The Commanders brief their teams, and the job of packing up begins in a day in which no new cases arrive. Eric directs his team through the process of cleaning, organizing and packing their equipment and supplies into the three vehicles. They are now fully equipped and supplied, and everything fits snugly into its appointed place. Eric stands next to the vans to be sure that not one scrap of mud gets inside.

The last patient at the centre is a private from the Royal Canadian Regiment who has been shot in the liver. Frank Mills is on duty and operates at 0200hrs in the morning of October 10.

48. VOLTURARA

Operating in a monastery.

Sunday, October 10, 1943

No.1 Field Dressing Station, No.1 Field Surgical Unit and No.1 Field Transfusion Unit depart at 0900hrs and drive the eight miles to Volturara. The 2CFSU team follows two hours later, leaving a small nest of FDS staff to look after the 23 patients remaining in Motta, pending their evacuation. The road to Volturara is the worst they have encountered –so steep and narrow that on several occasions they have to stop the larger vehicles and take several tries before making it around the switchbacks. They cover the eight miles in one hour.

Sure enough, their new location is a large monastery, with a chapel and a number of other buildings. The monastery was deserted several months ago, but for some reason has not been looted. The No.4 FA crew has done a good job cleaning it up, so it is easy for the arriving teams to move in and prepare for action. They have turned the chapel into a large ward, and it currently holds about 50 patients. Other buildings are set up as wards, and one large dormitory building houses the medical teams. The kitchen is huge and ancient, and an interesting challenge for the FDS kitchen staff.

They set up the OR in a large, airy room attached to the chapel so that it is convenient to the large ward. The electricity does not work so they set up the generators. Fortunately the water system does work. As is their agreed practice the first FSU to arrive sets up the OR with their own equipment, instruments and supplies, and is ready for work as soon as possible. Thus Frank Mills is ready to go by the time Rocke arrives, and they agree to continue on the same 24-hour schedule. The 2CFSU team takes over at 1800hrs, bringing their own instruments and supplies with them, but using the equipment installed by No.1 FSU.

There are no new cases, so Rocke's team has time to go over the patients in the wards and help out as requested.

October 11-12, 1943

The 2CFSU does one abdominal case in the late afternoon, and then the No.1 FSU team takes over. They handle a moderate but steady inflow of patients over their 24-hour shift, including four abdominal cases and five cases involving extremities – wounded arms and legs. The patients are all muddy and cold, shivering in the chilly fall air and the damp interior of the unheated monastery. The most unfortunate is an officer with both feet irreparably damaged. There is just nothing to be saved, and they amputate them both. One of the orderlies is weeping with rage as he wheels the unfortunate man out of the OR.

The rest of the team is not feeling any better. This has been the last operation of their shift. They are tired beyond understanding, not just from this shift, but also from the lingering effect of their 48-hour marathon session back at Foggia. They all feel the tragedy of this operation, and they can think of nothing to say about it. They clean up silently, and then Frank tells them to go and get some food and then lots of sleep.

Frank wanders through the courtyard of the monastery in the early evening mist, the light rain falling lightly on him completely unnoticed. He enters the canteen and gets a mug of tea. Several groups call for him to join them, but he shakes his head and sits down in a quiet corner. He stares at the steam rising from his tea, his chin resting in his hand, his eyes half closed. Frank is totally exhausted and close to the dark edge of despair. This last damn, bloody operation has knocked him back. All he can see is gloom and blood and hopeless pain and sorrow. He starts to think about the Lieutenant who has lost his feet. His name is Broderick. He comes from Alberta, and he was still playing hockey when he joined the army. *Now what the hell is he going to do...the poor guy is...*

"Sir," says a voice close to his ear. He turns to find his batman Tuff Wallace standing beside him with a very worried look on his face. "Sir, I've asked Major Robertson to come over to see you. He's just returned from a trip back to Motta to check on our patients still there. He's picking up his tea now." Rocke appears beside the table as if by magic. As he sits down he turns to Wallace and says "Tuff, there's a bottle of brandy in my kit bag in my room. Would you please get it for me?" Tuff hurries away and Rocke turns to Frank.

"I've heard about your last case, Frank. What a terrible sadness! You must be feeling pretty down about it."

Frank looks up at Rocke, who is looking back at him with a concerned, tentative look in his eyes. Frank also notices people at other tables glancing at him and perhaps listening in. He doesn't give a shit.

"It's bad, Rocke. It's bad. The war is just plain bad, and I don't think it'll ever end. All we're ever going to see is mud and blood and rain and stumps of legs. I'm finding it damn hard to take just right now."

"Listen Frank, I…"

"Jesus, man, this is the worst I've seen! Ever. Anytime. You and I have seen almost everything over these past few months. Torn up stomachs and crushed legs and guys burned and blasted to pieces. There was a poor Brit back at Foggia who had his balls shot off, and I thought that was as bad as it gets. But I don't know…that poor guy today! When I finished those two stumps I just thought *what the bloody hell is this anyway? Why is this happening?* Here was a young, tough guy, a good officer and a good athlete, and now he has to spend the rest of his life on stumps, for Christ's sake. In a wheel chair. That's if he lives, of course. And hell, I don't know if he'll want to live after this. It's tough enjoying life when you're flat on your ass, you know. And he's an athlete. Good luck! "

He is interrupted by Wallace returning with the bottle of brandy. Rocke thanks him and asks him to move to another table but to stick around.

"I know how you feel. It's just so damn tragic, and there's nothing we can do about it but just keep working. Here, have a shot of this stuff. It'll do you good." He pours a huge shot into Frank's tea, and a small shot into his own. They sip their tea. Then Frank takes a mouthful, winces, and swallows it down.

"I know, I know. But it's just such an awful battle all the time. My guys are just about out of it they're so tired, and those wounded just keep on rolling in, and we know that we have to deal with them now, right bloody now." He takes another big gulp of his tea.

Frank's words are like hammer blows on Rocke's ears. He is not feeling all that swift himself, but he sees in his friend the dangerous start of serious depression, brought on by stress and nourished by exhaustion. Frank Mills is as tough a man as Rocke has ever met, but every man has his limits, and Frank has reached his. Foggia was obviously the straw that broke his back.

"That's right Frank, and we do. Now listen, you fellows are still recovering from that 48-hour session you had in Foggia. You were beat after that and should have taken more time to rest at Motta. Well, you'd better take more time to catch up now, because it's not going to get any easier for us, and we can't handle it if you're not your usual lively self."

"Oh, I'll be OK. It's just that..."

"Right, Frank. You will be. But now that you've had a nice sleeping pill it's time you went to bed." He calls Wallace over to the table.

"Wallace, please escort Major Mills to his room. See that he gets to bed right away, and that nobody disturbs him until tomorrow."

He turns to Frank. "OK pal, off you go. You'll be good as new tomorrow."

Frank gets up, mumbles his thanks for the drink, and moves away under the guidance of Tuff Wallace. They cross the courtyard to the dormitory building. Frank has a brief pee stop on the way to his room. He takes off his trousers, sits down on the bed to take off his boots, and lies out flat on his back. He is snoring loudly by the time Wallace can get a blanket over him. He sleeps without moving for the next 18 hours.

Rocke stays put in the canteen, sipping his tea and fighting an intense internal battle with despair. Until this moment he has not realized how important the sense of teamwork and camaraderie is to his own strength and ability to do the demanding job expected of him. Frank has become a close and valuable friend. They support each other in handling caseloads, share ideas, instruments and equipment, and drink together. This is not a good time to lose Frank. But...what if Frank can't sleep and breaks down? What then?

He has had feelings similar to the ones just expressed by Frank, but so far not as strongly. There is a sense of helplessness and despair that creeps up on him sometimes after a long day of operating. It comes at him as a feeling that...*this will never end; every day of my life when I wake up there will be a long line of groaning, bleeding soldiers waiting to be saved. Blood everywhere, and pain, pain, pain...* He has always managed to overcome it, usually by simply sleeping and regaining his strength and, with it, renewed sense of purpose. He just hopes that Frank can pull out of it. He has actually worried about Frank ever since he heard about the marathon session in Foggia. It is simply not possible to go through something like that and then just carry on normally. Frank and his team seemed to do so, but as it turns out they were relying more and more on adrenalin, and the horror of this last operation exhausted even that.

49. RICCIA

A silly little post with little to do.

McKenzie finds Rocke deep in thought in the canteen and tells him that No.4 Field Ambulance is ready to move out. They go outside and bid farewell to the FA, which is moving forward to a place called Riccia. The town is just 25 miles from Campobasso, which is now under active assault by the Canadian forces. This places the Field Ambulance in a convenient position to provide direct support to the troops entering Campobasso, and also moving the wounded swiftly back down the line of evacuation past Volturara and Lucera.

There are no immediate surgical cases for them, so they start ward rounds and a slate of post-operative procedures. Rocke comes to the bed where Lieutenant Broderick is still sleeping peacefully, unaware of the fate that awaits him. He knows that much of the post-op work with Roderick will be simply keeping up his will to live.

The 2CFSU does four operations that night, interspersed with a two-hour break to watch a movie shown by the Field Dressing Station.

Wednesday, October 13, 1943

The morning is quiet for the 2CFSU. Around 1230hrs Frank wanders into the wards and greets Rocke like his old self. "Many thanks Rocke," he says. "I really did need that sleep, and your superb cognac (big wink) helped a lot!"

"How are the rest of your men?"

"I think we're all just fine, thanks. In fact, we're planning to put on a big Thanksgiving dinner this evening. The FDS is helping us cook a turkey and a chicken and pie and all sorts of goodies. Would you chaps like to join in?"

"That would be great. Many thanks. Let's get McKenzie and Wallace together to sort things out."

Unfortunately for these plans a call comes through an hour later for the 2CFSU to move up to Riccia to join No.4 Field Ambulance. They express their regrets and pack immediately while Frank's team takes over surgery duty. The 2CFSU team say a fond farewell to the monastery at Volturara at around 1515hrs and arrive at Riccia at 1730hrs.

Riccia is a small, quite primitive village well off the main road between Volturara and Campobasso. It has been badly damaged, and as usual the local citizens are just now starting to creep out of their hiding places to welcome the liberators. At first glance there seems to be no food in the village, but secret stores of food are starting to appear.

Once again the medicals are housed in an abandoned schoolhouse, but this one is in very sad shape. It has been ransacked by the locals and is battered and dirty. The electricity and water systems are inoperable, forcing the medical units to fire up their generators and to rely on water from the village well.

The Field Ambulance has allocated a large, gloomy room as the operating room in the building, and it takes two hours of hard cleaning by the drivers and OR assistants to bring it to an adequate level of cleanliness. The drivers carry out their usual Fly Patrol, continuing on to other parts of the building as requested by Major Tisdale of the Field Ambulance. By 2030hrs they have a light dinner served up efficiently by the Field Ambulance kitchen. They can't help thinking of the turkey dinner currently being enjoyed back down the road.

Just as they are finishing dinner a jeep rolls up and lets out a newcomer to the unit. He reports to Rocke as Private Sammy Smart, here to replace driver Victor Kraft. The team welcomes him, and Eric takes him off to brief him and show him the vehicles. As the evening progresses Peter Tisdale keeps up on the progress of the war via his wireless set, making frequent announcements. It seems that the Canadian 1st Infantry Brigade has reached the outskirts of Campobasso, and there is fierce fighting as they move into the town. There is only one surgical case to be done during the night.

October 14-19, 1943

In spite of all the reports of heavy fighting just ahead, there is very little for the 2CFSU team to do. The medical centre in Riccia has been set up mainly to support the 3rd Infantry Brigade, which is still being kept in reserve, so there are few problems for them to deal with. They average about one operation a day and are bored silly. Riccia has little to offer in the way of diversion, and there is only so much they can do repairing and cleaning their equipment. Campobasso has fallen on the 14th, and they hope that they will be sent there soon. On October 15 they learn that No.1 FSU is moving up to Campobasso, with No.1 Field Transfusion Unit to follow soon thereafter, to a building already opened up by No.9 Field Ambulance.

On the same day the No.2 Light Field Ambulance, serving the tank brigades, sets up in Riccia. It has been having a difficult time as the three tank brigades, the Ontario Tanks, Calgary Tanks and Three Rivers Tanks, have been widely dispersed in different actions. For this reason tank crews wounded in battle are generally served by the medical groups of the infantry regiments that the tanks are supporting. At present No.2 LFA is dealing mainly with patients from the tank brigades that are not committed to action.

They hear that Campobasso is still subject to intermittent German artillery fire, with some shells landing very close to the medical centre. On Sunday the Field Ambulance radio reports on a great church parade in Campobasso, with detachments of the 2nd Canadian Infantry Brigade and a squadron of tanks adding to the show. It is reported as a real celebration for the Italians, freed at last from the German occupation.

On the 18th Rocke, Jack and four others from the 2CFSU drive up to Campobasso to visit the Canadian Medical Centre there. The town is in a shocking state, with rubble everywhere and very few buildings intact. There are, however, already signs of renewed life as local citizens walk the streets greeting the Canadians with smiles, tend their wrecked properties, search for lost articles and mementos, and open their shops and bring out hidden supplies to sell to the depleted population. There is a feeling of hope in the air in spite of the occasional explosions of artillery shells and the ear-splitting responses from the Canadian guns stationed on the outskirts of the town.

The Canadian Medical Centre is located in a large college building, and there are several side buildings on the modest campus. No.9 Field Ambulance has commandeered one of the side buildings that overlook the large parking lot for its operations. Sleeping quarters for all are in the second side building. In the main building there is a lot of space that Major Mills, Colonel Bowman and Captain Scott have divided up logically into a substantial hospital facility, anticipating the arrival of a Field Dressing Station and 2CFSU, at a minimum. Rocke finds the operating theatre the best he has seen so far – large and bright, well supplied with electricity and water, and already spotlessly clean. He catches Frank between operations and they have a mug of tea in the canteen while Rocke's colleagues tour the whole facility.

"We've been quite busy here," says Frank. "Nothing like it was back at Foggia, mind you, but five or six operations a day and lots of post-op work to do, plus helping the Field Ambulance to screen its customers as they come in. We're seeing quite a number of German prisoners now, and of course there's the usual line of locals…you probably saw them when you came in."

"That I did. This seems like a really good set-up. The OR is terrific. I envy you the work. We have nothing to do back in Riccia and it's really getting on our nerves. I take it we're there to support the 3rd Infantry Brigade, but they aren't sending us many patients."

"Yes, well I think you'll be up here soon, and we can get back on our shifts. There's a few bars and restaurants opening up or almost open in this town, and Basil is making sure that there will be an officers' club soon, so it's a pretty good place to be. An army chap told me yesterday that the idea is to make this a Canadian leave centre, as it's likely that we'll all be around here for quite awhile. It'll be OK once they can move those damn German guns out of range! And of course, when they can drum up a lot more women!"

"Well, if it's women you're after don't come to Riccia. I've only seen one since we arrived there, and she was older than my mother."

"Send her here. We're going to need all we can get! Actually it's no joke. Our whole army has been on the road for several months now without hardly even a look at a woman, and lots of the men are going crazy. Not to mention the officers! It's classic, isn't it? You know exactly what will happen. More and more local women will be drawn into prostitution, and there'll be lots of messing around, and the VD unit will be up to its ass in business."

"Absolutely right, Frank. And there's not a damn thing we can do about it."

"I know. Oh listen, Rocke, I haven't told you, Brigadier Arnott, DDMS of the British 13th Corps, visited us a few days ago. He was very thankful for the work we did for them at Foggia, but he did say that after we left some of our abdominal cases were moved back to the Casualty Clearing Station too soon, and were in pretty bad shape as a result. He was reminding us of the one-week rule...politely of course, as it was their chaps who actually moved them too soon. Which reminds me, have you heard from that Brit you had to move out of Agira because of the flies?"

"Not yet, so I'm really starting to worry. I know I did the right thing getting him away from the flies, but still, I wish I didn't have to do it."

"Well Rocke, maybe he's just a lousy correspondent."

50. CAMPOBASSO

Back to the big time in a major Canadian centre.
Jack Leishman gets jaundice.

Wednesday, October 20, 1943

At last! Orders arrive for No.4 Field ambulance and 2CFSU to move to Campobasso. Major Tisdale is as pleased as Rocke is at this move as his people have been as bored as Rocke's in the Riccia backwater. They pack up everything except for enough supplies and equipment to maintain a small nest of patients still not ready to move, presided over by a group of unhappy Field Ambulance staff. The medical convoy departs Riccia, waved off by a few grateful citizens, and arrives at the Campobasso Canadian Medical Centre at 1745hrs.

Rocke and Frank agree to their 24-hour shift routine, but starting at 0800hrs each day. No.1 FSU will continue its present work, and 2CFSU will start at 0800hrs tomorrow. Frank's team has set up a very efficient OR, so 2CFSU can leave much of their equipment in the van.

Thursday, October 21, 1943

Colonel Playfair, the ADMS, pulls up to the Campobasso Canadian Medical Centre at 1015hrs and is met by Colonel Bowman, the senior officer at the centre. Bowman escorts him on a tour of the facility, and then they join all of the officers in the canteen for briefings and discussion.

"You have noticed that the German shelling has stopped. That's thanks to the efforts of our troops moving the Germans back over the Biferno River." Colonel Playfair strides in front of a large map pinned to the wall. "This has put them out of range, which is good, but it is also keeping our men busy holding them there. So that's where your patients will be coming from for the time being. I don't know as yet where we will be headed next, but for now Campobasso will be our home – ours and a whole lot of our soldiers on leave.

"We already have you fellows set up here. With two Field Ambulances here, plus two FSUs and the Transfusion Unit we have lots of capability. Peter and Basil, I would like to have a separate word with you later concerning coordinating the work of your Field Ambulances.

"Bill Clendinnen is closing up shop at Foggia today, so you should have No.2 Field Dressing Station here by tomorrow evening at the latest. That will give you all the strength you need to handle anything that comes in. Mind you they'll be a bit tired. I'm sure you've all heard about the volumes of sick and wounded they've been dealing with over the past few weeks. Frank, you and Bill did a wonderful job back there. The Brits will be forever grateful!

"Anyway, the flow of patients slowed down a lot beginning about a week ago, and Bill has managed to evacuate a lot of patients back down the line to the British Casualty Clearing Station at Barletta, out on the coast. The sick are all now flowing to No.5 Field Dressing Station that is still at Lucera. We can handle all wounded from the fighting here now, so it's time for Bill's group to join you here. I'm also leaving No.1 FDS at Volturara in that delightful monastery, as a staging post for evacuation. I have also decided to move Doug Sparling back to strengthen some hospitals, and Major Harry Francis is replacing him as Commander of No.1 FDS.

The American Field Service Ambulance Company has agreed to move patients from here to Volturara. Harry's people will transition them to a British motor ambulance convoy for the ride back to British stations at Foggia, and then farther back to Barletta. I should say that the Americans are doing a splendid job for us. They're all volunteers, you know, raised by an outfit called the 'Society of Friends' and, fortunately for us, attached to the 8th Army. They came to us with the 13th Corps when we started across the Foggia plain, and have been doing a fine job, bless their hearts."

"Sir, how about patients who are evacuated but can probably return to active duty?" asks Don Young. "Will they still be sent all the way back to Barletta?"

"Good point Don. I've ordered No.5 Field Ambulance back at Lucera to function as a convalescent centre for all ranks, so that should hold quite a few men closer to the action while they recover. Now then, how many patients do you have here at present?"

"Around 150, Sir," replies Colonel Bowman. "We're admitting 20 or so a day, and we have capacity for at least 300, so we should be fine. I'm also in touch with the chaps over at the British Casualty Clearing Station here in town, and we are agreed to move patients back and forth if there are any problems of overcrowding."

"Good show, Basil. How about Germans and local patients?"

"We have 12 Germans at the moment, and a pretty steady line of locals coming in for treatment. Most of them are out-patients, and only 10 are actually staying here…surrounded by family, of course!"

"Right," says the ADMS. "And finally, you must be delighted that I am located right here in town at divisional headquarters. So you can look forward to frequent visits."

They all laugh, and the session is concluded.

Friday, October 22, 1943

There are no new cases. Following ward rounds, Rocke and Jack drive back to Riccia to visit the two patients they have left there. They are progressing well. In Campobasso the rest of the crew spend most of their time at the cinema. Campobasso is quickly developing into a lively town for the Canadians. There are three cinemas and a vaudeville theatre, a 'Beaver Club' for the men and an 'Officers' Aldershot Club', not to mention numerous bars and restaurants opening up around the town. The only thing that is missing is the crowd of women that every soldier on leave wishes to find when in town.

The Field Ambulances are, meanwhile, busy supporting the troops holding the banks of the Biferno River, and this is a particularly harrowing day for Pte. Ted Walls.

Ted is well and truly exhausted. He and his mates have been carrying stretchers in rough country for months now. Their job is a challenging combination of long distance running and weight lifting. They walk or jog for miles looking for wounded located either in Regimental Aid Posts or in the field, and then bring them back; a one mile 'carry' may be, in total, a 2 or 3 mile hike. And that's not the end of it. Even the rides in the ambulances, many of them jeeps with racks on them for the stretchers, have been tiring as they move over bumpy roads and the stretcher-bearers go through contortions to keep the wounded in place and stable.

A pressure that Ted never thinks about, but that is very real, is the emotional stress of dealing every day with terribly wounded Canadians and Brits. In every action, every single time, he feels the sharp pain of mixed fear, worry and sympathy that goes with helping the wounded. Add to all of this the numerous work details in the stations, both ordered and voluntary, and Ted has every right to feel 'a little puffed', as he puts it.

But today is especially tiring – so much so that at the end of it the Sergeant actually gives him a few days off to rest. Today Ted has had to deal with his latest and worst case of shell shock. The patient's name is Sergeant Jim Garr.

James Prentice Garr from Canmore, Alberta has achieved military success and is proud of it. He joined the Princess Patricia's Canadian Light Infantry regiment as a private in 1939, a month after the war broke out. A sturdy 24 year-old foreman in a meat packing plant, he quickly showed his strength and leadership qualities during the training in Alberta, and by the time his unit was posted to England he was a Corporal. He excelled further in England and was promoted to Sergeant in early 1943.

Throughout the campaign in Sicily Jim Garr was a superb leader of men, a quintessential Sergeant. He was precise and disciplined in managing his unit, a detailed and complete reporter to officers, and above all a tough and fearless leader in battle. He pushed his men hard and expected the most out of them, but always led by example. The Sergeant was always the first to charge forward, the last to retreat. He would move up and down the lines of his unit bellowing, encouraging, ordering and sympathizing – whatever was the best formula to make them do their best. Nobody was really close to the Sergeant, but everyone liked him.

As his unit moved up the toe of Italy and through its 'ankle', Sergeant Garr started to change. For the first time he felt fear. Sicily had been every bit as violent and dangerous, but he had simply ignored the danger and fear and done his job. Now in Italy, however, it was different. Somehow the sense of threat woke up with him in the morning and stayed with him all day, no matter what the unit was doing. He started to worry about artillery fire when they were in camp or on the road. Shellfire of any sort brought him to the early stages of panic, which he fought down by focusing hard on his men.

Jim Garr didn't sense the change because it came on him gradually, over several weeks. Suddenly it seemed natural to be 'concerned' about dangerous situations, which just happened to be everywhere, most of the time. This fear made him less decisive in his planning, and in dealing with the men. He started to hesitate in leading, and to be preoccupied with minor issues. The men started to notice the change, and they worried about it. As his unit moved through the Foggia plain, constantly engaged with the enemy, his condition went rapidly downhill.

He found that he was constantly exhausted – almost too tired to do his job. He lost his appetite, and was short and angry with the men. He had trouble sleeping and would wake up in the middle of the night sweating and nauseous. He would get up in the morning tired and often dizzy. Everyone was tired and stressed in this critical stage in the campaign so the men, while they noticed that the Sergeant was not up to snuff, figured that he was just the same as them, plus a bit more pooped due to his responsibilities. The one thing they did notice with real concern was his lack of boldness in action. He often showed fear, and actually looked terrified at times.

The officers started to notice it in his uncharacteristic silences during briefings and his lack of responsiveness to orders. The Lieutenant asked him once if he was OK, and he replied "yes" because he thought that he was, you know, just a bit tired. Then, when he withdrew his men prematurely in a brief skirmish near Volturara the Lieutenant knew that something was wrong with Garr and decided that he had better have a chat with him. But they moved on quickly and there was no time for the chat.

Today they are in action near Baranello, west of Campobasso, when Sergeant Garr breaks. His company is under mortar fire, pinned down in ditches next to the road. They are returning fire with some effect and waiting for the Sergeant to give the order to move out to join other units moving slowly forward on both flanks. But the Sergeant is not giving any orders. The sight of a Private soldier next to him taking a bullet in the leg and rolling in the dirt, grunting in pain, breaks the last vestiges of his sanity. Jim Garr sits in the bottom of the ditch facing backwards, his eyes wide with fear, yelling incomprehensibly into the wind. Private Harry Mason, who has rushed to help his comrade with the shattered leg, looks at Garr and calls, "Sarge, are you OK?" But to no effect. Mason then calls to the Corporal that the Sergeant… " must be wounded or something 'cause he's not moving and he sounds crazy." The Corporal tells Mason to stay with Garr and the wounded man, and shouts the order for the company to move on.

Ten minutes later Ted Walls and four other stretcher-bearers come jogging along the road and jump into the ditch. "Hi soldier, I'm Ted Walls. We're from the No.9 Field Ambulance helping your medical guys in this sector. What's up?"

Two of the bearers are already tending to the wounded Private. Sergeant Garr continues to stare and yell. Pte. Mason, now sitting with his arm around Garr's shoulders, tells Ted what has happened. "Oboy," says Ted. "That's shell shock, really bad. Has he been kind of weird lately?"

"A bit," replies the soldier, "but nothing like this. But yeah, he has seemed scared of things lately. He ain't the same guy we had in Sicily."

Ted moves to the other side of Garr, gently taking his arm to establish contact. "Yep, that's how it happens. They start by getting some fear in them, and it grows and eats away at them, and then they snap. Just like the Sergeant here. Soldier...what's your name?"

"Harry Mason".

"Harry, we're going to need your help getting him back to the ambulance. These are the toughest cases to handle. They don't bleed, but they're very sick. They're totally bonkers and you never know what they will do. It's really good to have someone they know help us move them out. The ambulance is just about 300 yards down the road, so you can catch up with your guys soon."

The group climbs out of the ditch, which is no longer under fire. Four of the stretcher-bearers lift the wounded Private on the stretcher. Ted and Harry hold Sergeant Garr firmly by the arms and talk quietly to him as the party moves back along the road. Ten minutes later they arrive at a makeshift Casualty Collecting Post set up by the Field Ambulance to coordinate movement of wounded out of the area.

They place the wounded man in his stretcher on the rack of the jeep ambulance waiting there, already with two other wounded aboard. Ted and Harry Mason put Jim Garr in the front seat, where he sits tamely, staring into the distance. Ted thanks Harry, who says a quiet good-bye to his Sergeant, turns and jogs back toward the fighting. The bearers agree that it is time for this ambulance to head back to Campobasso as there is another one on the way and anyway this one is pretty well loaded. Ted climbs into the seat directly behind Sergeant Garr to keep an eye on him, next to the orderly/bearer who is tending the wounded in the stretchers. The other stretcher-bearers rest beside the road, awaiting the next ambulance and their return to the fray to search for more customers.

The driver starts the ambulance on the bumpy road back to Campobasso. This area has been cleared of enemy but is still within their artillery range. It had been strongly defended by the Germans, and they have left a legacy of mines embedded in the road and in nearby fields. Advance units of the Canadian army have placed crude markers on the edge of fields known to be mined.

As the ambulance grinds slowly through a riverbed next to a collapsed bridge and up onto the road on the far bank a stray artillery shell explodes 100 yards up ahead. Sergeant Garr screams. As the driver stops the jeep momentarily to assess the best way around the crater Garr jumps out of the ambulance and runs into the field next to the road, passing blindly the marker showing that this is a minefield.

Ted sees the marker but doesn't hesitate. Sputtering with anger and yelling an oath that includes all swear words known to the English language he leaps from the jeep and sprints after Garr, the orderly/bearer hard on his heels. "Jesus, Ted, we're in a bloody minefield you know," screams the orderly. "This guy is really nuts!"

"Yeah, right. OK. So keep right behind me, and I'll try to follow his trail as closely as I can. That way at least he'll blow up first!"

They are both quick and strong and Garr is staggering, and within 200 yards they have the Sergeant in their grasp and the three of them are standing together in a small group, the bearers holding the Sergeant firmly around the shoulders and waist. Garr is now silent but staring wildly around. When their pulses have returned almost to normal the bearers walk the Sergeant carefully out of the field, following precisely their own incoming footsteps. They place Garr back in his seat and bind him securely in place with ropes from their emergency supply.

The rest of the trip is uneventful aside from frequent screams from Jim Garr. At the Canadian medical centre in Campobasso an orderly with special training in shell shock takes the Sergeant away for rest and treatment that starts at the centre and moves through the Corps Exhaustion Unit at Foggia all the way back to a hospital in England. Sergeant Garr's war is over and Ted Walls is very, very tired.

The officers at the centre have seen many cases like this, and without exception the shell shocks make the medical doctors uncomfortable. As the ADMS told them back at the briefing in Valguarnera, these 'exhaustion' cases are wounded in a very real sense, but not in a way that the medical doctors can deal with without special training. They see what appear to be healthy soldiers removed from the fighting without a scratch on them. It doesn't seem fair to the 'real' wounded, but yet, well, who would want to be in such a condition? These poor guys are out of control; they have lost themselves and are adrift God-knows where. The story is that it will take some of them a long time to recover, and some will never be the same again.

October 21 – November 22, 1943

The 24-hour shifts work well for the two FSUs at the Canadian Medical Centre. Their operation caseload is surprisingly light. They average two to three operations a day, plus the usual course of post-operative work and consultations on new patients arriving at the centre from the fighting around the Biferno River. The one case that does exercise them considerably is a small Italian boy who has picked up a mine and suffered the consequences. Fortunately the mine was a dud that produced only a minor explosion so the boy is alive, but it has had a devastating effect on his hands and arms, and on his face. The family is distraught, and keeps the drivers busy consoling them with tea and food while their child is on the operating table.

The centre is, however, busy with a constant stream of patients suffering from illnesses such as malaria, dysentery and jaundice, and it has a relatively constant patient population of around 300. The 2CFSU team is itself faced with some medical challenges.

On November 1 Jack Leishman is admitted to the No.9 Field Ambulance ward with a high temperature, dosed with quinine for the expected malaria. He is discharged on November 5, but by November 11 he is feeling terrible, rejects almost all food and is a definite yellow colour, and is re-admitted with jaundice. This event has the effect of cancelling a leave to Naples that had been planned by the unit. The No.1 FSU team subsequently goes to Naples on leave November 13-16, increasing the disappointment felt by Rocke's group.

OR assistant Johnny Pyke also spends time in the ward, suffering from a recurrence of a malignant tertian malaria that he had suffered in Sicily. On November 15 it is clear that he will not recover sufficiently to return to duty, and he is evacuated. Pte. Daniel Pritchard joins the unit on November 17 to replace Pyke.

There is little news in Campobasso about the progress of the troops, although it is generally understood that things are moving slowly due in large part to the muddy conditions brought on by heavy rains, and also by the active demolition work of the Germans. There is, however, an air of expectancy – of things happening – and lots of speculation and gossip. In the second week of November Rocke is told to expect to move out with No.4 Field Ambulance on an unspecified mission, but on the 10th he is told that this had been postponed. The Field Ambulance does however depart on November 16 in support of the 3rd Infantry Brigade, which is now known to be involved in an attack along the upper Sangro River.

The medical centre receives visits from several military VIPs during the month. On November 5 Major General Chris Vokes, Commander of the 1st Canadian Infantry Division, inspects the centre. He finds the entire set-up satisfactory and spends considerable time chatting with convalescing wounded patients. They have two meetings with the ADMS to discuss various medical issues. They also enjoy a session with Colonel R.G. Donald, Surgical Consultant to the British 8th Army who last visited them in Agira. He goes over the surgical cases with the Canadian doctors, and also tells them that there is now some hope that small amounts of penicillin will be available to them in the near future.

The weather alternates between sunny and cool, pleasant weather and miserable rain and cold. In their off-hours the Canadians enjoy the local entertainments that include a steady flow of American movies.

Tuesday, November 23, 1943

Jack is lying flat on his back with eyes closed at 0815hrs when most of the other patients in the ward are sitting up and reading, finishing their breakfast, or in a few cases walking about to stretch their legs. Rocke and Eric stand by his bedside, masks over their faces, looking at Jack's yellow-tinted face. Jack is very thin from several weeks of uncomfortable temperatures and muscle-aches and fitful eating. The drip in his arm is now his only reliable source of nutrition.

"Eric," whispers Rocke, "I've talked to a couple of the other doctors here, and they agree that Jack just isn't getting better as he should. I'm damned worried about him. It looks like we'll have to send him back to hospital, and I hate the thought of losing him. But it's better to take action now than run the risk of losing him permanently by not getting him all the care he needs."

"Yes Sir, I agree. It's been great having Captain Leishman here, but we're all very worried about him. Where will he go if we send him back from here?"

"I'm not sure. I assume they'll send him via Lucera where No.5 FDS has their set-up for jaundice and malaria, but after that they'll have to decide what hospital to send him on to. My guess would be Sicily, but you never know."

Jack opens his eyes. "What are you two muttering about?" He raises his head, winces, and lets it fall back on the pillow. "Christ, I feel awful!"

"Jack," says Rocke, "we're talking about getting you out of here to a real hospital so that you can get better. You actually look as bad as you feel, and the lads here are agreed that you're just not progressing like you should. So I've decided to evacuate you today."

"I hate to desert you but I must admit that you're right. Hell, I'm looking yellow and pissing red, and I want to eat but just can't seem to. But I hate to leave the unit. We're a great team and I've enjoyed every minute of it…well, almost every minute."

Rocke turns to Eric. "Would you please get Captain Leishman's things together and arrange for evacuation on the next shipment out?"

"Yes Sir," says Eric. He turns to Jack. "Captain, we're going to miss you a lot. You take care of yourself." He salutes and leaves.

Rocke sits on the edge of Jack's bed and they talk quietly. Rocke promises to write Trudy a note about the jaundice and how Jack will be better soon. Jack gives Rocke some thoughts about management of the unit. He also asks Rocke about who will replace him.

"I've seen Shorty Long here, over at the ADMS Headquarters. You may remember Shorty. He was a few years after me at McGill, but I met him once or twice in Montreal. He's a good chap, and I know he'd rather be in the field than headquarters. So I'll probably ask for him."

Jack opens his eyes at this. "Hey, you've been thinking about this haven't you?"

"I sure have Jack. You know, while you've been snoozing here and having a grand time I've been worrying about you, and that means worrying about what we'd do without you. The answer is, of course, that we have to have a replacement. But also of course, we'll welcome you back the moment you're up to it."

Jack drifts off to sleep and Rocke leaves. At 1430hrs an evacuation ambulance is waiting at the front door with a place for Jack. The entire 2CFSU team is waiting by the van as Sammy Smart and Matt Curran carry him out of the centre on a stretcher and place him in the ambulance. Jack is only half awake, but he manages a thin smile and a weak, "Thanks fellas. See you soon." Their reply is a jumble of "Good lucks" and "See you Captains", finished off with "Keep your hands off the nurses, Jack," from Eric, which has them all smiling grimly as they wave the ambulance away.

51. CIVITANOVA

A small post in support of a diversionary attack.

Wednesday, November 24, 1943

At 1100hrs the ADMS orders Rocke to proceed immediately to join No.4 Field Ambulance at a place called Civitanova del Sannio, northwest of Campobasso. The Field Ambulance has been supporting the 3rd Infantry Brigade in an assault in the region of the upper Sangro River designed, it appears, to fool the Germans into diverting valuable troops from the key coastal area. The Field Ambulance has been relying on a British FSU for its surgical needs, but that unit has now moved away and Peter Tisdale has asked for a Canadian FSU to come and help out.

Eric supervises the loading, and they depart at 1345hrs. The distance is only 25 miles as the crow flies, but along the winding mountain roads it is much farther and they arrive at 1700hrs. Major Tisdale greets them, out of the pouring rain on the porch of the abandoned house that they have taken over for the Advanced Dressing Station. It is a relatively new house with a lot of rooms and very little damage. It has water service, but the electricity service is off and the Field Ambulance generators are hard at work.

"Hello Rocke," says Peter, smiling through his cloud of pipe smoke. "You know, this is a bit like it was back at Bompalazzo, when you were sent to help us and we had nothing for you to do and no instruments to do it with anyway. Now we have all the instruments and supplies we need, but there seems to be a lull in the flow of patients requiring surgery. I'm delighted you're here as this could change very quickly, but right now you can take your time getting set up. In fact, why not join us for supper first, before you set up shop?"

"Jolly good, Peter," says Rocke. "Let's do it." By 1900hrs they are ready to operate, but have no patients requiring surgery. Rocke and the orderlies join Tisdale for a tour of the two wards that have around 40 patients in them, half wounded cases and half disease cases.

November 25 - December 2, 1943

This is a period of virtually no surgical activity for the 2CFSU. The diversionary action comes to an inconclusive end and the Canadian troops are moving down to the coastal plain. Captain Shorty Long arrives on November 25, replacing Jack Leishman as Second-in-Command of 2CFSU. He and Rocke are friends, and he fits in nicely with the team. On December 1, a clear and cold day, Rocke leads his team on the first route march they have suffered since Scotland. Actually they are extremely bored by this time, so the march really isn't so bad after all, in spite of the rain.

But they know that this lull won't last much longer. Big things are brewing out on the east coast. Word is that the Brits are having an awful time advancing up the coast, and that the Canadians are being called in to help out. They are sure that they will soon be part of the show again.

52. THE BATTLE OF ORTONA BEGINS

The start of the historic battle on Italy's Adriatic coast.

November 28 – December 9, 1943

The town of Ortona, on Italy's Adriatic coast of Italy, was a popular summer vacation spot for many Italians, who liked to call it 'the Pearl of the Adriatic'. It was not meant to be the focus of the Allied assault up the eastern side of Italy and the scene of an historic battle for the Canadian Army, but that's what it turned out to be.

Montgomery's plan was for the British Army, which included Divisions from Canada, India and New Zealand, to drive north across the Sangro River, sweep past Ortona and take the important coastal port of Pescara. They would then turn westward along the main road across the Italian boot and approach Rome or get at least as far as Avezzano, 50 miles east of Rome, before halting for the worst months of the winter. This would force the Germans to move troops from the Gustav line protecting Rome from the American assault from the south, in order to bolster defences against the British Army moving in from the east.

It was, as it turned out, too bold a plan for two reasons: the weather, and the strength of the German defensive tactics. From the start of October the weather in the eastern part of Italy was highly unpredictable, often rainy and cold, and almost insufferably cold and wet by December. This was hard on the attacking Allied forces, and equally important it often slowed and even stalled their tanks and other heavy vehicles, which were essential to the success of the venture.

The German defensive tactics were clever, well designed and carried out with great efficiency. They established strong defensive positions in places ideally suited for defence such as riverbanks and valleys. They would defend the positions fiercely, often launching wild counter-attacks, until it became clear that they would be overrun. They would then retreat to the next strong position, destroying bridges and roadways as they went. These tactics caused substantial delays in the Allied advance, and heavy casualties.

Thus what Montgomery had foreseen as a swift advance up to Pescara turned out to be a drawn-out slugfest, massively costly to both sides. As the Allies inched their way northwards Montgomery saw that he must set a more realistic objective for the current campaign, and although still speaking of Pescara, he settled on the small coastal town of Ortona. The town had railway access and a fine harbour, so it could serve as a supply base for the coming assault on Rome from the east, a base that they sorely needed in light of the length of the supply lines from Sicily and North Africa. Anticipating this, the Germans had destroyed the rail lines and the harbour, but these could be repaired. Montgomery felt that Ortona could be taken quite easily, and the Allies could then consider their options for further action from that base. What they did not realize was that the Germans, fully aware of the strategic importance of this small town, were determined to defend it at all costs.

The Allied advance in the last week of November was launched by the British 8th Army centred on three Divisions: the British 78th Division, the 8th Indian Division and the 2nd New Zealand Division, and preceded by a massive artillery barrage. They crossed the Sangro, but the crossing for the British and Indian Divisions was strung out endlessly by the flooding out or demolition of all bridges in their sector, so that all vehicles had to use one pontoon bridge built by British engineers. Many of the infantry crossed the Sangro on foot bridges built by the engineers. The Indians then moved four miles inland before turning north. The New Zealanders crossed even farther west. It was hard fighting right across the front as the Allies approached the Moro River, the last major river before Ortona, which had heavy German fortifications on its northern side.

The British 78th Division was by now an exhausted force, having suffered more that 10,000 casualties since the start of the Sicily campaign, with 4,000 of them coming in the battle to cross the Sangro. In anticipation of this, Montgomery issued orders on November 25 for the Canadian 1st Infantry Division to move from the Campobasso area to Termoli, 20 miles south of the Sangro. From Termoli they then moved north to a position behind the British 78th, with a view to relieving them as soon as possible. The British refused to be relieved until they had taken the last coastal town south of the Moro River and driven the Germans back across the Moro. The town was called San Vito Chietino.

This they achieved on December 3, and by the end of December 4 the Canadians had taken over the British positions on the southern bank of the Moro

River. That night the pontoon bridge over the Sangro washed out, further slowing the advance.

The Canadian task was to force a crossing over the Moro River and secure Ortona, some two miles beyond its mouth. The 1st and 2nd Infantry Brigades opened the attack on the night of December 5. On December 6 the 1st Canadian Armoured Brigade began to relieve the British armour that had remained in the line under Canadian command, and moved to support the infantry in the Moro crossing.

The German 90th Panzer Grenadier Division offered savage resistance, and it was December 9th before the Canadians secured a firm bridgehead on the north side of the Moro. This attack included an artillery barrage of historic proportions on December 8. Having crossed the Moro, the Canadians still had much work to do to push the Germans back towards Ortona, and to secure the key towns of Villa Rogatti and San Leonardo.

The Canadian medical units followed the troops out of the Campobasso area on December 1, seeking the most strategic locations to set up their facilities in support of the offensive. Their vehicles were stuck in the massive traffic jams involved in the Sangro crossing, but by the end of December 3 they were in business right behind the fighting troops. The town of Rocca San Giovanni, just south of San Vito Chietino, seemed a logical place for them. It was south of the Moro River and just out of the range of German artillery. ADMS Headquarters staff decided that the large municipal building that had been vacated by the retreating Germans and used by the British medical units would be satisfactory, and ordered the Canadian medical units to make it their first medical centre in the Ortona struggle.

No.5 Field Ambulance was the first unit on the scene. Finally released from its fever and jaundice duties at Lucera, the team arrived on December 2 to find a rather dark and cramped building, not well suited for medical work but obviously the best thing available. The No.28 British Field Surgical Unit was still there to help the Canadians set up and to facilitate the transfer from British to Canadian medical services. The Field Ambulance established its Advanced Dressing Station in the building, and the next day sent a company forward to San Vito Chietino to operate a Casualty Collection Post

No.9 Field Ambulance arrived late in the day on December 3 in convoy with No.1 Field Surgical Unit and No.1 Field Transfusion Unit. They set up immediately, and Frank Mills did his first operation there on the morning of December 4. The Field Ambulance stayed in reserve.

No. 4 Field Ambulance and 2CFSU, coming from Civitanova, arrived on the scene on December 6. The 2CFSU joined the medical centre in Rocca, relieving No. 28 British FSU. The Field Ambulance waited in reserve at Rocca until ordered to send a company to set up another Casualty Collection Post just north of San Vito, across the small Feltrino River and closer to the Moro, on December 8.

The Field Dressing Stations were initially more involved in treating and evacuating existing British casualties than in taking in fresh Canadian casualties. On December 4 No. 2 Field Dressing Station arrived at Casalbordino, ten miles south of Rocca and farther inland, to help the overwhelmed staff of the British Advanced Dressing Station there look after a large number of British patients.

At the same time No. 1 Field Dressing Station arrived on the scene from Volturara and took over another British Field Dressing Station in Fossacesia, just south of Rocca. The patient load, mainly British but increasingly Canadian, was also heavy there, but sufficiently under control that Major Francis was able to send 12 orderlies to assist in the care of post-operative patients at the Canadian Medical Centre at Rocca.

As of December 8, therefore, all of the Canadian medical units were gathered in Rocca or in the immediate vicinity. The Field Ambulances were up front supporting the Canadian advance, the Field Surgical Units were in place in Rocca to operate on the seriously wounded, and the Field Dressing Stations were located slightly farther back tending to mainly British casualties and facilitating their evacuation.

The workload at Rocca was heavy from the outset. The Canadian station there admitted over 900 British and Canadian casualties of all types up to the end of December 10. On the 9th alone there were 230 admissions. It was therefore vital that evacuation of patients should be carried out as quickly and efficiently as possible. Evacuation from this area was mainly to the British Casualty Clearing Station at Vasto, 20 miles south of Rocca. Patients were sent by road if possible, although the bottleneck at the Sangro caused serious problems, and for a week had to be supplemented by seaborne evacuation from Fossacesia Station to Casalbordino Station, and thence by motor ambulance convoy to Vasto.

53. THE LONG, SLOW ROAD TO THE BATTLE

There is heavy traffic on the road to Ortona.

Friday, December 3, 1943

"Looks like your route marching days are over for awhile," grins Peter Tisdale, emerging from his radio room in the Advanced Dressing Station at Civitanova. "Orders have just come through for us to head down to the coast to a place called Rocca San Giovanni. From what I can gather our Division is there to replace the Brits in the move northwards to Pescara. ADMS says that the Brits have been advancing but have taken a frightful beating in the process and need some relief. We're to be part of a medical centre at Rocca, and I guess we'll move north with the troops from there."

"Good," says Rocke. "It'll be just fine to get away from this bloody rain and cold, and maybe even to have some work to do! Let me get Eric going with the loading, and then I'll call Shorty in here and we can go over the maps."

Orders given, the officers huddle over their maps while all around them there is the controlled chaos of packing and loading in the teeming rain.

Peter traces out the twisting mountain road from Civitanova northeast to the coastal road south of Vasto. "We'll be sharing the road with some of the units from the 3rd Brigade, so it's going to be slow going. We'll be passing through towns like Agnone and Castiglione that have been liberated just days ago. I'm sure the locals will be delighted to see us, but we'll have to keep our eyes open for mines and booby traps."

"How about the patients here?" asks Rocke. "I think you have about 25 in the ward?"

"That's right. Fortunately we have no really serious cases in the ward, so we can take the patients with us and drop them off at a Field Dressing Station along the way. Evidently there's one at Fossacesia out on the coast, and we'll be going right by it on the way to Rocca."

The units have a quick lunch, complete packing, and move out in convoy at 1400hrs. The 18 vehicles of the Field Ambulance stretch ahead of the three 2CFSU vehicles. Gazing through the streaming windshield of the surgical van, Rocke sees that the front three or four trucks in the line actually disappear in the rain and heavy mist that encircles them. The FA is still, however, an impressive array of equipment with its jeeps, ambulances, jeep ambulances, the one poor, streaming motorcycle, and of course the vital water truck. That truck alone was worth its weight in gold back in parched Sicily. Even here, with constant rain, it is the essential source of potable water for the unit and their wounded.

There are no 3rd Brigade troops in sight. It is a terrible day for driving, made worse by the horrendous condition of the road they are travelling. It is a secondary road, quite well built, but it has suffered from the recent fighting and is an obstacle course of rubble and potholes. The lead van has an observer with binoculars keeping a sharp eye on the road ahead for mines and other obstructions, and seven times he diverts the convoy around suspicious sites.

At just after 1700hrs they reach the outskirts of Agnone, a small town situated next to a mountain on the banks of the Verrino River. They have taken three hours to cover 20 miles. The convoy halts and Peter consults with Rocke. It is almost pitch black outside now, and with the pouring rain visibility is very poor. They agree to stay here overnight. Military police from the Canadian 3rd Infantry Brigade direct them to a TB sanatorium and nearby school that are suitable for accommodation in Agnone. After several false starts they find the facilities and billet there for the night along with troops from the Carleton and York Regiment, with officers in the sanatorium and other ranks in the school. They are warmly welcomed by the staffs of the two buildings, who are thrilled to be invited to share some of the Canadians' food cooked in the facility kitchens.

Saturday, December 4, 1943

The medical units tag on to the tail end of the 3rd Infantry Brigade convoy heading down to the coast to join the action to replace the British in the drive to Pescara. Driving at almost walking speed through continuous wind and heavy rains, it takes them nine hours to cover the 72 miles to the coastal road at Vasto.

The coastal road is one long traffic jam, with every known type of military vehicle moving along it at the slowest of slow speeds: mainly Canadians heading north; occasionally British heading south. During one long stop two miles before the turn-off to Casalbordino, about 10 miles south of the Sangro crossing, Rocke talks with a military police officer. The man is standing helplessly beside the road, his traffic control duties useless in what is in effect a huge parking lot.

"What's the hold-up, soldier?" asks Rocke. "Is it just traffic or is it more serious?"

"Sort of a bit of both, Sir," comes the reply along with a smart salute. "The Sangro is flooding and has just washed the bridge away, so we're all at a standstill, and it's going to take a while to repair it as the water is so high. You might still have a mile or so to go before you'll have to stop completely and wait, but I would suggest that if you spot any good place to spend the night you should take it."

"Many thanks," says Rocke, returning the police officer's salute as Pete Monroe moves the truck ahead 50 yards before slowing to a crawl again. The Field Ambulance is ahead of the FSU, so Rocke says "Pete, I'm going to jog ahead and give this message to Major Tisdale."

"Right Sir," says Pete, stopping to let Rocke out. Half an hour and one mile later they follow the Field Ambulance into a large orchard on the left side of the road. It is a comfortable looking peach orchard with lots of room for the two units to set up their tents and their cooking stoves.

The rain has stopped by the time Rocke steps out of the surgical van and stretches his cramped muscles. He is delighted with the lack of pounding rain and with the warmer air that is here – it must be at least 5 degrees warmer than it was up in the mountains. He tells Eric to set up the campsite, and then he and Shorty visit Peter Tisdale at the FA camp to discuss the situation.

"It looks like we're going to be here at least for tonight and maybe longer. I wonder how long it takes for the engineers to build one of those bridges?"

"I don't know, Rocke, but it's damn frustrating being here. The ADMS just told me via radio that they're really busy up front and he wants us there as quickly as possible! But what the hell can we do?"

"Nothing, Peter. So let's just enjoy ourselves here. The weather's a lot better than it was up at Civitanova, and there's no shelling, so we might as well rest as best we can. We'll be busy soon enough! Come on over for a drink if you like. I still have some of that cognac, and it's tasting better every day. And the men found some wine at one of those stops on the way down here earlier today."

They spend a pleasant evening with some drinks and a good, hot dinner. The ground is still wet but the tents are dry and the 2CFSU team has a long and restful night.

Sunday, December 5, 1943

The medical units are up and about at 0800hrs and anticipating something happening, but there is no sign of movement on the road outside the orchard. It is still a massive line of vehicles pointing north, most of them empty with their occupants camped in orchards and fields along the road. After breakfast the teams pack the vehicles once again, and then they sit around and wait for the traffic to start moving forward. The weather stays dry and relatively warm so there is impatience but no complaining. Several military units in nearby camps see the red crosses on their vans and send men over for minor first aid – change of bandages and treatment of cuts and bruises for the most part, plus one soldier who burned his left hand trying to fry bacon for breakfast.

At 1600hrs a despatch rider comes down the line telling all units along the way that the bridge will not be ready for at least another 12 hours, so orders are to stay where they are. Peter Tisdale radios the news to the ADMS who is with the medical units up ahead in Rocca, and is rewarded by the first serious stream of cursing that he has ever heard from Colonel Playfair. They unpack the tents and set up for another comfortable night on the road to the Sangro River.

Monday, December 6, 1943

The situation is identical to yesterday, except that it is raining again, and a cold wind is coming off the ocean and inland through the peach trees in the orchard. The medical units are ready to go at 0900hrs, but it is not until 1600hrs that a rider roars into the orchard and tells them to get back into the convoy, still behind the 3rd Infantry Brigade troops who have been languishing in a field on the other side of the road.

It takes them five hours to drive the 11 miles to the new bridge over the Sangro. Some of the medicals get out and march along the road just to get the exercise.

The scene at the bridge is serious chaos – *a bit like Montreal at rush hour,* thinks Rocke as they edge through a mass of parked vehicles and other military equipment, all awaiting their turns to reach sufficient priority to make the crossing. Rocke has no idea why his unit has priority over some of them, but as they finally have their wheels on the bridge he senses the heavy hand of the ADMS at work. This means that there is a lot of medical work to be done at Rocca and forward, and the ADMS has pulled strings to get his people up there to do it.

54. ROCCA SAN GIOVANNI

The first Canadian Medical Centre in support of the troops fighting for Ortona is a busy, grim place.

Once past the bridge the convoy moves ahead at a slightly faster pace, but it is still 2200hrs before No.4 Field Ambulance and 2CFSU pull up in front of the Canadian Medical Centre at Rocca. Rocke huddles with Frank Mills and the Commander of the No.28 British FSU about setting up and assignments. They agree that the Brits will move out at first light, Rocke will set up to replace them, and the two Canadian FSUs will return to their 24-hour shift routine on the old system starting at 1800hrs each day. Frank tells Rocke that there is a good space where he can have his own operating theatre in a house across the street. If he takes it there will be two separate operating rooms, making it easier to service them and keep them clean. They settle down to sleep in the spare rooms in the house. No.4 Field Ambulance stays parked and loaded at the medical centre, awaiting orders.

Tuesday, December 7, 1943

The house is small but nicely arranged, ideal for a surgical theatre.

War Diary

Set up equipment in a small but quite conveniently arranged house with a warm resuscitation room (large fireplace), a good-sized wash up room adjoining the theatre. We have in addition a small kitchen

*that we use as a sterilizing room, having set up our new sawyer stove
in it. It works well. We start our 24-hour stretch at 1800 hours.*

The 2CFSU team sets to work at first light, cleaning and scouring the house and setting up their equipment and instruments. The drivers carry out a modest Fly Patrol, and McKenzie stocks the kitchen with tea and food supplies. Eric is thoroughly pleased with the set-up and is grinning as he takes Shorty Long on his inspection tour.

Rocke and Shorty, accompanied by orderly Jimmy Price, spend the morning at the medical centre assisting with the intake of wounded and going over the potential cases for surgery on their shift. Due to an unusual pause in the inflow of patients there is only one case that evening – the last quiet day they are to have for a long time.

December 8 – 9, 1943

The caseload seems to grow by the hour. Ambulances jam the front of the medical centre, either bringing in new casualties or bringing out treated cases to take them back to the Casualty Clearing Station at Vasto. Many are sick or lightly wounded, but there is now a solid stream of candidates for immediate surgery. The surgeons note that the wounded are generally in as bad shape as they have seen since the start of the campaign.

War Diary

December 9, 1943
*Major MacLennan visited us and found us doing an amputation
on a case of gas gangrene. In the period 9-10 Dec. we did 6 cases.
Both teams note that the degree of shock exhibited in these cases is
very great. Several cases have died in the resuscitation room.*

"It's hard to put your finger on it," says Frank to Rocke as they share a quick tea break between shifts. "It's not that the wounded back in Sicily were exactly in good shape, what with the dehydration and the sore feet and all. But these fellows coming in now just seem to be stretched to the breaking point as well as being wounded."

"I agree," says Rocke, munching on a biscuit. "They all seem to be very tired, and of course cold and wet. I've heard that the fighting to get over the Moro is terrific, so there's a lot of exhaustion and fear as well as exposure to deal with. And there's the constant shelling in both directions. Hell, it gives me problems even back here just listening to the big guns. I've never heard such a racket. One soldier told me it's one of the biggest barrages we've ever had. A big thing for our cases seems to be to keep them warm. They crave the warmth. They keep asking for more blankets, and it's proving difficult to get them away from the fireplace in our ward."

"Hey, that's right! You have that fireplace don't you? Now how the devil did I miss that?" Frank chuckles, sips his tea, and turns serious again. "The big thing for us to watch for is shock in the patients. I had one lad on the table a couple of days ago and he was still shivering with cold and shock. He was badly wounded and needed urgent attention, but I had to send him back to the ward to settle down and warm up. I was afraid that if I'd worked on him as he was it would have been worse than waiting another hour for him to quiet down."

"Right. In fact, we'd better remind our orderlies about this and make sure they read up on dealing with patients suffering from cold and shock." They finish their tea and go their separate ways. It is just after 1800hrs. Rocke's team is now on duty, and he returns immediately to '2CFSU House' to scrub for their first case who is, to Rocke's surprise, a Forward Observation Officer from the 2nd Field Artillery Regiment. Rocke is surprised because he doesn't think of artillery troops as being much exposed to enemy small arms fire, but here is a living example of just how wrong he is. Eric gives him a quick education on the subject.

"This guy was way up ahead of his unit spotting for them and directing their fire from a low ridge overlooking the Moro River. A sniper got him, as you can see, right in the shoulder. He told me that snipers just love to hit FOOs because they cause so much trouble for the Germans. I guess there's nothing more useless than inaccurate artillery fire, and nothing more useful than accurate fire. So anyway, this lad got it in the shoulder and he says that it bowled him over backwards and he rolled down the hill away from the sniper fire. Which probably saved his life…well, as long as we can patch him up, that is."

There are other surprises during the shift. One case is a padre from the Seaforth Highlanders who comes to the operating table with his right arm hanging by a thread – a flap of skin and some torn sinew. One of the orderlies who bring him in says that the padre was blown up by a mortar shell while helping carry stretchers for the regimental medical teams working around San Leonardo. "There are two others from the same stretcher crew waiting for surgery as well, Major. The story is they were right up in the middle of the battle when they were hit." After the stretcher crew Rocke operates on an engineer who had been involved in protecting a bridge built by Indian engineers across the Moro River in front of Villa Rogatti, and repairing it after artillery or mortar hits. He learns that many engineers have been killed or wounded in this vital action, and over the next 24 hours he and Frank see several more of them. Their injuries are all from mortar or artillery strikes, with the Germans trying hard to sabotage the bridge that has been so desperately built and defended by the Allies.

The 24-hour shift system for the FSUs is working well. Shifts start and end at 1800hrs each day. The FSU on duty operates or is ready to operate for the next 24 hours. If they do not have a case on the table they clean up, eat, assist in the wards and catnap. The FSU coming off duty generally eats and sleeps during the night, and then spends the day up to shift time doing consultations and post-operative work in the wards, cleaning and prepping for their shift, eating and resting. There are occasions when the weight of case loads has both teams operating at the same time, but they try to avoid this as the 24-hour system is demanding enough, and consultations and post-operative work are surprisingly hard work and time-consuming.

The surgeons are very aware of the care they must take to deal with the fatigue that is involved in the 24-hour system. It is one thing to stay awake for 24 hours. It is quite another to have to perform tense, delicate and high-precision work throughout that period, with virtually every operation a life and death situation. The entire team must be alert and accurate throughout the shift, striving to give the same level of care to the last patient as to the first. That last patient is, after all, just as susceptible to a mistaken incision or infection from a poorly sterilized scalpel as is that first patient.

In this situation the batman once again proves his worth as a member of the team. He is there with a hot cup of tea for the OR team after an exhausting two-hour operation. He has fresh linen to replace bloodied gowns, snacks at any hour of the day or night, and a ready notebook to record patient records and events for the war diary. He wakens an OR assistant grabbing a catnap at 0345hrs between operations, and makes sure that the wash station is clean and ready to go.

The drivers also are invaluable, even without driving chores and with their vehicles sitting repaired, serviced and ready to go. They guard the vehicles and move them as required to make way for ambulances and other military traffic. They play an essential role in running the surgical theatre as a clean location, continually cleaning and sweeping, washing walls and floors and swatting flies. They prove themselves to be efficient mouse trappers. They carry supplies and equipment wherever and whenever required, move cots and stretchers around as instructed, and help the orderlies move the patients to and from the operating theatre. They are also the messengers of the unit, keeping close touch with other medical elements in Rocca to ensure coordination of efforts. On several occasions they use the large lorry as an impromptu ambulance to help evacuate patients back to Vasto.

55. THE GULLY

The troops encounter a major obstacle keeping them from the gates of Ortona.

December 10 - 19, 1943

With Villa Rogatti, San Leonardo and other key points north of the Moro River secured, although still risky and under artillery fire, the Canadian command knew that it was time to launch a direct attack on Ortona itself. It would send the troops across a narrow ravine and onto the road running southwest from Ortona to Orsogna, well inland. This would take some more hard fighting, but they felt that once they controlled the road they would be able to march into Ortona relatively easily. Modern armies did not generally like to commit to house-to-house fighting in urban areas, and the Germans would move out and form their next defensive line north of Ortona.

This plan was based on two wrong assumptions and was hopelessly optimistic. The first wrong assumption was that the 'narrow ravine' that appeared so innocent on their maps would not be a significant obstacle. It was, in fact, a deep natural ravine running parallel and approximately 200 yards south of the Ortona/Orsogna road. Dubbed 'the Gully', it constituted, in effect, a straight-line moat protecting the town of Ortona. The Gully was three miles in length, 200 feet deep and about 200 yards wide at the coast, narrowing to about 80 yards around San Leonardo. It was full of vineyards, and in wet season had a stream running through it. The Germans saw it as the perfect natural setting for defence and fortified it accordingly with strategically located gun pits and shelters on its southern slope. These defences were almost impossible for the Canadian artillery to hit, and were ideal bases for defence of the southern side of the Gully, preventing the Canadians from even approaching it from the south, much less crossing it. They took advantage of its dense vegetation to conceal their defensive manoeuvres, and used the Ortona/Orsogna road for communications and to move armour and reinforcements quickly and easily up and down the line on the north side of the Gully.

The second wrong assumption was that the German opposition was weakening, and that as soon as the Canadians started to advance the Germans would retreat past Ortona without offering significant opposition. It was true that the 90th Panzer Grenadiers had suffered terrible losses in the actions at the Sangro and Moro Rivers, but this did not mean that they planned to give up. More importantly, the German command had decided to make a serious stand at Ortona, and at this very moment was rushing the tough, experienced fighters of the 2nd Battalion 3rd Paratroop Regiment to shore up the defences. Kesselring was determined to prevent the Canadians from taking Ortona 'at all costs'.

And then there was the weather. There was now cold, steady rain for extended periods, icy winds, and mud everywhere. It was a terrible setting for an offensive.

General Vokes was being subjected to strong pressure from Montgomery's headquarters to take Ortona quickly. He sent the Canadian Brigades forward in a series of suicidal frontal attacks on the Gully, and they were thrown back with such substantial casualties that the capability of the Canadian units to continue the attack was steadily weakening. The first sign of success came on December 12 when elements of the Seaforth Highlanders crossed the Gully at its top end, to the west of the main German defences, aiming at the village of Casa Berardi on the Ortona/Orsogna road. This made the command realize for the first time the potential wisdom of circling around the Gully rather than trying to take it by frontal attack. They gradually adjusted their sights to this approach, but it still took until December 19, and many more casualties, before the Canadians had control of the Ortona/Orsogna road at a vital crossroad two miles out of Ortona.

As the battle at the Gully proceeded it was time for the medical units to move closer to the action, and on December 11 the ADMS launched a general shift forward of medical installations. He had his Field Ambulances set up Casualty Collection Posts across the line of battle to siphon the wounded back from the Regimental Aid Posts and, when necessary, directly from the field. He also kept a substantial portion of the FA strength in reserve and ready for a quick move into Ortona itself.

No.5 Field Ambulance moved the farthest west, with its company at the Casualty Collection Post at San Vito moving to Sant' Apollinare and the remainder of its staff also at Sant' Apollinare, on wheels in reserve and ready to move into Ortona.

A company of No.9 Field Ambulance established a Casualty Collection Post across the Moro at San Leonardo. This post was extremely busy and under frequent shellfire. The remainder continued in reserve at Rocca.

No.4 Field Ambulance maintained its Casualty Collection Post north of San Vito. The remainder of the FA opened an Advanced Dressing Station at San Vito in the place vacated by No.5 FA's Casualty Collection Post.

The three Casualty Collection Posts now began to evacuate the wounded to this Advanced Dressing Station at San Vito rather than Rocca.

Meanwhile the ADMS strengthened the facility at Rocca by moving No.1 Field Dressing Station, finally relieved from its duties at Fossacesia on the 11th, to replace No.5 Field Ambulance as the base unit at the Rocca Canadian Medical Centre. The Field Surgical Units and Field Transfusion Unit continued to work there.

As No.4 Field Ambulance's Advanced Dressing Station at San Vito was still subject to enemy shelling, the ADMS ordered that casualties should not be retained there longer than absolutely necessary. Until December 16, therefore, all casualties arriving at San Vito were transferred elsewhere as rapidly as possible: Priority 1 and 2 cases, those requiring resuscitation and/or urgent surgery, to Rocca; priority 3, all other casualties, to Vasto; seriously sick to a British Field Ambulance at Cupello; minor sick to No.2 Light Field Ambulance now stationed at San Vito Marina; and exhaustion cases to a treatment centre established in Rocca.

On the 16th the situation in the Rocca station was intolerable, with the number of patients held by No.1 Field Dressing Station rapidly approaching the maximum capacity of the wards. Although San Vito was not yet safe from enemy artillery, the ADMS decided that he had to move some of the operating work forward. Thus he sent 2CFSU and No.1 Field Transfusion Unit forward to set up there at the Advanced Dressing Station run by No.4 Field Ambulance. No.1 Field Surgical Unit joined them on the 19th, whereupon No.1 Field Dressing Station at Rocca ceased to admit any but exhaustion and venereal disease cases.

No.2 Field Dressing Station, having finally cleared the British wounded out of the station at Casalbordino, was placed in reserve near Rocca. The ADMS would have liked to have the units in reserve more actively involved, but there was a serious lack of space for medical activities in Rocca due to the destruction and to the presence there of large numbers of headquarters people, all requiring places to stay and to work.

December 10-14, 1943

The battle is raging just a few miles away. The din of the artillery is almost constant – there are Canadian artillery units as close as San Vito, and in breaks during night duty the medicals can go outside and watch the barrage light up the sky. The medical centre at Rocca is deluged with casualties requiring either immediate surgery or at least intensive medical attention.

The Field Surgical Units work continuously, either operating or, in their off-shifts, sorting and diagnosing, examining and re-dressing post-operative cases. The Field Transfusion Unit is in a constant state of crisis with blood supplies running short, and new supplies almost always late or arriving just in time from the Casualty Clearing Station at Vasto.

War Diary

December 11, 1943
We were busy all day trying to get our cases re-dressed and straightened up. Starting in again at 1800hrs we did 6 cases. They are nearly all difficult cases and abdomens have been numerous – no less than 7 of these in the past 4 days.

No.1 Field Dressing Station, the host unit of the centre at Rocca, is driven to a state of near-collapse by the influx of wounded. Every nook and cranny in the building is jammed with wounded lying on stretchers or, in many cases, on blankets on the floor. Every case is serious. Every patient is in pain and uncomfortable, and needs a level of attention that the harried orderlies and doctors simply cannot give him. The gas heaters spread around the building keep some of the cold and damp at bay, but there is a constant call for blankets and they are often not available, or blood spattered and awaiting their turn for a visit to the overworked laundry run by the Service Corps in a nearby building.

Harry Francis would like to be doctoring, but he finds himself spending most of his 18-hour days managing a very large and complex medical factory. The raw material for the factory is the flow of wounded coming straight from the battlefield via the Advanced Dressing Station at San Vito. Through the triage process at San Vito they have been selected because they have that vital combination of characteristics: they are so seriously wounded that they must be treated immediately, but if that happens they have a reasonable chance of surviving.

The output of the factory are patients ready to be evacuated back to the Casualty Clearing Station at Vasto, and then probably beyond. Very few of these patients will ever see action again. Their war is over, but it will take most of them months or even years before they can enjoy this release. Decisions on evacuation are amazingly difficult for Harry and his team to make, even with the advice of the surgeons readily available. As doctors they want to keep patients until they are clearly well enough to travel comfortably and safely. As managers, however, they have to evacuate patients much sooner than that because there is simply not enough room to keep them at Rocca. With patient inventory full (and no other ward space available in Rocca), and with new raw material flowing in daily, there must be a matching output via evacuation. The decisions are causing Harry nightmares.

The nightmares are shared by all of the medicals in the centre, surgeons included, due in part to the conditions in which the patients must survive. These are war heroes and they deserve to be clean and warm, in comfortable beds in warm, bright, cheery wards with trained nurses hovering over them and trays of delightful, healthy food served whenever requested. Instead they are cold and dirty, many still in their muddy uniforms torn to expose their wounds. Some have been bathed or partially bathed by the orderlies, but there is not enough time or water or facilities to do the job properly, even with the welcome assistance of a Mobile Hygiene Section that appears occasionally, between visits to the regiments. The patients are on uncomfortable stretchers or blankets on the floor, their bodies aching from the hard surfaces and their inability to move around. Many are cold, and the food that they receive is warmed up army rations, often inappropriate for their condition.

It is an emergency ward gone mad. The hope that every patient clings to, and that all of the medicals pray for, is that he will get sufficiently better quickly so that he can get into that ambulance and move to Vasto and then a hospital beyond. The trick for Harry and his fellow officers is to avoid being swayed too much by sympathy for the plight of these patients, and to make their decisions based on solid medical grounds.

"Something has to give, Rocke," says Harry as they move through their ward rounds in the immediate post-operative section of the centre. "You and Frank are producing too many serious post-op cases, and we're just about out of room for them."

Rocke moves away from a sleeping patient, having checked the large bandage over the man's stomach. This is one of his star cases – a gunner from the 8th Indian Division who suffered a huge gash across his abdomen when a shell exploded close to his gun, sending a mass of shrapnel into the labouring gun crew. They were working so close to the Canadians that it was a Canadian medical team that came to the aid of the crew. They thought initially that the man had been almost torn in half and was dead, but he was alive and incredibly tough. They brought him to San Vito, and within hours he was on the operating table in Rocca. Rocke gives him a 50/50 chance of survival.

"I know, Harry. We're giving you a very heavy load to take care of, and of course most of them have to stick around for a while. Particularly the abdominal cases like this one, and we seem to be getting a lot of them. Frank and I think it would make sense for at least one of us to operate up at San Vito. That would take some of the strain off you here. What do you think?"

"It's a question of space. If they have more space up there, then yes, I would agree. I'm meeting with the ADMS at 1100hrs today. I'll see what he thinks."

Two hours later Harry finds Rocke in the evacuation area of the centre, assisting with the re - dressing of a thigh wound before the lucky soldier departs for Vasto.

"Colonel Playfair agrees about moving one of you fellows up to San Vito. He's been thinking about it for a couple of days now, but has hesitated because there has been too much shellfire there. But he says that the action is almost out of range now, so he's going to send you and the transfusion guys up there on Wednesday. That gives you a day to sort things out with Frank."

56. SAN VITO CHIETINO

The 2CFSU sets up even closer to the fighting.

Wednesday, December 15, 1943

War Diary

St. Vito. Moved up today to join 4 Cdn Fd Amb. This town is near the present front line. We left Rocca at 1400hrs and arrived at St. Vito an hour later and were set up in a small school by suppertime. We did our first case at 2130hrs and were busy the next 10 hours doing 4 cases.

The Advanced Dressing Station in San Vito Chietino is a deserted and badly battered schoolhouse. It is a square, brick, three-storey building with about one quarter of the windows blown out. Miraculously, the electricity and water systems both work, thanks to the engineers who had come through with the first wave of Canadians to prepare the town for headquarters staff and medicals. Leaving aside the kitchen, washrooms and cloakroom area there is space for one room for operating with a tiny room next to it for wash station, sterilizer and cot for catnapping, two examining rooms near the main entrance on the second floor, and ward space for about 100 in very cramped conditions. The Field Dressing Station has set up a crude but functioning laundry in the basement, which also has racks for storing supplies and equipment.

There are still occasional explosions in San Vito from German mortars and artillery, harassing the units behind the Canadian front lines. The 2CFSU team learns quickly to ignore them, although it is impossible to forget them completely.

They find that the room in the schoolhouse designated as OR has been used for a variety of first aid purposes and is consequently dirty and untidy. Eric directs them in their now-familiar clean-up drill and Fly Patrol while Rocke, Shorty and the orderlies accompany Peter Tisdale on ward rounds.

"You aren't much better off here than Harry is back at Rocca," says Rocke as they climb the stairs to the top-floor wards. "You aren't full to capacity yet, but there's an awful lot of patients here and many of them look mighty uncomfortable."

"I know, Rocke. It's the damndest thing trying to keep up with such a stream of wounded. We have to give the new arrivals immediate attention for obvious reasons – they're often bleeding and in serious pain, so we need to stabilize them before we can even decide where to send them next. It's always a relief when we can send then down the line direct to Vasto. What I mean is a relief that they're not so badly wounded, but also of course that we can get them out of here quickly. But then there's the badly wounded ones who need more work here, and then have to go over to Rocca for treatment or operating. We've actually done a few minor operations here, but nothing big. The trick is to move them through quickly enough to have space to handle the intake."

"Right," says Rocke. "Well, it's going to get worse now that we're here, because you're going to have to keep patients we operate on for longer. And I think Frank will be joining us here soon, so then this place is really going to be loaded."

"Heaven help us!" replies Peter. "Well, I guess we'll just have to do what we can. If only we had some more orderlies so that we could look after the patients better. You know, wash them and keep them cleaner and a bit more comfortable, not to mention just getting to them sooner when they come in! Or better still, send us some nurses! Real, live, trained nurses who can show these orderlies how it's really done, and boost their morale a bit." He shrugs as they move into the first wardroom. "But on to more practical things…your guys are fixing up the OR I assume. Our drivers can show yours where the sleeping quarters are. We have a beaten-up house about a block away."

Rocke and Shorty inspect the OR, which is small but now shining clean, and has two extra lamps hooked directly to the unit's generator in the surgical van, parked outside the window. It is pitch black outside as they go to the kitchen for supper, and then it's time to scrub for the first case. Just before 2100hrs the Canadian artillery battery on the outskirts of San Vito opens fire with a terrific salvo. Looking through the wards Rocke can see several of the patients covering their faces in fear, both present and in memory. One of them is shaking visibly. The noise of war, still so close at hand, is yet another problem to be dealt with by these men, so terribly wounded and deserving of some peace.

Thursday, December 16

Cold and rainy, as usual.

Rocke wakes out of an exhausted sleep at 1100hrs, grumbling that three hours sleep is just bloody well not enough. He is, however, delighted to find a bag of mail for the unit waiting for him, and the team has its usual brief quiet period while they catch up on news from home. Rocke has another lovely picture of the family, and lots of stories from Rolly about Tam's exploits at school and how Ian refused to wear a rain hat. This gives him a smile, although the familiar ache of loneliness haunts him until he finishes the letter, places the picture next to his bed, and looks at the other official looking envelope addressed to him.

It has a British army envelope and letterhead, and he starts to read it dully without even checking the signature first. But as he reads his mood lightens wonderfully.

> *"Dear Major Robertson*
> *I am writing to tell you that I have now recovered fully from my wound that you operated on back in Agira, in Sicily. I was in the hospital for about five weeks, and then at a rehab centre for another month, before being posted back to my unit that is now in Italy.*
> *I am sorry to have taken so long to write you, but I wanted to be sure that I was fully recovered first, and we have been very busy here in Italy.*
> *Thank you for your wonderful work, and for saving me from the flies! Please give my best to Matt Curran and Jimmy Price and Bill McKenzie.*
> *Yours sincerely,*
> *Jon Robson (Pte)"*

Rocke has tears in his eyes as he calls for McKenzie, shows him the letter and asks him to tell the others.

Then it's up and to work starting at 1300hrs. The artillery noise is continuous and very distracting, as well as being upsetting to many of the patients. At 1615hrs they are in the middle of an operation on a mangled foot when there are sounds of live explosions close by the hospital. They carry on the work, but Shorty can't help wondering out loud if the Germans are counter-attacking and might even overrun San Vito. McKenzie puts his head in the door and tells them that a few German shells have landed in the village and, through hellish bad luck, have struck a platoon of soldiers from the Hastings and Prince Edward Regiment who are in town for a brief respite – showers, a hot meal and distribution of Christmas parcels.

Rocke and Peter Tisdale hear the details from a Sergeant from 'B' Company of the Hasty Pees who is supervising the transport of the casualties to the medical station. "It's a terrible bloody business, Major. These guys were here for a break, and this is supposed to be a safe place! Then 'wham!', a shell lands right beside the truck and kills one lad and wounds six others. So we were carrying the wounded men over here and we just got to the village square when another shell landed right on top of us. Four more men are dead, and now as you can see we have most of the No.12 platoon wounded. Five men dead and 29 wounded, and all in this 'safe place'! Safe, my ass."

"Unbelievable!" says Peter, pressing a hand to his weary forehead. "Sergeant, we're going to head over and sort out the wounded right away. I've already seen at least one who will need surgery immediately. Meanwhile I'll have an orderly look at your arm. You didn't quite escape yourself, you know." The Sergeant looks down at his left arm, soaked with blood from a shrapnel wound just below the shoulder. "Christ, I hadn't even noticed that!" he mumbles.

The 29 new patients fill the building to its capacity and then some. There are now stretchers in the hallways, tripping the orderlies as they rush about their frantic rounds.

December 17 – 19, 1943

The 2CFSU is busy throughout the period with the exception of one unusual lull in new cases on December 17, with only one operation all day.

The team pitches in to help in the wards, and Shorty runs a much-needed outpatient clinic for the local inhabitants of the town. Some of them have been living in caves for months to avoid the Germans. They are hungry and malnourished, and many have small wounds suffered when running through debris-strewn streets to avoid capture or artillery fire. Every patient is treated to a sandwich and cup of soup.

On December 19 the unit sleeps until mid-afternoon, having worked throughout the previous night. After doing one case they have supper, and shortly thereafter the three vehicles of No.1 Field Surgical Unit pull up to the hospital building and Frank Mills walks in to see Peter Tisdale and Rocke.

"Welcome Frank," says Peter. "You're just what we need to be really busy! Now we can have a 24-hour stream of new cases with nowhere to put them!"

"Hi Peter," replies Frank with a grin. "I knew you'd be pleased to see us. But now listen, Playfair knows about your problems here and is doing everything he can to speed up the evacuation system. I'm here now because he thinks we should concentrate operating in one place. He's sending a bunch of orderlies from No.2 FDS along as well to help out in the wards. No.2 FDS is sitting in reserve in Rocca waiting to move into Ortona as soon as possible. Which means that you, Peter, are running a Field Dressing Station right here, as well as an ambulance operation. Congratulations!"

Peter is mulling this over when Rocke joins in. "Peter, this is going to be rough for you, but all I can say is that we are here to help you in any way we can when we're not operating. My orderlies and OR assistants are terrific with patients. They'll focus on the immediate post-op patients, of course, but that should at least take a bit of pressure off your fellows."

Rocke and Frank agree that they will go on 24-hour shifts, with Frank starting at 1800hrs tomorrow. Frank has his team check out the OR and move in their supplies and any extra equipment they may require, and they head off to the sleeping quarters. The 2CFSU team return to the OR and prepare to work on a young soldier from the Hasty Pees who has a burst appendix.

57. ORTONA STREET FIGHT

Bitter house-to-house fighting in the streets of Ortona.

December 20 – 28, 1943

There are differing views of when the Battle of Ortona actually began. Was it at the fight to cross the Sangro? The Moro? Or was it the assault from the north bank of the Moro that was supposed to proceed quickly into and through Ortona, but was stalled for 10 days of vicious fighting at the Gully? Or was it just the fighting in Ortona itself? No matter what the interpretation, there is no doubt that the eight days of fire and brimstone in Ortona was the climactic phase of a battle that was one of the finest displays of Canadian courage and victory ever recorded in the annals of war.

When the British high command reset their sights for the pre-winter campaign from Pescara and Avezzano to Ortona, they held back on artillery and air bombardments of the town as they intended to use it as a transport and supply centre for the continuing assault north, and east towards Rome. They fully expected that the Germans, having lost the Gully to the Allies, would slip through Ortona to establish a defensive line farther north. The German army had, after all, learned a very hard lesson in the horrors of house-to-house fighting in Stalingrad, and were unlikely to try it again here.

Wrong. The German high command gave orders to stop the Allies at Ortona at all costs, and that is what they tried to do, at huge cost to the structure of the town. Before the war Ortona had been a popular vacation spot for Italians. For years after the war there was little there for anyone to enjoy. The seriousness of the German resistance was measured by the fact that they threw a complete Parachute Division into the battle. These were battle-hardened and well-rested veterans who were skilled in every aspect of this type of fighting. The Canadians were certainly battle-hardened, but were also battle-weary and seriously un-

der-strength due to the heavy losses in the Sicily/Italy campaign. It was a tough match-up.

As the Canadians turned the end of the Gully and established themselves on the Ortona/Orsogna road, the Germans withdrew into Ortona and prepared their defences with a view to making every inch taken extremely costly to the attackers. They turned their dreadful experiences in Stalingrad into good ideas as defenders in Ortona.

The start of the action was innocuous and misleading. On the evening of December 20, Canadian officers from the Royal Canadian Regiment and the Royal Canadian Engineers walked up the Ortona/Orsogna road and into the southern edge of Ortona. They were looking to see if the road was mined, as the intention was for a combined infantry and tank force to enter the town in the morning and roll from one end of it to the other. They proceeded about 200 yards into the town without seeing any sign of a mine or a gun, and returned to their units optimistic that they would at least be able to gain a strong foothold in the town.

The next morning proved them wrong. The soldiers from the Loyal Edmonton Regiment who launched the attack were under intense fire even before they reached the edge of the town. Some did get in, just, but the Germans engaged them immediately. The Seaforth Highlanders had better luck on the right flank, getting well into the town before meeting some stiff resistance. The Three Rivers Tanks supported the infantry, but soon realized that the Germans had blocked roadways in a way that their tanks could not move down many side streets, and must often move forward with their flanks unprotected. They were halted on main thoroughfares by huge piles of rubble, some of it from a cathedral that the Germans had destroyed for the purpose. The enemy had spiked the rubble with mines for good measure.

The streets were riddled with mines and the buildings with German machine gun nests and deadly snipers. Every building was booby-trapped. Carefully placed obstructions in the streets forced the Canadians to move in predictable directions and paths, often into pre-selected killing grounds.

Many of the civilians in Ortona were hiding in railway tunnels running under the town. The Germans were completely familiar with this system, and used it to give them mobility in moving men around the battle area, and as resting places. They would launch lightening raids within the Canadian positions, having infiltrated there via the tunnels, surprising the Canadians with devastating machine gun fire from behind or the side before disappearing again into the tunnels.

For several days the Germans actually felt that they could hold the Canadians almost as long as they wished.

As the days progressed the Canadians had to use ingenuity and a heavy dose of courage to proceed against the well dug-in enemy. In house-to-house fighting the initiative came from the individual fighters, often totally out of touch with their Commanders. They may have started as a group with specific orders, but they were soon out there on their own, perhaps within occasional sight or hailing distance of comrades, but dependent on their own courage and strength to stay alive and to advance.

Moving from house to house was a hazardous proposition, as they had to go around the intervening wall to get at the next house. The Germans in that house would lie in wait, and shoot at the Canadians as they made their moves. The Canadians developed a system that they called 'mouse-holing' to help them do so. They would blow a hole in the intervening wall or walls at mid-floor level, and pour through the hole and up and down the stairs to kill the Germans while they were still stunned. It worked well, enabling them to move through streets much more quickly than previously. They also used their tanks and anti-tank guns to blast buildings concealing German defenders.

Reinforcements for the depleted Canadian units were arriving periodically, many of them coming straight from training and with no combat experience. The danger of putting such inexperienced troops into such a battle scene was often cruelly demonstrated, occasionally in a most dramatic fashion. In one case a group of 20 reinforcements literally marched into Ortona, right down the centre of a major street, and was immediately destroyed by mortar fire before an officer in the town could shout a warning for them to get the hell out of line and into cover.

While the battle was raging in Ortona, General Vokes launched on December 23 an offensive to surround Ortona by pushing troops around to the north. Just as at Stalingrad where the Russians had succeeded in surrounding the German army and destroying it, so the Canadians hoped to surround them here and kill them or force their surrender or, at the least, their rapid withdrawal from Ortona to avoid capture. This offensive, like the assault on Ortona itself, was bitterly contested by the German paratroopers and slowed by terrible weather that rendered tanks virtually useless for several days.

In spite of heroic efforts to serve Christmas dinner to the troops, there was no lull in the fighting on Christmas Day. Both inside the town and on the ridges to the west, Germans and Canadians spent the day trying to kill each other. The *flanking action had taken the Highlanders a mile within the German lines, and the Germans were taking their threat seriously. By now the Royal Canadian Regiment had joined in the flanking movement, and on Christmas Day they took heavy casualties. In Ortona the Germans used flame-throwers for the first time – a deadly new twist to an already horrible scene.*

But they were still gradually giving ground, and in the flanking movement the Canadians were finally able to bring tanks into play, giving them forward momentum. In later years it was learned that starting around December 26, German reports to their high command greatly exaggerated the strength of the Canadian forces. They were making excuses for losing.

But they hadn't lost yet, and after a particularly deadly mine explosion in a building virtually destroyed a platoon of Loyal Edmontons, the Canadians in Ortona sought vengeance by turning more and more to heavy explosives to destroy whole buildings containing Germans, rather than trying to roust them out in combat. General Hoffmeister called up the PPCLIs, who had been held in reserve, to strengthen the offensive in Ortona and help to finish the job quickly.

The Germans withdrew from Ortona during the night of December 27. On the morning of December 28 the town was silent. There were no enemy in sight, and the Canadian troops soon found that the Germans had abandoned the town during the night. Civilians started to appear out of caves and tunnels and basements. The Canadians secured the town, and many soldiers just lay down where they were and slept.

The Canadian medical units remained virtually static during the battle in Ortona, with two exceptions. No.5 Field Ambulance upgraded its Casualty Collection Post at Sant' Apollinare to an Advanced Dressing Station, and took over responsibility for triage from No.4 Field Ambulance in San Vito. This meant that No.4 FA could focus on resuscitation and urgent surgical cases.

No.2 Field Dressing Station moved from reserve in Rocca to occupy buildings in Sant' Apollinare with capacity of 80 patients, and opened to receive a proportion of the minor sick.

Severe casualties from both the battle in Ortona and the flanking action around Ortona flowed through the Regimental Aid Posts and the Divisional Field Ambulances to the Canadian Medical Centre at San Vito Chietino.

58. THE GENERAL

General Hoffmeister visits the medicals in San Vito.

Monday, December 20, 1943

There is a pause in the flow of serious casualties to the medical centre in San Vito. Rocke and Shorty and three of the men drive to Rocca to pick up laundry and some mail, and to visit their post-operative cases. They are doing well, and all are longing for the day when they can be evacuated to some place more comfortable. Harry tells Rocke that with the FSUs now located at San Vito his evacuation program is running much more smoothly.

"In fact," he says, "Playfair has us focusing now on VD and exhaustion cases. How's that for a combination of problems? I must say I can understand the exhaustion business. I've seen lots of cases and the poor guys really are a mess. So we're getting some psychiatric help, and we'll have roomfuls of shell shock cases to handle. But VD? Where the hell do these guys get a chance to catch VD? There's hardly a woman to be seen around here!"

"Well I guess there must be," replies Rocke with a wry grin. "Our soldiers are damn good you know, and they can spot a woman at 500 yards! We all can. But some of the men are really especially good, and I guess we've passed through enough small towns with bars open to give them the opportunity they need. In fact, back at Horsham we had a patient who had been at Dieppe, and got himself a light wound in the leg and a heavy dose of gonorrhea! He was heading up into the town when he heard a call from a window, and there was the love of his life! So while our soldiers were being pummelled in the town, he was being pummelled in bed! He left only when he heard his unit retreating down the street outside that window!"

300 .∴. WHILE BULLETS FLY

"Right. Well, so they have a nice screw and then, a couple of weeks later, 'presto', they come and see Uncle Harry for some treatment. Actually it really is too bad, Rocke. It's taken some really fine soldiers out of action, and these are guys who have fought long and hard and deserve to go home with a medal rather than the drip. And we have all types in here: one Lieutenant, a Quartermaster, several Corporals and lots of Privates. This morning we even took in a despatch rider from the ADMS staff. You may remember him – Billy Santer? He was all over the place back in Sicily, and we've seen him several times in Italy. He's come down with a very serious dose."

"Oh yes, I remember Santer," says Rocke. "I'd heard that he was having some luck, and some of the men were very jealous. Well, they won't be now."

"Anyway, on to other things. How's the surgery going at San Vito?"

"We have a good surgery set-up. We've had lots of work to do up until today, when there seems to be a lull. I hear that the assault on Ortona is just getting underway, so we should be heating up again in the next day or so. The big issue for us is lack of space and orderlies, just like it was here a week ago. Peter is handling big inflows every day. Many of them don't need operating, thank heavens, but they all need intensive care and the orderlies are running themselves ragged trying to keep up. My men are pitching in whenever they can, as are Shorty and I, and Frank will be doing the same as soon as he has some time. You know the scene. We have a great big emergency ward going full tilt, but manned by under-trained orderlies. It's really tough on the patients, but it's all we can do at the moment. We're still under occasional shellfire, so we can't expect nurses to come along and help out. I just wish we could!"

Back at San Vito No.1 FSU takes over the operating room and begins its 24-hour shift at 1800hrs.

Tuesday, December 21, 1943

The No.1 FSU team has had a night of modest activity – two operations, one on either side of midnight. They have another mid-morning, and then do clean-up and ward service until their shift ends at 1800hrs. Rocke's team takes over just as a new load of wounded arrive at the centre, and three of them are slated for surgery. It is a busy night.

Wednesday, December 22, 1943

Frank Mills and Captain Tovee visit Rocca to check on their post-operative cases. The 2CFSU team has a busy day of operations and ward work, and are happy when the No.1 FSU team takes over at 1800hrs.

Thursday, December 23, 1943

Several days ago Rocke applied for a short Christmas leave for his team at the No.1 Canadian General Hospital at Andria, back down the coast between Foggia and Bari. This would mean hard duty for Frank as he would have to do all surgery from the proposed departure on December 23 to return on December 27, but he has graciously agreed. It would, after all, make up for the leave to Naples that Frank's team had taken from Campobasso, and that Rocke's team had been denied due to Jack Leishman's illness. They both hoped that there would be a lull in the fighting at Christmas.

Permission came through yesterday, and at 1430 hrs the 2CFSU team plus Captain Ed Tovee, Frank's Second-in-Command, pile into vehicles, leaving only driver Sammy Smart to watch over their things in San Vito. Frank waves them away and then returns to his work.

At 1615hrs Frank is nursing a cup of tea between operations, staring out the window at a truck below that is burning fiercely. Orderlies are dousing the side of the building with buckets of water to keep it safe. The truck has been parked next to the open-windowed wall to protect the people inside from shrapnel. Five minutes ago it took a direct hit from an artillery shell. Frank shudders at the thought of that shell landing 20 feet to the left. It would have taken out the entire centre.

His batman bursts into the room to tell him that General Bert Hoffmeister has just arrived at the medical centre, and Major Tisdale has invited Frank to join him in hosting the General. Frank is surprised and thrilled. The Commander of the 2nd Canadian Infantry Brigade has already gained legendary status for his inspirational leadership. It is typical of the General that he would take the time to come to the centre to visit his wounded troops.

Frank rushes down to the front entrance where Peter is greeting the General and his Aide. General Hoffmeister is very tall and young looking, and for some reason is dressed as a private. Then Frank remembers that senior officers who stay close to the action often 'dress down' to avoid the unwanted attentions of German snipers looking for important targets. His next thought is that Peter looks terrible, spattered with blood, pale and dishevelled. He realizes that he probably looks the same, for the same reasons. He salutes, and Hoffmeister returns the salute and then smiles and shakes his hand.

"Hello Major. It's nice to meet you at last. I've heard so much about you and Rocke Robertson; is he here too?

"He's just gone off for a short leave, Sir," replies Frank.

"Right. Well gentlemen, I thought I'd look in on some of my men. Major Tisdale, you have a very big operation here. It's lucky that shell missed the building!"

"It is indeed, Sir," says Peter as he leads the small party into the first ward. Hoffmeister stops at the doorway, a look of consternation on his face as he stares at the crowded, bloody scene of wounded men and scurrying, grey-faced orderlies. He regains his composure and begins his tour through the room. The patients have been told who their important guest is, and they do their best to smile and answer his questions. The party moves through all of the wards in 20 minutes, and stops on the front doorstep for final words.

"My God, Peter, I had no idea you were up against it like this," says Hoffmeister, his face flushed and worried. "You must have almost 100 patients there, all of them serious, and the poor guys are jammed in like sardines. In fact some of them seem to have been waiting a long time to get fixed up. What's the status? Can you handle it? What do you need?"

"Well, Sir," replies Peter, picking his words carefully. "We could use a new building and a few more doctors and warmer weather and faster evacuations. Of course that's not possible, but what we really need are nurses. Real, trained nurses, Sir. Those poor orderlies in there…you know most of them have first aid training at best. They're doing their damndest and working themselves to death, but we're dealing with really complicated cases, and it just isn't enough. Some trained nurses would be an absolute godsend."

"I can understand that Peter, but this is still a war zone, and as you know nurses are not permitted to work in war zones."

"I know, Sir," says Frank. "But as Peter says the situation here is critical. And most of the nurses I know would be perfectly willing to come here to work, and to hell with the regulations."

Hoffmeister pauses to think. The doctors gaze at their feet.

"Right," says the General. "Gentlemen, why don't you send a request down the line of hospitals for some nurses, and reference me. Let's just see what happens. OK, I'm off. Thank you both for your time." They salute, he salutes, and he steps into his jeep and is driven away. Frank and Peter rush to the radio room of the medical centre and send out the request.

59. CHRISTMAS LEAVE

The 2CFSU team enjoys some leave back at the CGH located in Andria.

The 120-mile journey to Andria takes five hours on roads now much clearer of traffic than previously, and the 2CFSU team arrive at the hospital and are welcomed by Rocke's old colleague Cam Dickison, now a senior surgeon at the hospital.

"Hello Rocke. Welcome to civilization! Hi Shorty. Great to see you again. And you must be Captain Tovee. Welcome. And also hello to the Corporal and all of you chaps. We have a good place for you to stay, and I think you'll find a few more sights to see here than in San Vito. The Colonel is away doing something or other so he'll see you in the morning. Let's get you settled, and then perhaps Rocke, you and Shorty and Captain Tovee will join me at the officers' club for a drink?"

They are in front of a modern two storey Italian civil hospital near the centre of the town that looks like a superb location for the No.1 CGI. However Cam climbs into a jeep and leads them about half a mile away from the hospital to a schoolyard with two buildings on it, a junior and a senior school. They get out at the second building that Cam describes as 'staff quarters', and find small, simple and clean rooms waiting for them. Rocke asks Cam to tell Corporal Branch where the bright lights of town are so that he can lead the men there, and then the officers climb into Cam's jeep and drive to the officers' club.

The club is an old restaurant on the town square. It has some damage but is in reasonable shape, and the Italian owner is all smiles as he shows them to their table and delivers the first bottle of wine.

"This is a bit of alright, Cam. Here's to you," says Rocke. They raise their glasses in a toast. "It looks like you have a pretty good set-up here…lots of space at the hospital, and good facilities in the town?"

"That we do, Rocke. This town took some serious damage, but the locals have brought it back to life very quickly. It's really quite amazing to see their spirit after taking such a beating for so long. We arrived here in late November, straight out from England. We opened our doors on December 1. The big building you arrived at is the main hospital, and it's really a treat to be there. It was built just a few years ago, and is modern and well laid out and equipped. It's very bright and cheery, and all the beds and furniture are there and in grand shape. The plumbing is a bit dodgy, but there's some British engineers stationed nearby who have promised to fix it up soon. The operating theatres are a work of art. I'll show you around tomorrow. Oh, and you'll enjoy the slogans. The Fascists wrote their slogans on the walls in the wards: 'Credere, Obbedire, Combattere', which means 'Believe, Obey, Fight'. Nice eh? Sounds like a marriage vow…which reminds me Rocke, Thelma sends her love.

They laugh, and then Shorty pipes up. "How many beds do you have here, Cam?"

Cam explains that they have 600 officially, but have had to add another 200 to keep up with the work. From the day they opened they have been overrun with patients, just as it has been over at No.14 CGH at Caserta, which opened a few days after Andria. They receive a full flow of patients from the Ortona area – the serious wounded plus all the other ones who don't need front line operating, and for a short while they were taking in quite a few Brits as well. The CGH at Andria is called a 'line of communication hospital', which means that they take them all in, sort them out, and evacuate them as quickly as they can. They send the Brits back to their hospital at Bari, and the Canadians over to Caserta. Since they opened they have had almost 2,000 admissions and 1,200 discharges or transfers.

"The rest are with us, and we're working like hell to move them through because we hear that Ortona is pretty tough going and we can expect to have a lot more coming in. The 600 beds are in the main hospital, and the overflow beds are in the senior school building. In the staff quarters building we have all of our accommodation plus some examination and rehab rooms and offices. It's really quite a show. And what we have and you don't have are nurses, and thank God for that. We couldn't hope to cope with this flow of wounded without the nurses."

"You're damn lucky," says Rocke as he calls for the next bottle of wine. "We sure could use some, but there's still quite a lot of artillery fire landing in the town. Tell me, are you doing much surgery?"

"A lot more than I expected. I thought that you fellows would be doing most of it up front, but we've found a whole lot to do back here as well. Of course we have secondary work on your patients, re-setting and secondary suturing and the like. But we also find that many of the troops who have been sent via triage straight here with relatively minor injuries aren't quite as minor as expected, and require some sort of fix-up. So yes, it's a busy place."

The conversation drifts on to comparisons of service in the two locations. Two bottles later they head back to the staff quarters to sleep.

Friday, December 24, 1940

Christmas Eve at Andria starts with everyone sleeping in late, thoroughly tired from the previous day's long drive and evening's festivities. They manage to drag themselves up to have lunch, but there is already the languor of relaxation setting in after months of tension, and while the officers wander through a tour of the hospital, stopping to greet previous cases, the other ranks head back for more snoozes. Then it's a walk through the town to test the bars, and back for dinner and a movie in the evening.

The officers finish their rounds and then join a cocktail party hosted by Colonel Ruddick, the officer in charge of the hospital. Matron Nel Swanson is still with the hospital and still her old self in spite of the departure of Sergeant Hank Money several months ago. She has taken up with a new lover, a Captain anaesthetist, still enjoys her gin at the parties, and still runs a good, albeit social, ship. Dinner happens sometime during the evening.

Saturday, December 25, 1943

Christmas is a business day for the hospital at Andria, but not for the group on leave from San Vito. They relax and snooze, eat grand meals in the canteen and stroll about the town. In the afternoon they visit their post-operative patients in the wards, seeking to spread some Christmas cheer to the wounded soldiers. In the evening there is an all-ranks dinner and dance, complete with turkey and stuffing and lots of wine. A feature of the event is the performance by Cam Dickison on his accordion. He is an accomplished player, and was fortunate to be able to ship the instrument to Italy concealed in a container of medical supplies. It is a fun and relaxing time.

Rocke and Cam share a table with Nel Swanson and her anaesthetist lover Captain Ron Furlong. They are a happy, lusty couple and Rocke feels envious, as do the 75 other people in the room. They are also garrulous and fun, and Rocke enjoys dancing with the famous matron. At the table they compare notes about life in a hospital such as this, and in a field unit. The comparison is an interesting one.

The hospital is very large and extremely busy with a huge variety of patients, from seriously battle-wounded to VD cases to all sorts of illnesses. At least it has a stable work environment for the staff, with levels of cleanliness and efficiency similar to those at hospitals back home, and with the nurses to make it so. The FSU is much smaller, but also very busy and with generally miserable working conditions. All of its patients, by definition, are seriously wounded. The hospital people are interested in Rocke's stories of life in the field, and far from being repelled by the conditions, generally feel that they would be happy to be posted up front. The talk turns to home and families, and everyone gets a bit misty-eyed, and it's jolly fun.

Sunday, December 26, 1943

There is a church parade in the morning for troops and medicals in Andria. A company of Canadian reinforcement troops for the 2nd Infantry Brigade are in town en route to Ortona, and put on a splendid show of drill and spit and polish in the town square, to the delight of a substantial crowd of local inhabitants. The staff from the hospital is considerably less impressive, and Rocke is somewhat embarrassed by the show that his 2CFSU team (including himself) puts on. Their drilling is very rusty, and their uniforms shoddy. He consoles himself with the thought that…*we've come from an action area, so what the hell do people expect?*

He watches the manoeuvres of the reinforcements with pride mingled with a strong dose of sadness. He knows full well what they are getting into, and what a slim chance most of them have of surviving it. They are lambs to the slaughter – raw, hastily -trained soldiers with nice uniforms, heading into an inferno where only the tough, experienced veterans have any realistic hope of surviving. There are simply too many tricks of the trade to be learned, and in Ortona there is no time for learning. You either know what you are doing or you die…or at least meet Rocke at the operating table.

He thinks of an operation he did just days ago on a young soldier brought in with reinforcements for the Seaforth Highlanders. The man was no more than 19 years old, with a fresh uniform and shaven face. Within minutes of moving into Ortona with a small squad of experienced Seaforths he had been too slow in seeking shelter in a doorway and taken a sniper bullet in the groin. He had 10 minutes of war, and then a lifetime of pain and regrets. *I wonder how many of the fresh faces marching here today will be on my table within a week? Dammit to hell, what a stupid bloody waste!*

He fights the sense of depression that seems to come all too easily these days. *It just seems so hopeless - so many people trapped in a nightmare of violence and death, with seemingly no way to get out of it except on a stretcher or in a coffin.* He looks around the square, and sees in the far corner a young Italian couple watching the parade. She is a lovely young woman, or would be with some food and care and better clothes than the ragged dress she is wearing. He is tall and gaunt, with a haunted look in his eyes. Yet they are holding hands and watching the parade with tiny smiles at the corners of their mouths. This is clearly the beginning of hope for them. Heaven knows what they have been through. It clearly has not been nice, but now they are amongst friends who look tough and well organized and are here to rid the land of their enemies. Rocke's depression lifts simultaneously with an unsoldierly misting of the eyes – whether tears of sadness or happiness or relief he has no idea. Probably a mixture.

The padre drones on for a while. Captain Tovee plays a beaten-up piano for a hymn that everyone knows by heart and then, suddenly, the rain comes down in sheets and the padre's hurried blessing is followed by a stampede for cover.

After lunch the team has a leisurely afternoon, most of them revelling in the chance to snooze without fear of a call to service. That evening the officers are hosted in a casual dinner by the officers of the hospital while the other ranks hit the town for a spot of 'relaxation'.

Monday, December 27, 1943

Rocke accepts Colonel Ruddick's invitation to give a seminar for the staff on field surgery. His initial impulse is to bring along just the officers, but he then decides to bring the whole team, and in the end he is glad that he does.

His 10-man team plus Captain Tovee face 35 hospital staff, mainly doctors and nurses, in a large meeting room on the main floor. Rocke leads off with thanks to the hosts for the warm welcome the 2CFSU team has received. He says how nice it is to be back in a hospital again after months driving around in a truck, and the answering smiles show him that the Christmas spirit is still alive here, and he can keep the session light and enjoyable.

He starts with an over-all description of the concept of the FSU, and how it works with the other field units to provide medical services right up close to the fighting troops. He describes the main categories of wounds that they deal with, and some of the main medical issues that arise when operating in primitive conditions. This starts a lively discussion, with particular focus on the subject of the 'hand-over' of patients from the field units through the Casualty Clearing Stations to the hospitals: patient preparation, transport problems, the handling of records, stabilization of patients on arrival at hospital, and so on. The audience is mesmerized by Rocke's description of the incident of Pte. Jon Roberts and the flies at Agira.

After coffee Rocke turns it over to the others to have their say on whatever subject they think might be of interest. Ed Tovee quietens the room when he describes the 48-hour operating blitz that the No.1 FSU went through at Foggia. A religious man, he ascribes the ability of the team to survive such a marathon of surgery to 'the grace of God and a lot of strong, black coffee'.

Shorty Long talks about the hazards of anaesthetics in uncertain field conditions. He reminds the audience that the team is often dealing with soldiers fresh from the field, in very uncertain physical condition (dehydration, exhaustion), usually with some level of morphine in them, and quickly and sometimes not too expertly prepared for surgery. The precise dosage of morphine and its timing are usually question marks in spite of the best efforts of stretcher-bearers and other field personnel to record and report. These uncertainties add a dangerous dimension to the anaesthetic process on the operating table.

Rocke then asks Eric to describe how the unit sets up and packs and moves around the countryside, and this starts a session of wonderful story-telling and comedy. Eric talks about the three vehicles and their functions. He is interrupted by Pete Monroe saying, "Corporal Branch is assuming that the damn things work at all." All eyes turn to Pete, and he produces a flood of stories about the finicky nature of the vans and the amazing experiences he has had with army repair depots, and especially those bandits back at Reggio. Eric finally stops him and gets back onto the subject of mobility and set-ups.

When Eric describes the different sorts of structures they have used as operating theatres, Matt Curran pipes up and has the crowd in stitches with his graphic description of a 'Fly Patrol, Sicilian style'. This brings Dave Finley into the act, giving a brief but very amusing presentation on 'the scientific aspects of magazine manipulation for fly control in operating rooms'.

To Rocke's surprise even Bill McKenzie, the silent and efficient bat-man, comes to the fore with a wonderful, meandering talk that he starts by saying "Oh yeah, you think these guys are important? Let me tell you what I do." He describes the horrendous conditions of some of the wash stations he has had to set up, and how the surgeons and OR assistants "still go through the whole scrubbing act, even when the water looks like bad soup." He tells them how to wake up an officer in the middle of the night (give them a nudge and tell them the coffee's ready), and how this differs from waking up Corporal Branch at the same hour (very, very politely or there's hell to pay). He describes the dangers of tropical insects and animals, illustrating the point with the story of Jack Leishman's long night at Valguarnera trembling in fear of a stray belt under his bed.

Rocke figures that this is a good way to end the session, and besides it's lunchtime and they are still on leave. He finishes the session with a reminder to everyone that the job that they all have, from field unit through to hospital, is saving lives, and that this will be successful only if they are all in it together and work as a team. He thanks the Colonel once again for the hospitality, the Colonel thanks the team for the presentations, and the session ends.

After a jovial lunch in the canteen, the team packs up and loads the van. There are handshakes all around, and they head off back towards San Vito at 1430hrs. They stop in at Barletta to pay their respects to the British

Casualty Clearing Station there, have dinner at a restaurant at San Severo, and arrive back at San Vito at 2100hrs.

Rocke tells his team to wait for instructions, and then he and Captain Tovee go into the building and up to the operating area where they find Frank sipping tea, resting after a particularly sinister abdominal case. He is very tired. He greets his colleagues, says that he hopes they have had a good time, and tells them that he has been going flat out since they left, and is damn tired. And that there is one more case lined up for the night.

"Well done, Frank. Now then, what's say we take over now and you and your gang get some rest? We'll take it through until 1800hrs tomorrow, and then we'll be back on shifts."

"No thanks," replies Frank. I think we have just one case tonight, and then it should be quiet. You've had a long day too."

"OK. Oh by the way, has the Christmas mailbag come in yet?"

"No it hasn't, and we're all pretty upset about it. I just hope it comes in soon."

Rocke is just starting down the stairs when Frank calls after him. "Oh by the way, I have some good news for you. We're going to have some nurses here soon."

"What?" shouts Rocke. "What do you mean? What happened?"

Frank describes the visit of the General and says that within two days of their sending out the request for nurses they had received an offer of four nurses from the British hospital at Bari to come to San Vito. Evidently they had a meeting and called for volunteers, and every nurse in the hospital had volunteered, and four had been selected and should be arriving soon.

"That's terrific!" says Rocke. "I didn't hear about your request at Andria. I wonder if they received it? They might have, but they're going flat out there so probably decided not to respond. Anyway, that is wonderful news. Four British nurses! Well done Frank!"

He goes out to the lorry and tells the team the good news, and they return to their lodgings in a very happy mood.

60. WAR ZONE

An artillery shell comes a bit too close for comfort.

Tuesday, December 28, 1943

At 0730hrs Rocke is slowly waking up when there is the sound of loud explosions towards the town centre. It sounds like an air raid – an infrequent event now with the Allies controlling the air, but still an occasional problem. Rocke is half awake when a cannon shell bursts through the ceiling of his room, passes over his bed and rips out of the side wall, leaving jagged holes in both places. He leaps out of bed and stands looking at the hole in the wall, his mind racing. His main thought is that while the medicals simply ignore the shellfire around them in San Vito, sort of vaguely assuming that it's not really meant for them, this brings home very dramatically the fact that it really is bad stuff and they could easily get hurt whether it's meant for them or not.

Another thought is relief that this was not an artillery shell or they would all be blown to smithereens by now. He notices that there is a commotion outside the widow. He looks out at the surgical van parked under the window and sees a neat shell hole in the roof of the cab, and three of his team standing looking at the vehicle.

He hurries into his clothes and rushes outside to inspect the van. The only visible damage except for the roof of the cab, which he can't see from the street, is the shattered windshield. He sees that the hood over the engine is up and prays that the engine is OK. Eric Branch, Pete Monroe and Sammy Smart are standing beside the van, looking shaken and talking in loud, relieved voices. As Rocke approaches they stop chattering and Rocke gets the first word in. "That shell went right through my room! Talk about a close call! How are you chaps? Anybody hurt? How's the van?"

It is the new man Sammy Smart who finds his voice ahead of the others. "We're all OK, Sir, but it was damn close. Eric and I were in the cab and Pete was checking under the hood when the shell came through. It missed us by inches! You can see how it went – through the roof, out through the windshield and into the ground right there." He points to a small furrow in the ground close to the left front wheel. "Thank God it didn't explode!"

Eric is now standing on the running board checking the damage to the roof of the cab. He finds a neat hole right in the middle of the big red cross painted on the roof – the insignia designed to protect the vehicle from enemy attack. "Sir, that pilot must have been blind not to spot our red cross up here. It was in plain view. It looks like he was deliberately aiming at the van! Just like the van that was hit over at the centre. Either they're stupid or desperate or I don't know what!" The others chuckle at this, but quietly. The thought of German planes deliberately targeting medical vehicles is intolerable. It is simply not done.

Before returning to his room Rocke asks Eric to arrange for repairs to his room, and to have the drivers repair the van as quickly as possible.

The 2CFSU team have their breakfast and then head out on their various tasks. Rocke takes Shorty Long and the orderlies for ward rounds at the medical centre. At 1135hrs Peter Tisdale stands in the middle of the biggest ward and announces that the Canadians have taken Ortona at last. There is a moment of hushed silence and then a wild burst of applause and cheering.

The 2CFSU team start scrubbing at 1730hrs for the first operation on their shift: an artillery gunner who, in a moment of carelessness after carrying and loading heavy shells for six hours non-stop, had lingered too close to the violent recoil of his gun and paid the price with five broken ribs and numerous internal injuries. It is a busy night filled with the cruel, bloody aftermath of the battle.

61. MOPPING UP

Military activities to secure Ortona and beyond.

December 29, 1943 – February 28, 1944

The enemy had vacated Ortona, leaving a seriously damaged town with piles of booby-trapped debris and a heart-rending collection of destroyed buildings, including some that had been of great beauty and historical interest. The local citizens started emerging from their caves and tunnels and basements, cautiously welcoming the Canadians as they searched for their homes in the ruined streets.

The enemy might be gone from the town itself, but they were not far away, and German artillery and mortar shells still whistled down on the town. The Canadians knew that they must drive the Germans farther north to get them out of range. The objective was to push the German paratroopers across the Riccio River and to secure the land south of the Arielli River, which would then be the next important objective on the road to Pescara.

The major problem faced by the Commanders of the 1ˢᵗ Canadian Infantry Division was the serious condition of their fighting troops. The nine regiments of the Division and the Armoured Corps had been badly mauled in the fight for Ortona, and offered limited potential for further offensive action pending substantial rest and reinforcement. Still, there was a job to be done, and it had to be done quickly because worse winter weather was now forecast. General Vokes called on the troops in the best condition to finish the job.

He ordered the Carleton and York Regiment to complete its circle around Ortona and to approach the coast road from the west. The objective was a craggy fortress on the coast called Torre Mucchia. On a raised promontory jutting into the sea, the fortress was of strategic importance in controlling the coast highway south of the Arielli River. The promontory was designated Point 59.

The PPCLI regiment moved through Ortona and up the coast road to join in this engagement. Further to the west, the 48ᵗʰ Highlanders and the Royal 22ⁿᵈ Regiment were sent to clear the enemy out of San Tomasso and San Nicola and secure the road to Tollo.

These objectives were finally achieved, but at further serious loss of life and wounded. Point 59 was taken on January 4,1944. The next two months saw one further serious offensive when the 11ᵗʰ Infantry Brigade was ordered to relieve the 3ʳᵈ Brigade on the right flank of the Ortona salient. Their objective was to push the enemy back from the Ricchio River to the Arielli Valley, but their attack launched on January 17 was unsuccessful. Other than that, action throughout January and February was limited in the main to patrolling and preparing for the spring offensive. This work plus continuing German artillery and mortar fire and the atrocious weather itself took their toll of dead, injured and sick. Over the period February 1 to March 7 Canadian battle casualties were 120 killed and 585 wounded.

On December 29 No.5 Field Ambulance opened an Advanced Dressing Station in Ortona, and No.9 Field Ambulance moved into Ortona from San Leonardo as a mobile reserve unit. On January 4 No.2 Field Dressing Station moved from Sant' Appolinare to San Vito to replace No.4 Field Ambulance as the host of the Canadian Medical Centre. No.4 Field Ambulance moved elsewhere in San Vito to look after minor sick, VD and exhaustion patients. On the same day No.1 Field Dressing Station closed its operation in Rocca, transferred its patients to No.4 Field Ambulance and moved into Ortona as a mobile reserve.

The centre in San Vito enjoyed an historical first for the RCAMC when on December 29 it welcomed four British nurses to help out with the overpowering patient load. They continued to operate in San Vito throughout January and most of February, handling a steady but slowly decreasing flow of serious casualties from Ortona itself and then the actions around Point 59 and the Riccio River, the Tollo Road actions and the winter patrolling. At the end of February the Commanders of Canada's first two Field Surgical Units were moved on to other responsibilities.

62. THE NURSES

Four British nurses arrive at the medical centre in San Vito.

Wednesday, December 29, 1943

The 2CFSU team completes its fourth operation of the day at 1115 hrs. The medical centre is bursting at the seams with patients, all in some sort of pain and many extremely uncomfortable as well. It is cold, their bedding is messy, and the orderlies are at their wits end trying to help out in what seems like an impossible situation. The 2CFSU team is very tired, having worked throughout the night, as usual on very serious cases that fill them with tension and hope and angst all at the same time, and call upon all of their skill and nerve.

With the OR cleaned up and ready for the next case, Rocke steps out the front door for a breath of air just as a jeep pulls up bringing four nurses to the centre.

Nurses! For Christ's sake! Unbelievable!

The nurses are attractive and smiling, and have a crisp air of bright and confident efficiency. They are dressed for work, and each is carrying her nursing kit.

Peter Tisdale sees them as well and comes running out, and the two Majors salute and then shake hands and greet them warmly. Wally Scott also joins them on the run. "Welcome to our centre, ladies," says Peter. "I'm Major Peter Tisdale, OC of the No.4 Canadian Field Ambulance, and this is Major Rocke Robertson, OC of the No.2 Canadian Field Surgical Unit. Oh, and here is Captain Wally Scott, OC of the No.1 Canadian Field Transfusion Unit. We are delighted that you are here."

"Thank you, Major," says the nurse who has stepped out in front of the others. "We are here from the British hospital at Bari. I'm Captain Anne

Bennett, and may I introduce Lieutenants Teresa Montgomery, Annette Heuchan and Petra Marconi. Lieutenant Marconi speaks Italian."

Everyone nods and smiles. Everyone knows how exciting and important this moment is for the Canadian medical service located in San Vito. Everyone knows that they are breaking new ground with nurses in a war zone, and everyone just loves it.

"Right, Captain Bennett. This lovely building is, as you can see, our medical centre. We have living quarters in several houses along the street, and my batman will be happy to take you there and help you get settled in."

"We are settled enough, thank you Major," replies Captain Bennett. "Let's get to work. We have our working uniforms on and our kits with us. Your batman can take the driver down to the quarters and put our bags there."

"That's fine, then" says Peter. "Rocke, Wally, let's take the nurses for a quick tour of the building, and then we can discuss assignments."

They climb the steps and enter the building. There in not a sound to be heard; every patient and every medical staff member is holding his breath, waiting to see the British nurses. The air of tense anticipation in the rooms turns to relief as the nurses walk through the wards, looking around very carefully, saying warm "hellos" to patients and orderlies alike, and firing polite but strong questions at the officers.

The tour over, the group gathers in an examining room to discuss assignments. Rocke and Peter are both preparing to make suggestions, but Captain Bennett beats them to the punch. "May I make a few suggestions, gentlemen?"

Before they can reply, she does so. "I have some thoughts about the surgery area, Major Robertson, but you do seem to be doing fine, so for the moment I suggest we focus on the wards. We can be of some considerable help in the post-operative area. That is of course a very delicate and complicated nursing area, and I am sure your orderlies there would appreciate some assistance. I would propose to put Lieutenant Heuchan there as she has extensive experience in post-op. The next most needy area seems to be patient admission. They are arriving very dirty and messy, and it looks like the orderlies are having trouble deciding how to handle them, especially when they arrive in groups. I suggest that I start in there with Lieutenant Marconi. We can perhaps improve the procedures so that you can do your triage more quickly, and get the serious cases looked at sooner. When we have done some work there we can join Lieutenant Montgomery in the other wards. I would like to go over all of the systems with the orderlies as I think we could save them a lot of time and bother, and have the patients more comfortable too. What do you think?"

Peter, Rocke and Wally are speechless. They can already feel a burden of worry lifting off their shoulders.

"That sounds just fine, Captain," says Peter. "Rocke?"

"Oh yes, that sounds just fine. But please do come and see the OR when you have some time. We may be doing fine, but I do have some questions. Wally?" Wally just nods.

"Of course we will, Major Robertson. Right, now let's get at it." The nurses salute and disappear into the wards, leaving the doctors grinning at each other.

Rocke goes back to work and does two more cases before Frank takes over the duties at 1800hrs. Frank is very excited about the arrival of the nurses and says that he has already heard about the good work they are doing. The nurses, it seems, are full of energy and very good ideas, the orderlies are following them around like puppy dogs, and some of the patients are actually smiling!

In the kitchen for a quick dinner, Rocke sees Bennett and Montgomery enjoying a bowl of soup. Six orderlies are with them, firing questions and thoughtfully absorbing the answers. They move to clear a space near the nurses for Rocke, but he waves them off and watches the conference from afar. He is almost finished his meal when Petra Marconi comes into the room and drops into a chair beside him. She has washed up but her blouse is stained with mud and blood, which she covers with a large napkin before attacking her soup.

"How's it going, Lieutenant?" asks Rocke. "You look a bit tired."

"That I am, Major Robertson. I must say you have a challenge here. I've never seen such a mess when that batch of troops came in this afternoon. They were from the Loyal…something?" "Loyal Edmontons," says Rocke. "Right, the Loyal Edmontons. They looked like they had been crawling in mud for days. Their uniforms were ripped and a complete mess, and for some of them the dirty uniforms were stuck right into the wounds. They were in terrible shape, and it's not easy to clean them up when everything is so crowded and the facilities are so limited. Those orderlies have been doing miracles here!"

"Yes," says Rocke, pleased with the compliment. "The orderlies are really a fine bunch. As you've probably found out most of them have very little training, and they're also very tired. It's been non-stop for quite a while now. But tell me, how can you help them do a better job?"

"It really comes down to training and instinct, Major. I find that I can look at a wounded man just brought in and I know instinctively what his problem is, and what we can do for him right away. And that can be quite difficult you know. For example if he is groaning and in terrible pain an orderly without formal training, like most of them here, will very likely hesitate to handle him until a doctor comes along, whereas I know that we can handle him a certain amount, and what we can do to make him more comfortable and ready for treatment. It takes knowledge and a lot of faith in what you are doing, and that's what nurses' training gives us. There's gut feel involved as well, of course, but it helps if gut feel has some training and experience to back it up!"

They both smile at this, and Rocke thanks his lucky stars, for the hundredth time, that General Hoffmeister paid them that visit.

Out in the wards there is a palpable difference in the atmosphere. Where there had been cold and fear and exhaustion there is now a sense of warmth and confidence and energy.

The nurses leave the building at 1030hrs, completely exhausted but excited and satisfied with their first day in a war zone. Peter Tisdale escorts them to their quarters and thanks them yet again for volunteering.

Thursday, December 30, 1943

As he leads ward rounds in the morning, Rocke watches the nurses at their work. He is amazed by the change in atmosphere in the building, reflected in the faces of workers and patients alike. The nurses move quickly and efficiently, yet they seem to have time for everyone – the doctor with a suggestion, the orderly with a frantic question, the patient with an aching back and parched throat, desperately in need of attention. Things are straightening out. Nursing tables are cleaner and better organized. One orderly is on continuous water duty so there is no more gasping for a drink. The wards seem cleaner and brighter. An orderly is actually heard humming to himself!

Excerpts from Rocke's notes written after the War

From the moment they had their sleeves rolled up and started to work it was clear that something was happening in the ward that hadn't happened before - that couldn't have happened before because there hadn't been anyone there who had the gift that these women had, of being able really to nurse, to comfort, to reassure, to encourage, to do all those things that nurses can do, and can do best while simply taking care of the patient's creature comforts.

I've called this a gift, and so it is, this ability to nurse, but it is one that must, in order to be fully effective, be developed by experience. This group of nurses that I came to admire so greatly as they showed us up for the oafs that we were as far as nursing was concerned, had gained their experience in a British hospital a good many years before the war. I venture to say that they had had practically no so-called scientific training. A touch of anatomy and physiology perhaps, a fairly extensive practical course in decorum probably, but no real science as curriculum people like to think of it.

I doubt that they knew what a red blood cell was, but they knew whether a patient's colour was good or bad. They knew nothing about fluid shifts or membranes, but they knew at a glance whether or not a patient needed water and they knew how to get him to take it. They probably wouldn't know anything about an electro-cardiogram machine but they deduce a lot from feeling a patient's pulse. They probably had never heard of Applied Psychology but they could out-perform most psychologists, I have no doubt.

It was a treat to see them moving down the ward in their first swing to see what needed to be done. A look and a word or two with each patient and they decided exactly how to handle that boy from there on. In this their judgement was virtually infallible. In short, they had their own ability to make people feel better, and the men felt it and responded, and the results were wonderful to behold. The men relaxed. They started to sleep a bit - to eat a little - to recover.

It was a great experience for all of us to see this quality that I have been trying to describe at work in such a dramatic fashion and in so concentrated a form. Such an extraordinary opportunity seldom arises. I hope that it never does again.

The day passes quickly. It includes a brief but informative meeting of the officers at the centre with Captain Bennett, who gives a report on the work of the nurses so far, and recommendations for further action. They include one major item, namely adjusting the layout of the centre to improve the flow of patients through the various wards, and in particular to keep traffic away from the immediate post-op area. Aside from that they include a number of items concerning hygiene and patient care, and especially routines for turning patients and getting them up and moving about to avoid bed sores and muscle collapse. All recommendations are accepted immediately. Peter Tisdale tells the meeting that the hour that Nurse Marconi spent earlier in the day in the outpatient clinic for locals had been brilliant. "You should have seen their faces when this foreign nurse started chatting away with them in Italian. It was terrific!"

63. WINTER VISITING

Rocke visits medical units based in Ortona.

Friday, December 31, 1943

The 2CFSU team is on duty until 1800hrs, and does three operations during daylight hours following two the previous night. The patients are no longer from Ortona itself except for one poor soldier from the Seaforths who has managed to blow himself up relieving himself in a booby-trapped bathroom while checking houses for survivors and documents. They are now coming in from the fighting going on north and to the west of Ortona.

The weather is absolutely miserable, with freezing rain, sleet and snow the order of the day. Arriving patients are wet, filthy with mud and chattering with cold, and virtually every patient in the draughty building is calling for more blankets. The drivers are kept busy stoking the wood-burning stoves around the building that are serving as heaters. Firewood is easy to come by with so many wrecked buildings in the town. The surgeons find it an interesting challenge to operate with cold hands.

The nurses are hard at work, seemingly impervious to the cold. "It's rather like at home," says Mary Montgomery to Eric at one point when he asks her if she is warm enough. "You know, we don't have central heating there either, so we're quite used to bundling up when it gets cold like this." Eric grins, thinking fondly of his toasty-warm house back in Montreal.

The No.1 FSU team takes over at 1800hrs, and Rocke and his colleagues head for the kitchen for some dinner before final ward rounds. The cooks have put some local wine on the table to celebrate the New Year, and they enjoy it immensely. That is all the New Year's celebration that there is at the San Vito Chietino centre. Frank and his team celebrate the New

322

Year in the midst of a desperate operation to save the life of a soldier riddled with shrapnel at the fight over Point 59, north of Ortona.

-/-

The winter months are quite busy for the surgeons at San Vito despite the relatively low level of fighting going on up the east coast of Italy. There is a steady flow of patients requiring surgery, and the two FSUs average a total of four or five operations per day, with occasional very busy days and some days with no operations required. Over the two months the pressure of work does, however, slowly decline, and the teams can spend more time helping in the wards.

Fortunately the weather improves somewhat starting the second week of January until the start of February, when the cold, wet weather returns with a vengeance.

Life at the San Vito centre has become more like working in a small, draughty, poorly equipped hospital than in a mobile FSU. The teams can focus on their medical work without worrying about their mobility, and they have more time for other activities that include enjoying some of the attractions of San Vito. It has been developed somewhat as a leave centre for the troops, and there are movies and some bars open.

Monday, February 7, 1944

The 2CFSU team is off duty until 1800hrs, and Rocke decides to visit Ortona. He, Shorty Long and Eric take a jeep and driver Peter Monroe and, with clearance from 2nd Brigade headquarters, drive into the town, or rather what is left of the town. The three-mile drive takes them right along the coastline, and they stop at the famous Gully to see what it looks like. Now that all is quiet it looks innocent enough, although there are signs of the past conflict everywhere, from torn vineyards to burned-out military equipment and several destroyed German fortifications.

"Christ, it's an eerie sight," says Shorty. "It's so quiet except for the wind, yet you can almost hear the battle, can't you? Look at the muck down there in the vineyards. Imagine slogging through that stuff!"

"And yet they did it, Sir," says Eric. "Those poor bastards had to run through that mud and just hope that they wouldn't be shot and disap-

324 ∴ WHILE BULLETS FLY

pear into it, like they did in the Great War. I talked to one lad, one of the Edmontons, who said that he was so bloody tired by the time he had run through that mud that he was almost glad when he was hit and could lie down and rest! Not exactly, of course, but what he was saying was that with the rain and the mud and the wind it was almost impossible to concentrate on actually fighting. They were fighting the weather as well as the Germans."

They pass beside the southernmost part of the town and enter it on the road that takes them straight into the main square, or 'Piazza Municipali' as it says on the one sign left standing. A main street stretches away to their left, and ahead and to the right are the town hall and main downtown area. Everywhere there is devastation.

"Good Lord," is the only thing Rocke can think of to say as they stand beside the jeep, staring around them. The weather is dry and much warmer for a change. They walk through the square, past the town hall, and gaze in awe at the very large cathedral, now a massive pile of debris with only bits of the walls still standing. It seems to symbolize the barbaric treatment that this small seaside town has received at the hands of the two armies.

An officer from the Loyal Edmonton Regiment sees their jeep with the red cross on it and joins them as their guide. He takes them up and down several streets talking about the action that brought about such terrible destruction. The man is lean and tough looking. He is clearly proud of what his regiment accomplished in driving out the Germans, but also somewhat chagrined at the cost of it all.

When they have seen enough Rocke says "Thank you, Captain. Could you show us where the No.5 Field Ambulance has its dressing station?"

"Yes, Sir," comes the reply. "If you get back in your jeep and drive a short way down that large street over there, you'll find it about two blocks along."

"Thank you, Captain. And good luck." They salute, and the group returns to the jeep and drives to the Advanced Dressing Station. It is easy to find because it is surrounded with ambulances and other military vehicles. They park and walk into the building, one of the few still standing amidst the rubble. The sentry directs them to the canteen that has been set up next to the kitchen, and they find the Commander of the unit, Major Bob Fulham, just sitting down for a cup of tea with Major Don Young, who has been promoted and taken over No.9 FA from Basil Bowman, and Harry

Francis, Commander of No.1 FDS, both of whose units are in Ortona in reserve status. They invite the visitors to join them, which they do, Eric and Pete diplomatically taking chairs at a separate table.

"Bob, this place is appalling," says Rocke after the round of greetings. "Imagine the people here, living in this place and seeing it destroyed like this. Even the cathedral has been blasted! What's it like working here, gentlemen? Are there still lots of mines and booby traps around?"

"I can answer that easily," says Young. "It's the shits working here, and yes, there are lots of mines and booby traps still around. We're camped over on the far side of the town, in reserve as you know, and even so we lost one man yesterday. He was helping Bob's men searching though some rubble for bodies and he must have touched a mine. It blew the poor guy to pieces. Nothing left to send back to you and Frank to sew back together."

"That's awful. Bob, have you had any casualties here? Or you, Harry?"

"Not so far, thank God," replies Bob. "Actually we're not doing much in the town right now. Our ambulances have been working more up north and to the west, covering those actions. It's been pretty hot there, but we haven't taken any casualties ourselves since we moved in here. Oh, and Don's people have been terrific helping us move people around, and particularly back to you folks at San Vito and beyond."

"We've been OK too," says Harry. "We're in reserve, like Don, and we're also helping out searching for bodies and dealing with minor medical stuff for the troops here in town. But the main thing we're doing here is running a clinic for the locals. I'll tell you Rocke, they're a sorry lot. Do you know half of them have been living in caves and tunnels for months now, and the other half in basements! They were all desperate to keep away from the Germans to avoid the slave labour. The Germans had them building the fortifications that our lads had so much trouble attacking. A lot of them were out of food and in very bad shape when we got here. Some of their stories are really sad – men leaving to search for food and never returning, or caught in artillery fire…that sort of thing. Our men are running a damn fine soup kitchen, I'll tell you."

Rocke sips his tea. "We've had about five cases of locals from Ortona over the past couple of weeks, as you know. Mainly mine explosion cases, which are really brutal. I did one young man a couple of days ago who will have to live the rest of his life with no feet. How's that for someone who makes his living in the vineyards? Our local clinic has been pretty active too. We've been really lucky to have a nurse who speaks Italian."

"Which speaking of," interjects Don, "how's it been with those nurses? You've had them there since the end of December. How have they fitted in? Any problems?"

"Good Lord no. Far from it. They've been just terrific. Boy, are they efficient! They arrived and went to work right away. We were ready to give them orders and instructions, but it turned out the other way around. The boss, Captain Bennett, took one look around and then told us what needed to be done...and did we agree?"

The group are all chuckling. They can visualize a bunch of crisp, efficient British nurses wading into a building full of grimy patients and tired doctors and orderlies. No contest. There would be no nonsense, and things would bloody well be done right or else!

"Well," Rocke continues, "we agreed in two seconds, and off they went into that awful building. In one day they had the place completely reorganized, all clean and efficient...well, as clean as it could be under the circumstances. The orderlies were working like crazy and much more confident, and the patients were even smiling. A couple of days ago I talked to one lad from the Seaforths who was in a lot of pain and not doing well. I asked him how he was feeling and he actually grinned and said "Sir, I feel a lot better. It's just great to have a mother here to look after me!"

"Wonderful!" says Harry. "We all know how the nurses run things in the hospitals back home. Now they can come and tell us what to do right here in the war zones! But Rocke, have there been any problems with them living there? You know, personal issues? Any concerns for their safety?"

"We always have concerns for their safety, but not from any danger in the town itself. It's just that the shelling and strafing by aircraft that we had until the Germans moved out of Ortona is still sort of with us in spirit. You know, we can't believe that it has gone away completely, and we'd just hate to have them injured in any way. As far as the town itself, they couldn't be safer. Hell, everyone loves them! The soldiers and walking wounded know what they are about and damn near worship them, and the locals really appreciate their work in the clinic. Particularly Petra Marconi, of course, with her Italian. So they are sort of local royalty, with everyone looking out for their welfare."

"How about romances?" asks Bob. "Surely you've had some wild dances and parties and all sorts of guys are involved with them? Come on Rocke, give us the dirt!"

"Sorry Bob, no dirt to tell. Even though two of them are quite attractive, well, they're just too busy and we haven't had time for socializing. I hope that will change because they deserve to have some fun. I'll keep you posted, OK?"

They laugh, and then Harry asks Don, who has been in contact recently with Division headquarters, "What's going to happen here, in the war? Do you think we're going to make a push towards Pescara soon? There's still the Arielli River to go before then. And a few others too."

"Right Harry, the Arielli, and then the Foro, and then the Alento, and lots of gullies too. I don't have the answer for you – the generals haven't yet learned to consult me too closely. But it seems to me that with the mauling our regiments have taken over the past few months, plus the big fight the Germans are continuing to put up, plus the God-awful weather, we could use a while to rest and get some reinforcements in place and trained, and wait for some dry weather so that we can use our tanks again. You know, I don't think that even one of our nine infantry regiments is even close to fighting strength right now!"

"I'm not surprised," says Shorty. "When you see the stream of wounded coming through San Vito, and you think that this is only the really seriously wounded and there's many more who don't need operating, and the walking wounded and sick and the like who you fellows take right past us, and of course the dead, it's a wonder that there's anyone left to carry a gun."

"They're rifles, not guns, Captain Shorty," says Don, flashing an ironic salute, and they all laugh.

"Well, if all this is true, then it looks like you folks will be enjoying the delights of Ortona for a while," says Rocke. "Lucky chaps. We'll just have to put up with San Vito, with its new cinema and those bars that keep on opening all over the place. And of course, dances with the nurses!"

"OK Rocke, now you just finish your tea and bugger off," laughs Harry, and they all get up and leave the canteen. Rocke and his team return to their jeep and head back to San Vito, arriving just in time to grab a sandwich before going on shift at 1800hrs. Rocke tells Frank Mills about their visit to Ortona, and Frank says that he'll probably do the same in a day or two. Things are very quiet at the moment in terms of new cases, so it's a good time to look around.

64. PENICILLIN!

The units in San Vito receive small supplies of penicillin. Exciting results.

Monday, January 10, 1944

War Diary

...Lt. Col. Jeffries (of the British Penicillin team) arrived in the late afternoon and gave a lecture on penicillin after supper. He gave 100 grams to each FSU for local application on wounds.

The Colonel is very specific about how these tiny samples of the new wonder drug are to be used. "Clearly we don't have enough for you to spread around to anyone who has any indication of infection, or might have infection. Indeed, we have indications that penicillin is effective on infection once started, but not in preventing it from starting, so don't use it in cleaning out wounds, no matter how severe, if there is no infection there. You can apply the penicillin either in a sodium salt powder in solution, injected near the wound, or in a calcium salt solution using this special atomizer that we have developed for the solution. As you can see there is a very limited supply of the calcium salt solution and it is very potent, so you are ordered to use it only on gas gangrene cases. The reason should be obvious – these cases are hard-hitting and can kill within a day, so you have to apply the drug in the most rapidly usable form."

The doctors at the centre are ecstatic that the new drug, so long expected, has finally arrived. They set up a system to monitor all patients who receive penicillin treatment, as they know that they will be asked to report on it.

Tuesday, January 11, 1944

The surgeons apply penicillin to several wounds during the day, but the most dramatic application comes at 2130hrs when Nurse Heuchan reports that a recent amputation patient of Rocke's has developed gas gangrene in the stump of his leg, and by the time they discovered it there are signs of rapidly developing infection in his abdominal wall and loin. His blood pressure has plummeted, he has a raging temperature and he is irrational. In other words, he will die soon unless something miraculous happens.

Rocke tells Eric to assemble the team and get the patient on the table immediately. He brings out the atomizer and the vial of calcium salt solution of penicillin, and puts what he hopes is the correct amount of solution in the atomizer. Shorty applies the anaesthetic to the incoherent patient. As soon as it takes, Rocke slashes the flesh in the middle of the most infected area and then gently, carefully, sprays the penicillin solution into the wound. He applies dressings to the new wound and sends the patient back to the ward hooked up to intravenous feeds, with instructions to his staff to keep a careful watch on him.

The patient is a marked man. Everyone in the medical centre, whether doctor, nurse, orderly, patient or even cook knows that a man with a horrible infection that will kill him very quickly has been treated with the new wonder drug. They know that the curse of infection is always there and voracious in its appetite, and that it never gives up its victims easily. So if the treatment works here, then there's a brighter future ahead!

Wednesday, January 12, 1944

"Eric," says nurse Teresa Montgomery over an early morning cup of tea, "do you think the penicillin is working on Pte. Donegan? I haven't seen him yet this morning. What's happening?"

"So far as we can see, it's so far-so good. We don't see any signs of spreading, but you never know. You had better take a real good look at him this morning. All I can say, and I've looked in on him every hour all night, is that he doesn't seem to be any worse."

"That's fantastic," says Teresa. "I will. Bloody hell, can you imagine what this means if he comes through? All that horrible infection crap under control?"

"Now Teresa," says Eric, smiling benignly, "I didn't know you swore! I thought you nurses were sent from the good Lord himself and had nothing but good words for everything!"

"Right Eric, and 'stuff you old son' as we say back in Birmingham. So anyway, if you have finished your sacred tea, why don't we go and see how young Donegan is doing?"

"Good idea," says Eric, and they head for the ward that is the centre of attention of the whole building.

To the untrained eye, Donegan is a very sick man, probably on death's door. He is deeply sedated, ashen grey, and seems to be shrinking into the bed. To the trained eye of Teresa Montgomery and the hopeful eye of Eric Branch he is, yes, a sick man, but he is definitely not on death's door. She feels his forehead; it is cool. They change the dressing and find, to their joy, that the glow of infection has actually retreated! The angry red of yesterday has faded overnight to a dull pink. As they are changing the dressing Donegan opens his eyes and gazes at them. He then utters those memorable words: "Jesus Murphy, what hit me?"

"You stepped on a mine, Pte. Donegan, and I'm afraid you've lost your leg," says Teresa in that voice full of realism, sympathy and hope that only nurses can conjure up. "You've had some infection too, but we've given you some penicillin and it looks like it may have solved that problem."

"What's penicillin?" mumbles Donegan.

"It's the new miracle drug that fights infection, and we just received it two days ago. So what do you think of that?"

Donegan has no opinion to express. He is fast asleep.

They turn away from the bed and find Rocke standing quietly behind them.

"How does he look, Lieutenant?"

"He looks better, Sir. A lot better. He's clearly not out of the woods yet, but I'd say that so far we're winning. The inflammation has subsided in all areas, although it hasn't yet disappeared completely. I think his temperature is down to almost normal, and he is coherent. I'm just about to take his blood pressure."

"That's just wonderful news," says Rocke. "Please do keep me informed of progress. Now then, Eric, we have another case coming up, and we'd better take a look at him now."

As the day progresses, so does Pte. Donegan. At noon he wakes up and asks for food. His temperature and blood pressure are both back very close to normal, and although he is drowsy he is able to talk coherently to the patients in neighbouring beds. He has come to understand the miraculous nature of what has happened to him, so that in spite of losing a leg he actually feels lucky. He lapses back into sleep after ingesting half a bowl of soup, just as Frank Mills looks in on him.

Meanwhile the medical centre is going through its usual busy day. Rocke's team has two more cases before their shift ends at 1800hrs. Frank's team takes time out of its ward rounds and clinical duties to bid farewell to Captain Tovee, their Second-in-Command who is returning to Canada, and then to welcome his replacement, Captain Ian Davidson. Rocke receives a letter from Jack Leishman saying that he has recovered fully from his jaundice, and should be able to return to the 2CFSU in the very near future.

At 1730hrs Rocke examines Pte. Donegan, who is now awake and surprisingly chipper for a man who has just lost a leg. Rocke is overjoyed that the man is capable of being chipper. After all, without penicillin Donegan would be dead by now! He tells Donegan that the infection has all but disappeared, and that if he is careful and does everything that he is told, he should be able to get home and live a long life.

At 1815hrs Rocke and Shorty go with Teresa Montgomery and Anne Bennett, the two nurses off duty, to the officers' club where they share a joyful bottle of champagne to celebrate the miracle of Pte. Donegan and all that it means to the future of their profession.

-/-

The No. 1 FSU team take a much-needed leave to Bari and Naples in mid-January. Penicillin treatments continue while supplies last, and Rocke finds that cases where penicillin in calcium salt powder solution is applied to wounds the results are generally satisfactory. It is difficult to know for sure, however, as most cases are evacuated soon after treatment, and record keeping once patients are away from San Vito is almost impossible.

He applies penicillin in sodium salt solution to five cases of gas gangrene. Two are too far gone by the time he treats them, and die. The others show positive results.

Jack Leishman returns to action in mid-January, posted to the No. 1

Canadian General Hospital at Andria rather than to San Vito. In a brief visit to San Vito he tells Rocke that while he wished he could be back with the 2CFSU, there is so much to do at the hospital that he doesn't have any time to worry about it.

February comes in cold and wet. The centre at San Vito receives word that there is to be a conference in Ortona of the 1st Division Medical Society, hosted by the No.9 Field Ambulance, on February 10. The surgeons will be called upon to report on the success of their applications of penicillin. Rocke and Frank agree that Rocke should attend as Frank will be on duty at that time, and also because Rocke has had more occasions to use penicillin in serious cases.

65. FINAL ACT

Rocke gives a presentation on the use of penicillin.
The Colonel tells him that he is being posted to a Canadian
hospital at Caserta. He leaves the 2CFSU.

Thursday, February 10, 1944

Rocke and Shorty Long have an early breakfast at the centre and then drive into Ortona for the 0900hrs start of the conference. It is a large gathering held in a huge hall in a deserted but only partially destroyed school. Rocke knows about half of the officers there, although only a few, like Don Young and Peter Tisdale, are really close friends. The head table is impressive, with the ADMS Colonel Playfair flanked by Lt.-Colonel W.E. Mace and Lt.-Colonel W.J. Boyd, two senior officers less well known to the field officers but still very influential in the medical service. Colonel Playfair welcomes the nine Majors and 22 Captains in attendance, and lays out the agenda for the meeting. He says that he would like to meet with some of the officers after the meeting, and that his Aide will inform them during the tea session following the meeting, which should be over by noon at the latest. He then opens the session by calling on Rocke to report on his personal experience with penicillin.

"Thank you Sir. First I should remind you that we have only had penicillin, and in limited amounts, for less than a month, so I can't give you too much detail. We have, however, been able to give it a good try.

"Major Mills and I have treated around 55 cases of operative wounds with the calcium salt powder in solution, injected near the infected area. These were cases with moderate to quite severe infection already under way. We tried to set up a system to monitor all of the results, but we realized, of course, that most of these patients would be evacuated too quickly for us to be able to see the results except for a very short period. And we weren't in a position to hold them back just to monitor them – San Vito is not a comfortable place to stay if you can possibly get out.

"Virtually all of them were in improving shape when they were evacuated, which was a positive finding for the medicine. This also applied to the five cases of post-operative infective wounds that we treated with the powder. They seemed to be doing well also. We did manage to keep tabs on 12 cases that were serious enough for us to hold onto for long enough to observe the total effect of the penicillin. In 10 of these cases the effect was very positive – the infection disappeared completely and the patient was in good shape when finally evacuated. In the other two cases the effects were less evident. There seemed to be some lessening of the infection, but then it re-occurred. We think that we might have administered incorrect dosages in these cases, but can't be sure. On the whole, however, this part of our experiment with penicillin was highly successful.

"We did five cases using the sodium salt solution applied directly to the wound with an atomizer. We could have done more, but we were limited by the available supply of penicillin. Under orders we used this method only in cases of gas gangrene. The first case had very dramatic results. This was a leg amputation that developed a virulent gas gangrene that had already spread to his loin and abdominal wall by the time we found it. We treated him immediately by slashing the main area of infection in the stump and applying the penicillin, and a day later the infection was totally under control and he was in much better shape. We evacuated him about 10 days later, and by then he was clearly on the way to a full recovery – with only one leg, of course.

"Several days after that first case we had another, this time with an arm amputation, and we had the same highly successful result. It was very dramatic to see the infection subside so quickly in a patient threatened directly with a painful death.

"Then we had two cases in succession where the results were not so positive. One was another leg amputation, the other a severe wound in the shoulder. In both cases the gangrene was very advanced when they came to us. The penicillin seemed to have some positive effect at first, but it simply couldn't drive out the infection completely, and in the end both patients died. There is some research to be done here concerning dosages and application procedures for advanced cases.

"Finally, we had our fifth case four days ago, a shattered hip and torn thigh that had turned gangrenous, and the infection had started to spread down the leg and also up into the abdomen. But we seem to have treated him in time, because as of today he is doing fine and seems to be recovering well."

Rocke concludes with some remarks on dosages and application techniques, and passes around for observation a tiny specimen of the sodium salt solution and the special atomizer.

"Thank you Major Robertson," says the ADMS. "Before I open the floor to questions, Captain Midgley, I think you have some technical comments on penicillin application?" Captain Midgley speaks for some time on a number of detailed issues concerning penicillin, and then there is a lively discussion, with Rocke and Captain Midgley fielding the questions.

The conference moves on to other topics, and at 1140hrs the ADMS declares the meeting closed and invites the participants to join him and other senior officers for tea. Rocke is just out of his chair when Colonel Playfair's Aide taps him on the shoulder and says that he is to meet the ADMS in an adjoining small room, set up as an office for the occasion, in 15 minutes.

With tea in hand and two hastily eaten sandwiches under his belt, Rocke sits down in front of the Colonel's desk at 1155hrs precisely. The ADMS is in great spirits and draws heavily on his pipe as he opens the discussion.

"Well Rocke, you've come a long way since those pleasant days in England rushing around the countryside looking for pubs, eh?"

"We certainly have, Sir. It's been an incredible time. I've done more surgery in six months than I would have done in 10 years at home. And Frank's the same. It's certainly an interesting way to go to war."

"Right. Well, you and Frank have done a fine job right from the start. I've been very aware of the conditions that you've been working in, but that's the idea of the FSU, isn't it? So there's been nothing for it but to just let you do your thing and see how it works. I've kept a close eye on your records, and I can say for certain that you two have saved hundreds of lives – I don't have the count of your operations here in front of me, but it's a very large number and a very impressive recovery rate. You and the transfusion chaps, and of course the Field Dressing Stations and the Field Ambulances, have been a terrific innovation – so much so that we already have several more FSUs here in Italy, and are forming a whole bunch more in England for the big push into Europe from the north, whenever that takes place."

Rocke smiles and relaxes. "Thank you, Sir. It has certainly been a adventure, and I am delighted that you consider it such as success."

"Right. Good stuff. Now then, I take it that the British nursing sisters have been a help?"

"Oh yes, Sir, they certainly have. It's absolutely amazing what they have done for us, both medically and in terms of morale. As you can imagine the orderlies have been thrilled to have such highly trained people to give them some guidance, and as for the patients, well they have been much happier with such terrific nursing. Not that the orderlies haven't done a good job, Sir. I'm not saying that. But as you know most of them have had very little training and..."

"Yes, yes, I know what you're saying, and I agree. So much, in fact, that you will be receiving four Canadian nurses tomorrow to replace the Brits. You have probably heard of this?"

"Yes Sir, we have, and we're planning a smashing party tomorrow evening to thank the British sisters for their wonderful work and to welcome the Canadians. I hope you can make it?"

Colonel Playfair smiles and sucks on his cold pipe. "Perhaps, Rocke. But the real importance of this is that we've established the precedent of having nurses in war zones, and it's my hope that we can make this a general rule. It seems to work so very well, and the nurses are very keen to be closer to the action."

"Jolly good, Sir," says Rocke, grinning as he finishes his tea and places the cup on the desk.

"Now then," says the Colonel. "Looking ahead, I have some plans for you and Frank. The war is stalled for the moment, and you fellows haven't been mobile for quite some time. But as soon as the weather improves we'll be back at it for sure, and things will get very busy again. I have decided to use this lull to make some changes in our field units. As you know I put Jack Leishman back at the hospital at Andria rather than returning him to you. What I am doing is changing the guard in the field units to give some other chaps a chance to have some time in the field, and also to get you experienced fellows into the hospitals to help run things there. Your experience with the most severely wounded will be extremely valuable to them.

"So Jack is already at a hospital, and Shorty Long is gaining good experience under you. Ed Tovee is on his way back to Canada to do some important work there, and I have Ian Davidson learning the ropes under Frank. I'll be sending Frank as Surgical Specialist over to help set up the No.15 CGH near Caserta in about 10 days. I'm not yet certain whom I'll send in to replace him, but Davidson can do the job until I find the right man. Please don't mention this to Frank; I'll be telling him when he comes to see me tomorrow.

"As for you, Rocke, I'd like you to do the same for the No.14 CGH, which is also at Caserta. As you probably know, Sandy MacIntosh is Head of Surgery there, and he is looking forward to your arrival, especially to help with chest cases. We have this big build-up there for the assault on Rome. So I think you'll find it interesting. I have my eyes on David Johnson to replace you. I think you know him – he's at No.14 right now, and he could use some time a bit closer to the action."

Rocke sits quietly staring out the dusty window at the driving rainstorm. His world has changed just like that, in the course of one brief conversation. He is to leave the field and move back to the much more civilized world of the hospital. But then, isn't the hospital, so close to Rome, really in the field too? Well anyway, so what if it is or isn't? This is the army and that's where he's going.

"Right, Sir. When will I be posted there?"

"In a couple of weeks. I'll get your orders to you as soon as possible."

They both rise. The ADMS comes around his desk and they shake hands.

"Thank you, Sir."

"Thank you, Rocke. Well done."

Rocke leaves the office and finds Shorty, and they head back to San Vito Chietino.

Saturday, March 4, 1944

Shorty Long's War Diary

Major Robertson left this morning for #14 C.G.H. and was driven there by Cpl. Branch and Dvr. Monroe. Came on duty at 1800hrs and did six cases during the night.

Afterword

The Field Surgical Unit concept proved its worth in Sicily and Italy. During the eight month period described in this book the two FSU teams performed some 700 operations, not including the numerous incisions of abscesses, changes of dressing and other minor procedures. Forty-seven percent of these operations were on the more serious abdominal and chest wound cases, and the overall mortality rate was 15 percent. The credit for this remarkable record was shared by the skill of the surgeons and their teams, and by the fact that the mobile system meant that the wounded soldiers could be on the operating table while they still had a reasonable chance of survival. Almost a quarter of the cases were operated on within 5 hours of being hit, and 60 percent within 10 hours, and these time periods include the often lengthy delays in the field, from the time the soldier was wounded to the time he could be rescued and carried to a Regimental Aid Post.

By the time of the Normandy landings in June 1944 there were 11 Canadian FSUs in the field. Along with 11 Field Ambulances, four Light Field Ambulances (for armoured brigades), 15 Field Dressing Stations and four Field Transfusion Units, this represented a very substantial mobile medical service in support of the Canadian troops.

Rocke Robertson and his colleagues returned to Canada at different times, and most pursued distinguished medical careers. The training and lessons learned in the war served them well in their peacetime work, accelerating their experience and giving them insights into the medical issues involved in increasingly crowded, overworked domestic medical facilities.

Rocke's experience was a good example. After three months at No.14 Canadian General Hospital in Caserta he was sent back to England in a large convoy, arriving one month after the Normandy landings. He was assigned to the No.6 CGH at Farnborough, once again dealing with heavy influxes of casualties from the fighting in Europe. In late September he was offered the op-

tion of returning to Canada, and he accepted it gladly. In October he sailed to New York on the Queen Mary, along with 10,000 other troops, and then took the train to Montreal.

Promoted to the rank of Lieutenant Colonel, he was posted to Vancouver as Head of Surgery at the Shaughnessy Military Hospital. He was discharged from the army in October 1945, and began a distinguished career that saw him Chief of Surgery at Shaughnessy and the Vancouver General Hospital, and Professor of Surgery and Chair of the Department at the new medical school that he helped found at the University of British Columbia. In 1959 he was appointed Surgeon-in-Chief at the Montreal General Hospital and Professor of Surgery and Chairman of the Department at the McGill University Medical School. In 1962 he was appointed Principal and Vice-Chancellor of McGill University.

The skills that supported Rocke's remarkable career were either developed or at least honed in the war. As learned so dramatically in England, Sicily and Italy, surgery is not a stand-alone activity taking place in operating rooms. Rather it must be viewed as a continuum of activities, all of priority importance.

The first key activity is speed of access. There is a clear inverse correlation between the time it takes to get an injured patient on the operating table and the chances of having a successful operation.

The second key activity is diagnosis. Rocke was well known for the personal interest he took in all patients, where he demonstrated the application of the hard lesson he learned in the war that you must 'use your head' when diagnosing. The most obvious diagnosis is by no means always the correct one; you should not be distracted by secondary symptoms.

The third key activity is the surgery itself. It must be done quickly and efficiently, taking all of the surgeon's attention no matter what the conditions or circumstances.

The fourth key activity is post-operative care. His horror of infection as exemplified by the deadly gas gangrene, and the wonders of the new miracle drug penicillin, drove his research in wound healing and treatment of antibiotic-resistant infections that won him international acclaim.

The war experience also gave him unforgettable insights into the emergency function in the medical system: the need for judgement-based triage and for coordinated and managed emergency facilities. Back in Canada he was a pioneer in modern emergency care.

The medical services in an army represent the curious, violent contradic-

tions of war. Most of an army is dedicated to killing or wounding the enemy, yet the medical services represent the other side of the coin — the sanctity of life and freedom from pain; compassion in the midst of violence and hate. These contradictions can shine through the most pressing and complex war situations. This was brought home to Rocke in a most dramatic fashion during his voyage from Italy back to England. As told in his own words...

Rocke's Memoires

A remarkable episode on the return voyage. A large convoy - many merchant ships and a host of battleships and destroyers. On the first morning out I was called to see a young English sailor who had a ruptured appendix of a couple of day's duration. He was obviously going to be ill for a long time and our supply of intravenous fluids would only last about three days.

I spoke to the captain. He told me to notify him when we were about to run out of fluid and he would take action. When the time came, a signal was sent to the admiral of the fleet who issued an order. The fleet stopped moving and a destroyer moved among the vessels picking up cases of intravenous fluids. By the time the exercise was completed we had enough fluid to last a month.

While all this was going on, I lifted the boy up so that he could see through the porthole that all the ships were standing still. He was overcome when it was explained to him that this was being done for him, and all that he could think of to say was "coo lummie!". When we landed at Liverpool he was improving and I had every hope that he would recover.

Terminology and Organizations

Military life is full of jargon, titles and acronyms. The following is a quick reference.

The Armies

The invasion of Sicily was carried out by the 2nd Corps of the American 7th Army and the 13th Corps and 30th Corps of the British 8th Army. The Canadians were involved as a unit of the 30th British Corps.

When they moved to Italy the Canadians came under the 13th British Corps. The invasion force that landed at Salerno, south of Rome, was under the command of the American 5th Army and consisted of the 6th US Corps and the 10th British Corps.

The Canadian force consisted of:

· 1st Canadian Infantry Division
- Canadian Armoured Corps: 4th Reconnaissance Regiment
- The Royal Canadian Artillery
- The Canadian Infantry Corps
  ◊ Saskatoon Light Infantry (brigade support group)
  ◊ 1st Canadian Infantry Brigade
    * The Royal Canadian Regiment
    * The Hastings and Prince Edward Regiment (the 'Hasty Pees')
    * 48th Highlanders of Canada Regiment
  ◊ 2nd Canadian Infantry Brigade
    * Princess Patricia's Canadian Light Infantry Regiment (the 'PPCLI')
    * The Seaforth Highlanders of Canada Regiment
    * The Loyal Edmonton Regiment

◊ 3rd Canadian Infantry Brigade
   * Royal 22e Regiment (the 'Van Doos')
   * The Carleton and York Regiment
   * The West Nova Scotia Regiment

Infantry Regiments were divided into Companies (A,B,C, etc). Companies were divided into Platoons (1,2,3, etc).

1st Canadian Armoured Brigade
- 11th Canadian Armoured Regiment (Ontario Tanks)
- 12th Canadian Armoured Regiment (Three Rivers Tanks)
- 14th Canadian Armoured Regiment (Calgary Tanks)

Corps of Royal Canadian Engineers
- 4 companies

Royal Canadian Army Medical Corps
- Units under the 1st Canadian Infantry Division

Medical Units

The Royal Canadian Army Medical Corps (RCAMC), a unit of the Canadian Army, had over-all responsibility for medical services to the Canadian forces.

The regiments had their own medical officers and orderlies assigned to them and under the direct authority of the regimental commands: to care for wounded in the field of battle, and to bring them out of the line of fire to Regimental Aid Posts (RAPs) where they would be given basic first aid and then picked up by Field Ambulances. From then on the wounded would be under the care of units operating under command at Division level. The senior officers involved were:

DMS   Director of Medical Services, Canadian Military Headquarters, London.

DDMS   Deputy Director of Medical Services – senior officer at Corps level.

ADMS   Assistant Director of Medical Services – senior officer at Division level.

The main operational units involved were:

CGH   Canadian General Hospital – hospital unit set up in Canada and then sent to Europe to set up and serve wherever needed.

CCS   Casualty Clearing Station – major field medical unit coordinating between mobile units up front and hospitals back in secure locations.

RAP   Regimental Aid Post – emergency aid post set up by regimental medical staff as close to the fighting as possible.

FA   Field Ambulance – mobile unit to bring wounded from RAPs to field medical units and beyond to CCSs and CGHs.

CCP   Casualty Collecting Post – temporary post set up by an FA to assemble wounded for evacuation.

FDS   Field Dressing Station – small, mobile field hospital.

FSU   Field Surgical Unit – mobile operating room (OR).

FTU   Field Transfusion Unit – mobile blood service unit.

ADS   Advanced Dressing Station – set up by an FDS to serve the wounded in a forward area..

ASC   Advanced Surgical Centre = FDS + FSU + FTU in the same location.

CMC   Canadian Medical Centre = ASC + FA; a full-service medical set-up.

IAN BRUCE ROBERTSON was born in Montreal and grew up in Vancouver. He studied at McGill and Harvard, and pursued a career in international government and business. With his wife Bonnie he lived and worked across Canada, in the United States, and in the Philippines, India and Singapore. They now live on Vancouver Island on Canada's west coast, where Ian is a full-time writer. While Bullets Fly is his first book.

ISBN 142513512-9

9 781425 135126